So Much for My Happy Ending

KYRA DAVIS

So Much for My Happy Ending

MIRA®

MIRA

ISBN-13: 978-0-7783-2351-8
ISBN-10:   0-7783-2351-X

SO MUCH FOR MY HAPPY ENDING

www.MIRABooks.com

Printed in U.S.A.

To my friends, Brenda, Jackie, Mika, Annie,
Shawn, Cheryl, Barbara and Eleanor;
when things were at their worst you provided me with
moral support, child care, martinis and Victoria's Secret
gift certificates. Thanks for keeping me sane!

ACKNOWLEDGMENTS

I want to thank my agent Ashley Kraas and editor
Margaret Marbury for making this book possible.
I also want to thank Will Pizzalato for helping me figure out
what Tad does for a living and my family for taking care of
my son so that I had the time to write this book.

PROLOGUE

May 2001

By the time most of us have reached college graduation we've entertained a few not-so-pleasant "what if" scenarios. What if I don't land my dream job? What if I don't earn enough money to pay for future Botox injections? What if I don't ever meet Mr. or Ms. Wonderful? But I think it's the rare individual who thinks, What if I inadvertently marry a bipolar sociopath?

And yet here I am…in my own unique marital hell. That's what I get for not thinking outside the box. Once upon a time the only images the term *mentally ill* evoked were those of derelicts, third world leaders and my mother. Now, of course, I know better; almost everyone is crazy. I firmly believe that the key to maintaining a good relationship is to choose a partner who is just as crazy as you are—no more, no less. It was this matchmaking strategy that made Bonnie and Clyde the twentieth century's top supercouple.

I'm minorly crazy myself. For instance, I have often considered trying to get a measure on the California ballot that would prohibit the distribution and sale of ugly shoes no matter how comfortable they may be. God created foot surgery for a reason. So I should have gone out and found myself a man with a swollen-foot fetish. Did I do that? Oh, nooo. I had to hook up with Mr. Hyde; except instead of tearing people apart with his bare hands my husband's weapons of choice are ill-begotten MasterCards and manic spending sprees. That wasn't supposed to happen. Now Winona Ryder, she'd make a good match for my husband; they could be the all-American couple on weekdays and do their grand-theft thing on weekends. She could make it work. I can't.

The worst part about this whole mess is that it blew up right when I was on the verge of my very own identity crisis and now I've had to put that off. The really ironic part of all this is that I married Tad because I thought he would bring stability into my life. He was the ingredient I needed to be part of a normal family. Now *I'm* the one who has to offer that stability for *him* because he has gone so far off the deep end that my staying grounded is the only way I can keep our world from spinning out of control. I can no longer afford to spend the day window-shopping in uncomfortable shoes. I can't be bothered with the pros and cons of last-minute holiday shopping. I can't just stroll into the Museum of Modern Art and spend an hour staring at my favorite Chagall. Because Chagall makes me *feel,* and if I allow myself the luxury of emotion I will be so overwhelmed with terror that I will become completely unable to function.

It's difficult to reflect on the past while in survival mode, but I think it might be important to have an understanding of how

I got myself into this predicament. It may prove useful when I finally have time to have my breakdown. Or maybe I could use it to help me get things back under some semblance of control. If I really press myself I can remember. The warning signs were there. No neon signs, mind you, just little sparks at the end of a very long string. Funny that I could have been blind enough not to realize that the string was a lighted fuse.

THE
ENGAGEMENT

ONE

October 2000

Utopia. I wasn't sure how I got there, but there was no question that Utopia is where I ended up.

No one around but the brown-haired, green-eyed Adonis who brought me here. The stars were twinkling above the Golden Gate Bridge, the Legion of Honor glowing behind us. The night was relatively mild (which in and of itself was a small miracle considering the fall season), the champagne was Cristal and the caviar beluga. I felt Tad's fingers thread themselves through my mane of wavy dark-brown hair as he cuddled closer to me on our little bench on the cliffs.

"God, you've got to be the most exotic and beautiful woman I have ever laid eyes on."

I squeezed his hand and leaned in a little closer. I'm not so conceited as to think of myself as beautiful, but *exotic* is a good word.

I'm probably black. Maybe part Native American—that would explain my hair. My father was a one-night stand who my mother describes as being gorgeous and ethnic, so on the college applications I just checked all the boxes, and let affirmative action do its thing.

"April, you know how much I love you, don't you?"

"Mmm, hmm, right back at ya." I wasn't very good at mushy so I tried to push my chest out a little more to compensate for my lack of poetry.

"I want to fill my life with moments like this. I want you by my side holding my hand, telling me your funny stories, smiling at me with your beautiful mouth." Tad gently took hold of my chin and guided it up in his direction. "I want that every day of my life. And I want to do the same for you. I want to make you laugh. I want to protect you and support you in your struggles and ambitions. I want to be there day after day, year after year, so that I can remind you of how incredible you are."

There was something practiced about that speech. I shivered a little. Was it getting colder?

"April…" He moved off the bench and bent his long legs so that he was balancing on one knee. "April, I want you to marry me." He pulled a ring box out of his leather jacket and carefully opened it, revealing a rock that was a little smaller than the Hope Diamond. "Will you marry me?"

Not so perfect.

I stared at the ring and tried to force my heart to rise out of my stomach. Tad and I had been dating for three months. Only three months. That wasn't long enough. I knew that. It was in every *Cosmo, Vogue* and *Mademoiselle* I had ever read. Never get engaged before dating for a year. Dr. Laura said three years was the ideal. I'm not a big Dr. Laura fan but in this case she might be on to something.

"April, did you hear me?" The lilting romanticism that had affected his tone was being ebbed out by a note of tension.

I nodded, not quite ready to speak. He was a wonderful guy. I had never loved anyone like this before. Hell, I had never loved any man, period. I was twenty-six years old and while I had lusted, craved and to a lesser extent obsessed, I had never loved until Tad.

"April, this isn't the most comfortable position in the world… Do you think you can give me an answer this year?"

"I thought I was going to get to change my last name."

"Excuse me?"

"All my life I've dreamt of getting married and changing my last name from Silverperson. No one should be forced to have the last name Silverperson."

"April, your mom *could* have changed your name to Silverwoman." Oh yeah, that was definitely tension in his voice. This was not a topic he wanted to reexplore now, but I needed to stall for time so I could think. He was just going to have to suck it up and deal.

"It should have stayed Silverman. I don't see why I should have to suffer just because she has a thing for Gloria Steinem."

"So, I've offered you the ideal solution. Marry me and take my name. Say yes, April."

"Showers. You want me to change my name to April Showers? That's your ideal solution?"

"Fine, keep your name. Better yet, go down to city hall and have it legally changed back to Silverman. Change it to Beelzebub. I don't really care, just say yes so I can get up—I think my knee's in a gopher hole."

I lifted my eyes upward and located Venus shining steadily in the sky. That was Tad, vibrant, constant and secure in his place in the universe. He could be my Venus. I should just do it. What the hell, we could have a long engagement. I'd never heard Dr. Laura say anything about long engagements. I struggled to find my voice. *Come on, April, you can say it.* "I…um… Yeah, okay, let's do it."

"Let's do it?" Tad raised a thick beautiful eyebrow. I thought I saw a flicker of amusement dance across his features. It's a good thing he found this funny because I was scared shitless.

I swallowed hard. "Let's get married."

Before I could brace myself for his reaction I found myself being pulled down to the ground. I felt his pectorals press against my breasts and his mouth close around mine. Oh yeah, I had definitely made the right decision. When Tad finally allowed me to catch my breath, I giggled and caressed his five o'clock stubble. "I thought you wanted to get up."

"I changed my mind."

"Hmm, I'm not up on my prewedding etiquette, but I think you're supposed to put the ring on my finger before you ravish me."

Tad laughed and raised up enough to slip the diamond onto my hand. He held it above us so that the clear stone seemed to become one with the constellations. "We're getting married."

The first person I had to tell was my grandmother. I desperately wanted to be able to tell her in person but I simply couldn't wait until I had time to travel down to Carmel. I called her at seven the next morning, which would be early for some people but not for a woman who made her living as a baker. I sat on the couch, my feet tucked underneath me, the phone pressed tightly against my ear, and waited for her to pick up.

"Hello?"

"Bobe? It's me." Tad strolled into the living room and handed me a cup of coffee. How could you not love a man who went out of his way to feed your addictions?

"*Mummala!* You remembered my birthday."

"Oh, well yeah, like I'd forget your birthday." It's amazing how big of a loser I could be. "Your gift is coming, it's just that it was… It was out of stock, so it's going to be a little late." Tad shot me a scornful look, just in case I wasn't already drowning in shame.

"*Pfft!* What do I need presents for? I have everything I need, a nice apartment, a nice cat and a granddaughter who never forgets to call."

"Well, I do have a birthday surprise of sorts. I was thinking that maybe you'd like a grandson who remembers to call, too, or at least a grandson-in-law."

"April!" I could practically see her stormy eyes twinkling as her wrinkled face bunched up into a grin.

"He proposed last night. So I guess I'm not going to be an old maid after all, huh?"

"*Hmmph*, an old maid. That Tad should be thanking his lucky stars for landing such a catch. So when's the wedding?"

"Bobe, he just proposed yesterday. We haven't set a date. But when we do, you have to promise to make the cake. You know I can't get married without one of your famous wedding cakes."

"For you I'll make it extra fancy. So where is the groom-to-be?"

"Right here."

I handed the phone to Tad, who tucked it between his face and shoulder as he warmed his hands over his coffee. "Bobe— can I call you that? I've always wanted a bobe."

I'm not sure what Bobe's response was, but Tad seemed to

think it amusing. "Well, I promise that I will take good care of her. I'll make it my mission in life to see that she wants for nothing and that she'll always be safe and well."

He knew how much power the word *safe* held for Bobe, and I was touched that he would think to use it. Tad had such a knack for pinpointing the words people needed to hear. He chatted with her for another few minutes before handing the phone back to me.

"He's a good boy, a real mensch," she said. I could hear a tea-kettle whistling in the background. "So when will I get to congratulate you in person?"

"Soon, Bobe, I just have to arrange to get two days off in a row so I can drive down there."

"It's been so long, *mummala*. I miss you."

"I miss you, too, Bobe. It'll be soon, I promise."

I placed the phone back in its cradle and grinned at Tad. "She really likes you. I think you might be her favorite goy."

"I thought that honor went to Cary Grant."

"Cary Grant isn't a goy, he's a god. Big difference." I leaned over and brushed my lips against his. "I've gotta go to work."

"Sure you can't be a few minutes late? I think this relationship needs a little more consummating."

"Since when have you ever been able to consummate anything in a few minutes?"

"Good point." He gave me another, more lingering kiss. "After tonight's dinner then?"

I wrinkled my nose. "God, I wish you hadn't insisted on having my mother over. Wait a second. Did you plan it this way?" I asked as Tad was guiding me out the door.

"It'll be the perfect time to tell her. Now, off you go, you don't want to keep the shopaholics waiting." He gave me one more kiss goodbye before closing the door.

I took the bus to Union Square and went in the employee entrance of Dawson's, the high-end department store where I worked as the Sassy department manager. Normally I find the narrow hallway leading to the employee elevator rather stark and claustrophobic, but today it was kind of comforting. Last night my entire life had changed, but Dawson's would always be my one constant. If an archangel descended from heaven to announce that the end of the world was coming in twelve months, the main concern among the staff at Dawson's would be what impact this would have on next season's skirt length. Not that it would be an unimportant issue; I mean, if you can't put a little effort into looking good for the apocalypse, then what the hell's the point?

When the elevator got to the top floor I waved my smaller-than-a-breadbox handbag in front of the guys in security so that they could see I wasn't bringing down anything large enough to stuff a lot of merchandise into. The handbag was actually a privilege reserved for managers and those above them. The sales staff was required to keep their possessions in a clear plastic bag. Everyone was guilty at Dawson's until proven otherwise.

People who don't work retail always assume that security checks and all of that stuff happens on the first floor of a building, but in large specialty stores that's rarely the case, at least not in cities like San Francisco. The ground floor is prime real-estate and thus too important to waste on employees. It's where all the foot traffic is. That's why the bulk of it is always devoted to everyone's top money maker, cosmetics. So us worker bees were forced to enter through the employee entrance on the bottom floor that had nothing other than a pathway to one employee elevator; go up to the very top floor, which was devoted to things like offices and break rooms; get checked in and then take another employee elevator down to the sales floors. Security was a big deal at Dawson's. Convenience wasn't.

I nodded to a few of the other managers on my way to my department and immediately started in on my routine, which consisted of recording new merchandise, setting the floor, checking my selling cost, coaching Dorita and Laura—the two employees I had scheduled for the first shift—and trying to stay present and cheerful, despite the fact that in the hours before my lunch break there were only five sales that were offset by two rather large returns. When I came back from lunch, the department was completely devoid of customers and Dorita and Laura were standing in the front looking like Swiss soldiers guarding the Vatican.

"Still slow, huh? If you need a project…"

"We could straighten and size the Versus jeans on the back shelf?" Laura finished for me. "Yeah…Dorita started that."

"Great, did you finish it?"

Dorita's chiseled features scrunched up into a grimace. "I didn't have a chance. Liz showed up. She's waiting for you in the back room."

"Shit." So not what I needed at the moment. I regarded the door leading to the stockroom that doubled as my office with a mixture of trepidation and annoyance. Liz was the store manager and one of the several people I reported to. Last I checked, all of my buyers were pretty happy with me, so it was inevitable that Liz would think I was doing something horribly wrong. I pushed my way past the untouched racks of clothes and entered Dante's Inferno.

"Hi, April, sorry to hit you with this just as you're getting in from lunch, but I came onto your floor a few minutes ago and there were only two salespeople out and one of them was in the back section."

I forced myself to smile at the anorexic blonde glaring at me from my office chair. "Yeah, I just talked to her about that. Was she neglecting any customers?"

"That's not the point! She's supposed to be in the front of the department greeting people."

I never understood this strategy. How was one supposed to greet invisible people? And in a retail setting, how could the absence of customers not be the point? "I'll work with her on it. It won't happen again."

"Good, when traffic is bad like this we need to be at our best. Has your staff been calling their personal customers?"

Probably not. "Absolutely."

"Good. Remember, the important thing is to control your controllables." Ass kissing was the only controllable that held any importance at Dawson's. Do it well enough and you could get placed in a department that was virtually guaranteed to make its numbers.

"I stopped by to talk to you about the Appreciation Meeting Wednesday. Last month I didn't feel like our store was peppy enough. What do you think?"

"We could have been peppier."

"Oh, I'm so glad we agree." She pulled gingerly at her pink lapels. "Wednesday, I really want everyone to get into the spirit. We're the flagship store, and I know the regionals expect us to really raise the bar. We need to be cheering, clapping—the whole nine yards. In fact…" Liz reached for something under my desk— *Please God, let it be a hara-kiri sword.*

It wasn't, it was a pom-pom. A pom-pom. "I got all the managers two of these. Mickey's the regional who's going to be conducting the meeting this time, so when she introduces our store I want all of us to stand up and say:

> 'Oh Mickey,
> Our store's the best,
> Our sales put others to the test,
> Hey Mickey!'

And then, we'll wave our pom-poms in the air."

Where the hell was the hara-kiri sword?

"April? What do you think?"

"I think you can't get much peppier than that."

"Great! I knew you'd be into it."

As a little girl I had dreamt of being a curator for New York's Whitney Museum. Now, instead of collecting fine works of art and rubbing elbows with the cultural elite, I was playing with pom-poms and taking poetic license with bad '80s tunes. Funny how life works out.

"Well, I'll leave you alone so you can get on the floor. Remember, all bodies up front and don't forget to call your personals!"

I plastered my Miss America grin on my face and held the door open for her.

Liz froze in place. "What's on your finger? Are you engaaaged?"

"Yippee?"

"Oh my God, you are! You're engaged!" She started jumping up and down waving her French manicure in the air like an autistic Barbie. She pulled me into a forced embrace and then suddenly released me. "You're not pregnant, are you?"

That's what I loved about Liz, she was all about tact. "No, my eggs are currently unfertilized."

"Oh, goody!" She was jumping and hugging again. "Well, you just be sure and tell me what days you need off for the wedding and honeymoon. Just don't take off time during any of the four big sales, or the two weeks preceding them, of course. Oh, and I guess it goes without saying that I can't give you any time off around the holidays, but other than that I'm totally flexible. I'm just so excited for you!" She gave me one final excruciating squeeze before leaving me to search for her next victim. I really hated my job.

I silently joined Dorita and Laura in the front of the department and spent the rest of the day trying to figure out how we could call our personals while standing fifteen feet in front of the phone. Unfortunately, it wasn't enough of a dilemma to fully distract me from the two months' salary resting on my finger. I glanced down at my hand. Actually, if that was two month's salary, Tad was doing a lot better than I had realized.

Tad was one of those start-up tech guys or at least that was what I told everyone; it was a little more complicated than that and I'd be lying if I said I fully understood his job. He said he brought different types of technology manufacturers together so that they could make tech products for other manufacturers. He always tried to explain it to me by using a cell phone as an example. If Nokia decided that they wanted to make a phone that featured advanced video games and had an address book that could hold up to five hundred phone numbers it had to go to one outside company for the memory chip and another for the game technology. Tad represented several different kinds of tech companies that complemented each other and then presented them

as kind of a package deal to companies like Nokia. Again, I
didn't really understand it, all I knew was that it was a little
nerve-racking considering that of the large number of start-ups,
the majority were failing these days. Tad's business, SMB, seemed
to be one of the few that was still going strong. The office space
said it all. They were located in the heart of San Francisco's financial district. Tad had two partners at SMB, Sean Miller and
Eric Bradley, but apparently they had all agreed that Tad should
be the one to negotiate the lease. The man was an expert at
getting what he wanted. And to top it all off he was a great
dancer, not to mention well-read and fluent in three languages.
The man was amazing, and I was marrying him. How could I be
anything less than ecstatic?

"Hey, honey, how much for a hand job?"

I turned and looked up at the wiry six-foot man standing next
to me. "I'm sorry, we don't do that here, manicures are given up
at the spa."

"But my cuticles need rubbing now! Come on, rub my cuticles.
Just one little rub?"

I rolled my eyes. "Honestly, Caleb, I'd stick my boot up your
ass if I didn't think you'd enjoy it so much."

He laughed and for the first time I noticed that he had
once again cut his impossibly thin strawberry-blond hair.
Caleb was always applying a new thickening product to it but
there was no question that he was destined for baldness. Caleb
frequently quibbled that when that happened (thanks to his
weight and his distaste for gyms) he would look like a prisoner
of war, to which I would respond, Americans *like* prisoners of
war. We make them darlings of the media and elect them to
the senate. If it wasn't for the months of torture everybody

would be signing up for a gig. Plus I had no doubt that Caleb's sparkling complexion, impeccable fashion sense and beguiling personality would always make him a hot commodity and there were a lot of men who agreed with me on these points. He thrust his Rolex in my face (a gift from a former sugar daddy). "Six thirty-five. You've put in your required overtime. Let's blow this pop stand."

"I don't know, I've been 'spoken to' by Liz. I think maybe I should stay extra late to make an impression just in case she's still around."

"Mmm, hmm, and which is the largest-volume department?"

"Cosmetics."

"Who's the cosmetics manager?"

"You are."

"So if it's acceptable for me, the cosmetics manager, to call it quitting time after a ten-hour day, don't you think that it's acceptable for the manager of some little chickwear department like yours to do the same?"

"Condescending references aside, yeah, I guess you have a point." I looked around my department: two employees and one customer looking through some of our inappropriately revealing careerwear. Assuming my salesgirls didn't kill each other in order to get the commission, everything was under control. "Wait for me, I'll get my purse."

I went back to my office, jotted down some notes for the closing staff and grabbed my bag. By the time I got back out to the floor, Caleb had collected a big red hairball, otherwise referred to as Allie. There was more to the lingerie manager than her hair, just not much. She swore that she was both over five feet and a hundred pounds, but I suspected that those figures were obtained while wearing heels and a lead-filled parka.

Caleb waved me over. "Hey, April, come over here and feel Allie's water bra."

"Oh. Is that what's different?" My hand hovered over her chest. "Isn't it against regulations to feel up co-workers on the premises?"

"Not if it's in the interest of furthering your product knowledge," Allie corrected.

I retracted my hand without squeezing. "I think I'll hold off until we get to the elevator."

"Good idea," Caleb agreed as we walked to the employee elevator. "Give the boys watching the security camera an early bonus."

The metal doors opened and we scooted inside. I reached out to push the button for the top floor but Caleb grabbed my hand and stared at my ring finger.

"Oh my God, you're pregnant."

"You know, Liz jumped to that same conclusion."

Allie snatched my hand away from Caleb and held it inches from her face. "Holy shit, April, it's like the Rock of Gibraltar!"

"Hel-lo! We're just sitting here in an unmoving closed elevator. Don't you think one of us should press the button?"

Caleb grabbed my hand back. "Have you done the rainbow test?"

"The rainbow test?" Allie questioned.

"You're supposed to hold your ring up to the light and if it casts a rainbow…"

"It means you have a good-quality diamond," I finished.

"No, it means you're a closet homosexual. Get with the program, honey."

"So why are we just finding out about this now? Why didn't you call us the minute he put the ice on your finger?" Allie demanded.

"It just happened last night and you two are the first of my friends that I've told, so relax. By the way, we're still not moving."

"You waited almost twenty-four hours to tell us, and now you're impatient because we've been sitting in an elevator for two minutes," Allie said, completely mystified by my unreasonable behavior. "How did Mommy Dearest take it?"

I started kneading my handbag with my fingernails. "I haven't told her yet."

"Why on earth not?" Caleb asked.

"She'll tell me not to do it."

"You never listen to your mother," Allie pointed out, "why should you start now? I know, tell her that the morning before he proposed, you read in your horoscope that you were supposed to say yes to a very important question."

I nodded thoughtfully. "That might work. She's coming up to have a late dinner with Tad and me at his place tonight, so we'll see how it goes."

The elevator door opened and a woman from housekeeping stood before us. "Are you going up?"

"We were thinking about it," I explained. The woman looked confused, so Caleb reluctantly ushered her in and pressed the top button. We stood there silently for the thirty or so seconds that it took us to go up two floors. I assumed Caleb and Allie were formulating their list of questions about the proposal. My thoughts had already switched to my impending dinner.

My mother had only met Tad once before and it had not gone well. Like an idiot, I had neglected to warn Tad about my mother prior to their introduction, so he had done everything that a suitor is supposed to do when meeting his loved one's parent. He put on a sports coat, shined his shoes, bought her a lovely potted orchid and made a point of calling her Ms. Silverperson. As far as my mother was concerned, he might as well have been wearing a sign that said, "Hello, I am the next Rush Limbaugh." Now I had to tell her that I was marrying the man she had come to refer to as "The Great White Hope."

The doors opened once again and we all headed for security where we held open our bags for inspection like the common criminals they presumed us to be.

"You know this really is very cool." I assumed Allie was referring to my engagement, not the security search. "Still, you should have called us right after saying yes."

"Forgive me, but it seemed like an inopportune moment to call you two, seeing that I was busy having sex and all."

The security guy looked up.

"Yes, that's right, I was having sex with my new fiancé. I know that's kind of personal but considering that you are currently rifling through my Tampax, it just doesn't seem like inappropriate conversation." I snapped my purse closed and walked briskly to the exit elevator.

Allie and Caleb quickly caught up. "Tell you what, why don't I give you two ladies a ride to your respective destinations and April can fill us in on everything in the car? Tad's still at the Pacific Heights place, right?"

"Mmm, hmm." How much money must Caleb be making to be able to pay for parking five to six days a week?

The cool breeze hit us as we walked out of the building. I loved this moment. I spend the days cooped up in a completely artificial environment: no windows, no fresh air, everything's pretty and tame, and then I walk out the door and there it is—my city. San Francisco. Locals racing down the sidewalks pulling their leather jackets around them, cars honking at each other, shivering T-shirt-wearing tourists taking pictures of minor traffic accidents, and the occasional drag queen. Everything's in motion, everything's excessively real. It's the moment I look forward to every time I go to work at Dawson's…leaving.

Caleb tugged at my sleeve and we crossed to the garage. "So when's the big event?" he asked.

"Not sure yet. It's going to be a long engagement, so you'll have plenty of time to figure out what makeup you'll need for me and the bridesmaids."

Caleb shook his head as he held open the door of his Toyota. "Honey, I expect to *be* a bridesmaid."

"I am not wearing the same dress as you," Allie said, climbing into the backseat. "Our coloring is completely different. Why the long engagement anyway? If you want to make a life together why not just start ASAP? Life's short."

"We've only been dating three months. It's going to be a long engagement."

Caleb gave me an almost imperceptible nod of approval before switching his focus from the radio, which was now set to an '80s modern-rock station, to his hair, which he tidied with the help of the rearview. "I can't believe you're marrying a man I barely know," Caleb grumbled. "I've only hung out with the two of you three times."

"I've only hung out with them twice and you don't see me giving her a hard time about it," Allie said. "April's a great judge of character. If she says Tad's the one then he's the one."

"Yes, yes, but *why?*" Caleb asked. "What makes Tad a Prince Charming anyway?" he asked, pushing the car into gear. "Is it that he's named after everybody's favorite soap opera character?"

"Tad Martin's not my favorite," I said. "I think Todd Manning is these days."

"Todd Manning? He just sold his own baby on the black market."

"Yeah, that's been kind of a problem for me, but he's just so tortured and lost. It's kind of endearing."

"Okay, you two are scaring me now." Allie pulled herself forward so that her face was between Caleb's and my seats. "Are you saying that Tad has some cute sociopathic tendencies that turn you on?"

"No, no, Tad is very sane. He would never sell anyone's baby. He's actually very…um…righteous."

Caleb winced. "Okay, you say righteous and I think Pat Buchanan."

"I mean righteous in a good way. He has a very clear ethical and moral code. When he sees or hears of someone doing something that is inherently wrong, he speaks up. There aren't many people who do that nowadays."

Caleb gave me a sideways glance. "Give me a for-instance."

"We were sitting at one of the outdoor tables at the Neighborhood Café when a very attractive Asian woman walked by." I focused on the dusty film clinging to the window. "There were these two redneck tourists sitting near us and one of them called out, "Hey, I never had Chinese before, how about a free taster?"

Caleb maneuvered us around a cable car. "You have to cut some of these tourists a little extra slack," he said. "The pickup lines that work on their livestock don't always go over too well with the Homo sapien chicks."

Allie and I cracked up and I eased back into the leather seats. "Anyway, Tad stood up for her. He went right over to their table and chewed them out. Told them their behavior was repulsive and pathetic and that he was leaving so he wouldn't have to share air space with them."

Allie slapped her hand against the upholstery. "This guy fucking rocks. Tell more."

"Tad took my hand and started to lead me out of there, but one of the guys followed us and challenged Tad to a fight. The jerk was, like, four inches shorter than Tad and looked as if he lived off deep-fried cheese sticks, so it wouldn't have been much of a contest, but Tad took the high road. He just said, 'Look, I don't want to fight you, but you've got to know that you can't treat people like that. Not women, not Chinese—no one.' By now there's a crowd around us and the manager had to come out and break it up. The two guys were asked to leave and everyone cheered Tad. It was awesome."

"Shit…" Allie collapsed back into her seat with the satisfaction of someone who had just watched a good sex scene. "I think *I* want to marry him."

"Well, if he ever discovers a long-lost twin, I'll send him your way."

"Okay, you really need to cut back on the daytime drama." Allie leaned forward again. "But I do think it would be fun to have a wedding. Most men are pretty much the same, when you get down to the nitty-gritty. Maybe I'll just pick one and throw him into a tux." Caleb double-parked across from Allie's Russian Hill apartment, and she pointed to a man with dark hair falling to his shoulders walking out of her building. "There, I pick that one."

Caleb shook his head as we watched Allie's future husband pause to light a cigarette. "He's too pretty to be straight."

"So? I didn't say I wanted to have a romantic relationship with him, I said I wanted to marry him. Two totally different things— ask my parents."

They were both wrong. The one thing I was sure about was that my marriage to Tad would always be romantic; I mean, the man had memorized the first forty-two of Shakespeare's sonnets. I also didn't think the guy in question was too pretty to be anything; in fact, just the opposite.

For some reason, we all became quiet as we watched him take a few long drags of his cigarette and walk into the darkness. When he was completely out of sight Allie heaved a big sigh and pushed the car door open. "As tempted as I am to chase him down and throw a lasso around his waist, I've really got to head up. There's a carton of Ben & Jerry's in the freezer and a bottle of Baileys in the cupboard and I don't feel comfortable leaving them alone for long periods of time. Call me tomorrow and give me the dirt about dinner."

"Okay, but in case I get busy just assume it was awful."

Caleb waited for Allie to get inside before directing the car toward Pacific Heights. "So you're engaged to Gandhi. But, tell me, how does he treat you?"

My grin widened. "He worships me."

"Hon, lots of men worship you. Look in the mirror."

I shook my head dismissively. "Not my body or my appearance. *Me.* He's always romancing me, telling me how considerate and fun I am. He's not possessive but he's protective. I guess you could say he's a little paternal."

"Oh, here comes the Freudian psychoanalysis."

"It'd be pretty hard for me to marry a man like my father, considering I've never met him."

"So you find a guy who fits the bill and you're marrying him? I read somewhere you're not supposed to do that."

"He's not a father figure, but…come on, Caleb, it's what every woman wants. To feel safe, protected, taken care of. I mean, yeah, I want to hold on to my independence, and Tad would never take that from me." I waved my hand in the air as if trying to grasp the right words. "Everyone should have somebody who will go to bat for them. I've got that in Tad."

Caleb gave my knee a little squeeze. "I'm glad you're happy, but just so you know, I'll always stick by you, too." He stopped the car in front of Tad's. "Are you ready for this?"

"No."

"Well, you're gonna have to get out of the car and deal, I have a date in twenty minutes."

"Is this your version of sticking by me?"

"This is my version of forcing you to face the music. Now go take your pill and call me in the morning."

I stuck my head between my hands. "I hate pills."

"Give it a rest. It's not like you're dining with Hannibal Lector."

He was right; it was just my mother. And if she hated Tad, so what? I hated most of *her* friends. This would just even the playing field. I gave Caleb a kiss on the cheek and climbed out. I mean, really, how bad could it be?

TWO

"Goddess, is that you?" I heard Tad's voice filter through the intercom.

"Yep, that's me. Goddess of the underworld."

There was a buzz and I pushed open the door and headed up the three flights to his apartment. Halfway up, the scent of my impending meal overwhelmed my senses and caused my stomach to rejoice. However, as I continued my climb I stopped rejoicing and focused on new and more disturbing observations. Tad was waiting for me at the top of the stairs. He was wearing a plaid shirt, untucked, and a pair of jeans that I had never seen before, although they definitely were not new. They had a rip in the knee and the rest of the fabric looked so worn I was sure that a few strokes of my hand would result in hole number two. He was also wearing sandals. Tad never wore sandals. Tennis shoes, dress shoes, boots. Once I had seen him wear a pair of boat shoes— but no sandals.

He extended his hand to me and kissed my palm. "You look gorgeous, as always."

"Thanks, you look…interesting. What's with the new getup?"

"When in Rome…" Tad shrugged his shoulders nonchalantly. "Speaking of which, your mom showed up early. She's very… Gothic today."

"Gothic? Explain Gothic."

"You'll see." Tad led me into the apartment and presented me to my mother, who was lounging on the love seat fondling a glass of wine.

"April!" She gracefully rose from her seat and held her arms out in anticipation of a hug. Tad was right, she was gothic. She had added deep purple highlights to her curly dark hair and she was wearing a black crushed-velvet sheath dress and a jaggedly cut crystal pendant that dangled between her breasts. I have long since given up questioning my mother's fashion choices, so her outfit didn't really shock me. What did take me off guard was Tad's apartment.

His decor had always been tasteful if a little barren, but today he had done something completely different. There were candles everywhere, thick beeswax sticks held in new beaded candle-holders by the windows, floating tea lights on top of the low bookshelf; plus, there was a batik sarong that I had never seen before hanging on the wall, and a little brass Hindu god sat cross-legged in the middle of the coffee table. It was like he had raided the clearance section of Pier One Imports. He had moved the dining table into the middle of the living room and, along with place settings, had decorated it with a dried fall-flower arrangement (wisely he placed this away from the candles). As far as I knew, the only dried thing he'd ever previously kept in his home was a boxful of raisins. My mother cleared her throat awkwardly and stretched her arms out a little more since I obviously wasn't getting the hint. I forced my mouth closed and gave her the expected embrace.

"Mom, I'm...I'm glad you could make it." I was having a really hard time focusing. Were we listening to Sinéad O'Connor?

Tad silently handed me a glass of wine, which I downed in two gulps. I shot him a questioning glance, to which he responded with a sly wink. Maybe Tad really did have a long-lost twin and this was him. Not a good thing; long-lost twins were always evil.

He rested a hand on both mine and my mother's shoulders. "So, are you girls hungry?"

"Women," my mother corrected, her hazel eyes narrowing. "We stopped being girls at eighteen."

"Wow, I can't believe I said that. You are absolutely right, that was really insensitive of me."

I did a quick double take. He was so totally evil-twin guy. My mother however was completely pacified. "We all have little slips of the tongue now and then." She tried to toss her somewhat immobile hair. "How about it, April, you ready to *mangiare?*"

"By all means." Mom and I took our seats while Tad excused himself to get the first course.

"I was wrong about Tad," my mother confided in what qualified as a stage whisper. "He's wonderful. If you two break up, I might go for him myself."

"This must be what Kendall feels like when introducing guys to Erika Kane."

"Huh?" My mother shook her head uncomprehendingly.

"Nothing. Look, Tad and I are not breaking up. He is a great guy, just not necessarily the guy you think he is."

"Oh, I know, I know, he explained everything to me. Last time, he was just trying to make an impression. I guess he thought I was going to be one of those Doris Day moms or something. This—" my mother made a sweeping gesture to direct my attention to the miniature fire hazards surrounding us "—this is the real him."

"Everything going okay here?" Tad asked as he placed some adorable little grape-leaf-wrapped mystery food on our plates.

"Not really," I said. "I'm kind of getting this *X-Files* vibe, except instead of turning into an alien or zombie, it seems you've morphed into the pre-Republican version of Sonny Bono."

The fine lines on mom's forehead deepened. "The *X-Files?*"

"Get a television set," I shot back impatiently.

Tad offered me a tolerant smile. "I think somebody had a bad day at work."

"Or maybe she's menstruating," my mother offered. "Honey, it's very important that we embrace the moods that are part of a woman's cycle. If you need to scream, cry or howl at the moon, you do it."

What I wanted to do was give them both a whack upside the head. I took a steadying breath. Tad was trying to please my mother. So what? It was nice of him, irritating as hell, but nice. Time to offer an olive branch. "I'm not menstruating, Mom, but I did have a bad day at work. I'm sorry I snapped."

My mother gave me a knowing nod, clearly she was clinging to her menstruation idea.

"No need to apologize," Tad said, although I hadn't really been talking to him. He then turned to my mother. "April and I have news."

If I had been hesitant to make the announcement before, I was loathing the prospect now. A few hours ago I had been nervous about our engagement but at least I had been enthusiastic about Tad.

"Oh, me, too…" Mom put down the fork before it had a chance to touch her food. "And it's big."

Now I was really scared. My mind raced to figure out what Mom was about to spring on me. I didn't think she was pregnant; there were some mistakes even my mother refused to repeat. Nor was she going to confess to a lesbian love affair, because considering everything else she'd done in her life, that really wouldn't be all that newsworthy. I squeezed my eyes closed. *Please let it not be another commune.*

"I have found religion."

I opened one eye. "You've rediscovered Judaism?" I asked hopefully.

Mom shook her head vigorously. "No, no, no. This is much more revolutionary than that. I now belong to the Temple of the Earth Goddess."

Maybe a commune wouldn't be so bad. "Is this…temple… Does it require human sacrifices?"

"Don't be silly. It's a new movement that started in Santa Cruz. We already have almost two hundred members in our congregation. You see, we Children of the Earth—that's what we call ourselves—believe that all these so-called environmentalists have it wrong. It's not about respecting the environment, it's about worshipping it. We need to be kissing the ground we walk on and hugging the trees, not figuratively but literally. We have no right to kill the spiders that come into our homes. Every animal, insect and slug is part of the Earth Goddess's holy creation. If an ant enters our home we should feed it, not smash it, or worse, spray it with an evil poison created by our oppressors."

"Our oppressors?"

"Proctor & Gamble."

"All righty then." I looked to Tad for support, but he was listening to her with an expression you would expect most people to wear while listening to a State of the Union address being delivered by a president they'd voted for. I placed both hands on the table and tried to center myself. "So let me get this straight. If you find an ant on your coffee table, you show it where you keep the bread?"

"Exactly!"

"So, your grocery bill has gone up since you joined this church?"

"Temple. I would never join a church."

"Of course not, but a pagan cult, that's okay."

"It sounds fascinating," Tad said. "I've always felt that too many people get so wrapped up in the biblical religions that they lose sight of life's true essence."

I sat there gawking at him. He had "always" felt this? By "always" did he mean for the last five minutes?

He tapped his finger against the edge of my mother's plate. "You should taste your appetizer, Kate, I think you'll like it." At least he didn't immediately offer to sacrifice his table to the termites.

Mom gently pierced her food with her fork. "Is it vegetarian?"

Tad offered her a display of pearly whites. "Vegan."

"Okay, that's it." My chair crashed to the floor as I jumped to my feet. I glared at Tad. "I don't know if I need to take you to an exorcist or a rehab clinic, but if you don't snap out of it right now, this engagement is off!"

My mother clapped her hand over her heart. "Engagement? Honey, are you two getting married?"

"Not unless…" But no one was listening to me. Tad and Mom were hugging and kissing. She was choking back contrived sobs and he was laughing like an idiot. Finally Mom turned to me and placed her hands on both of my cheeks.

"Oh, honey, I'm so happy for you." She sighed and cocked her head to the side. "Of course, you know how I feel about the institution of marriage, but if you believe that you need a piece of paper to bind you together then so be it. The important thing is you have found a truly wonderful man and I just know that the two of you will be happy."

"I'm not happy."

"That's wonderful, sweetie."

Why was I even there? If I had skipped dinner and sent an inflatable sex doll in my place would anyone have noticed?

Tad righted my chair and held it out for me gallantly. "I know we all have a lot to talk about, but at this rate our food is going to spoil before we taste it."

And then I did something unspeakably horrible. I sat down. I didn't scream at them for ignoring me; I didn't rail against them for showing so little regard for my feelings; I just sat down and ate my dinner. I listened to my mother tell Tad about the sixty or so holidays observed by the Children of the Earth: one for the fish, another for the invertebrates and so on. I stared blankly at Tad as he asked about the power of rose quartz. I did flinch when my mother asked if we would consider allowing her to marry us on a nude beach at midnight, but actually found myself mollified when Tad told her that I had the final say when it came to the wedding arrangements. I idly wondered what new narcotic had brought about my mother's current sense of enlightenment, because when it came to my mother there was almost always a drug involved, but I didn't express my concern. Every once in a while I'd throw out a question but I didn't push it when they were evaded, or out and out ignored. This was all wrong. Tad was supposed to be the sane and stable part of my life that made me feel safe. He was not supposed to be my mother's twin. But I couldn't get myself to challenge him now. If he sided with her against me and she saw it... I just wasn't strong enough to handle that. By the time dinner was over I felt nothing but a dull resentment directed not only at them but also at myself.

Finally the torture session came to an end and Mom stood up to make her farewells. "You two just have to come down to Santa Cruz soon. If you let me, I'll arrange a time for the priestess to bless your union. It's a lovely little ceremony, and all you have to do is stand there and drink the wine when she hands it to you. You will come, won't you?"

Tad squeezed her hand. "Of course, April and I will call as soon as we can coordinate our schedules."

Mom gave us both another kiss and then skipped out of the apartment, leaving me with the alien-vegan life-form that claimed to be my fiancé.

Tad turned to me for the first time that evening and reached out to squeeze my waist. "I think she likes me now."

"Well, at least somebody does."

"Oh, come on." He pulled me in a little closer. "All I did was tell her what she wanted to hear. What's wrong with that?"

"What's wrong with that?" I pushed away from him and crossed my arms in front of myself protectively. "Whatever happened to being yourself?"

Tad blinked his eyes in apparent incomprehension.

"Look at this place." I shoved a bowlful of potpourri under his nose. "This isn't you. If I wanted to marry the male version of my mother I'd find myself a Hari Krishna guy and be done with it."

I thought I saw a flash of anger cross his features, but I wasn't done yet. "And what about the way you treated me at dinner? You acted as if I wasn't even there. Worse, you acted like I didn't matter. Did you hear me when I asked you about the apartment and your newfound interest in astrology? I mean, if you don't respect me enough to take me seriously, maybe we really should rethink this—"

"Give me a fucking break!" I stepped back as if avoiding a physical blow. Tad had changed again. Not into the man that had proposed to me last night but into something new. Something really, really angry. "So I wanted to impress your mother, so the fuck what? If your mother was a normal person, I'd have put on a suit and called her ma'am. Would you have had a problem with that?"

"Actually…"

"I proposed and you said yes. Did you mean it or not?"

"Of course I meant it, but—"

"But what? I mean so little to you that one bad dinner is enough of a reason to end it? Or are you so insecure that you can't handle my taking the time to focus on someone else's needs, even if that someone else is your own mother?"

"No, but—"

"Why the fuck do you think men give women roses?"

"What?"

"Why do men give women roses? Why do we arrange candlelight dinners and give you cards with little hearts on them? Do you think that we do it because we secretly love sweet frilly things?"

"I don't know…"

"We do it because we want to make the women we love happy. We want to make them smile. Tonight I wanted to make the woman-I-love's mother smile, and you're bitching me out for it."

When this argument started I was pretty sure I had a legitimate point. Now I was totally confused. Had I been in the wrong? Did I owe *him* an apology?

"Look, I guess I just, I…" I faltered and looked around for something to help me find my bearings. "Maybe I overreacted."

Tad nodded but didn't say anything.

"I'm…I'm sorry."

He sighed and rubbed his eyes. "It's all right. I know you're tired." He stepped closer again and pulled me to his chest. I felt suffocated.

"Tell you what," he continued, "why don't we blow out these stupid candles and cuddle on the couch. Maybe we can even have a little more wine, and if you want, I might have a few ants we can murder."

"Okay." I managed to force a smile. Something very strange had just happened, and for the life of me I couldn't figure out what it was.

At five-thirty the next morning I woke up in Tad's bed alone. I had vague memories of finishing off the remaining wine and Tad helping me to the bedroom. I was pretty sure that he had joined me. I pushed myself onto my elbows and tried to get a handle on the situation. From the living room I could make out the sound of fingers tapping against a keyboard. I threw a jacket over the oversize T-shirt I was dressed in and went out to investigate.

Tad glanced up briefly from the computer and smiled appreciatively. "You look good. You should go pantless more often."

"Tad, it's not even six. What are you doing?"

"I've got an idea. Your mom said that her temple has almost two hundred active members, and there are almost as many holidays. That's a lot to keep track of, don't you think?"

"I prefer not to think about it."

"The obvious solution is a calendar. The Jews have one, right?"

"Well, yes, but our calendar is actually numbered differently…"

"I'm talking about a calendar featuring different landscapes and nature scenes and noting all the holidays. And if we sold it at twenty bucks a pop, twenty times two hundred, that's four thousand dollars, babe."

"First of all, I'm pretty sure there's a law prohibiting entrepreneurial activity between the hours of midnight and 6:00 a.m. Secondly, *almost* two hundred members is not two hundred and you have to assume that some of them are related to each other and living in the same house and thus only need one calendar. And thirdly, what the hell do you mean *we?*"

"But I'm sure that within the next few months their membership will have increased by ten or twenty percent. It is Santa Cruz after all, and you know how many freaks live there."

Funny, I would have sworn I'd made three points. I leaned over his shoulder and studied the photo he had pulled up. It was one he had taken while hiking in Hawaii. It really would be beautiful on a calendar.

"I've been sorting through my photos. So far I've found five that I think would work. Oh, and I made up the calendar months for the next year."

"How long have you been working on this?"

"Since two-thirty."

I blinked. "You've been up for three hours? Tad, you haven't slept in two nights."

He got up and kissed me gently on the lips. "Sleep is for the lazy."

"Hey, I like being lazy."

"And I like watching you sleep, so it's a win-win." He glanced up at the clock hanging over the fireplace. "I have to get showered and changed. I want to be at the office early this morning."

I really was in awe of him. I could survive on six hours of sleep, but anything less than that turned me into the Bride of Frankenstein, inarticulate and mean. Tad walked past me to start his morning rituals as I rubbed the sand out of my eyes. It was probably a good idea if I practiced being as unproductive as possible during my free time. That way Tad and I could balance each other out. Theoretically, this should have been a good day to try out that game plan since it was technically my day off, but in a pathetic attempt to make myself seem dedicated I had agreed to come in to set the floor with Marilyn, my casual-sportswear buyer. So I really only had forty-five minutes of lazy time before I had to throw myself together and run. I fell onto the couch and flipped the channels until I found E! television's behind-the-scenes look at *Three's Company*. I make it a point never to waste lazy time.

THREE

By the time Marilyn and I were done, all of my less-expensive and slower-selling merchandise (the things she bought) were up front and my higher-ticket hot sellers (the things Blakely, my careerwear buyer bought) were in back. Of course, I wouldn't have to worry about it for long because by the end of the day Marilyn would be on a plane to L.A. for a vendor show. Blakely would be back in town by tomorrow afternoon. In other words, I would be doing another major floor change in less than twenty-four hours. I bet this didn't happen to museum directors. I tried to imagine myself in an elaborately furnished office at the Whitney with two curators in front of me.

"April, this is unacceptable. Everyone knows that the Monets I bought are far superior to the crap this bimbo picked up, so obviously it's my purchases that should be on the first floor."

"Excuse me, but my Picassos kick your Monets' ass."

No, I was sure museum directors weren't subjected to this.

"April…April, are you listening to me?" Marilyn was standing in front of a display table, her stocky but fashionably dressed frame becoming dangerously rigid.

"Hmm? Yes, of course. I was just…" I faltered for a moment. "I was just thinking how those jeans are going to blow out now that the customers can really see the cut. Putting them on the mannequin was really a stroke of genius." I had begun to use the term *genius* way too liberally.

"Thank you." She turned to admire her handiwork. "So you'll coach your team on the FAB for the jeans and the leathers?"

I knew that in this case FAB stood for the "feature advantages and benefits" of the merchandise because God knows there was nothing fabulous about it. "I'll coach them."

"Good." She glanced at the salespeople who were busily clearing the empty fixtures and racks off the floor before the doors opened in five minutes. She then took in my own faded jeans and T-shirt. "I take it you're not working today."

"I just came in for the floor change."

"I'll go up in the elevator with you." Of course there was no "Wow, April, it was so great of you to come in on your day off." It was only natural that Dawson's would expect me to give up my life since they had already purchased my soul for the low-low price of forty-five thousand a year.

I gathered my things and we walked across to the elevator. "So what's new with you these days?" Outside of "hello" these were the first nonbusiness words Marilyn had spoken all morning.

"A lot actually." We stepped into the elevator and went up toward the sixth floor, where the security check and buyers offices were located. "Tad proposed a few days ago."

"Did you know that Don hasn't even mentioned marriage and we've been dating six friggin' years?"

Definitely not the response I was prepared for. I toyed with the band of my wristwatch. "Well, he obviously loves you otherwise he wouldn't still be around..." We stepped off the elevator and paused by the doors. "I'm sure he's just waiting for the perfect moment."

"Bull. He's a little chickenshit who doesn't have the guts to make a commitment."

I heard the musical notes of my Nokia floating up from my purse and I plunged my hand in for it with unprecedented enthusiasm. "Really important call," I explained before looking to see what number was on the screen. "Got to take it."

"Whatever."

I watched her stomp down the hall toward her office. I clicked Talk and held the phone to my ear. "Hello, darling, missing me already?"

"The Ritz had a cancellation," Tad said.

I remained silent for a beat.

"April, did you hear me?"

"I heard you, I'm just trying to decode your message. Just answer yes or no—are the kidnappers there with you?"

Tad laughed. "The small ballroom at the Ritz, April. It's available for the Sunday of Martin Luther King's birthday."

"And you wanted to throw him a birthday party? That's sweet, but you do realize he's dead, right? I'm just saying 'cause getting him there might be a problem."

"Very cute. I think I want to book it. What do you say? Are you up for putting together the wedding of the year in a three-month time span?"

"No." I hung up the phone. I was fairly sure he was kidding

but just in case he wasn't it was better to avoid the conversation all together. My phone rang again but I forced myself to ignore it. If I didn't have to list my many objections to his proposition, he wouldn't be able to break them down.

I snagged the new *InStyle* from the break room and left Dawson's in favor of the café a few doors down. I had gotten on the scale that morning and I was three pounds thinner, so I figured I'd celebrate by adding a chocolate-filled croissant to my normal espresso order. My phone rang again as I was in the process of being rung up. My fingers itched to pick up but I reached for my wallet instead.

The lanky freckle-faced cashier looked up from the register to regard my musical purse. "Is that your phone?"

"Yes. Do you have a problem with that?"

The cashier wisely didn't answer and took my money instead. The ringing stopped. I sat at a vacated table that was adorned with the crumb-filled plate left by the previous occupant. My cell was at it again. I pulled it out and tapped my fingers against the screen flashing Tad's number. What if there was an emergency? Maybe Tad really had been kidnapped and his outrageous request had been a clue meant to inform me that he was being held hostage at an overly priced hotel chain. I had to answer it.

"We are not getting married in three months," I said in lieu of hello. "And we are not having it at the Ritz-Carlton. These are nonnegotiable points."

"The Ritz is perfect. Every woman wants to get married at the Ritz."

"Are you trying to tell me that I'm not a woman, or that you are one?"

"April, I want this to be perfect. You're the best and you

should have your dream wedding, complete with a long flowing veil and a lavish reception…at the Ritz."

"Sweetie, that was Joan Rivers's dream and, lucky her, she had the money to live out that fantasy through her daughter. My mother's dream is that I shack up with some stagehand who can get her free passes to Lilith Fair. Even if she had the money she wouldn't pay for this, and I don't want to go into major debt just so that I can wear white after Labor Day at the Ritz."

"Don't worry about money, we can afford to splurge. Come on, April, you only get married once."

"Yeah, but bankruptcy lasts a lifetime."

"April," the deceptively gentle female voice came from behind me. "Taking a break already or is this your day off?"

I shifted my position so I could stare up at Blakely's lightly tanned features and tried to mask my horror. "I'll call you back," I whispered into the phone and quickly hung up. Blakely was hardly the most annoying of the Dawson's buyers, but she was high up there on the evil scale, and if she had gone to my department and seen her merchandise in the back section she was probably ready to smack me with a cloven hoof. I squirmed slightly in my seat. "It's my day off, and speaking of which, isn't it yours, too?"

"Mmm, hmm. I just got in from New York. I'm completely spent but I have a nail appointment in an hour so I figured I'd pick up a latte and check out your floor while I wait."

I stared at my espresso and forced myself to say the words I knew she expected. "Care to join me?"

"Love to." Blakely gracefully assumed the seat opposite me and used a silk fingernail to nudge the abandoned plate farther from her person. "I really am glad to have run into you. I've been wanting to discuss something."

"Oh?" That sounded like something that could take the better part of an hour.

"What do you see as your future at Dawson's?"

I considered the question. Either she had already been on my floor and wanted me to step down or she was trying to prime me for a promotion. I swallowed the coffee, along with my pride, and gave her my practiced answer. "I love Dawson's. This isn't just a job for me, it's part of who I am and I hope to take advantage of every opportunity for advancement available to me."

The flicker of amusement in her eyes told me she recognized B.S. when she heard it, but the rest of her countenance remained unchanged. "This, of course, is just between you and me."

I knew immediately that she had told at least five other people. "Of course."

"There are no open assistant-buyer positions at the moment but…I don't think Cherise is very happy in her job."

I looked away from Blakely and focused on the scratch on the table. She and I both knew that her assistant was about as happy as any mother of a two-year-old cardiac patient could be. Cherise needed her job; she needed the money, the insurance and the outlet. She was also good at what she did, but Blakely felt she had a bit too much attitude, which is another way of saying she was too black. Blakely had inherited Cherise from her predecessor and she'd been gritting her teeth and bearing it for the last thirteen months. Of course, I was pretty ethnic myself, but I didn't braid my hair or harbor a crush for Puff Daddy, so as far as Blakely was concerned I was the perfect answer to the EOE dilemma. It was obvious where Blakely was heading with this and it was unethical and offensive. And I *really* wanted to be promoted.

I ran my finger along the rim of my cup. "Has Cherise said anything about wanting to leave?" I knew damn well she hadn't.

"I can just tell. You know she's taken over three weeks of vacation time in the past year. We're only supposed to have two."

Her daughter had heart surgery, you bitch! "I think she's had a lot going on but I thought things were calming down for her. She always seems so dedicated."

"Trust me, she's not the picture-perfect employee she pretends to be."

Now, *this* was a code I could translate. I played with my hair self-consciously and let out a little yelp as my ring snagged a stray curl.

Blakely's eyes zoomed in on my ring finger. "You're engaged."

"Yesss." Why was it so many people forgot to put congratulations in front of that sentence. I tugged a little harder and freed my ring, then held it up proudly as the disembodied hairs hung limply from its prongs.

"How wonderful." Blakely seemed more concerned about the hairs than the ring, which goes to show that we shared at least some of the same priorities. "Most men don't understand how important a woman's career is to her. You're fortunate to have found one who does."

"Tad knows that I'm a workaholic by nature. It's one of the things he loves about me." Damn, I had gotten so good at this code talk. My next job was going to be as a political speechwriter.

Blakely visibly relaxed. "So have you two set a date? I always love winter weddings. The gowns they design for the season are always so much more regal than the ones they put out for spring."

"We haven't set a date, but it's definitely going to be a long engagement." My Nokia started ringing again.

"Go ahead and answer it," Blakely instructed. "I have to order my latte anyway."

It occurred to me that I shouldn't need her permission to answer my cell phone on my day off, but sadly I also knew I never would have had the guts to answer without it. I waited until she had gotten up to purchase her caffeine before pressing Talk.

"I don't have time to argue this with you. I'm with Blakely."

"I thought this was your day off."

I glanced over at Blakely. Two people were ahead of her in line, and from the look of impatience on Blakely's face, I'd say their life expectancy was rapidly decreasing. "It is, I ran into her by chance."

"Lucky you. Listen, April, you didn't get a bat mitzvah, you didn't have a sweet sixteen party and you said you had a lousy prom. We all deserve to be spoiled occasionally and you never have been. Let me be the first person to do that for you. I promise you won't regret it."

Oh, *melt*. Blakely moved one position up in what was turning out to be a very slow-moving line. I was still unsure if I wanted a big wedding, but I was very clear on wanting Tad to spoil me. How could I say no to this? Of course, there was the three-months part to consider. Maybe Allie was right. Maybe the long engagement was just an unnecessary postponement of happiness. I had to think about this. "How long do we have to decide?"

"I have to let them know today."

"Forget it." I hung up the phone. Tens of thousands of dollars we were going to have to commit to this and he wanted me to treat it as an impulse buy. Blakely was finally being waited on but I could tell by the way that she was repeatedly stabbing the countertop with a fork that the service left something to be desired. I made a note to myself to never piss her off while in the presence of utensils.

It took Tad a full three minutes to call me back. "I just booked it."

I couldn't speak. Was he joking? Guys forgot to give cards on your birthday, they spilled red wine on your favorite Pottery Barn rug, they had sex with your college roommate, but they didn't book reception halls without express permission. No way was he serious. "You didn't really. I mean, this is a joke, right?"

"Nope, they have my credit card number and they're gonna use it. I told you I was going to spoil you, and I meant it."

"And I told you I didn't want you to do this. Call them back and tell them no."

"No can do. There's a five-thousand-dollar cancellation fee."

"Are you kidding me? Call back right now! If you call back minutes after making the reservation I'm sure they won't charge you."

"Maybe not, but I'm not canceling. You'd better start dress shopping—we're getting married in three months." The line went dead.

Blakely approached with her latte. The fork had been retired. "The cashier is a complete retard. I had to repeat my order four times before he got it right and all I ordered was a half-caf-nonfat-no-foam-vanilla latte."

"Uh-huh."

Blakely's eyes narrowed slightly. "What's wrong with you?"

"Huh? Oh, nothing." I shook my head, trying to clarify what had just happened. "I was just talking to Tad about wedding stuff. We, um, I think we set a date."

"Oh?" Blakely sipped her half-caf-nonfat-what-the-hell-ever coffee. "And what would that be?"

"Um, this January. January nineteenth."

Blakely put her drink down and folded her hands on the table. "Usually, when people talk of having a long engagement they are referring to a period of time that extends further than three months."

"Really? I didn't realize that." I winced as soon as the words left my mouth. It was never a good idea to use sarcasm with the person in the best position to promote you. "Sorry, it's just pre-wedding jitters. But it will be better this way... This way I'll have the whole wedding thing out of the way by the time any positions open up in your office." Boy, was that a stretch.

"Right." Blakely wasn't buying it but she also obviously didn't care. "So you would take the position if it were offered to you."

For a brief moment my problems with Tad took a backseat to the immediate issue of my career. I toyed with the corners of my napkin. What would be worse, working for Liz, the demented cheerleader, or Blakely, the female version of Satan?

"April?"

"I'd take it." I had already sold my soul so I might as well report to the big guy.

"Wonderful." Blakely's lips curled up. She could now get rid of Cherise and avoid a lawsuit. If Blakely's plans worked out it was going to be hard not to hate myself for allowing her to use me in order to hurt someone else. But if Blakely really wanted to fire Cherise she was going to do it no matter what I did or didn't agree to so I might as well let myself be used. At least that's what I was going to tell myself. "I'll let you know as soon as something becomes available. I probably won't make any changes before the quarter's wrapped up but that's just a few short months away." She checked her watch. "Oh no, I don't think I'm going to have time to check out your floor after all."

"You're kidding? I was really looking forward to getting your input."

After spending another ten minutes playing politics with Blakely, I raced back to my department to do a floor change during business hours. This was a major no-no and if Liz had come down from her office to see me stripping mannequins and running over customers with four-ways of leathers she would gouge my eyes out with a cheap mascara wand.

I checked the time. Two-twenty. I had spent the better part of my day off working. Normally that would have been enough to make me want to scream, but now I found myself longing to coordinate another outfit, write another schedule, plan another special event—anything other than think about what went down between Tad and me earlier. The worst part was nothing did go down. We didn't get in a fight. I mean, what was I so upset about? That he wanted to spoil me with a big wedding at the Ritz? Most women would kill for that problem.

The exhaustion I'd been staving off finally took its hold on me. I couldn't figure this out right now. Right now I just needed to go home, watch the soap that I'd taped and go to bed early. And my illusive troubles with Tad? Well, in the words of Scarlett O'Hara, tomorrow is another day.

I took the J train home. I dropped onto a seat and put my coat next to me to discourage others from getting within touching distance. There was a Latina in her midfifties sitting across from me, staring out the window, although there was nothing to see but the concrete walls of the tunnel. There was nothing outwardly original about her, but I found myself nonetheless reaching into my tote bag for my pocket sketch pad. She was wearing a pale-blue skirt suit that she probably picked up at Mervyn's or some such place and the briefcase on her lap was severely frayed at the corners. She had probably been beautiful in her youth. She would still be so now if she didn't look so damn depressed. It was palpable really, each line in her face was testimony to the years and layers of living beneath—and no doubt hundreds of life's little disappointments. She didn't notice my sketching. She just sat there staring at nothing. There was no gold band on her hand nor was there a tan line or skin depression to give evidence of past commitments.

That would never be me. I didn't love my job but I did love Tad—nonexistent problems be damned—and now I would have him forever. He was my "at least." You know when things go wrong in your life, your friends always bombard you with "at leasts." "So your love life sucks, at least you have your work" or in my case vice versa. You knew you were in trouble when people resorted to, "At least you have your health." If I ever got there, I was going to go out and catch myself a very unhealthy terminal illness.

Whenever the news media interviewed individuals who were on their death beds they frequently said that they wished they had done more with their lives, but they *never* said that they would willingly give up their loving family in exchange for a clean bill of health. It's why masochists cut themselves; people would rather be consumed by pain than depression.

My subject got off at the Civic Center exit, leaving me with a half-finished portrait. I longed to work with models like the ones in my college art classes. But I digress. No one made money as an artist. I certainly wouldn't have. I had made the pragmatic choice. And I could still be a star, if only recognized by the other tortured souls within Dawson's.

I got off the subway at the Castro exit. There were no depressed people in the Castro. Or if there were they hid it under Estée Lauder for men. I walked through the sea of gay couples until I came to my Edwardian apartment building. Tad was standing outside the door holding a single red rose.

I held my hand out in a stop-in-the-name-of-love gesture. "Whatever you want to do, I'm not up for it."

Tad smiled and looked up at the sky, "God, I haven't even married her and already she isn't up for 'whatever.'"

"Tad, I'm tired. I don't want to go out to dinner, drinks, dancing or any of the other spontaneous outings you're famous for, and I'm sure as hell not up for talking about the Ritz."

He stepped closer and brushed the petals of the rose against my cheek. "So why don't you tell me what you are up for."

"Watching my soap and going to bed."

"And what do you expect will happen in good old Llanview today?"

"Well, for one, I expect Jessica will find out that the man who's been tormenting her family and recently married her twin sister is really her father."

Tad scrunched up his nose in distaste. "He married his daughter?"

"No, his wife and his daughter are twins but they have different fathers."

Tad opened his mouth, then closed it.

I tried unsuccessfully to suppress a smile. "Yeah, I know, I haven't figured it out yet, either."

"And you were going to try to solve this medical mystery on your own? Good God, woman, are you mad?"

I giggled and felt myself involuntarily leaning in to him. He reached behind me with his free hand and stroked my hair. "If you let me come up I might be grateful enough to make popcorn."

"I'm not sure that the ninety seconds it takes to throw a bag of Orville Redenbacher in the microwave is enough of an enticement for me."

"Foot massage?"

"We have ourselves a winner."

In my dream there was a monster trying to get into my room. I couldn't see him but I just knew he was terrible, like something out of a high-tech science-fiction movie. I could hear his claws scratching against the wall. I knew that I needed to run but it was so dark and I couldn't see which way to go. I had no idea how to defend myself from this thing. Could it be killed? Defeated? His claws just kept moving—*scratch, scratch, scratch*— and bit by bit the wall began to crumble. Specks of plaster began to fall onto my eyes.

I blinked and adjusted my vision to the darkness. My room. I could make out the outline of my robe hanging on the back of a chair near the window. I could feel Tad's body next to mine. It was just a dream. Except for the scratching sound…that was real. I felt the flutters of panic in my stomach. *Stupid, it's obviously not a monster. A rat maybe?* I immediately became more alert; a rat in my bedroom would be infinitely worse than a monster. It was so dark I couldn't really see Tad's features, but I became aware that he had used his pillows to prop himself up into a sitting position and I could tell by the way he was ignoring me that he thought I was still asleep. With as little movement as possible I looked in the direction of where the noise was coming from. Tad sat perfectly still, with the exception of his right arm. He was scraping fingernails against the wall behind him. He just kept running them up and down, up and down in a heavy, methodical movement—*scratch, scratch, scratch*—all the while staring into space.

The rat scenario started to sound more appealing. What the hell was he doing? From where I lay I could see a neon-red three shinning on the face of my digital alarm clock. How long had he been at this? *Scratch, scratch, scratch.* Okay, this needed to stop. I closed my eyes again and rolled over with a slight moaning noise, hoping that the fear of waking me would stop him. The noise ceased, and for a brief moment there was a silence that probably should have been comforting. Then I felt the covers become heavier as he piled his share on top of me. The floor creaked as he walked out of the room.

He was just anxious. That was all. It had been an eventful week and now we were going to be married in three months. Everyone has a few nervous tics; no big deal. I heard the muted tones of the television set float through the closed door. All's well that ends well and if I could just let everything go and relax I could still get a few hours' sleep before work. I lowered my lids once again and tried to visualize some of the paintings from Chagall's Blue Period. Something about the coolness of his paintings during those years always relaxed me. I felt my limbs get heavier until everything took on that surreal quality it always does when one is on the verge of unconsciousness. The sound from the television seemed to become softer and more melodic, and I barely stirred when the scratching noise started up in the living room.

FOUR

It is amazing how stressful it is to be spoiled. If Tad had just agreed to neglect me my life would be one hell of a lot simpler. Not that I wasn't flattered by Tad's efforts to make our wedding the event of the century, but surely there had to be at least one Bay Area wedding professional whose portfolio we didn't need to see.

Caleb eyed me from the passenger seat as we headed toward Club Red. "Not to be a backseat driver, but maybe it's not such a good idea to zone out while changing lanes."

"We're not dead, so stop complaining," I shot back. I heard Allie giggling in the backseat. "Did you know that *Modern Bride* says you need twelve months to plan a formal wedding?"

"*Modern Bride* is full of shit," Allie said. "Look how much you've gotten done this last month, and you still have two to go. Besides, Tad's helping, right?"

I grunted in response and used one hand to discreetly adjust my halter top. Tad had been working day and night on business proposals and forecasts in the hope of convincing his partners to expand SMB but he still found plenty of time to be involved in every wedding decision. Actually, he *made* most of the wedding decisions; I was just the lucky girl who did the legwork. I know there are women who pray for those particular burdens, but all I wanted was to get married and be part of a "normal" family for once. I didn't want a guest book with its very own attendant.

I stopped for a red light and glared into the starless night sky. How I got roped into being the designated driver was beyond me, since no one in the car needed a drink more than I did.

"Why do you think women obsess over their weddings?" I tried to make the question sound casual, but the answer was very important to me. If I knew why other women felt compelled to spend—oh, what were we up to now?—thirty-five thousand dollars on a single party, I might be able to get into it, too.

Caleb slipped the Chap Stick he had been applying back inside the pocket of his leather jacket. "I actually have a theory about that."

Allie laughed and adjusted the spaghetti strap of her daringly low-cut camisole. "I can't wait to hear this."

"Okay, here it is. Most women spend their first twenty-some years of life dreaming about a prince falling hopelessly in love with them, putting the glass slipper on their size-seven foot and taking them to his panoramic-view palace. Then they get older and think, 'Hey, how is a glass slipper going to support a hundred and thirty pounds of muscle and body fat?'"

"Yeah, that's it," Allie said. "We grow up and start pondering the inaccurate physics of the Cinderella story."

"After the marital knot has been loosely tied," Caleb continued, "they find out that castles are expensive and most of them are cold and moldy, and Prince Charming is having an extramarital affair with Camilla Parker Bowles. The only part of the fairy tale that does ring true is that many of us do have the privilege of living with rodents in the attic, and if you sniff enough ammonia they *will* start talking to you."

Allie and I exchanged looks in the rearview mirror.

"But on their wedding day the fantasy comes to life. Women get to pretend that they are about to ride off into the sunset and live happily ever after. In short, it's the last day women can live in complete denial, and *that* is a day worth cherishing."

"Jesus, Mary and Joseph!" Allie threw up her hands in disgust. "Here's an idea, instead of a reception, why don't we just stage a mass suicide after the ceremony?"

"It would be apropos," Caleb agreed.

Allie rolled her eyes. "You are one sick little monkey. Hey, hey, look—that car's pulling out."

I pulled into the parking space and reached across Caleb to pull the free passes to Club Red out of the glove compartment. I studied the Grateful Dead-like graphics on the glossy 3x5 cards. "Allie, are you sure about this place?"

"Absolutely, you guys are gonna love it."

Caleb pushed his shoulders back slightly, as if preparing for battle. Allie was infamous for taking us to places that we absolutely didn't love. The only reason I hadn't put up more of a fight this time was that she had told me that the headlining band would be a great choice for my reception. But as I looked at the passes I had my doubts.

The club was only three city blocks from our parking spot, which wasn't a problem for Caleb since his jacket was part of his ensemble, but was a major inconvenience for Allie and me who had risked hypothermia in order to exercise the right to be sexy. Allie folded her arms across her chest as we got out of the car. "Jesus, my nipples are going to chap." Caleb smiled and draped an arm over each of us.

"What's the name of the band again?" I raised my voice so Allie could hear me over her chattering teeth.

"Dig—Jeremiah's the lead singer. You remember him, right? He's the pretty one I wanted to lasso."

"The closet case," Caleb clarified.

"Right." My breath was coming out in little dragonlike puffs. "You know, Jeremiah doesn't really have that wedding-singer look to him."

"Just listen to him—if his music doesn't do it for you at least you'll have a chance to see him get all sweaty under the hot lights."

Caleb nodded. "Stage sweat is so much sexier than gym sweat."

We reached the club and hopped in place as the doorman collected the cover from the two couples in front of us. When I stepped into Club Red I immediately froze in place while I took in the scene in front of me. The space itself was large, with low ceilings and a small, cramped stage. Everywhere around me people between the ages of twenty-one and twenty-nine were waving their fists in the air and thrashing their heads in time to the violent beat of a grungy-looking alternative-rock band.

I grabbed Allie's arm. "Are you kidding me?" Even though I was standing three inches away from her I still had to scream.

Allie lightly patted her hair to make sure it still had that hard-to-achieve messy look. "This isn't Dig. They're up next."

"But it'll be the same type of music, Allie."

"What's your problem?" she asked impatiently. "You liked Nirvana."

"But I didn't want them to play at my wedding!"

Caleb leaned in. "Look at these people…" He waved his hand around the room. "They're all a bunch of flaming heterosexuals! My God, what is this city coming to?"

I started to laugh but that resulted in a secondhand-smoke coughing fit. I checked my watch. Surely I could fit in one or two strong cocktails and still have time to sober up for the drive home. "I'm heading for the bar, who's with me?"

"You guys go ahead," Allie instructed. "I'm going to see if I can get closer to the stage."

Caleb and I pushed our way to the bar and we both ordered shots with beer chasers. I somehow lucked out and scored myself a stool.

Caleb held up his shot glass for a toast. "To easy listening."

We slammed our drinks just as the band onstage finished its last song. I rubbed my fingers against my ears in hopes of relieving some of the ringing. "Do you believe all that stuff you were saying about marriage?"

"Somewhat," Caleb said. "I think it's certainly true for some people. But there are the rare success stories out there."

"But the fairy-tale part… You really don't believe in fairy tales?"

"Why would anyone want to?" He stepped a little closer to me to allow another patron access to the bar. "Fairy tales are so predictable. Life is much more exciting."

"Well, call me a traditionalist, but I want a big strong man who will love, and for the most part, give me a happily-ever-after."

They were announcing Dig now, and Caleb raised his voice to make himself heard over the cheers. "Listen, wanting something and wanting to want something are two very different things."

I instinctively jerked away from him. He didn't know what he was talking about. I knew what I wanted. It was what I had always wanted; what everybody wanted.

My thoughts were interrupted by the sound of an electric guitar, but unlike those of the last band, these notes were actually melodic. My eyes were automatically drawn to the stage where Jeremiah, whose skin was already on the glistening side, was a few paces back from the mic. His head was down and his hair hid his face. Just then the drums set in. He looked up slowly and slid forward. I wasn't sure if it was from smoking or genetics but his voice definitely had a gravelly quality to it. Yet the notes still sounded pure, sultry. The guitarist was strumming a little harder now but not enough to detract from what Jeremiah was doing—which was seriously sexing up the audience. He had his feet shoulder width apart and he was grasping the microphone stand with both hands. He was barely moving but somehow… God, what was it?

I sat there mesmerized for the rest of the set. I didn't have to worry about carrying on a conversation with Caleb since he had zoomed in on the bartender's bisexual tendencies. Several of the songs were a little too hard-core, but about one out of three was fantastic. Jeremiah was fantastic. At one point he let out a guttural moan and I felt a certain throbbing in my groin that I usually only felt while watching Brad Pitt movies. I bit down on my lip. No way was that man singing at my wedding.

At the end of the night Allie and I abandoned Caleb so he could help the bartender "close" and went to an all-night burger joint so we could fulfill our daily allowance of saturated fat.

Allie leaned forward over a plate of fried onion rings, putting her chapped nipple at risk of exposure. "Tell me those guys didn't rock?" The Long Island ice teas she had consumed before leaving the club had left her diction with something to be desired.

"They rocked," I confirmed. "They must be playing pretty regularly if Jeremiah can afford a two-bedroom in your building. Or does he have roommates?"

"He has four." Allie dipped an onion in ketchup. "He's so hot. All dark and dangerous, kind of disturbed… God, I'd love to use him as a weapon against my parents."

I smiled and chewed on an ice cube. "He looks Mediterranean or something."

"Italian, I think… He's got those dark intense eyes. The kind of eyes you want to look into while being tied to a bed." Allie's eyes took on a kind of glazed look before she brought her attention back to clogging her arteries. "Speaking of which, how much time did Liz give you for your honeymoon?"

"I'm taking eleven days off, so after you subtract the wedding and travel time we'll have eight days in Spain." Now, *that* was something I was looking forward to.

"You should've chosen France."

"We've been over this—Tad's fluent in Spanish, and I've always wanted to see Gaudi's cathedral. Spain will be perfect."

"When planning a major vacation you should always pick the location that's best able to cater to your passions. You're passionate about art and fashion, so you should go to France."

"Ah, so does that mean your next vacation spot will be a liquor store?"

I gasped as I felt Allie's foot make contact with my shin. "That hurt!"

"Yo, Allie, thought that was you."

Allie almost spit out her onion ring at the sound of Jeremiah's voice.

I looked up and tried not to seem awestruck. He was so not

my type. He was too short (five-ten, tops). He needed a haircut,
a new pair of jeans, some dark glasses to hide those insanely sexy
eyes… I shook myself slightly and looked to Allie to see how she
was going to respond, but she appeared to be choking.

Jeremiah bent down a little. "Hey, are you all right?"

"She'll be fine." Serves her right for kicking me. I thrust my water
in her direction and offered my free hand to Jeremiah. "I'm April."

"Uh, hi." He accepted my hand but still seemed a little preoccupied with Allie's struggle for life.

"Allie, can you say anything?" I asked.

"I think I'm dying," she wheezed between coughs.

I turned back to Jeremiah. "You see? If she can talk she's
not choking. Really, she does this all the time. Your band was
great tonight."

"We've been better." He looked uncertainly at Allie, who was
quickly recovering and using her regained strength to glare at me.

"Would you like to join us?" I waved my hand toward the seat
next to Allie. He might have been off-limits for me but if Allie
could get him naked she could give me enough details to flesh
out my fantasies.

Allie managed a flirtatious smile and scooted over. "Where's
the rest of the band?"

"They're at some lame-ass party. Not that I got anything
against smokin' a little weed and listening to Bob Marley, but the
guy throwing it has some serious issues. I figured I'd just grab a
bite and chill for a while."

Well, this was perfect. I had found a guy who could have been
spectacular wet-dream material and he had to screw it up by
speaking. When was I going to learn, never let them talk.

Allie gave him an understanding nod. In her world, adolescent drug addicts were acceptable dating material. "So, Jeremiah's an unusual name. What's your last name?"

"Bullfrog."

Allie and I were silent.

"Nah, I'm just shittin' ya. It's Ramano. My dad's Italian. How 'bout you guys? Wait—" he pointed a finger at Allie "—I know your last name. It's O'Riley, right? I saw it on your mailbox."

"Gosh, usually I wait until the third date before I let a guy check out my box," Allie teased. I wanted to slap her.

"My name's Silverperson."

"Silverperson? Now who's *shittin'* who?"

"You do realize that *shittin'* isn't actually a word."

Allie gave me a warning look but Jeremiah started cracking up.

"It really is Silverperson," I said. "My mom changed it to reflect her feminist ideals."

"No way, are you—"

"Please don't say it."

"—kidding me? I was gonna say kidding me."

He waved over a tired-looking waitress, her 1950s-style uniform bunched slightly at the hips. "Do you need a menu?"

"Nah, just get me a cheeseburger, garlic fries and a milk shake. Thanks."

I discreetly took inventory of Jeremiah's fit physique. To find evidence of God's favoritism toward men one need only look to the difference in the metabolic rate between the two sexes. I sneaked a peek at my watch. I might be able to hurry Allie out of here if I helped eat her onion rings. I was tired, and curling up next to my tall, sexy, *literate* fiancé was sounding pretty great right about now.

Allie dipped her finger in my ice water and sucked off the

liquid suggestively. Jeremiah seemed unmoved. "So, Jeremiah's a cool name. You ever go by Jerry?"

"Nah, people hear Jerry and they think Seinfeld. Or Garcia if they're a former dead head or something. And, you know, Jeremiah is a better name for a rock star."

"Oh, so now you're a star?" I asked.

Allie threw me another glare but I ignored her. If I ended up driving him off, she could thank me after her brain cells started working again.

"Nah." Jeremiah grinned and propped his foot up on the booth he was sitting on. "But I'm a great wannabe and that's got to count for somethin'."

I laughed. "Kind of like the—"

"Offspring's song," he finished. "I'm pretty fly for a white guy. That pretty much sums it up."

Allie giggled. "Have you always wanted to be in a band?"

"Since I was a kid. As soon as I heard Hendrix I knew what I was all about."

Allie shifted so that her body was fully pivoted in his direction. "Then, how come you only play your guitar for a handful of your songs?"

He flashed a broad grin. "'Cause I suck at it."

I burst out laughing. He hadn't been bad but he certainly wasn't the best in his band. "So maybe the question needs to be reversed," I offered. "If you think you suck, why do you play at all? You have two other guys in the band who can really play."

"Dallas and Gary, yeah, they rock. I play because I love it."

I blinked. "I don't get it."

"You don't get it?" Jeremiah repeated. He paused as the waitress brought his food. "What's not to get?"

"Well, I assume you want the band to hit it big."

"Ideally."

"And you have a great vocal style and you have two great guitarists, so why would you want to lower the band's performance level by playing an instrument at which you don't excel?"

"April!" Allie chastised.

"It's okay, even my biggest fan has gotta admit that I'm no Hendrix." He turned his attention back to me. "You know, I got a college degree. You know what I majored in?"

"I'm guessing it wasn't English."

"I majored in accounting," Jeremiah said. "You're looking at a fully licensed CPA."

"You're shittin' me."

"No, I'm not *kidding* you. It was my dad's idea. I always had a good head for numbers and I've been doin' his taxes since I was sixteen, so he figured, 'boy should be an accountant.' I got my degree at Sac State. I made the dean's list and everything."

Now even Allie looked worried.

"After I took the exams I went on all these interviews and I got a couple of good job offers for some serious bucks."

"Is that CPA-speak for a competitive salary?"

"Something like that. I could have had a good income, decent hours, benefits and as much job security as you can get nowadays. But the more I thought about it, the more down I got. It's not that I don't want to have the money and weekends off, but if I have to choose, and let's face it—" he shook a fry at me "—we all gotta choose, I'd rather be poor and performing. So I got another certification, this time as a personal trainer. Now I work part-time for shitty wages and play full-time for really shitty wages. So, after giving up all that security, I am going to stuff my guitar in some storage unit all because some guys in my band are better than me? Fuck that. I'm strumming that motherfucker until I get to the level I wanna be at."

Allie had scooted over to the edge of the booth farthest from him; I knew she hadn't gotten over the accountant thing. I was more shocked by the philosophy behind his lifestyle. "What if…" I faltered, not even wanting to utter the words on the off chance my question hadn't occurred to him. "What if you fail?"

"I can't fail. I've already succeeded."

"But you just said you weren't making any money."

"It's not about the money. I've succeeded because I'm pursuing my dreams, man. And even if I never cut a record with Maverick I still got that. I'm never gonna do that 'what if' shit. I'm fucking living the 'what if' right now."

I stared at him in bewilderment. "What planet did you say you were from again?"

"Didn't you read the book, babe? We're all from Mars."

FIVE

Five weeks had passed since that late-night dinner with Allie and Jeremiah. This meant there were only three weeks before D-day. I tried to breathe out the stress as I sorted through the ecru-colored envelopes that had arrived the day before. I placed the acceptances and the rejections in separate piles on the empty seat next to me on the Muni train. I had read in *Modern Bride* that every bride should designate a special place to work on her wedding planning. I looked around me and studied the teenager with the pink-and-green Mohawk sitting in front of an elderly woman clutching a grocery bag full of not-so-fresh fish. I might be able to find a less smelly special place if I had even a second of spare time. Thanks to the holidays and an upcoming inventory count, I had been able to take all of two days off in the last month, and if that wasn't enough to make wedding planning difficult I was also in the process of moving. One of Tad's acquaintances was relocating to San Luis Obispo and he was renting his

Laurel Heights home to us for the low-low price of twenty-five hundred dollars a month. It wasn't a horrible rent considering the area and the fact that it was a house instead of an apartment, but it was still a big change from the eleven-hundred-dollar rent I was used to paying. I had thought that moving in with Tad would have been more of a monumental occurrence. Since the first night—he had made me a spectacular dinner that we had eaten picnic style while sitting amongst the large cardboard boxes on the dining-room floor—we had been working so much that it didn't feel like I was seeing him any more than I had before. That was a week ago and all the boxes were still there. I had gotten up this morning at five so that I could go back to my empty Castro apartment and clean it before the beginning of my closing shift in hopes of earning back my full security deposit. But just focusing my eyes seemed to take more energy than I had left.

The train pulled to a stop at the Civic Station exit and I glared at the woman entering, who was eyeing the seat next to me. Let her sit with the fish eater; I needed the space.

Stupidly I double-checked the mail to make sure I hadn't missed a return-address label with the name Showers on it. The chance of that was pretty low considering no one from Tad's family was invited. His decision, not mine. Any objections I had to the omission were silenced two weeks earlier. Just thinking about that day made me squirm in my plastic seat.

Tad and I had been at the Beach Chalet enjoying a late-Sunday lunch. From our table we could see the restaurant parking lot and the waves crashing onto Ocean Beach across the highway. I remember thinking it was the perfect moment to broach the subject.

"Maybe you should send your parents a note telling them

about me—about us," I had suggested. "Even if they refuse to come at least you will have given them the option."

Tad took a long sip of one of the restaurant's original brews. "Trust me, it's not an option they want, and I have no intention of sitting back and listening to them insult the woman I love."

"Maybe they won't. Maybe your estrangement was the push they needed to see the world differently."

"Racists don't change." Tad seemed more concerned about the seagull perched on his car than our conversation.

I used my fork to push the remnants of my salad around on my plate. "You loved them once, Tad."

"That's not the point now, is it?" I hated it when Tad became angry—he always got so…intense—

"Maybe you should just call them. Tell them that you're marrying a woman who…well, who appears to be black and is most definitely Jewish, and if they can accept that then you would really like it if some of those burnt bridges could be rebuilt. I mean, what could it hurt?"

"Jesus Christ, April, what the fuck is wrong with you? These are people who blame the Jews for everything from the death of Christ to the loose morals of Hollywood. They refer to Dr. King as an immoral troublemaker and they think César Chávez is some kind of specialty salad."

"Yeah, I got that, but—"

"Do you think this is easy for me? They're my parents, for Christ's sake! I loved them—part of me always will—but I can't stand by and idly watch them act superior based on some accident of birth."

"And I totally respect that, but—"

"And now I'm at a point in my life where I've finally accepted the situation for what it is and here you are dredging it all up again by questioning my judgment."

I had fallen back in my chair and stared at him as he stabbed his steak. At what point had my good intentions turned into an assault on his judgment? "Tad, you know I believe in you, and of course I trust your judgment…"

"Then why do you have to question everything I fucking do? My God, do you really think so little of me? How could you think that I would turn my back on the people who raised me if I hadn't exhausted every other avenue? I've spent every moment we've had together learning about you, trying to know you the way only a soul mate could, and now I find out that you haven't bothered to get to know me at all. That's great, April. That's just fucking great."

The woman at the next table had looked at him pityingly and leaned over to whisper something to her friend as I slipped farther down in my seat. The worst part had been that, although I thought the anger directed at me was unfounded, I was so confused I didn't know how to challenge him. Or, maybe he was right and I was pushing too hard. At this point, I just wanted the conversation to end.

"I'm sorry. I didn't mean to insult you or attack your character. I do know you, and of course I trust you. I'll try…I'll try to make sure that always comes across."

Tad had reached across the table and stroked my cheek. "I love you, April, more than I ever thought possible. It's just that sometimes you make things more complicated than they need to be. From now on it's just you and me. My parents are not a part of that equation."

So there would be no replies from the Showers family. I was

now one stop away from Union Square and I quickly stuffed the cards into two large manila envelopes and used the silver bar next to my seat to pull myself into a standing position.

It was only 11:00 a.m. when I walked into my department, which was just sad since I wasn't scheduled to leave until 9:30 p.m. Sally and Laura were busy with their customers. Laura was trying to convince a pudgy middle-aged woman that it really was perfectly acceptable to wear a sheer nylon top that was two sizes too small. "You'll look like you're coming down a runway," she gushed. She caught my eye as I headed to the back room to put my purse down. "April, Blakely's back there. She's kind of in a weird mood."

Spectacular. I tried to brace myself for the unknown and went back.

Blakely was going through the customer holds, scrutinizing the tag on each item and then violently thrusting them aside. "They're all up-to-date," she spat. "Every one of your holds is up-to-date!"

"Um, thank you?"

"And the back stock is perfectly organized. Your whole stockroom is perfect!" From her tone it was clear that perfection wasn't all it was cracked up to be.

"I usually take a few minutes before opening to go through this area," I said carefully.

"You're even a minori— You're…you're… You went through sensitivity training."

Well, at least one of us had. "Blakely, is there a problem?"

"Yes, the problem is that you would make the ideal assistant buyer! Goddamn it!" She pressed her palms into her forehead, apparently trying to push her brain back in.

"Blakely, I'm sorry but I'm having a hard time following…"

"Cherise is pregnant. Pregnant! I was going to Human Resources today to tell them I would be letting her go and she hits me with this before I have a chance! Now if I so much as demote her it will look like I'm doing it because of the stupid brat she's carrying."

As opposed to the ever-so-ethical practice of demoting her due to her ethnic identity.

"God, that little bitch couldn't have timed it better if she'd planned it. Oh!" She took in a sharp breath and pulled her hair back with a force just short of scalping. "Do you think she did? Do you think she planned this?"

I shook my head uncomprehendingly. "The pregnancy? I don't know, maybe?"

"Then she knew!" Blakely started pacing the cramped space. "She knew she was going to lose her job and she came up with a way to hold me off!"

"You think that Cherise got pregnant in hopes that it would buy her a few more months as your assistant?"

"Of course! Why else would she do it?"

So many sarcastic remarks were flooding my head I actually felt dizzy.

"Well, it's not going to work. She'll be gone by the time she reaches her third trimester."

"You know," I ventured, "I'm in no real hurry—"

"By the third trimester, April!" Blakely threw one more disgusted look at my perfect holds and stormed out.

I fell into my chair and took in a deep breath. Was it me or had the HR director gone to the local sanitarium and offered all the inmates a job?

"April?" Sally's voice floated through the intercom. "Your mom's on line one."

"Is she calling to request an application?"

"Huh?"

"Never mind, I got it." I pressed the appropriate flashing button and picked up. "What's up, Mom?"

"April, hon, how are you? I was just straightening up and I came across your wedding invite… I don't think I'm going to be able to make it."

"What?"

"The priestess from the Temple of the Earth Goddess is holding a retreat that weekend and I think it's important that I be there."

"You've got to be kidding me! Have you been smoking?"

"I don't see what that has to do with anything."

I pressed the receiver to my chest and quickly counted to ten before bringing it back to my ear. "Mom, I want you to put the bong down and listen to me. I am your only child. I am getting married in less than three weeks. Your absence is not an option."

"Hon, I've done a lot of soul-searching on this. You know how I feel about you…"

"Well, I'm beginning to get an idea."

"And I really do love Tad, but I feel I need to take a stand."

I threw my free hand up in the air. "Against who? Me?"

"Against the institution of marriage, silly. Particularly since you're having the wedding at the Ritz. God knows how you talked Tad into that. It just epitomizes this entire capitalist culture we live in. Everything's been commercialized, even our relationships. It goes against my Marxist ideology."

"Your Marxist ideology." I wanted to reach through the phone and just strangle her. "Well, if you've become a Marxist I'm assuming you will no longer be a congregant of the Temple of the Earth Goddess."

"I can be both."

"Oh, but *Das Capital* says you can't. I'll pick up a copy for you the next time I'm at Borders." I pulled out a pencil and started twirling it between my fingers. "So if you're not going to be worshipping bugs anymore then you won't need to go to the priestess's retreat, which means there's no longer a scheduling conflict. Why don't you come to the wedding and wear a big sign that says Down with Capitalism? I'll be pacified and Karl will be smiling down on you from…well, he'll be smiling at you from wherever it is atheists go after they die."

"April, I just recently had my chart done. It said I needed to get more in touch with my spirituality and my own ethical belief system, and going to this wedding just interferes with both. I can't conscientiously be there to celebrate your choice to enter into a capitalist institution that encourages women to give up their freedom. I am sorry, but try to understand. I have needs, too."

"You're really not coming," I whispered.

"I'll see if I can make the rehearsal dinner. Oh, and tell Tad that everyone at the temple can't wait to see the calendars."

"Calendars?" I asked weakly. I couldn't believe she was doing this to me. She actually hated me.

"The calendars for the temple. And he said he would be making posters and bumper stickers, too. He really is clever, and so spiritual. Are you sure you wouldn't rather just live together? I have such a hard time seeing him confined by something as conventional as a marital—"

I hung up the phone. I didn't owe her any courtesies. How could she possibly think it was okay to not come to my wedding? It had occurred to me that she might get strung out on 'shrooms that day and lose the mental capacity to find San Francisco, but

I hadn't expected her to *plan* not to come. It just felt so mali-
cious. I squeezed my pencil into my fist and tried to come up with
an explanation I could live with. Maybe it didn't have anything
to do with me. Maybe this was about…about…Bobe? Was it that
she didn't want to see Bobe? I could count on my fingers the
number of times I had seen them in the same room together for
more than the three minutes it took Mom to drop me off and
pick me up at Bobe's.

The last time, I had been six, young enough to think that my
mother's then Crystal Gale-length hair made her look like
Rapunzel rather than some hippy freak. I remember Bobe was
wearing dark trousers and one of her many polyester blouses
buttoned up to her neck, her silver hair pulled into a little bundle
that rested at the base of her skull. Howie the cat and I were
sitting on the beige carpet, drenched in sunlight coming in from
the sliding glass doors of Bobe's modest apartment. We watched
as she paced back and forth, wringing her hands like a character in one of those Rocky and Bullwinkle cartoons. She was
almost yelling. It had scared me to death. Mom was always
screaming, but until then I had never heard Bobe even project
to what would qualify as an "outside voice."

"Arrested! It's not bad enough that you should hitchhike,
that you take up with all kinds of strange men? Now you get
yourself arrested? Is this what I raised you for?"

My mom was sitting on the La-Z-Boy making a show of being
exasperated. "It was a protest, Mother."

"A protest! You call taking your clothes off and prancing
around in front of a police officer a protest?"

"It's a nude beach, Mom! I don't care if it's on the books as
being one or not, they have no right to force their puritanical

value system on the rest of us. I was taking a stand. You should try it sometime."

"Now you want me to take my clothes off, too? Listen, you have a daughter now—it's not right that a mother should make such a spectacle."

"It's called living Mother! L.I.V.I.N.G." Mom pushed the footrest down and sprung to her feet. "You put so much time and effort into becoming invisible you've forgotten how to live! Or maybe you never knew. Tell me, Mom, when's the last time you cut loose? When have you ever let yourself get wild and have a little fun?"

"Bobe can be wild," I said, somehow feeling that it would be up to me to point out their small strip of common ground. "She has a tattoo just like you! Show her your tattoo, Bobe. Show her the numbers on the inside of your wrist."

Whenever I hear the term *deafening silence* I think of that moment. It was like everything in the world just died for an instant. My bobe stood completely still, and my mother, despite the red rouge that she was wearing, seemed to lose her color. Then without warning, Bobe turned on her heel and walked into her room, slamming the door behind her. My mother pressed her fingers into the bridge of her nose before walking to the bedroom door and suspending a fist in the air in preparation to knock. She didn't.

I abandoned Howie and pulled on my mother's skirt. "Did she not want me to see it? But I think tattoos are neat, Mommy! Even if hers doesn't have any color."

My mother stared at me like I was some kind of exotic pet that she was a little squeamish about—it was a look I had become used to. "Get your coat, April, it's time to go."

It was a year before I figured out what those numbers meant and another year before I worked up the nerve to ask Bobe about it. I learned that she had spent most of the war in hiding with her younger siblings. When the war was in the last stretch, and the camps the most brutal, she was captured by the Nazis. I didn't ask for any more details. I didn't want to know. I didn't want to know what they did to her or in what manner her brother and baby sister were murdered. For that matter I never wanted to hear about the details of the car crash that had killed my grandfather twelve years before I was born. I didn't want to face the fact that the only person who had ever been protective of me had never really been able to protect anyone at all.

SIX

I tried to spend the remainder of my shift performing tasks that necessitated my being in the back room. It was the only way to hide the fact that I was barely keeping it together. I wrote up two of the three promotions that I would have to turn in during the coming weeks; I managed to e-mail the buyers a wish list of items that I thought would sell well in my department and which items I would be willing to give up; I wrote and rewrote the following month's schedule. But as much as I didn't want to admit it, I was duty bound to venture onto the sales floor occasionally. *I can do this. How hard can it be to get through one day?* I took a deep breath and walked through the door that separated my dark, windowless office from the artificially lit world of Dawson's.

"Excuse me, but when Sally gets back could you tell her that nothing worked?"

I turned to see a middle-aged woman with platinum-blond hair and an outfit that probably cost more than my car looking at me through blue contact lenses. "I had her go to the shoe department to pick out four or five pairs that matched the outfits I tried, but I've changed my mind. I left everything in the dressing room," she added needlessly; women like her never even bothered to rehang what they had tried on, let alone take it out of the room. "Oh, and Snuckums here had a little accident." She lifted up her Chihuahua, safely ensconced in the woman's oversize Gucci bag.

I grimaced at the thought of it taking a piss inside her purse. "Do you need some tissues or something?"

"God no, he didn't do anything in my purse. He went poo-poo in your fitting room. Didn't you, Snuckums? Didn't you go poo-poo in the fitting room? Yes, you did—yes—"

That was it. I had absolutely had it. I turned my back on the dog and her bitch and stormed out of the department, avoiding Laura's questioning gaze. I didn't stop until I got to Liz's office. The door was cracked open and I knocked, then pushed it open without waiting to be invited.

She was wearing a sky-blue suit over her white silk-ribbed tee (the Savoir-Faire department's item of the day). She offered me a vague smile and waved me to a seat. "Were we meeting today?"

"Liz," I sobbed, falling into a chair, "I know I'm going to have some time off in less than a month, but I've logged in one hundred and forty-five hours over the last two weeks, and I just can't do it. I have to have an assistant."

Liz calmly pulled open a file drawer at the bottom of her desk and started flipping through filing tabs. "I have to admit I was nervous when you said you were taking a full two weeks off for your wedding and honeymoon, but I'm really happy about the dedication you've shown recently," she chirped. "I always knew you had that Dawson's spirit."

Now, if Tad had come back at me with something like that I would have assumed that he wasn't listening. However, the statement from Liz was dripping with not-so-hidden meaning. It was my fault for taking the time off to begin with so if I wanted to be perceived as a team player I needed to shut up and put out.

I was trying to come up with a diplomatic way to tell her to go fuck herself, when she pulled out a thick folder labeled Sassy. "You know you have to have over four million in annual sales in order to qualify for an assistant. So let's set up a game plan that will help us reach that figure by the end of next year, okay?"

"Liz, the gross annual sales figure for my department last year was four point eight."

"Seriously?" She cocked her head to the side before locating the sheet listing last year's figures. "Hey, your right! So why don't you have an assistant? You know it really isn't a good idea to try to manage that kind of volume on your own, April. You could be missing growth opportunities."

My eyes rested on the letter opener lying on her desk. How many times would you have to stab someone with one of those before they bled to death. Eighty, ninety…

"April?"

"What? Oh, right," I said, shaking myself out of one of the most fulfilling fantasies of my life. "Does this mean you'll be telling HR that I have the go-ahead to hire an assistant?"

"Of course, April, you can always count on me."

In what alternative universe? I managed a tight smile and left the office. The hell with all of them; housekeeping could deal with the dog crap, I was going home. I collected my things from my office, rambled off some instructions to the remaining crew and took off. It only took me three minutes to get to the metro station and I almost kissed the J train when it arrived. I found an empty seat and as the train sprang back into motion I closed my eyes to better savor the budding sensation of calm.

I was only one stop away from the Castro when I realized I was on the wrong train. I was headed toward an apartment I no longer lived in. Now it would take me an extra half hour to get home. I sucked. I got out at my old stop for lack of a better alternative. There was no way I was going to get back on a bus or any other form of public transit before consuming a very strong alcoholic beverage. At least I was in the Castro, so I could go to a bar by myself and know that none of the men there were going to harass me.

I climbed the subway stairs that took me to street level and made a beeline to the Castro's version of a dive bar, which basically meant that none of the cocktails was served with umbrellas. There was a handful of men scattered throughout the establishment nursing their drinks and watching the male figure-skating competition that was being shown on the TV screens conveniently located in every corner. I went straight to the bar and ordered a Manhattan. I didn't really like Manhattans but the name sounded so sophisticated and I needed a little of that after my latest Alzheimer's moment. I welcomed the foul taste and the burning sensation the alcohol offered as it worked its way down to my liver. It took me a moment to realize that someone was watching me. I could feel it. I scanned the bar until my eyes rested on Jeremiah. He was sitting at the other end of the bar and he raised his pilsner in greeting before walking over to where I was sitting.

"I thought that was you," he said. He put his drink down next to mine.

I twisted in my seat to take in his attire—Doc Martens, black jeans and the same motorcycle jacket he'd been wearing on the previous occasion I'd seen him. "Jeremiah, don't tell me I lost my bet."

"I dunno, what's the bet?"

"I bet Caleb that you were straight, but here you are, wearing leather in a gay bar."

He laughed and pulled up a stool. "You won the bet. I came to the Castro to go shopping, and I can't shop while fully sober."

"That is the weakest cover story I've ever heard. What were you planning on buying? Chaps?"

Jerimiah shook his head, causing his brown hair to swing around his face. "No cover-up. A couple of male friends of mine are having a…um…an alternative wedding, and I figured that the Castro would be the place to buy the gift."

I wrinkled my brow as he finished his beer and motioned for the bartender to bring him another. "What exactly are you planning on getting them?"

"Dunno, a rainbow flag or somethin'."

"Oh God, please don't."

"Why, you got something against rainbows?"

"No, just tasteless gifts."

"Hey, I'm a guy. I don't know shit about buying wedding presents." He grabbed my hand and held it up in the air, his thumb pressed into the center of my palm. "You're getting married," he said, using his free hand to point to my ring. "What kind of presents do you want?"

I yanked my soon-to-be-married hand from his grasp and swallowed some whiskey. "Forks."

"Excuse me?"

"I want lots and lots of forks. Have you ever noticed that the forks are the first utensils to get dirty? You could have a drawerful of spoons and butter knives, and all your forks will be sitting in the sink waiting to be washed. If they registered for forks, you should definitely buy them."

"I don't think they registered at all."

"Then you're going to have to be a little more creative." I twisted myself a little more in his direction.

"Maybe a slotted spoon?"

I giggled and took another sip. It always amazes me how much more powerful liquor is when you're tired and hungry. "You really are clueless, aren't you?"

"Maybe, but I got a cute ass. At least that's what that blond guy sitting in the corner told me a few minutes ago."

I laughed again. I hadn't seen Jeremiah since that time at the diner, although I had thought of him periodically. He was like one of those case studies I wrote reports on in psychology classes.

Jeremiah leaned in a little closer. "Tell you what, why don't you help me out. Come to a few shops with me and you pick out the gift. That way I won't make a jackass of myself."

"I hardly think that's appropriate," I said while checking out the redhead blonde who was checking out Jeremiah. "I don't even know these people."

"I promise not to put your name on the card."

"I meant I don't know what they like."

"Well…I know they like guys."

"You're kidding." I slammed my hand on the bar for emphasis. "You're telling me that your two male friends who are marrying each other are gay? And here I thought they were just looking for an excuse to wear white!"

Jeremiah chuckled and rubbed the stubble on his chin. "You're on fire today. Does that mean you're having a really good day or the opposite?"

"My mother's a heartless bitch and I work for the Evil Barbie Queen."

"So 'really bad' it is. What's your mom done to piss you off?"

"She's not coming to my wedding. She has other plans."

"No fucking way." Jeremiah shook his head and leaned his forearms on the bar. "That shit's messed up."

"Oh yeah." I slammed the rest of my drink and waved my empty glass at the bartender.

"My parents would like nothing better than for me to do something normal like get hitched. My dad's one of those guys who tries to live through his son. He's a blue-collar dude who hurt his back while doin' some handyman shit. Now my mom has to support him because he doesn't have any skills that don't involve manual labor. So he wanted me to have some white-collar accounting job. Man, when I told him I was ditching the accounting to start a band he seriously freaked out. Now he has this idea in his head that all I need is a good woman, some chick who will straighten me out and get me to a desk job."

Did I ask for this information? I ran my finger around the rim of my newly filled glass.

"Hey, but if you're feeling down that's all the more reason to come shopping with me. Shopping always cheers chicks up."

I made a small noise of disgust. "That is such a stereotype."

Worse, I was stereotypical. I *did* want to go shopping. Even though I rarely shopped the Castro when I was a neighborhood resident, I missed the stores now that they were so much farther out of my way. "I really need more information. What do your friends do?"

"My friend's a DJ and his, um…"

"Domestic partner?"

"Right, his domestic partner's a property manager."

I shook my head. "I don't think that helps me." I chewed gently on my bottom lip. "How did they meet?"

"In a photography class. They're both really into taking pictures."

I slapped the side of his arm. "I know the perfect thing!" I stuck a few bills under my glass, grabbed his sleeve and dragged him out of the bar and across the street to a New and Used Bookstore. "It has to still be here," I murmured as I scanned the display tables. "It's always here."

"What's always—"

"That!" I pointed proudly at the coffee-table book that I had salivated over every time I came to browse. "A book of photographs by Annie Leibovitz. It's contemporary, unique and it speaks to a shared interest. It's the perfect wedding gift."

Jeremiah flipped through the pages. "Jesus, these are great."

"Of course they're great. Do you think I would get all excited if the book was filled with crap?" I pressed my lips together self-consciously. My language had deteriorated in the short time I'd spent with Jeremiah.

Jeremiah didn't seem to notice. "I don't know you well enough to be able to gauge what gets you excited."

"You really are obscene, aren't you?"

"Hey, we're just friends, so it's all good."

We were friends? When had that happened?

He turned the book over and blinked at the price tag. "This book is thirty-three bucks."

"That book is a work of art. Stop being a miser and buy it already."

Jeremiah made a noise of distaste but he tucked the book under his arm and brought it to the cash register. I stood behind him and looked longingly at the Swiss chocolates that they had featured on the counter.

"Hey, can I take you out for an early supper as a way of thanking you for helping me?"

"It's barely five."

"I did say early, didn't I? Come on, I'm hungry and I hate eating alone."

Going home was the right thing to do. I still had some boxes to unpack, thank-you notes to write for last month's holiday gifts, bills to pay….

"April?"

"Yeah, I'll get some food with you."

Since the weather was unseasonably warm, we went to Café Flore, which has outdoor seating. It was nicely fenced, so it was easier to pretend that we were in a countryside café rather than a restaurant that was bound to eventually be demolished by a runaway Muni bus. Once we had ordered and picked up our food and beverages at the counter and found a table I asked the question that had been killing me since I met Jeremiah. "Did you really go to college?"

"I did indeed," Jeremiah said as he scooted his chair in.

"So at what point did you unlearn the English language?"

He made a show of wincing although it was obvious that I hadn't hurt his seemingly impenetrable self-esteem. "April, did you take a foreign language in college?"

"French."

"Were you any good at it?"

"I was good enough to get Bs in my classes but I'm hardly fluent. If pressed I could probably still manage to give a Parisian tourist directions."

"And if pressed I can speak proper English," he said with what I think was supposed to be an upper-crust accent but sounded more like a bad John Cleese impersonation. "I was even able to produce the very few grammatically correct term papers that are required of an accounting major. But unless called upon to speak in front of a large gathering of professors who are unfortunate enough to have the proverbial stick pushed up their literal asses I see no need to do so." He then added in his normal voice, "It ain't who I am."

I pretended to buy this as we began our light meal but I suspected that, while in college, Jeremiah's grammar was better than it was now, even when in casual setting. My guess was that hanging around with a bunch of stoned rockers had had its effect on him whether he was consciously aware of it or not.

Jeremiah was now pulling out the Leibovitz book with every third or fourth bite of his sandwich. "They're gonna love this. I know I do."

I shrugged and allowed the bubbles of my mineral water to tickle my tongue before swallowing. "Just don't get any mustard on it."

"Yeah, yeah, I'm being careful. You know, you got good taste, April," he said while looking into the eyes of Yoko Ono. "Are you into photography, too?"

"Art in general, I have a B.A. in art history. I wanted to be an art curator."

"But you don't anymore?"

I shrugged. "Believe it or not, it's a difficult job to get. I would have to go back to school for my Ph.D., and even then the odds of landing a curator position would be against me."

"What are you sayin'? You just gave up?"

"I didn't give up." Jeremiah raised an eyebrow at my involuntary rise in volume. I swallowed and tried again. "I put myself through school by working part-time at Dawson's. A few months before I graduated, Dawson's offered me a job as an assistant manager and I grabbed it. I thought it would be a good way to pay off student loans and save for a graduate degree."

"So this job is temporary?"

I shook my head. "Not anymore. Turns out I'm a good manager and I will probably make buyer soon. So now I'm a fashion girl. All's well that ends well."

"I gotta tell you, that ending sucks."

"It works for me," I snapped. "Besides, if I was trying to land a curator's job right now I'd have to relocate in order to land the first position available, and how could I do that while maintaining my relationship with Tad?"

"Your fiancé's name is Tad?"

"Tad Showers."

Jeremiah fell back in his chair. "No fucking way."

"Yeah, I know, that would make me April Showers. Obviously I won't be changing my name."

"No, it's not that… What I'm trippin' on is that I know Tad—we were buds."

"Really? When and what do you mean 'were'?"

"He had a thing with my friend Jackie."

"Shut. Up." I placed both my palms on the tabletop and leaned in. "Okay, you have to understand, I haven't met any of Tad's exes… Well, there's Jen Vesilind and…Cathy or Constance or something like that, but they don't count because he only went out with them three or four times each, but

Jackie—he's actually mentioned her! You have to tell me all the gory details."

Jeremiah pulled a pair of sunglasses out of his jacket pocket. He unfolded them and then folded them back up. "I'm not real big on gore. How's Tad doing these days?" There was an edge of concern in his voice that I found puzzling, but not distracting enough to get me off the subject at hand.

"He's fine. Tell me about Jackie."

Jeremiah unfolded the glasses yet again and put them uselessly on the table. "Jackie moved to L.A. about six months ago. I haven't talked to her for a while."

"I mean tell me about what she was like then!" Really, men could be so dense. "What does she look like, what were they like as a couple—the dirt!"

"Jackie's a hottie. Dark, long brown hair. She's kind of on the tiny side but she's toned, you know, one of those chicks with definition in her abs and shit." He took another bite of sandwich and I waited impatiently for him to continue. "She's a bit of a wild woman," he finally added, "and not the easiest gal to get along with. I've always made it a point not to get too involved in her love life." He met my eyes and then slumped slightly when he realized that I was not going to just let the subject drop. "Okay this is what I know. I was Tad's trainer for a while, that's how we met. When he got a load of Jackie he befriended me in order to get to her."

I shook my head impatiently. "Tad wouldn't do that. He's insanely ethical."

Jeremiah lifted his eyebrows as a silent indicator that he wasn't buying it. "It doesn't matter why we started hanging out. What matters is that we did and it turned out that we have a lot in common."

I pressed my fingers to my lips in order to keep myself from pointing out that apart from male genitalia, Jeremiah and Tad had nothing in common whatsoever. But it hardly seemed a point worth arguing.

"So he and Jackie hooked up and Tad and I became buds. When things didn't work out for them, Jackie moved out and Tad fell off the face of the earth. That's what I know." Jeremiah took a large bite out of his sandwich, oblivious to the fact that my heart had stopped beating.

"Did you say—" I stopped myself, not wanting to give away that I was so ignorant about the romantic history of the man I had agreed to marry. How could he have not told me that he had lived with someone before? Wasn't that one of the things couples were supposed to share with one another? I didn't need him to confess to the details of his first sexual experience, but to not tell me that he had lived with Jackie…

"Yo, you all right?" I refocused my eyes to see Jeremiah staring at me from over his sandwich.

"Fine," I said weakly. I smoothed my hands over my cotton-Lycra black skirt as if I expected to find a wrinkle.

Jeremiah took one last bite and then unfolded his glasses once more, and without putting them on gazed into their lenses as if the UV protective glass doubled as a crystal ball. "We should all get together one of these days." His words came out a little too slowly. "I haven't seen Tad for a while. I'd like to catch up."

A simmering anger was beginning to melt away my shock. "Oh, I definitely think that's a good idea. How about you drive me home tonight? Maybe we can surprise him."

SEVEN

It was eight o'clock when Jeremiah walked me to my door. He openly admired the exterior of our house as I fished for my keys. It wasn't all that impressive, but it was a house and that put it a step above the majority of the other San Francisco residences.

"Tad knows the owner—he's giving us a deal on the rent." I spoke in a voice that was barely above a whisper. I didn't want Tad to hear us. I wanted to spring Jeremiah on him the same way his former living situation with Jackie had been sprung on me.

I finally found my keys, and flung open the door. "Hi, honey, I'm home," I announced. I could hear the notes of a commercial jingle coming from the living room.

"Goddess, I've been wondering when you'd show up." Tad entered the foyer carrying two glasses of wine. He stopped short when he saw Jeremiah. I'm not sure what I expected, but I didn't expect him to look as if a ten-pound dumbbell had been dropped on his foot. Despite my anger I felt myself start to reach out to him, but then as quickly as it had come his expression of pain disappeared, washed away by something that looked like dull apathy.

"You remember Jeremiah, don't you, Tad? I ran into him in the Castro. He's the lead singer for Dig, the band Caleb, Allie and I went to see a few weeks ago. Isn't that just a big ol' coinkidink?" I waited to see Tad's reaction. Surely from my flippancy he could surmise that Jeremiah had spilled a few beans.

But Tad barely acknowledged my presence at all. "Jeremiah…" He made an apologetic gesture to indicate that the wineglasses made a handshake impossible. "I haven't seen you for a while."

"Over two years, man." Jeremiah stuffed his hands in his pockets and leaned against the wall. "You're lookin' good. Still working out?"

"When I have time."

I looked from one man to the other. Jeremiah's tone had changed. It had become more…cautious. And Tad… I looked back to him. What was going on with him? He didn't seem embarrassed or anxious, as I had originally hoped he would be. Whatever he was feeling was a lot less dramatic and a *lot* more disconcerting.

"Tad, aren't you going to offer your old pal a glass of wine?" My voice lacked the sarcasm that I had meant to relay. Tad silently handed a glass to Jeremiah and one to me before turning around and leading us into the living room before disappearing into the kitchen. He emerged a minute later with a glass for himself.

"Nice pad you got here," Jeremiah commented. "You still working for Nextel?"

"I started my own business." Tad sat down on the couch and stared at the television. Some documentary about forensic science was on the Discovery Channel.

"You finally did that, huh?"

Tad gave a silent nod of accession.

This was supposed to be a righteous moment for me. Tad had lied and I had brought Jeremiah home to make him sweat. But I didn't feel righteous and Tad wasn't sweating. He was barely responding to the fact that there were other people in the room.

Jeremiah cleared his throat uncomfortably. "All right, I don't want to be cuttin' into you two's quality time." He took a small sip of wine and placed the still-full glass on a box near the fireplace. "We should all go to dinner one of these days. Maybe this weekend?"

I waited for Tad to respond. He didn't. "I think both Tad and I will be working all weekend but maybe the weekend after that?" My voice came out an octave higher than normal. This was so weird; Tad and I had gone to dinner with Caleb twice, Allie once and several more times with his partners, with and sometimes without their wives. Why not go to dinner with Jeremiah? What was going on here?

"Sounds like a plan." Jeremiah smiled but it looked strained. He nodded at Tad one more time. "Good seeing you, buddy."

Tad turned his head slightly in his direction but didn't bother getting up. "See you later."

I escorted Jeremiah to the door. Jeremiah patted my arm absently as he stepped out onto the front walkway. "You got my number, right? You'll call to firm up our plans?"

"I'll call," I repeated.

"Or if you just want to shoot the shit." He smiled at me. "I'm always good for that."

"I don't usually shoot shit, but if I feel the urge, I know who to call. Good night, Jeremiah."

"'Night, April." He stood there for a few seconds as if deciding what his next move should be. Eventually he turned around and walked into the darkness.

I returned to the living room and noted that Jeremiah's glass had already been cleared away. Other than that, there was no indication that Tad had moved.

"Jeremiah told me you two used to be friends."

"Uh-huh." His eyes never left the flickering screen.

"He told me that you met Jackie through him."

"That's right." Again his voice lacked any indication of nervousness, anger…or emotion.

"He also told me that you and Jackie used to live together."

His eyes traveled to me, and for a brief moment he held me with his gaze. I felt an inexplicable chill travel up my arms. I watched as his eyes slid slowly back to the TV. "She stayed with me for a few weeks while she was in-between apartments. It was never either of our intentions that it be permanent."

Oh. I hadn't been prepared for a *reasonable* excuse. I toyed with the button of my coat, which I had yet to remove. "What was the deal with you two anyway?"

Tad's shoulders raised and dropped an eighth of an inch in what barely qualified as a shrug. "Jackie has issues. She's immature and a pathological liar."

I reached down to retrieve my glass of wine and finished half of it in one gulp. There were a million questions I wanted to ask but only one answer that I had to know immediately. "Did you love her?"

Tad's mouth curved into a sardonic smile. "I cared about Jackie a lot for a while but I never considered asking her to marry me. You're the only woman I've ever wanted to make that kind of commitment to."

The words were obviously meant to reassure me and they might have if they had been followed by a hug or a kiss, or even the touch of his hand. But Tad remained in his seat, watching a couple of guys in white coats analyze the fingernails of a corpse.

I shifted my weight from one foot to the next. "Tad…what is it? What's wrong?"

"Nothing, why?"

I hesitated. The question seemed simultaneously valid and ridiculous. "You seem—" I grappled for the right word "—down. You seem kind of down."

Tad mechanically reached for his wineglass. "I'm tired. I've been working a lot of hours."

That was true enough, another reasonable excuse, but…but what? He had a right to be tired. Hadn't I broken down in Liz's office today for the same reason? I looked down at my throbbing feet. Earlier today I had planned to unburden myself to him about Liz and more importantly about my mother's latest rejection, but after I found out about Jackie I had set my mind on having it out with him. Looking at him now, I couldn't imagine talking to him about any of those things.

"I'm tired, too." My response came too late to be considered casual. "I think I'll got to bed early… Care to join me?"

"In a bit."

I nodded and waited for something unknown, an explanation? A sign of tenderness? Finally I turned around and went to the bathroom to prepare myself for sleep.

I had woken up just in time to hear Tad's car pull out of the garage. It wasn't unusual for him to leave for work in the wee hours of the morning, especially recently, but considering his bizarre behavior of the night before his early departure felt like a method of avoidance. Not that I had a problem with avoidance, particularly since I didn't know what we were avoiding.

I went about my morning routine, and when I got to Dawson's it was unusually quiet. Liz was off, so I didn't have to deal with her reprimands for skipping out the day before (yet), and the customers were sparse. The few that did come in seemed to be set on returning unwanted Christmas gifts. By two o'clock we had done two thousand dollars' in sales and twenty-five hundred in returns. Just another reason why I hated the holidays.

It figured that on the day I desperately needed to be distracted I was forced to stand around and think. There was something that Tad wasn't telling me. Was it about Jackie? Jeremiah? Or was it something else entirely? When someone acted like that on *One Life to Live* it usually meant they had a brain tumor or a split personality. I tried to compare Tad's behavior to Victoria Lord's when she was having one of her many bouts of dissociative identity disorder. It didn't really fit. For one thing, Tad wasn't locking anyone up in a secret, previously nonexistent, underground room. The brain tumor seemed more likely.

"April?" I looked back to see Sally waving the phone at me as she credited another dissatisfied customer's MasterCard. "It's Marilyn."

I took the phone from Sally and stretched the cord so that I was still standing on the outside of the register. "Hi, Marilyn, how are you?"

"What the hell is going on?"

"I take it you've pulled up our numbers."

"Damn good thing I did. Do you have the department roped off or something?"

"Yes, I have it roped off and every time a customer comes within ten feet of the department I hold up a pair of your jeans and say, 'I bet you'd like to buy this, huh?' It's really driving them crazy."

There was a long silence on the other end of the line. I leaned back against the counter and rolled my eyes up toward the recessed lights. Sarcasm loses its therapeutic qualities when you're constantly having to apologize for it. "I'm sorry, Marilyn. I'm just feeling frustrated about all the returns."

"Are you even trying to turn them into exchanges?"

Again sarcasm was called for and yet perversely forbidden. "We're doing what we can. I have a few personal customers coming in later and they all love Hardtail and Versus jeans."

"Well, that's something. Remind your staff that they need to be selling a Michael Stars tee with every sale. Everyone needs a Michael Stars tee."

Everyone who's a size four with a B cup. "I'll remind them."

I hung up the phone and stepped behind the register to look at the credit slip for the last return. Eight hundred dollars.

"Excuse me, are you April?"

I looked up from the credit receipt to stare into the face of a future Playboy centerfold. Everything from her leather pencil skirt to the blond streaked hair that fell over the burgundy faux-fur collar of her tightly fitted sweater was pure sex kitten. I tugged at the sleeve of my own top self-consciously. "Yes, I'm April, can I help you?"

"Gigi Messinger." She reached over the counter and shook my hand a little too vigorously. "I sell in the 532 store. I just moved here from SoCal."

"Welcome to northern California. What can I do you for?"

"Is it true that you're looking for an assistant? Because if you are, I'm, like, totally your girl."

No way was I hiring someone named Gigi who referred to southern California as SoCal. "I am looking, but I've already had a lot of other people call about the job." Total lie.

"I promise you, I'm the one you want. My sales are, like, awesome. I've been a Dawson's Super-Seller every month for the last two years."

"Well, that's great, Gigi, but I'm looking for someone who has some managerial experience under her belt—this is a large-volume department and I demand a lot from my staff."

"I totally hear you." Gigi put her hand on her rather well-endowed chest for emphasis. "You don't want some slacker taking up space. I was the assistant in San Fernando Valley's Rhapsody department for a year before I moved up here. I figured it would be good for my career to move to a store that was closer to the buying offices—you know, get myself noticed and then get promoted. I've been at Dawson's for a total of two years and before that I was at Bloomie's managing handbags." She retrieved a folder out of her briefcaselike handbag and pulled out a résumé printed on pink marbleized paper.

Shit, she was going to make it hard *not* to hire her. I glanced down at the current month's schedule that was proudly displayed next to the register. In less than three weeks I'd be flying to Spain, and if I didn't hire someone for the assistant job by then I might as well draw a bull's-eye on my forehead and hand Liz a rifle. I took the résumé from her and scanned the information. "Why don't we go somewhere we can talk."

Gigi eagerly agreed and I took her to the more casual of the two Dawson's cafés and bought us both nonfat lattes. I couldn't help but notice the way the cashier was drooling when he handed Gigi hers, but she seemed oblivious.

"Love, love, love your floor," Gigi gushed as we maneuvered ourselves to a table with a view of the street below. "The way you have the Michael Stars tees mixed with the formal skirts—I mean, wow!"

I almost laughed, but one glimpse into her almond-shaped blue eyes told me that she was unfathomably serious. "Tell me exactly why you want this job."

"Are you kidding? Who wouldn't want it?"

I had to work extra hard not to throw my hand up in the air and scream, "Me! Me!"

"I mean," she continued, "this is the flagship store! This is where it happens!"

"Uh-huh. Where do you want to go with your career?"

"When I was a little girl I used to dream of being a buyer, but then I found out about merchandise managers and I knew that was the job for me, right at the top of the food chain. And to do it at Dawson's, God, can we say heaven?"

Merchandise managers were so far above department managers that it was hard for me to even contemplate the day when that position might be in my grasp. Buyers couldn't so much as go to a trade show without getting the approval of their merchandise manager, and the thought of someone with Gigi's temperament wielding that much power was more than a little scary. "You mentioned that you used to manage at Bloomingdales," I said. "Why did you leave?"

"Bloomies was cool but even though I love fashion I've never considered myself a New York type and..."

I waved my hand to indicate that she didn't have to

continue. Dawson's was one of the few top upscale large specialty stores that didn't have its corporate headquarters in New York, which would be important for someone who wanted to move up the corporate ladder but knew that she was too obnoxiously perky for the Big Apple.

"I must say, your enthusiasm is…overwhelming. As I'm sure you remember, assistants are expected to sell an average of $180 per hour worked."

"My SPH, sales per hour, has never dropped below two hundred and that includes the time I was an assistant in SoCal."

"I'll need you to work at least two nights a week, and most Sundays."

"I'm all over the nights-and-weekends thing."

"And I'll expect my assistant to be able to keep on top of the crew when I need to be off the floor."

"Of course, you'll never have to worry about anything."

I wish. "You must remember that assistants don't make that much on top of their commission. It's kind of a 'prove yourself' position."

"And that's exactly what I plan to do." Gigi leaned closer to my side of the table. If all models had skin like hers there would be no need for airbrushing. "I'm going to prove myself. While I was at the San Fernando store I helped plan five fashion shows in eight months. My sales are always the highest of all the salespeople in whatever department I work in. I have a personal trade that is so loyal they let me send them merchandise sight unseen just based on my recommendation. If you give me this job I will not only make your job easier, I will make it my mission in life to make you look good. After all—" she sat back and sipped her latte "—if you make buyer, and let's face it, the only reason anyone ever becomes a department manager is to get to the buying office, I'll be in the perfect position to take your job as department manager. The way I see it, it's win-win."

Gigi scared me. People on amphetamines usually did. But it was hard to argue with her dedication. This was her dream job, as sick as that was. I nodded and pushed my business card toward her. "Okay, I'm a believer. I've still got to interview the other applicants and I have to do reference checks, but you can count on my calling you in the next few days. If you have any questions before that—"

Gigi waved the card in the air. "I'll ring." She bounced up and extended her hand once again.

"Right," I said, shaking her hand briefly. "Either way, we'll talk soon."

I took advantage of Liz's absence and left Dawson's at five o'clock sharp. If Tad's schedule of the last few weeks was any indication, I would have a few hours alone before I would have to face him. I wanted to wind down before being forced to interpret whatever explanation he planned on giving me. I got home, made myself a gourmet meal of Top Ramen with hot sauce and then curled up on the couch with a bowl of popcorn and a murder mystery. I turned the television on so that the house wouldn't be too quiet. USA Network was having a Kim Basinger movie marathon. Currently she was having a sexual fantasy in her office, probably not the most opportune location. She should try working at Dawson's. That'd knock the sex drive out of anyone.

I heard the sound of keys scraping against the lock of the front door before finding the correct slot. Tad walked into the living room and threw his coat on the back of the love seat before bending over me to gently brush his lips against mine. The faint scent of wine clung to his breath.

"Wow, don't tell me you were drinking at the office."

"I stopped at a wine bar on the way home. It's been a long day." He lifted my legs and then placed them on his lap as he took his place beside me. "What are we watching?"

"*Nine and a Half Weeks.*"

"Really?" Tad's voice lifted with a note of enthusiasm.

"It's been edited for television."

"Oh," he said, his enthusiasm gone. "Sooo, it's just two hours of Mickey Rourke being an asshole."

I laughed and put my novel down on the coffee table. Tad was acting normal. So normal that I couldn't help wondering if I had imagined the tense mood of last night.

He started to massage my bare feet. "So, tell me, what's new with you? I feel like I never get to see you these days."

Clearly this was not a man who planned on explaining himself. I chewed my lip and considered bringing up the incident myself but realized I just wanted to sit here and enjoy getting my feet rubbed. "I interviewed a woman to be my assistant today, Gigi Messinger. She's got to be the sexiest woman I've ever seen in my life."

"Have you looked in a mirror lately?"

"Love you. No really, she's a knockout. If she worked in men's suits they'd have record sales."

"But does she have what it takes to be an assistant in a women's department?" he asked as he gently pulled on each of my toes.

"Maybe, she's done it before. There are a few things about her that concern me, though."

"Such as?"

"She's annoying—Southern California Valley Girl annoying."

Tad ran his thumb up the center of my left foot. "But you'll be working opposing shifts right?"

"Always. I'll probably only overlap with her twelve hours a week or so, and that doesn't include any lunch breaks or time I take off the floor to put together promotions and the like."

"That's not bad."

"No, but there's something else. She's very…ambitious."

"Good, then she'll work harder for you. Can't have too much ambition."

"Oh, really? Ever hear of Napoleon? And let me tell you something, if Napoleon had been a woman she would never have been defeated by the European monarchies."

"So, women are superior, is that it?"

"Just different. If Napoleon was a woman she wouldn't have been bad-mouthing the political system of the Brits and all the rest of them. She would have announced that while France and its, um, acquisitions should not be under a monarchy, the British monarchy is just lovely for the Brits. She would have gushed about how the two nations should be the best of friends and she would have baked them cookies for starters."

Tad nodded solemnly. "And considering the disparity between French and English cuisine, the cookies alone would have won the love of the king and queen."

"Exactly," I said, snapping my fingers in the air. "So the British would have loved Napoleonette. They would have invited her to parties and asked her for fashion advice and just when she had truly won their trust, *bam!*"

"Bam?"

"She'd invade! The English would be taken completely off guard because they would have thought France was their ally and before you could say 'fascist tyranny,' all of Europe would have been under one empire."

"So what are you saying? You think Gigi is going to stage a military coup and invade Canada?"

"No, I'm saying that she might be the type to stab me in the back."

"I see." Tad abandoned my left foot for my right. "Before we go further into this, might I say that your analogy was…excessively elaborate."

"I've always been a woman of extremes."

"Right. My other point is that you told me that Blakely has imminent plans to promote you. You don't have to be Napoleon, or Napoleonette, to see that the best strategy for Gigi is to do whatever she can to expedite that promotion so that she can step into your current job."

"Yeah, she mentioned something along those lines."

"If her references check out, hire her." I felt my jaw tighten; Tad's tone was a little too decisive considering it wasn't his decision to make.

"Maybe," I said vaguely.

"You need someone, April. You work way too many hours."

"Look who's talking." I slid into a more horizontal position as I enjoyed the sensation of his hands that were now working their way up my calf. "My mother's not coming to our wedding."

Tad's hands stopped. He looked into my eyes and immediately his face became the picture of empathy. "She actually said that to you?"

I nodded, not trusting myself to speak. It's always like that. You think you've blown something off and then you say it out loud and suddenly you're all choked up and pathetic.

"Goddamn her," Tad whispered, and leaned back into the cushions. "You realize this isn't about you."

"That's exactly what she said—that I wasn't considering her needs."

"What she 'needs' is a kick in the pants." He loosened his tie. "She's refusing to come to our wedding because it will remind her that she's always been alone, and she can't handle that."

I scooted myself into a more upright position. I hadn't considered that possibility. I liked it. With a little work I could convince myself of the idea and maybe even forgive her in a year or two.

"That doesn't make it okay," Tad continued. He reached out and gently caressed my hand. "Look, it doesn't take a shrink to see that your mother's a mess. She doesn't know how to manage her affairs, she doesn't know how to make a relationship work and obviously she doesn't know how to be a decent parent. But that's what makes you so incredible."

I shook my head. "I'm not following."

"She never offered you the guidance, emotional support or security that children are supposed to get and yet…well, look at you."

I looked down. I was wearing a Vivienne Tam shirt paired with a charcoal Vertigo miniskirt. Was this outfit the result of a bad childhood?

"It's not a fluke that everyone loves hanging out with you," Tad said. "You're fun, warm, generous and you know how to be a supportive friend. And perhaps more importantly, you know how to take care of yourself. You figured it all out on your own, April. You're…amazing."

"Oh. My. God. I so want to have sex with you right now."

Tad let out a gentle laugh. "Well, I think that can be

arranged." His hands gently stroked the insides of my thighs. "I noticed you didn't wear nylons today. Has Dawson's stopped requiring employees to wear them?"

"No it's just that I already took them off."

"Ah, one less barrier for me." His hands disappeared under my mini. I smiled as I felt his hands stroke the outside of my panties. "That's what I like about you Tad. You always get right to the core of the issue."

I could hear the rhythm of his heart as his chest rose and fell beneath my cheek and I ran my fingers over his taut abdomen. "And to think I was worried about coming home tonight." As soon as I said it I winced. Of all times to bring that up I had to choose now.

Tad sighed and propped himself up, using the pillows on our bed. "I was in a weird mood."

I didn't say anything.

"I called my parents."

Now, *that* I wasn't expecting.

"I knew it was important to you."

"So you called them...for my sake," I stated slowly.

"I love you, April, and if you want the opportunity to get to know my family then I want to be able to give you that."

I hesitated. Based on Tad's accounts of them, I wasn't at all sure I wanted to get to know his family. I just thought *he* should get to know them. "Did you reach them?"

"Yes."

Oh, that didn't sound good. "Did you tell them about the wedding?"

"They're not coming. They don't want an ethnic daughter-in-law and apparently they no longer want a son. I have been officially disinherited and disowned."

I gasped. "They really said that?"

"You think I would make that up?" he snapped. He stared fixedly at the blinds covering our window. "I just thought you should know that I tried. I tried for you."

A wave of guilt swept over me. Tad had closed the door on his parents before. He had worked through all that pain and heartache and thanks to me that wound had been ripped right back open. "God, Tad, I'm so sorry."

"It's not a problem. I'm over it." The expression on his face said differently.

"Really?" I sat up while holding the sheet over my breasts. It didn't feel like a nudity moment. "This is my fault. I shouldn't have pressed the issue."

"I need you to trust me, April," he whispered. "I need you to believe in me."

"Tad, I do." I lifted my hand to his cheek and gently guided his face in my direction. "I believe in you more than I've ever believed in anyone. I swear I won't question your judgment again." I hesitated for a moment. "Or at least...well, can I ask you something?"

"What?" he asked warily.

"Are you really going to start making religious bumper stickers for my mom's cult?"

Tad chuckled. "I never thought of it in those terms before. I did tell her I'd put together a small merchandise line for the temple, for a profit, of course." He reached over and tucked a lock of my hair behind my ear. "Do you not want me to?"

"I will pay you not to do it." I let the sheet fall a little so that it barely covered my nipples. I had the feeling I was going to need some ammunition in order to get my way. "It's bad enough that my mother's a pagan Marxist zealot, without my husband profiting off her neuroses."

He grinned and his eyes traveled to the edge of the sheet. "And what do I get if I agree to abandon this business venture?"

I let the sheet fall to my waist.

He grabbed my wrists and, with a quick move, pinned me beneath him. "April, you have yourself a deal."

EIGHT

The next three weeks blended together. I spent a good portion of time doing my chicken-with-head-cut-off impersonation as I ran around firming up plans with caterers, musicians and florists during my few hours away from work. The wedding was becoming incredibly expensive but Tad said that he had inherited a large chunk of money from his grandparents aeons ago and had put it in a Smith Barney account in anticipation of this occasion. What kind of guy put aside money for a future wedding? But that was Tad: Mr. Romantic. Still I convinced him that we didn't need to spend the money on a wedding planner. I had originally thought it was a totally needless expense. Now I was beginning to regret my decision.

In addition to all that I hired Gigi and spent an enormous amount of time bringing her up to speed so she would feel comfortable running things during the eleven days I would be gone. She was a quick learner, and if she wasn't such an annoying twit, training her would have been a breeze. I had one minor nervous breakdown during which Tad walked in on me pummeling a throw pillow. He took the opportunity to help me organize my to-do list and recommended that I postpone all our nonwedding social commitments (like dinner with Jeremiah) until after the honeymoon, to which I happily agreed. I had a bachelorette party where I had the pleasure of deep throating a cucumber and doing a body shot off a beefy male stripper with BO. When the wedding was twelve days away, Tad sent a dozen long-stem red roses to me at work. He sent eleven the next day, then ten and so on until I was down to one stress-inducing rose.

Now, as I stood in front of the mirror in a Ritz-Carlton hotel room just hours before I was to say my vows, I didn't feel stressed at all. Take note, panic and stress are very different things.

"You look like a princess." Caleb's figure came into range of the mirror. "And I don't mean the fairy-tale kind with ugly puffed sleeves. You're very Audrey Hepburn in *Roman Holiday*."

"Love that movie." I twisted slightly so that I could admire the white, delicately beaded bias-cut gown from a different angle. This would be a great dress for a curator to wear to a gala-type event. I imagined the people gazing at me with the appropriate mixture of admiration and envy. I could almost hear them whispering to one another, "Not only is she the best curator the museum's ever had, she has incredible style!" Another would add, "She's as lovely as the women in Renoir's paintings, except, of course, she's a good twenty pounds thinner!"

Caleb adjusted the silk straps on my shoulder. "Picturing yourself walking down the aisle?"

I blanched and turned to face Caleb. "I'm doing the right thing, aren't I?"

"Wedding jitters?" Caleb asked, lifting an eyebrow.

"If I turned around and bailed right now, would you support me?"

Caleb crossed his arms in front of him and looked around the room. "How much did this wedding cost?"

"A little under seventy thousand."

"I think it might be better if you just went through with it. If worse comes to worse, you can divorce and then you'll get to keep half the gifts."

I turned back to the mirror. "I don't believe in divorce."

"You haven't gone Catholic on me, have you?"

"I just think that people today don't take their wedding vows seriously enough. Once I get under that *chuppah* I'm going to swear in front of Tad, my friends and God that I will stand by Tad for as long as I live. No turning back, no matter what."

"Ah…" Caleb stepped back a few paces and sat on the armrest of a chair. "In that case, let me ask you this. If things between you and Tad never get any better than they are right now, would you be happy?"

I thought about that for a moment. Tad had his annoying quirks. Sometimes he got defensive for no reason and his refusal to function on more than four hours of sleep had majorly contributed to my need for undereye concealer. But he was also romantic, adoring, fun, witty and I loved him. Wasn't that what it all came down to in the end? I loved him and he loved me and that should be enough for anyone. "Yes," I said firmly. "I would be happy."

"Then let's get this party started," Caleb whispered. I examined his reflection. He looked resolute. I don't know what he had to be resolute about. I was the one about to make the biggest commitment of my life, a commitment that wasn't even legal for him to make to another man. I felt a sudden surge of jealousy.

Civil rights issues aside, there was something liberating about not having the choice of whether or not to marry. But then again I didn't feel as if I had the choice either. Maybe Caleb's and my situation had more similarities than I wanted to admit.

There was a rap on the door and then Allie used the key card I had lent her and poked her head in. "Guess who I found in the lobby?" she sang.

She threw the door open wide and made a ta-da-like gesture in the direction of the petite grey-haired woman at the door. "Bobe!" I tottered over to her in my stiletto heels and threw my arms around her neck.

"Let me look at you, *mummala*." She backed up and took in my ensemble. Her face crinkled into a warm smile. "What a beauty you are! A real lady." I smiled modestly and led her to the love seat. "I gave the cake to that Rose woman downstairs. I hope she knows what to do with it."

"She's the Ritz's event coordinator, she'll make sure it's stored correctly and served on time."

"So now you need an event coordinator?" Bobe shook her head in disapproval. "I don't understand it. Why all the hoopla? You couldn't get married in a nice synagogue or in one of those chapels? Now you have to get married at the Ritz with an event coordinator? It's not like you, April."

I rubbed her shoulder gently. Funny how both my mother and Bobe could disapprove of the same thing for such dramatically different reasons.

The thought of my mother threatened to give me a headache. I should've been thankful that she wasn't around to embarrass me, but I couldn't quite get myself there. I had really expected her to come to her senses. Couldn't she at least pretend to care?

I squeezed my eyes shut and took a steadying breath. *Focus on your blessings. Tad loves you. Tad will always be there.*

"I've got an idea!" Allie clapped her hands, oblivious to my change in mood. "Let's all have a glass of red wine!"

Bobe glanced at the clock on the wall. "So early? Before the ceremony?"

"You're right," Allie said. "We should start with white."

She pulled a corkscrew out of her purse (although there was one provided by the hotel right in front of her) and opened a bottle of Chardonnay that had been chilling in the minirefrigerator. She poured it into four elegant glasses and passed them out. "To April and Tad. May they have a life of happiness, love and just enough hell-raising and drunken debauchery to keep things interesting!"

Caleb's free hand went to his hip. "Did you steal that from *Martha Stewart Weddings?*"

"I've got to save the good stuff for the toast at the reception. Drink up."

We all raised our glasses just as another knock interrupted us. "Is the bride in there?" Rose's voice carried through the door. "They're ready for you to sign the Jewish marriage contract."

I saw Bobe blink away a tear. My choice to sign the *ketubah* immediately before the ceremony was a nod to the traditions she held dear. I glanced at the small group around me. "Okay, guys, it's showtime."

My small entourage followed me to the hotel room down the hall and Caleb pushed on the already partially opened door to reveal the rabbi, the best man and Tad standing around a table. As soon as Tad's eyes moved to me, his jaw literally dropped open. "Oh my God, you're breathtaking."

Maybe this princess thing wasn't so bad after all. I smiled and tried unsuccessfully to glide to his side. Tad took my hand and brought it to his heart. "I mean it, April. I'm actually having a hard time breathing."

I giggled and resisted the impulse to kiss him prematurely. This was right. The rabbi cleared his throat. My rabbi hadn't been available, but thanks to Tad's best man/business partner's sister-in-law's grandmother's recommendation we found the elderly and somewhat doddering Rabbi Gelfman. I listened as he rattled off a few words about the sacredness of marriage, and felt a renewed flutter of nerves. The rabbi handed me the pen and I looked at the contract. It was in Hebrew, so I couldn't read it. Sometimes it was better not to know what you were getting into. My hand wavered over the line where I was supposed to sign. I looked up and saw Caleb, who was looking rather rigid. He was worried about me. I shifted my gaze to Tad, and he looked back at me with so much love that I knew there was nothing to fear. I watched my hand write my name and then I handed the pen to the man I was going to spend the rest of my life with.

THE
MARRIAGE

NINE

I stood by the window in our room at Hotel Nouvel and watched the sporadic droplets of rain gently tap down on the streets of Barcelona. Such an interesting city. It was as if thousands of modern western conveniences and sensibilities had been put in a time machine and dropped on a sixteenth-century world. The archaic stone buildings were now wired with very advanced security systems. Scantily clad women danced in bars just a stone's throw away from where kings and queens had once ruled over impoverished serfs. And the nights! Children playing in the streets at a time when most American children would have been tucked into bed, street performers doing provocative Latin dances—it was like every evening welcomed in a new festival. Unfortunately, there was nothing festive going on within the walls of my room. I looked over my shoulder to confirm that Tad was still buried in the book he had been reading for the last two hours.

"It's barely a sprinkle," I noted. "Besides, I think there's some-

thing romantic about walking the streets of Spain in the rain—
Hey, that rhymes!" I held out my arms grandly. "The rain in
Spain falls mainly in the…"

"I'd rather not." He didn't even bother to look up from the pages.

I dropped my arms. "That must be a good book."

He shrugged and turned the page.

"Do you think I'd like it?"

"I don't know."

I turned back to the window; the view was a lot more lively
than the person on the bed. The wedding had been wonderful.
Tad had written such beautiful vows and we had continued to
dance even after the last of our guests had gone—right up until
the band had finally packed up to leave. We had gone back to
our suite and engaged in the most intense sex of my life. But my
favorite moment had come the day after the ceremony when we
had stopped briefly at our home before heading to the airport.

Tad's things were all moved in while many of mine were still
in boxes earmarked for storage, but it was the stack of gifts that
drew my attention. Caleb had been kind enough to drop them
off at the house after the reception, and the silver and floral
wrapping paper was now too much of a temptation to resist.

"Okay, I got my passport, we should get going," Tad had said,
but he, too, was attracted to the bounty.

"Just one," I had pleaded.

"I thought we were going to wait until we got back. Something
to look forward to."

"One." I looked at him and tried to flutter my eyelashes, which
predictably caused a lash to fall directly into my eye. Tad had
tried not to look amused as I cursed and delicately extricated it.

"Just one, April, we have to get to the airport." We both

broke into enormous grins, the kind Charlie wore before entering the chocolate factory. Then we dived for the present. We knew exactly which one. It had the most metallic wrapping and was beckoning to us from the top of the stack. The card was from the parents of Tad's college roommate. Together we ripped off the paper and I used my fingernails to break the tape sealing the plain brown box. I reverently pushed aside the tissue and we leaned over to see what was waiting for us.

Neither of us said anything at first. Finally, I pulled it out and held it up for our examination. "What, um… What is it?"

"Well, I'm no art major," Tad had said, "but I'd say it's a ceramic rabbit."

"Is it…the Easter Bunny?"

"On a really bad day." That was it. We were in tears laughing. I remember suddenly falling in love with that rabbit because it represented all the stupid stuff that Tad and I were going to be able to laugh at together. The moment, the wedding, everything—had all been perfect. But here in Spain, for no apparent reason, it wasn't.

I climbed onto the bed behind him and massaged his shoulders. "Let's go on an adventure tomorrow. We'll get on a train and go to the south of France, Nice maybe. We'll find some little dive hotel, spend the night, get some sun, it'll be fun."

"Okay."

"Would you rather stay here? Or we could rent a car and drive around the countryside. And we could try to find a little pension and do the whole bohemian-lover thing."

"Okay."

"Are you even listening to me?" I smacked my hands against his back and bounced off the bed.

"I'm trying to read a book."

My throat tightened. It would have been better if his tone had hidden an explosive anger or a cold rage, anything other than this lethal detachment.

"Well, forgive me for expecting you to pay attention to me on our honeymoon. Correct me if I'm wrong, but wasn't it you who wanted to come here?"

Tad shrugged again and resumed reading.

My jaw dropped. I had no idea how to respond to this. Hit him? I was pretty sure the domestic-abuse laws were a lot less stringent in Spain. I thrust my hands in my pockets to better resist temptation. "Tad, what's going on?" I strained to keep my voice steady. "Why are you being like this?"

"Look, I'm jet-lagged and I just want to read quietly for a while. Can I please just do that?"

His jet lag looked a lot like depression. That was just great; my husband had gone into a depression within forty-eight hours of marrying me. "We're going to the countryside tomorrow," I announced.

"Fine."

"I'm going out to see some more of the city."

"Fine."

I waited for him to ask if I wanted company. When the offer didn't come I grabbed my purse, yanked my coat out of the closet and made an unsuccessful attempt to slam the weighted hotel door. I took a minute to center myself while standing in the hallway. I had left my gloves on the bed stand. I looked back at the closed door and considered going back for them. I shook my head and quickly buttoned up my coat. I wasn't going in there. It felt more appropriate to have cold hands. I hurried down the corridor and turned the corner just as the elevator doors were about to close. "Hold it, please." The man inside pressed the open button just in time and I slid in. My fellow passenger was a well-dressed gentleman in his mid-forties with thinning hair; probably French or maybe Dutch. I would have struck up a polite conversation if he hadn't been so busy impolitely undressing me with his eyes. I gave him my best I'm-so-insulted look, but secretly I was relieved. If Tad abandoned me, I still had enough allure to have an affair with a womanizer.

When the doors opened I quickly strode out into the cold, late-morning air. I tried to focus on the Gothic architecture as I walked, or the street vendors, or anything outside of myself. *It's going to be fine*, I silently chanted over and over again. But at the same time another nagging voice kept reminding me, *He's barely touched you since you got off the plane, barely looked at you*. I stuck the nail of my pinkie finger between my teeth and then yanked it out before I could damage my Egyptian-Bronze polish. The trick here was to take everything at face value. He said the problem was jet lag, so I was going to believe him. I just never realized that being jet-lagged could have such a major effect on a person's personality. But it was temporary.

I stopped at the outside of El Museu Picasso. The one mental escape I could always count on was art. The paintings were exhibited in three medieval mansions, which I found odd, considering Picasso's fierce modernism, but the juxtaposition was an appropriate reflection of the overall city. I eagerly handed over my euro dollars to the admissions clerk. There was nothing as awe inspiring as viewing the works of a master in person. Their essence simply couldn't be conveyed in a photograph no matter how high the quality of print. I moved slowly through Picasso's pieces from his young-adult years; so much simpler than his later works, but that was predictable. Everything always got more complicated with age. And yet Picasso also became bolder, even stronger.

After spending a good hour admiring the paintings from his Rose and Blue Periods I approached some of his more avant-garde paintings. There was one in particular that caught my attention. It was of a woman whose features were cracked apart with a few daring strokes of the paintbrush. I found myself staring into her misplaced eye. I felt my teeth break the flesh of my chapped lips. If Picasso were painting Tad's portrait, how would the famous artist have put together the pieces of Tad?

Hours later I went back to the hotel. Tad was sitting at the edge of the bed staring at the wall. His eyes moved slowly in my direction as I let the door close behind me. There was no sign of recognition, no silent or spoken greeting, nothing. He just moved his eyes back to the empty space in front of him.

"Tad?" I whispered. "Tad, what is it? What's wrong?"

"I'm jet-lagged."

I hesitated before inching closer and letting my fingertips rest on his shoulder. "What's going on with you? Please, tell me."

He rose to his feet without acknowledgment and then robotically walked past me to the bathroom and closed the door. I stood in the empty room, unable to take my eyes from the spot he had just vacated. *It's going to be fine*, it's going to be fine. But the other voice was overpowering my mental mantra. *This is so not fine!* I had to get a grip. We needed to talk. Communication is the key to all successful relationships, right?

"Tad?" I called out without moving. "Tad, I..." *Say something poignant, make it clear that you're reaching out to him.* "I...I think

I'm going out again…I really want to see Gaudi's cathedral." Or I could go the opposite route and flee. There was no answer from the bathroom. I left the room, putting as much distance between me and Tad as I could in a flat minute.

The next day things were better—sort of. I never again caught Tad staring at a blank wall nor was he locking himself in the bathroom or even in the hotel room. He stayed by my side as I toured such sights as the Casa Museu Gaudi and Palau de la Música Catalana. We skipped the trip to the countryside but he allowed me to take him to some of the city's bars and restaurants. I never took him to the nightclubs. At no point during our trip was the mood ever appropriate for celebratory activities. I never even felt as if he was really with me—he was just a stranger by my side indulging me out of obligation. The highlight of our trip was the plane ride home.

I buckled my seat belt and pretended to listen to the flight attendant as she went over the complicated instructions of using a plastic oxygen mask. Tad was reading another book—his fourth that week. So he didn't travel well, no biggie. It didn't mean anything. Of course, Caleb would violently disagree with that. I tried in vain not to flash back to that conversation.

"You've *never* taken a trip together?" Caleb had dropped his sandwich onto his plate on the break table and scooted his plastic chair an inch forward. "Have you completely forgotten the cardinal rule of dating?"

"The cardinal rule of dating, let's see…always shave your legs within eight hours of having sex?"

"The other one, never commit to anyone you haven't vacationed with. April, everyone knows that if you don't travel well together the relationship is doomed to failure!"

I remember giving him a patronizing smile and finishing the rest of my Diet Coke. "I'm a little dyslexic, so I had to reverse the process to suit my unique learning style. Now that I know the relationship's a success I can count on having a rocking time on our vacations."

The plane started its slow journey to the runway. I popped in a stick of gum and wordlessly offered another piece to Tad. He politely declined. I could see that he wasn't angry with me, nor did he seem worried or stressed. With so many emotions that I could rule out, why was it I couldn't put my finger on any of the emotions he was actually feeling? The plane paused and then I felt the vibration of the engine and the fast momentum as we raced forward and lifted into the air. I reached into my purse and pulled out my own novel. *Everything's going to be fine*. After all, there was no alternative.

Two flights later we landed at the San Francisco airport. Allie met us at the gate with a bottle of single-malt scotch wrapped in a big purple bow. "Welcome home!" She threw her arms around me, then Tad. "Was it awesome?"

Tad nodded absently. "Yeah, it was great."

"Yeah?" Allie linked her arm with mine and led us toward the baggage claim. "Did you ever leave the hotel room?"

Every chance I got. "There's a lot to see in Barcelona," I said vaguely.

"Right, like all those dark handsome Spanish men. I hope you kept her well satiated, Tad, 'cause I know there was some heavy competition."

I knew she felt her ribbing was harmless since in her mind we had just spent the last eight days gazing into each other's eyes.

Tad didn't seem bothered by it. He simply dismissed it the same way he had been dismissing me. I made myself smile and tried to absorb some of her enthusiasm. I wasn't going to tell her the truth. The baffling disappointment of the last few days was going to stay locked inside me.

We reached the baggage carousal and watched the various pieces of luggage slide into sight. Allie elbowed me as Tad stepped forward to retrieve our bags. "You must have worked that man over day and night with all that good lovin'. I don't think I've ever seen anyone so spent."

"Mmm." I couldn't meet her eyes.

"Just don't expect it to continue this way. The honeymoon period never lasts."

Thank God.

TEN

And to think I had worried about going back to work so soon after my return. Who the hell cared how sleep deprived I was as long as I had something to distract me from the recent changes in my husband. My *husband*. I leaned against the wall as I waited for the employee elevator. I had expected those words to be so soothing. I had assumed marrying Tad was going to provide me with the sense of security that came along with being part of a normal family. But we weren't normal. Every day, I was becoming increasingly aware that Tad wasn't normal at all.

Although the night of our return had been somewhat less than horrible. After checking his e-mail Tad informed me that a major manufacturer he hoped to represent was one step closer to signing with SMB. That was the most forthcoming he had been since the wedding. We ordered Chinese food and he had eaten his share while reviewing files on the computer. I hadn't been feeling well lately so I let most of my food sit. Most people came back from their honeymoons with a tan. I came back with stomach upset.

The elevator at Dawson's finally arrived and when I got to my floor I found Gigi folding some twinsets into the shelves on the back wall. "Ohmygawd, you're back!" She flipped her hair out of her eyes before pulling me in for a quick hug. "Wow, you look so great! Was it wonderful? Tell me everything so I can be green with envy."

"What can I say? It was…it was unbelievable. And of course Barcelona was gorgeous."

"No way! The Custo designers are from Barcelona! But I thought you went to Spain."

I laughed. "Right, well, at the last minute we decided to go to Barcelona instead." It wasn't until I saw the blank look on Gigi's face that I realized she wasn't joking. "Barcelona's *in* Spain, Gigi."

"Oh, it is? I just figured you'd go to Madrid. You know, a lot of fashion comes out of Madrid, too."

"You don't say." I managed a tight smile. "What are you doing here so early? You know we don't have to be here until eight."

"Early bird catches the promotion," she sang. "We didn't get any new merchandise today—weird, huh? Our shipments lately have been totally light. I asked Marilyn if we could get a double-size run of Juicy Couture next time and she seemed into it…"

I nodded and made mmm, hmm and uh-huh noises while Gigi launched into a monologue designed to demonstrate that she hadn't let a single thing fall between the cracks during the eleven days of my absence.

"Well, Gigi, I must admit I'm impressed," I said as soon as she paused for a breath. "You've obviously been running a tight ship."

"I am, like, so glad you think so. I am totally excited to be part of your team and—"

"And my team and I are happy to have you," I interjected quickly. I needed to stop her before she started making me nostalgic for Tad's silent treatment. My eyes wandered toward my office door. "Tell you what, why don't you finish setting the floor while I try to catch up on a little paperwork. I was supposed to do the schedule for the second half of February before I took my vacation days and I didn't so—"

"Don't even sweat February's schedule. I already did it and handed it in."

My head snapped back in her direction. "You did the schedule? Gigi, only managers are allowed to do the schedule."

"I'm totally with you. That's why I put your name on it. It's been approved by both Liz and HR, and I gave it to the girls yesterday, so we're good to go."

"No, no, we're not." I shook my head furiously. "Gigi, I need to be the one doing the schedule. I use it to keep track of selling costs and figures and…and everything. It's not something I can delegate and it's certainly not something that you can do for me without asking!"

Gigi lowered her head slightly and peered at me through her long lashes. It was a look that had undoubtedly inspired forgiveness and leniency in countless numbers of straight men and quite a few lesbians, but it did nothing for me. "Where's the schedule?" I asked through gritted teeth.

"On your desk. I'm so over-the-top sorry, April. I totally thought I was doing you a favor."

I sighed and looked down at my shoes. Maybe I was overreacting due to the stress that I had been under. If Liz and HR had approved the schedule it had to be fairly decent and I could always tweak it here and there in order to accommodate selling costs. And if Gigi had wanted to undermine me, she wouldn't have put my name on it. Gigi was now giving me her "I'm-a-sad-little-sex-kitten" look. I sighed again. "It's all right. Just don't do it again, okay?"

Gigi's pout turned into a toothy grin. "Gotcha, the schedule is totally your deal."

Out of the corner of my eye I could see Dorita and Sally approaching the sales floor and I took the opportunity to walk away from Gigi to greet them. The four of us set the floor as Gigi babbled about this year's "totally awesome new neckline." By the time the doors opened I was ready to smack her. "You should go home," I suggested. "God knows you've earned the break."

"I really don't mind staying. On your first day back I imagine you're going to need a lot of time off the floor to play catch-up."

"Well, thanks to you there's nothing to 'catch up' on."

Gigi shook her head. "I did, okay, yesterday but, like, for the most part I've been so busy learning the ropes that my sales have suffered a little and I totally want to make up for that today."

"If you're sure…" Gigi was definitely strange. A Dawson's assistant manager refusing a day off was kind of like a state penitentiary inmate refusing a weekend pass.

I watched as Gigi buzzed from fixture to fixture dusting the silver bars until they sparkled like fine jewelry. I motioned to Dorita to follow me into the back room.

"You know that of all my staff I trust you the most," I said as the door to my office swung closed behind us. "So you're the one who gets to fill me in on the dirt. How is the staff adjusting to Gigi?"

Dorita tucked her perfect curls behind her ears. "She's kind of…um…"

"Annoying?"

"I was going to say hyper, but *annoying* will work." Dorita smiled. "But she knows her stuff and no one's been able to get anything by her. You know how Sally will pretend to call personal customers while she's really calling her boyfriend?"

"She does that?"

Dorita blushed. "Not that often, not at all anymore, I bet. Gigi caught on right away and set her straight."

"Huh." I sat down in my chair and motioned for Dorita to take a seat, as well. I had been working with Sally for eight months and never caught on to the personal phone call trick. Gigi had been working with her for three weeks. "How is she with the rest of the staff?"

"Okay, I guess." Dorita swiveled her chair back and forth. "She can be a little sharky at times but then there are times when she'll go out of her way to help us build and close sales, so I guess it balances out—and I'm sure you saw our numbers for the last week."

I nodded and absently tapped my fingernails against my desk. The numbers had been great. I had picked a winner. Why did that make me nervous? "How are the big shots reacting to her?"

"Liz *loves* her."

"And Marilyn?"

"*Loves* her."

"How about Blakely?"

"Blakely *tolerates* her."

I started to laugh just as the door to the office swung open, banging against the wall as it did so. "You're back!" Liz exclaimed as if she had been under the impression that I had been in Spain applying for citizenship. She looked over at Dorita, who had shrunken away from Liz's self-perceived brilliance. "Am I interrupting a one-on-one?"

"No, no. Dorita was just filling me in on the requests from her customers." I waved a hand at Dorita, signaling that this was her moment to escape. Dorita quickly got to her feet and left me with Liz.

"So good to see you. I am so excited about Gigi. You really have an eye for talent, don't you?"

"I'm glad you—"

Gigi pushed into the room and glowed at Liz, who reached out and playfully punched her in the arm. "Hey girl, I heard about that seven-thousand-dollar sale you had yesterday! Way to go!"

Hey girl? Liz had never called me anything other than April. Well, that wasn't entirely true; for the first few months we worked together she called me June.

"I'm glad I caught both of you," Liz said. "I want to go over next month's promo. First off, kudos to you, April, for coming up with such a fantabulous idea!"

"Thank you," I said. "You know I've always thought that a wardrobing seminar during cruise season would be…"

"Predictable and stale?" Liz offered helpfully. "I absolutely agree, which is why I was so excited when Gigi came in with your alternative action plan. Timing-wise we're cutting it close, but I know if we put our heads together we girls can pull it off."

I sat in my seat, dumbstruck. I had no alternative action plan. The wardrobing seminar had been it. I looked at Gigi but she was now giving Liz one hundred percent of her attention.

"I've arranged for televisions to be brought in from several of the other northern Cal stores, plus we'll be renting a few so there will be a screen in every department involved, and of course we'll have the sports bar where most of the activities will take place."

Now I was completely lost. Was I going to be on television? Did Dawson's have a sports bar? Or was she referring to our wine bar in which the San Francisco Junior League members traditionally gathered to watch the Olympic gymnastics competition?

"I've talked to Shoes, and Accessories, and they're all set," Liz continued. "Oh, and Cosmetics, of course—Caleb is completely on board. PR will have the postcards sent out by the fifth of the month. Now, on your end, have you been spreading the word amongst your customers?"

Gigi went to the little table that constituted her desk and pulled out a sheet of paper with a long list of names on it. "I've been making the girls give me the names of the customers they've pitched the promotion to." She handed the list to Liz, still avoiding eye contact with me. "I also had them make a brief note about the feedback they've been getting. As you can see, everyone is totally stoked on the idea."

"Of course they are, it's genius!" Liz gave me an approving wink. I tried to look flattered.

"So from this survey it appears that the stars who have the most coveted looks are Halle Berry, Kiera Knightly, Reese Witherspoon and, of course, right on the top of the list is Charlize Theron— Why am I not surprised?" She turned to me. "You know, you would be a good one to help give women that Halle Berry style. You kind of look like her."

I flashed a fake smile. I looked nothing like Halle but we were both biracial, so I'm sure in Liz's eyes we were twins.

"Okay, but I don't think we should make this all about the nominees," Gigi said. "Just because Cameron Diaz isn't nominated doesn't mean we don't all want her look."

"How true, and what girl doesn't want to be as adorable as

Drew Barrymore, or flawlessly beautiful as Gwyneth Paltrow," Liz mused. "But April's already thought of that."

"I…have," I said slowly, trying extra hard to keep the question mark out of my voice.

"Okay, well, it's looking good." Liz smiled genuinely at Gigi. "April, don't you think that this poor thing deserves a break? Why don't you take the rest of the day off, Gigi. I'm sure April has everything covered."

"April made me the same offer but I feel like I should be here while she gets settled back in."

"Nonsense. You're settled, right?" Liz looked at me expectantly.

The one thing I wasn't was settled. "If Gigi would like to take the day off nothing's stopping her."

"Good!" Liz flung an arm over Gigi's shoulder. "I'll walk you to the elevator. Is that your purse?"

I watched as Gigi and Liz exited my back room, arm in arm. At least Gigi had the courtesy to give me an apologetic look and to mouth the words *I'll call* before the door shut behind her. I slowly lifted my hand to the phone and dialed the extension to Cosmetics.

"M•A•C counter, can I help you?"

"Is Caleb there?"

"I saw him a minute ago…oh wait, I think he's in a meeting with one of the sales staff."

"Page him."

"We're not supposed to interrupt meetings unless there's an emer—"

"This is an emergency. Page him and tell him April has a 911 up in Sassy."

"O-kaay," the girl said uncertainly. "A 911 in Sassy."

"Thank you." I hung up the phone and drummed my fingernails impatiently against the receiver waiting for Caleb to ring back.

Caleb didn't bother calling. It took less than ten minutes for his tall figure to materialize in my doorway. "If it isn't everybody's favorite princess. How's the fairy tale going?" He bent down and ruffled my hair before taking a seat opposite me.

I tried not to grimace. "Forget the fairy tale. We have more urgent matters to discuss."

"Yes, I got your message. What's a 911?"

"Hello? It's an emergency. What else?"

"If it was an emergency you'd be calling the police, not the cosmetics manager. Unless…don't tell me you found a wrinkle?"

"Caleb, when were you going to tell me that you and Gigi have been planning things behind my back?"

Caleb scrunched his face up into a kind of confused-slash-offended look. "I don't plan with Gigi. I don't talk to Gigi. It's women like Gigi that give coke addicts a bad name."

"Movie stars, lots of televisions, make-believe bars, is this ringing any bells for you?"

"If we're playing Pyramid I'm going to guess Betty Ford Clinic."

"Caleb! I'm talking about February's promo!"

"February's…oh, wait—are you talking about your Academy Awards promo? Gigi gave me your memo and I told Liz I'd do it. Why, did you not want me to do it?"

"There's nothing to do! It isn't my promotion!"

"Honey, I looked at the name printed on the top and I'm pretty sure you're the only Silverperson who works here."

"But I didn't write it! Gigi wrote it and she's passing it off as my idea!"

"Really?" Caleb straightened up. "Well, I suppose that makes more sense. That whole line—'Come to Dawson's to celebrate the stars and leave looking like one'—didn't exactly sound like you, but I was really confused when I read your comment about the sassy sex appeal of Britney Spears."

"Britney… Oh my God, my name's on *that?*"

Caleb leaned back in his chair until it creaked with strain. "So you're saying that Gigi sold the idea as yours…on purpose." He shook his head, mystified. "Either she's a woman with a lot of marketing savvy who adores you or she's stupid and hates you."

"She didn't know Barcelona was in Spain, if that's any help."

Caleb waved the comment off. "That's because she was educated in California. You know how most people are here— they think there's only one state between us and New York. You know the place I'm talking about." Caleb snapped his fingers as if it would help jog his memory. "That little rectangle state where Toto and Dorothy used to live. Anyway, I have no doubt that Gigi is ignorant about everything that doesn't directly pertain to her. When it comes to her career I bet she's one smart little diva. She knows what'll please Liz, she knows what'll sell, and she's willing to pull out all the stops to get you promoted quickly so she can take your job."

"So she's trying to pass her good ideas off as mine so that she can become the next Sassy manager? Rather extreme, don't you think?"

"Just because it's not your goal…" Caleb shrugged without bothering to finish the rest of the sentence. "Look, I'll show you the memo so you'll know what you supposedly thought up. In the meantime I think you should just go with it. Take all the credit and give Gigi little to none. That'll teach her to try to make you look good behind your back."

I held my hands up in the air as if to block the path of a heavy object. "I can't take this. I cannot take any more craziness. I walked in this morning looking for a little normalcy, just a little, Caleb. Is that really so much to ask? That people just act normal for one friggin' day?"

"At Dawson's?"

I brought my hands into a prayer position and pressed them to my lips.

Caleb studied me for a moment before leaning forward and squeezing my knee. "Spill."

"Excuse me?"

"Why is it you need normalcy? Did something happen on your honeymoon that didn't fit your Cinderella fantasy?"

I looked away quickly. "My honeymoon was great…perfect. It was everything you could ever want a honeymoon to be."

"Right."

I glared at Caleb. "I'm just cranky because I'm a little under the weather today, upset stomach."

"They say marriage does that to some people, but not usually until they've been in the institution for a good three or four years. Come on, April, tell Papa all about it."

"Everything's fine, Caleb, really." I checked my watch. "You know, if you really want to cheer me up you could sneak a few of those Lancôme gifts into my bag."

Caleb grinned. "You're obviously not that sick."

"What makes you say that?"

"Because you're still as devious as ever. You without a mischievous streak is kind of like a dog with a warm nose."

I pushed myself out of my chair and waited as Caleb collected himself. "I swear, Caleb, you always make the most flattering comparisons."

* * *

I stayed at Dawson's for as long as humanly possible, but thanks to Gigi and her efficiency, the only thing left for me to do after the first nine and a half hours of work was stand around on the sales floor and gush to customers about the season's new color palette. Unfortunately I found that I was too anxious and preoccupied to fake a passion for seafoam green, so I eventually dragged myself home.

It was a quarter after eight when I carefully opened the front door to my house and listened for clues to what Tad was up to. I could hear the computer's printer producing something. At least I knew he wasn't staring at a wall. I went into our guest room, which doubled as an office, and dropped my purse on the fold-up futon. He looked up in surprise and then smiled as he rose to his feet. "I didn't hear you come in." He wrapped one arm around my waist and pulled me closer to him. "I'm glad you're home—I was beginning to worry."

I felt a huge rush of air escape me as I exhaled for the first time in weeks. He was back! My Tad was back! I placed a hand gently on his bicep as if to assure myself that the man holding me was real. "I didn't think you would… I was afraid…"

I looked up at Tad's face, expecting to see comprehension, but there was none. He simply caressed my hair and leaned in for a soft kiss. I tasted the remnants of wine clinging to his tongue.

"I am this close to nabbing that supplier," he said, holding up his fingers to illustrate his proximity to success.

"That's great! Seriously, I am thrilled for you!" My enthusiasm was a little over the top but how could I help it? The evil twin had gone the way of all the other unpopular soap opera villains and now I had the man I married back in my arms. I went up on tiptoe and leaned in for another kiss, this time with added passion. Now that I had him back, I was going to make sure that it was worth his while to stay.

ELEVEN

Tad's mood continued to elevate in proportion to his income. He took me to Aqua to celebrate, and afterward we went to the Starlight Room where we attempted (and failed) to swing to the sounds of big band music. I didn't bring up the honeymoon. It was behind us as far as I was concerned, and that's where it was going to stay. In all likelihood the problem really had been jet lag. I would just make a point not to leave California by plane in the company of my husband ever again.

My mother had taken to telephoning my department every few days but I refused to talk to her. I found that this new strategy made her a lot easier to deal with—or not deal with, as it were.

And as much as I hated to admit it, the staff and the customers were having fun with the upcoming Celebrate the Stars promo. Gigi's idea had been better than mine. But I knew where Barcelona was, so I figured that made us even. My own lack of enthusiasm over the promotion was partly due to the fact that I was in the beginning stages of burnout. I kept reminding myself that if I could hang in there for a few more months I could make it into the buyers' offices. Tad was doing his part to make hanging in there a little easier by dropping off small gifts for me on my days off, so that I would discover them at the beginning of my next shift. It's amazing how a small box of Godiva chocolates can have such significant mood-elevating effects.

Two weeks had passed since my return and I really had nothing to complain about—except for one most likely little, but possibly huge, thing—which was why Allie and I were at Walgreens pricing home pregnancy tests.

"How could I have done this?" The question was posed more to myself than to Allie.

"Done what? Had sex with your husband?"

"Not been careful!" I grabbed the EPT test and dropped it in my basket next to the shower puff and dishwasher detergent. I was pretending that if I bought several items the clerk wouldn't notice the more intimate one.

Allie sighed and put a hand on my back, directing me toward the register. "We've all gotten caught up in the moment at one point or another."

"That's not what this is about! This is about my inability to remember to take a stupid pill in the morning. This is about my taking minocycline for minor acne, despite the fact that it says right on the warning label that it may lessen the effectiveness of the Pill! Because I couldn't deal with the idea of having a pimple, Allie!" I bit my lip and forced myself to smile at the cashier as he rang up the sale. He rang up the EPT with the same enthusiasm with which he rang up the detergent. I wasn't sure if I was relieved or irritated. Shouldn't he care that my entire future depended on the outcome of that test? Shouldn't the world be stopping right about now?

I signed the charge slip and Allie and I took the bus up to her apartment. It was only five-thirty. Tad had called me at work to tell me he wouldn't be home until well after seven. That would give me time to get my negative result, laugh with Allie about the close call and have a vodka shot. Or two.

The bus stopped a block away from her apartment on Russian Hill and I glared up at the sky as the heavy mist turned into rain. "It never rains when I'm wearing practical shoes," I grumbled.

Allie gave me a funny look as she unlocked the door to the lobby. "You *never* wear practical shoes."

"So it should never rain." I stomped up the steps and waited for her to open the door.

"You know you just started taking the Pill two months ago," Allie pointed out as she ushered me in. "I don't think it's abnormal to be late while your body's adjusting to it."

I sighed and peeled off my now-wet leather jacket. "You're right. I'm sure I'm not pregnant. I'm just pissed that I even have to entertain the possibility."

Allie was reading the back of the box. "It says you just have to pee on the end of the stick and wait five minutes or less for a minus sign."

I nodded. "I can do that." Allie handed me the test and I went into the bathroom to urinate on my stick. I left it on top of the toilet and went out to meet Allie in the kitchen, where she was putting a kettle on the stove.

I wrinkled my brow. "I don't understand—you're making tea?"

"When it comes out negative we'll celebrate by putting some brandy in it."

"You're so clever." I checked my watch. "Has it been five minutes?"

"I don't think it's been thirty seconds." Allie opened her cabinet doors to reveal a plethora of pilsners, wineglasses, whiskey glasses, margarita glasses and three ceramic cups. She handed me one that said "Congratulations Graduate" on it and took the one with her sister's wedding picture embossed on it for herself. "Tell you what, we wait until the water boils, then we'll take our tea into the bathroom together. As soon as we see the minus sign we'll come back for the brandy."

I leaned against the kitchen counter and tested the old adage about watched pots. It did eventually boil, although I was sure it took an hour and not the five minutes that Allie insisted had passed. We poured the water over a few anti-quated-looking tea bags and she put a new bottle of brandy down next to the sink with a definitive thump. "Okay, let's go to the potty room."

We walked side by side to the bathroom and simultaneously leaned over the test.

We were both silent for a moment. Finally Allie cleared her throat. "Well, shit."

I didn't say anything. I just stared at the blue plus sign.

Allie straightened up and leaned against the opposite wall. "You could take another test but the directions say that the only reason a person would get a false positive result is if they have some totally rare medical condition."

"Oh," I said, still not moving my eyes from the test. "I wonder what rare medical condition I have."

"April…"

"I'm not pregnant, Allie." I turned to her and tried to keep my voice from quivering. "Blakely wants to promote me to assistant buyer, did you know that?"

"Yeah, you mentioned—"

"And I'm going to take the job. I know it's not fair to Cherise but that's the way the world works. I'm going to be a buyer and Tad is going to continue to expand his business until we're both rich, and then in five years or so, *that's* when we'll have children. You see, we've worked the whole thing out."

"April…"

"I can't be pregnant!" I screamed before collapsing in tears. I sat on the toilet seat, one hand clutching my nonalcoholic tea and the other grabbing for the toilet paper to keep my nose from running.

Allie kneeled beside me and put a hand on my knee. "You know, it could be a lot worse. You're married, April, to a wonderful guy. Tad might be happy."

I shook my head. "We had things planned."

"Have you ever heard that old Woody Allen joke?" Allie asked while handing me a few more squares of Charmin. "If you want to make God laugh tell him your future plans. Really, April, it's going to be okay. It'll be better than okay, it'll be good."

"Oh, really?" I snapped. "Do you think Blakely and Liz will share your optimism?"

"Fuck Blakely and Liz. They don't have to know yet anyway. Didn't you tell me that Blakely was planning to fire Cherise within the next two months? Don't you see? It's perfect, April! You won't be showing by then and you'll take the job. By the time Blakely finds out there won't be anything she can do about it and you'll be off your feet for the last half of your pregnancy."

I looked up at Allie and pushed some of my hair away from

my face. "That could work." I lifted my cup and then lowered it without tasting the watery tea. "So I just have to deal with Tad."

"He'll be happy," Allie assured me. "Guys like Tad are always happy when they get their wives knocked up. Just wait and see."

I walked alone to the bus stop. It was eight o'clock at night and a cold wind caused the raindrops to sting as they hit my face. Allie had suggested that I take a cab, but some masochistic impulse had spurred me to decline. I sat on the wiggly seat under the Plexiglas dome and watched the street for the arrival of a Muni. I didn't even recognize the Suzuki that pulled to a stop in front of me.

"Yo, April, whatcha doin' sittin' out here in the middle of a storm?"

I squinted at Jeremiah, who was leaning over into his passenger seat in order to yell at me through the window.

"I'm building an ark," I answered.

"What?"

"I'm waiting for the fucking bus, you moron."

Jeremiah laughed and pushed the passenger door open. "I knew there was a reason I missed you. Come on in, I'll give you a ride."

I shook my head. "It's all right. The bus will be here soon."

"What the fuck are you talking about? The buses don't run when it's raining. It's in the Muni driver's contract or something."

"It'll come eventually. Really, it's okay. Besides, my house is totally out of your way."

"The whole city only covers eight miles. Come on, April, get in. The rain's fucking with my upholstery."

Like this was my fault? I started to put up another argument but stopped myself. What *was* I doing? Did I really think the rain was going to magically wash the pregnancy away? I lowered my head and rushed into Jeremiah's car, slamming the door behind me. "You know, your upholstery couldn't get much worse."

"Hey, don't knock the Suzuki. I bought it for five hundred dollars and it barely leaks."

I looked up at the beads of water clinging to the edges of where the convertible roof was loosely attached. "Did it occur to you that a roof shouldn't leak at all?"

Jeremiah grinned as he put the car into gear. "I was talkin' about the oil."

I laughed despite everything. Maybe the universe wasn't coming to an end. Maybe Allie was right and Tad would be happy. I put my hand flat against the window as if I could somehow draw strength from the wind howling outside.

"Hey, are you all right?"

I jumped slightly, then laughed at myself. For a split second I had forgotten he was there. "I'm going to be. I'm going to be fine."

Jeremiah gave me a funny look but didn't say anything else for the rest of the ride. He stalled the car in front of my house and I started to open the door. His arm reached out and stopped me before I could get out. "You sure everything's cool? You haven't had any problems with Tad or nothin', right?"

It was an oddly stated question—grammatical issues aside. If he thought I was upset because of a lovers' quarrel then shouldn't he have asked if Tad *and* I were having problems? "Things with Tad are great." I looked at his hand and he removed it from my arm.

He nodded slowly. "Okay, I was just checkin'. I know a lot of newlyweds have a tough time with all the transition shit. You know, we still have to go out to dinner, the three of us."

"Yeah, of course…I'll call you tomorrow and we'll set it up."

I bent my head down and ran to my front door. I waved at

Jeremiah one more time as I stepped inside and watched him take off. The house was warm, indicating that the heat had been on for at least an hour, and I could hear the sounds of tinkering coming from the kitchen. Shit, he had cooked. The last thing I wanted to do was eat.

"April, is that you?"

"No, it's an intruder." I tried to keep my tone light as I hung my coat and purse on the rack. "I'm here to attack you."

I looked up as Tad bounded into the foyer and swung me up into his arms. "Goddess, I missed you!"

"Wow, it's only been twelve hours, I'm flattered."

"That's all day!" he protested. "Come here, I've got to show you something!"

He threw me over his shoulder and took me into the spare bedroom where we had the computer set up. "Tad, are you on crack? Why are you so hyper?"

"Look!" He lowered me to my feet and spun me around so that I was facing a tall stack of papers. "That's my new business plan! By next year SBM will have tripled its income."

"That's great." *And by next year this bedroom is going to be a nursery.* "Are Sean and Eric on board with it?"

"Of course they will be, it's brilliant!" He giggled. "I'm a genius!"

"So they haven't actually seen the plan yet."

"I told you they'll like it," he snapped. "It's flawless, and there's more." He whirled around before yanking me forward into the living room and pushing me onto the couch. "Tom called. They're going to be offering an entrepreneurship class this summer at City College and he wants me to teach it!"

"But Tom's a professor not an administrator. Can he really make that kind of decision?"

"Tom carries a lot of clout there." I watched nervously as Tad zigzagged around the room. "He'll get me in. I already know what my curriculum will be. I bet I could convince them to offer the class on a regular basis. Maybe SF State will pick it up, or USF. This could be great! And the pay isn't bad either, not great but not bad. And I bet when word gets out that I teach business classes at reputable colleges and universities SBM will have more clients than ever!"

His level of excitement was so disproportionate to what was going on that I found myself actually recoiling a little. "Tad—" I tried to find the least inflammatory words possible "—don't you think that you're getting a little ahead of yourself? I mean, it's all great, but none of it has actually happened yet."

Tad's feet stopped moving and he pivoted his body in my direction. "You don't…you don't believe in me." The anguish in each of those words made me ache.

"No, no, I do believe in you."

"The hell you do!" The anguish was being ebbed out by notes of hysteria. I moved closer to the corner of the sofa. "I've put everything I have toward getting us here. Look around you! We have a house—"

"We rent a house."

"I drive a BMW. We were married at the Ritz. We just got back from Spain, for Christ's sake! And now you don't think I can do this?"

"I didn't say that, Tad."

"Yes, you did!" In a flash of anger, he took the ceramic bunny that we had been displaying on the end table and hurled it across the room.

There was a crash and then silence. We both just stared at the fragments of our first wedding gift. Then without a word Tad turned around and walked out the front door.

I tried to breathe, but doing so was a struggle. I sat paralyzed for several minutes while I tried to come up with some explanation for what had just happened. I jumped at the sound of the doorbell but was still too stunned to immediately get up and answer it.

"April, are you there?" I heard Caleb's muffled voice filter through the door. I closed my eyes; I had totally forgotten that I had invited Caleb to come over and claim some of my unwanted wedding gifts. It didn't seem possible that he could be here for something so normal on a day in which everything had been turned upside down and backward. I used the little strength I had left to push myself off the couch and let him in.

Caleb stood in a military-like stance and held his nose in the air. "I've come for your cheese plates."

"Packed up in the kitchen," I said quietly as I stepped aside to allow him admittance.

Caleb strode toward the kitchen but stopped when he was halfway through the living room. He knelt down by the shards of ceramic and carefully lifted what remained of a long white ear. "My, my," he murmured. "This is one dead bunny." He replaced the piece on the floor and turned to me. "Did you slip and drop it?" He used his fingers to make imaginary quotation marks around the word *drop*.

"Caleb…"

"Don't get me wrong. I'm not trying to make you feel guilty. While I never saw him in life, from the looks of his remains I'd say it was a mercy killing."

"Tad and I got in a fight."

The amusement in Caleb's face disappeared and he stood up. "Who threw it?"

"Tad," I whispered. "I mean, he didn't throw it at me or anything. He just got frustrated, and well…" I gestured toward the broken pieces and then fell back down onto the couch.

Caleb sat down beside me and rested his forearms on his legs. "What was the fight about?"

"I don't know."

"Come on, you must have some idea. People don't go around hurling ceramic rabbits through the air for no reason." He paused and looked back at the bunny remains. "Well, maybe they do if the rabbit looks like that."

"It wasn't about the rabbit, Caleb," I said between gritted teeth. "I came home and he was all excited about some stuff that he's trying to do with his business, and when I suggested that it might be a little early to be popping the champagne, he lost it on me… He killed the Easter Bunny." I put my head in my hands and started crying for the second time that day. What was going on? Why would Tad have done that?

Caleb clearly didn't understand the gravity of the situation. He shifted awkwardly in his seat and put his arm around me. "April, you do know that wasn't the real Easter—"

"You don't get it! I loved that hideous creature! He stood for something! And now something is going on with my husband and I have no idea what it is, and if that wasn't enough, I'm pregnant!"

Caleb gasped and pulled away so he could better see my expression. "Are you serious?"

"I found out just a few hours ago. I took the test over at Allie's and I was going to tell Tad but then he freaked out on me before I even had a chance! Caleb, I can't deal with this… I just…" I started sobbing again and this time Caleb took me into a full embrace.

"Hey, hey, it's going to be okay, honey." He gently rocked me back and forth until my sobs turned into quiet sniffles. "All right, one thing at a time. Let's start by thinking through this little argument you two had. You said he was excited about some work deal?"

I nodded weakly, having no energy or desire to go into the specifics.

"You know I'm always on your side, but let's try to put ourselves in Tad's shoes. He had some news that he was anxious to share with you, but instead of being excited for him you rained on his parade."

I pulled away. "It wasn't like that, Caleb."

"Of course it wasn't. You had news of your own that was one hell of a lot bigger, but Tad didn't know that."

"But he was just so intense, Caleb—both intensely happy and then, out of the blue, intensely angry."

"But he didn't in any way hurt or threaten you, right?" Caleb asked.

"No, no, he was just…angry."

Caleb sighed and squeezed my hand. "Maybe there was more going on than you realized. Maybe something happened at work and you said something that reminded him of that. After all, you had more going on than *he* realized, and my guess is that while he may have been extra intense, you were probably just a tad extra sensitive."

It was a good theory. It didn't hold up but I'd give him an A for effort. The problem was, I didn't know how to make Caleb really understand what I had just seen. I didn't know how to translate it into words.

"April?"

"Maybe you're right…" I bit my lip and tried to make myself believe it. "Maybe I didn't realize what he needed from me right then and I set him off."

"Now wait, it's not your responsibility to read his mind but if you can both put your egos aside long enough to admit that there were two people dancing this tango, you and Tad will probably be able to work all of it out tonight." He looked around the empty house. "Where is he anyway?"

"He stormed out."

"That seems a little…extreme."

I didn't say anything. Everything that had happened was extreme. I needed to talk to my husband. He was the only one who could give me an explanation capable of putting my mind at ease. "Caleb, I don't think you should be here when he gets back. We're going to need some alone time."

Caleb stayed seated. "You swear he didn't try to hurt you."

"No, the only things in danger here are our objets d'art."

"Honey, if that's art, I'm da Vinci." He put his hand on my belly and grinned. "So Miss April's gonna be a mommy. Remember, when the time comes, I get to give the child the ever-important first makeover. Unless of course it's a girl, in which case I'll teach her how to play baseball."

I managed a smile and pointed to the door. "Take your cheese plates and skedaddle. Tad will be back any minute now."

He gave me a quick kiss on the forehead before collecting his bag of goodies and leaving me alone to organize my thoughts.

I spent the next half hour formulating the words I would say to Tad when he walked in the door. An hour after that I had mentally thrown out that conversation and come up with a much more heated one that included topics such as how inappropriate it was to walk out on your wife for over an hour without telling her where you were going. Three hours later I was worried.

I stood in the living room in my nightgown and used my foot to trace a circle over the newly cleaned floor. Had he been mugged? Been in a car accident? Or was he really so angry that he had actually walked out on me?

But the last didn't make sense. It had been such a stupid argument. It hadn't even been an argument since I never had a chance to say anything. In my heart I knew he was coming back, but I also knew that the fact that it was taking him so long spelled trouble, and I had had enough of that for one evening.

At half past midnight I finally resolved to go to sleep. I had contemplated calling the hospitals but couldn't quite bring myself to do it. I lay awake in bed and stared at the wall in much the same way Tad had in Barcelona. I had long since given up planning our impending conversation. Now all I could do was replay the conversation we had already had in hopes of making sense out of it.

Eventually I drifted into an uneasy sleep, only to be awakened by the creak of the front door opening. I checked the time and then closed my eyes again. Now I was just pissed off, and if I allowed myself to lay into him, at one forty-five in the morning, I would never get any sleep. I listened to the sound of his footsteps as he worked his way through the house. They were heavier than normal, more clumsy. He finally got to the bedroom and, without opening my eyes, I could feel him standing over me. I also knew he had been drinking. It wasn't the smell, although I thought I picked up the scent of red wine, but it was the way he was breathing, and just something about his overall presence. He stood there for what must have been a full three minutes and with each minute I felt more of my annoyance being chipped away by a more powerful sense of trepidation. Eventually he did move away from the bed and I opened my eyes long enough to see his back retreat through the door. I looked down at my hand and noticed that I had the corner of my blanket clutched inside my fist. I lay there silently in the darkness and listened to the sound of scratching coming from the living room.

TWELVE

I got to work at 6:00 a.m. the next morning. I had dressed in the dark and crept past Tad's sleeping body on the couch on my way out. I told myself that slipping out was necessary because I couldn't very well get into a heated debate at a time when we both needed to be getting ready for work. But that was only part of my real reasoning. I didn't know what to say and I wanted to avoid saying or not saying it for as long as possible. So I threw myself into my work. I did a complete floor change, reorganized the stockroom, worked on "my" Academy Awards promotion—anything to keep myself from thinking about Tad or my newly occupied womb. But that was stupid—who could find out they were pregnant and not think about it the next day? I stood in the middle of the sales floor and put my hand on my relatively flat stomach. There was no way there was room for anything in there aside from the Philly cheese steak sandwich I'd eaten for lunch. Certainly a baby couldn't have crammed his way in. *A baby.* A good woman would be excited right now.

"I am excited," I whispered to myself. Why wouldn't I be? I got myself knocked up accidentally at a time when a pregnancy was pretty much guaranteed to fuck with my career, when the job I did have virtually guaranteed I would be cursed with varicose veins and when my husband was on a murderous, bunny-killing rampage. How could I be anything less than ecstatic?

At 7:15 p.m. I gave up the chore of inventing urgent tasks for myself and went home. I could deal with whatever was waiting for me there. God only gives you what you can handle. *Oh, yeah?* said my little voice. *Then how come there are so many suicides?*

My little voice seriously needed to shut up.

I had done the unthinkable and shelled out money for parking downtown, so getting home took a lot less time than normal, and to make things worse, our new home had a one-car garage and a mini driveway suitable for second-car parking, so I didn't even have the luxury of driving around the block for twenty minutes while I figured out what I was supposed to say. I literally felt sick as I pushed the door open. The sounds of "When a Man Loves a Woman" floated from the stereo. It was the song that played for our first dance at our wedding. I slowly unbuttoned my coat and went forward to investigate. Tad was sitting on the sofa pouring red wine into two pristine glasses.

"I heard your car pull in," he said. "I think you may need a new muffler."

"Oh?" I looked at the label on the bottle. Bonnie Doon's Cigare Volant, my absolute favorite wine, and I couldn't drink it. A new horrible realization took hold of me—I was going to have to stay sober for nine months.

He stood up and handed me a glass. "I thought you might want this."

"Mmm." I tortured myself by allowing a few drops to make contact with my tongue.

"I was pretty wound up last night. I just needed to take a long drive."

"Four hours long?" I asked, not bothering to keep the disgust out of my voice. "Where did you go—Nevada?"

Tad let out an exasperated sigh. "Let's not do this." His eyes traveled to my jaw, which was tightening by the second. He sighed again. "I drove around and at one point I stopped to get a glass of Merlot at that new wine bar in the Inner Sunset." He paused and then moved to my side and pushed a lock of hair behind my ear. "How did I ever get so lucky to have you? Do you have any idea how beautiful you are?"

Normally that pacified me for a while, but not tonight. We had things to talk about. Sweeping it under the rug would just give me an ulcer, and pregnant women weren't allowed to have those. "Tad…"

"I know the timing on this isn't perfect, but I got you a gift a while ago and I picked it up today." He swirled the red liquid in his glass. "I should probably wait until Valentine's Day, but I just can't." He jerked his head in the direction of the fireplace and I saw the flat two-by-one-and-a-half-foot rectangular gift propped against the wall. It was wrapped in that expensive wrapping paper that's made to look like some kind of nondecorative natural fiber.

"What is it?" There was no way I would let him just buy his way out.

He shrugged and walked to the opposite end of the room. I

hesitated before putting down my glass and carefully removing the paper. I gasped. I was holding a portrait of me and my grandmother. It was derived from a favorite photograph of mine, taken when I was four years old. I was curled up on her lap and she was holding a book in a way that allowed me to see the pictures while she told the story. The photo had so perfectly captured the love and tenderness we shared, that although I don't actually remember the picture being taken, I will always feel that I remember the moment. In the painting the sentiment had become even more acute. The artist had made Van Gogh-like swirls in the background, and the illusion of the two of us somehow melting into one another was at once heartrending and breathtaking. "How did you…"

"I noticed you always kept that photo on your dresser at your old apartment, so when you didn't immediately unpack it I sneaked it over to Sibella Brandeis."

"The woman whose paintings they show at Café Mode? Oh, Tad, it's incredible." I quickly brought the back of my hand under my eyes to wipe away the tears.

"You always remark on how much you like her work." I turned to speak but words failed me. No one had ever given me something so utterly wonderful.

"Here's the photo." He pulled his jacket off the back of the love seat and took a small manila envelope out of the inside pocket. "I have something else, too."

"Tad, this is more than enough, I…" I turned back to the painting. "I don't know what to say."

He briefly disappeared into the kitchen and returned with a gift the size of a shoe box and handed it to me reverently. I stared at it for maybe half a second before ripping into it. I opened the top and pulled out a white pig wearing a policeman's hat. I felt the corners of my lips twitch.

"I looked everywhere for something as ugly as that rabbit and this is the best I could come up with. And look—" he tapped the slot in its back gloomily "—he's a piggybank. The stupid thing actually has a purpose. The bunny just lived to be ugly."

"I love him," I said, the tears now too plentiful to wipe away with just a sleeve. "I love my ugly capitalist pig."

"Are you talking about me or the piggybank?"

I started laughing and he gingerly took the pig from me before enveloping me in his arms. "That's all I wanted. To hear you laugh." He kissed the top of my hair. "So are we good?"

"We're better than good," I whispered. "We're soul mates." Tad tilted my chin up with his fingertips and I could see the twinkle in his eyes.

I opened my mouth with the intention of saying something romantic. "We're also pregnant."

There was a silence in the room. Those were definitely not the words of romance that I had planned to say.

Tad took a step back. "Want to run that one by me again?"

I squeezed my eyes shut so that I wouldn't have to see his face. "I'm pregnant," I repeated. "I took the test yesterday and I got a plus sign. I'm pregnant."

I opened one eye and peeked. Tad had his mouth hanging open like one of those cardboard clowns at amusement parks whose teeth are designed to be knocked out by flying beanbags.

Finally he managed to bring his lips closer together, although they still weren't touching. "Are you sure about this, April? Is there any chance the test is wrong?"

"Is there any chance we won the lottery?"

"I didn't buy a ticket."

"Well, then our odds are about the same."

Tad turned his head toward the window. "I don't understand how this happened. Weren't you taking the Pill?"

Ah, good question. What should I tell him? Yes, I was taking the Pill but never at the same time of day and often not even on a daily basis due to my complete flakiness? Or should I tell him that the medication that I started taking for my mild acne had a warning label that I didn't bother reading? I felt a new lump forming in my throat and I tugged gently at the ends of my hair. "No birth control method is a hundred-percent effective," I said lamely. "I guess we just made love during a blue moon or something."

Tad turned his head back to me and his eyes searched my face. I felt my chin begin to tremble and I clenched my teeth in order to stop it. He took a step closer to me and slowly, gently, put one hand on either side of my face. "We're going to be parents."

Now it was my turn to drop my jaw. He wasn't panicked at all! He was in awe! Suddenly a huge smile burst onto Tad's face and he lifted me into the air and spun me around. "We're going to be parents!" he said again, this time with so much enthusiasm that even I had to laugh. He put me down on my feet and dropped to his knees in front of me, carefully raising my shirt so that it bunched around my rib cage. I felt the palm of his hand glide over my abdomen. Then his lips landed just to the right of my belly button. "I can't believe this. We're really going to be a family now. Our own family."

I ran my fingers through his brown hair, watching as it fell back into place. "I didn't think you'd be happy about this. After all, we said we'd wait."

"But it didn't happen that way," Tad said without a hint of

remorse. He stood back up and pulled me to him. "It will be wonderful, April. We're married, we have a house, my business is taking off and then, of course, there's you."

"Me?" I spoke the word into his shirt.

"Yes, you. This child is going to have you for a mother." He squeezed me a little tighter. "How lucky can a kid get?"

And the tears were rolling again. If I didn't get ahold of myself I was going to start a flood. But how could I help but be overcome? Tad wanted me to bear his children. I guess I had known that before, but to be able to feel his excitement now…to be surrounded by his love and respect for me… "I'm the one who's lucky," I said between sniffs. "I have the most wonderful husband in the world."

We made love that night and it was incredible. Tad had never been so gentle, so admiring…it was like I was some kind of living piece of art that was to be admired, explored and savored. I fell asleep as he spooned me, his hand protectively on my tummy.

That night I dreamed I planted a rosebush. Two seconds after putting the seeds in the ground the plant sprung roots, and vines and stems burst from the ground. Within minutes my whole garden had been completely taken over by this unruly plant. There were other things that were supposed to be in that garden: snapdragons, a tomato plant, an apple tree. I searched desperately for them all, but they were gone. There were only the untrimmed offshoots of my one remaining bush and they were covered in dangerous thorns. But the roses…my God, those roses were the most intoxicatingly beautiful things I had ever seen.

THIRTEEN

I pulled a copy of *What to Expect When You're Expecting* from the shelf at Borders and handed it to Caleb, who was already weighted down with an armload of books. "You already have that one," he grumbled.

"No, you're thinking of *What to Eat While You're Expecting*. It's the companion book to this one."

"April, you bought five books yesterday, you've selected eight books so far today and you're still shopping. The Library of Congress doesn't have this many books."

"Well I guess the buyers over at the Library of Congress aren't properly motivated." I pulled out a book by Dr. Sears and tucked it under my arm.

"Whatever happened to asking the moms and grandmas for advice? Or has that kind of thing gone out with the family sit-down dinner?"

"I'm waiting until the end of the first trimester to tell my family about the baby." I found yet another book and balanced it on top of the others Caleb was holding. The stack in his arms now reached his chin.

"Can we talk about this?"

I gave him a noncommittal shrug and he awkwardly directed me over to a reading bench where he happily dropped the books on the floor in front of us. We both sat down and silently stared at the pile for a few moments before Caleb spoke. "Usually when a woman buys this many books about pregnancy it's because she's thrilled to pieces about playing the mommy role but—" he made some kind of vague gesture with his hands as if he was trying to pick up some kind of psychic reading from my aura "—I'm not sensing a lot of joyous excitement from you. If anything, you seem…nervous."

"Are you using *nervous* as a euphemism for scared shitless?"

"Okay, we can go with that." Caleb put his arm over my shoulder. "Are you worried that you won't live up to the Donna Reed standard of motherhood, or is there something else?"

I picked at a thread that was sticking out of the thigh-high slit in my skirt. "Of course, what else would I be scared about?"

Caleb picked up one of the books and started casually thumbing through it. "You know it wouldn't make you a bad person if you were worried about the impact this was going to have on *your* life."

"I want this child to know that he or she is wanted," I whispered. "I don't want him to ever think otherwise."

"The way you did." Caleb closed the book and picked up another. "And right now you don't feel like you want him enough."

"Wow, Caleb, did you go out and get a degree in psychology while I wasn't looking?"

"No, but I watch a lot of *Oprah*." He tapped his finger against the book he had been perusing. "Listen to this. 'Many men don't bond with their unborn children to the same degree as their pregnant wives. This does not mean that they will be bad fathers. Many of these men turn into superdads the minute their children take their first breath. So don't worry if your husband isn't singing lullabies to your belly. We are all individuals and we all emotionally connect to our children at different times and in different ways.'"

"But Tad does sing to my belly."

"Mmm, so we have a little role reversal going on." He took hold of my index finger and placed it on the last line of the paragraph he had read. "'Different times and in different ways,' April. It doesn't matter if it's the mom or the dad, the message is the same. You can be a good parent even if you aren't overwhelmed by feelings of maternal love the minute a sperm makes contact with your egg."

I took the book from Caleb and stared at the words without reading them. "I'm twenty-six. I used to think that at this age I'd be getting ready to graduate with a Ph.D. in art history." I shrugged. "That's never going to happen. I'm going to be a buyer at Dawson's instead, and even that ambition will be left unfulfilled if Blakely finds out about this pregnancy before promoting me."

We both fell silent as we watched a harried-looking woman usher three small children to the escalator.

"You told me awhile ago that you didn't want to be a curator anymore," Caleb reminded me. "You said that you were happy at Dawson's."

"And you believed me?"

"No. But I was fairly sure you believed you."

I looked away from him. I didn't want to cry.

"Lots of moms go back to school, April."

I shook my head. "Pregnant or not, I was never going to be a curator. It's just that now I feel like I have to give up on the fantasy."

"You don't have to give up on anything." Caleb checked my expression to see if he was reaching me. He apparently surmised that he wasn't because he threw his hands up in defeat. "So what's with all the books?"

"I know this is going to sound terrible, but I'm pregnant because I behaved…irresponsibly."

"It doesn't sound terrible, just honest."

"Well, I'm going to be responsible about this. I'm going to eat the right foods, do the right exercises, select the right birthing center…the whole deal. This child is going to be well taken care of from day one."

"Uh-huh." Caleb pulled another five books off the floor. He checked the table of contents of the first one and turned to the page he desired. "'It is important that women maintain a diet high in complex carbohydrates throughout the length of their pregnancies,'" he read aloud. He picked up the next and turned a few pages before reading, "'Pregnant women should adopt a high-protein, low-carb diet.'" He reached for book three. "'If you're longing for a bagel and cream cheese, eat it, likewise if you have a hankering for prime rib.' Your body knows best…unless you're craving spicy foods, in which case you should throw yourself off the nearest bridge because you're most likely pregnant with the Antichrist."

"It doesn't say that."

"No, it doesn't, but you see my point. You could read each and every one of these books and all you're going to get is confused.

Find three that are written with a viewpoint you relate to and stick to those."

"So you're telling me that moderation is key. Huh, where were you when I was buying out the shoe department with Allie last week?"

"What do you mean where was I? There was a men's sample sale at the Fashion Center."

I went home with only two books and several grocery bags full of the foods recommended in the latest issue of *Fit Pregnancy*. Okay, there was a Twinkie in there, too. I unloaded it first and held it up to eye level so that I could better admire it. Not one of the pregnancy books had recommended Twinkies. But maybe that was the problem with today's youth. We were spoiling them with too much healthy food and exercise. Maybe we needed to toughen them up by teaching them how to survive the horrors of trans fat. I was using my fingertips to pull open the opaque plastic wrapper when the phone rang. It was a sign from God. I wasn't supposed to eat this. I almost threw the treat away but I couldn't quite get myself to do it. I ended up stuffing the Twinkie in my purse instead. That way it could be like the unsmoked cigarette carried around by a former addict as a badge of honor. I picked up the phone a second before the answering machine got it.

"Yello."

"April, it's Nick."

"Hey, Nick, what's up?" I hadn't talked to our landlord since before Tad and I had moved into his place. Tad dealt with all the little details of our life, such as paying the rent.

"Is Tad there?"

"Nope, he may not be for a while. Can I help you with anything?"

"Well, you could pay me the rent for starters."

"Oh…" I glanced at the calendar, February was more than half over. "I'm sorry, didn't Tad pay you yet?"

"Not for this month, and he's been late with it every single time. I know his business is going through a transition period but I can only be so lenient, even for a friend."

I dropped onto a kitchen chair. Why would Tad fall behind on the rent? "I'm…I'm so sorry. Tad's been busy, he must have done something silly like written the check but forgotten to send it out or something. He would never be late on purpose."

Nick didn't say anything.

I ran my nails up and down my leg self-consciously. "I'll send you a check today. Twenty-five hundred for February, and how much is the late fee?"

"You owe thirty-one hundred for February."

"Excuse me?" I was on my feet again. "I understand if you've attached a penalty for us being late, but seven hundred dollars is a little steep."

"I'm not attaching any penalty at all, although I probably should. Your rent is thirty-one hundred dollars."

"Are you even familiar with San Francisco's rent-control laws? You can't raise rent on existing tenants at a rate higher than, like, two percent a year. Give me a break!"

"I've been giving you a break by not demanding the rent when it's due. Your lease agreement clearly states that the rent is thirty-one hundred dollars. Now, are you going to pay me or are you going to find a new place to live?"

I couldn't believe this. I had only met Nick a few times but he had seemed like a decent and reasonable guy. Obviously my asshole radar had been malfunctioning on the days he'd been around. "I'm going to talk to Tad about this. If we owe you anything, we will pay you. Otherwise I strongly suggest that you rethink your extortion tactics because I *will* drag your sorry butt to court." I hung up the phone and ignored it when it rang again. He was so not going to get away with this. I started pacing back and forth across the hallway. Tad thought Nick was his friend. Maybe not a close friend but certainly not someone who would screw him over.

Who did he think he was kidding? Just because my name wasn't on the lease didn't mean that Tad hadn't told me exactly what it said. I walked into the guest room where we kept all our important files. I pulled out the top drawer of a wooden file cabinet with so much force that it almost came tumbling out. I reached the back of the files without being able to locate the lease. I then searched through the drawer beneath it. Finally I went to the drawer closest to the floor. I yanked it with the same force as I had used on the others, which almost caused the whole damn cabinet to fall on top of me. But the drawer didn't open. I tugged at it again, more gently this time. It was locked.

I fell back from my squatting position and sat on the floor with my knees sticking straight up in the air. Why had Tad locked the cabinet? I studied the lock and laughed. If Tad thought that lock was going to keep anyone out he had some serious gaps in his education. *I* could pick that. I was actually pretty good at picking locks. My mother and I had been evicted on two occasions when I was a kid. The first time it had happened the landlord had changed the locks on the apartment, so when Mom's boyfriend du jour escorted us back home from a weekend nature retreat we found ourselves unable to get to our things. Mom's boyfriend had used the opportunity to teach us both how to pick locks...so we would be "prepared for next time." I got to my feet and retrieved a bobby pin from the bathroom and stuck one end of it in the keyhole. "Easy peasy," I murmured as the drawer sprung open. I flipped through a few files that pertained to Tad's company. Finally I found the lease.

My eyes stopped when they got to the figure $3,100 per month.

I heard the front door open and close. "April?" Tad's voice traveled through the walls that separated us, but I didn't respond. I just stared at the lease.

"April." This time he said my name in the teasing manner of a lover expecting to play some kind of flirtatious version of hide-and-seek. Still, I was silent. I listened to the sound of Tad's footsteps as they moved through the living room to the kitchen and finally down the hall to where I was.

"Aha, I found you. Why didn't…" his voice trailed off as he looked at the paper I was holding.

"You fucking bastard." I barely recognized my own voice. I dangled the lease in the air, holding it by the corner as if it were a soiled handkerchief.

Tad was silent for a long time.

"You broke into the bottom drawer," he said flatly.

Was he accusing me of wrongdoing? Me? I felt my whole body start to tremble. "Don't go there. Don't even think of going there. You've been lying to me. I told you that I wouldn't pay more than twenty-five hundred for this place and you told me you talked Nick down. Why did you lie to me, Tad?"

"April…"

"WHY!"

"Don't talk to me like that!"

Was he kidding? He had been lying to my face for months and

now he was worried about my tone of voice? Like some disobedient little child who couldn't handle having his mommy yell at him? I could barely speak, barely even look at him. I thrust the paper forward in his direction. "Why?"

Tad looked at the cabinet. He gently took the lease out of my hand and then took the key to the file drawer out of his wallet. I watched as he returned the lease to its original location and then locked it in the drawer. He straightened up and slowly, so slowly, replaced the key. "I'm not going to talk about this right now."

He then turned around and left the room. I stood there in disbelief as I heard him turn on the television.

Something in me snapped. I rammed my hairpin back into the keyhole and grabbed all the files out of the drawer without bothering to look at what they were. I marched into the living room, creating a literal paper trail that led back to the guest room, and with one fluid motion I threw all the files at Tad, who was now sitting on the love seat. "You don't get to ignore this one, Tad. You lied to me and you are going to tell me why."

"Oh, am I?" His voice was full of bitterness. "Any idiot knows that you don't get a two-bedroom house with a garage in San Francisco for twenty-five hundred a month. We needed the house and I did what I needed to do to get it. You simply chose to believe what you wanted to believe."

"Hello? I believed what you told me. I was under the mistaken assumption that I could trust my husband!"

"Like I can trust you to take your birth control pill every day?"

My breath caught and I staggered backward. He couldn't possibly be throwing that in my face, not now. "You said you were happy about this pregnancy," I gasped. "You said you wanted—"

"I do, but damn it, April, we share the same medicine cabinet.

Didn't you think I would see the warning label on the minocycline? Didn't you think I would notice that you were popping the Pill at all different times of day? I knew this would happen. I knew you would fuck up on the birth control just like I knew that we were going to need a house with a room for a baby. You want to know why I lied to you, April? I lied to you because I didn't have a choice."

"Fuck. You." I turned around and headed for the front door.

"Don't you walk away from me!"

I turned to see Tad glowering at me. He was now standing up and his hands were in fists. It took him exactly three strides to close the distance between us. "You don't walk out on me. Not now, not ever."

I looked down at his fists and swallowed. He must have seen my reaction because he immediately opened his hands and allowed them to dangle limply at his sides. He took a small step back. "We're married, April. If you're upset, that's your choice, but you don't get to just walk out the door. You stay and deal with it. That's what married people do."

"Uh-huh, is that what you did on the day you broke our rabbit?"

"If you had asked me to stay I would have," he said dismissively. "I'm going to watch a little television to help calm myself down. I highly suggest that you pull out one of your art books and do the same."

I smiled and crossed my arms in front of me. "And I highly suggest that you stop telling me what to do before I go Lorena Bobbitt on your ass." I turned around and marched out the door.

FOURTEEN

My feet pounded against the pavement in keeping with the rhythm of my thoughts. *He lied to me, he lied to me.* I finally ended up in a little coffee shop located a few blocks away. I had neglected to take my purse with me but I had enough money in the pocket of my jeans to score myself a cup of licorice tea. I sat at a small dusty table tucked into a corner by the window and bobbed my tea bag up and down in the hot water. At least I had made a strong exit. The image of Tad's face when I had mentioned Lorena Bobbitt did give me some sense of vindication.

I also felt very alone.

If Tad and I had been dating I would have called it quits immediately. But we weren't dating, and as much as I hated to admit it, Tad had a point about how married couples were supposed to work out their problems. And if that wasn't enough to keep me tied to him, the baby I was carrying was. I put my hand on my stomach. "You're going to complicate everything, aren't you," I whispered. It was a horrible thing to say, but since there was a pretty good chance my soul was already slated for eternal damnation, I might as well admit the evil truth to myself; thanks to this child, nothing would ever be simple again. Like it or not, I would always be bound to Tad.

"I do like it," I said, this time to myself. I had no idea why he had lied to me and I couldn't think of one excuse he could come up with that would make it okay, but that didn't erase the love I felt for him. I thought about the painting of me and Bobe that was now proudly hanging above our fireplace and I felt some of the muscles in my neck relax.

Then I thought about the comment he'd made about birth control and they tightened right back up again. The worst part about that remark was that it was true. I had screwed up, but to point it out now, a day before our first appointment with the ob-gyn... Really, how could he?

I took a small sip of my tea and tried to pretend it was a Bloody Mary. Sadly, I couldn't even drink my problems away. I had thought that marriage to Tad would translate into a situation where, for the first time in my life, someone would be taking care of *me*. That's what I had signed up for.

But perhaps that was the problem. I had been so anxious to relinquish control of my life that I had allowed myself to be put into a position where I was continually lied to and manipulated. According to the fairy tales it wasn't supposed to work that way, but perhaps Caleb was right about fairy tales. Maybe you had to give them up after the last piece of wedding cake had been consumed.

I squeezed my eyes shut. I was majorly overanalyzing everything and I was giving myself a headache. I stayed long enough to finish half my beverage and started home.

It was then that I realized that in my fury over his lies about our rent, I had completely forgotten that I had even more to be angry about. Why were we late with the rent? The money was there; Tad's paychecks were better than ever now. I didn't know exactly how much was in Tad's accounts since, with the exception of one savings account, we kept our finances separate, but surely it was a high figure. How else would he have been able to pay for three cases worth of futures in Mondavi Reserve? Or the new laptop and car-stereo equipment he had bought last weekend?

Maybe having separate accounts hadn't been a good idea but every advice column I had ever read suggested it. It's easier to balance, maintains everybody's independence and so on. But perhaps when it came to finances Tad needed to be less independent, not more.

I would have to pull a Scarlett O'Hara and think about all of this tomorrow. I had enough on my plate right now and talking to Tad tonight had gotten me nowhere fast. He had a point about waiting until we both cooled down, but damned if I was going to admit that to him.

I arrived at our front door and was relieved to see that Tad hadn't locked it. He was lying on the couch watching the Discovery Channel again. I stormed past him, went into the bathroom and slammed the door.

When I was done I came out to see Tad sitting in the same place. I glared down at him. "Well, I've been gone for a full forty-five minutes. Have you had time to think up a better excuse yet?"

Tad didn't respond.

"What a surprise, you're ignoring me! That's definitely a big step up from lying to me." I turned my back and walked into the bedroom. I spun around one more time. "Oh, just in case you didn't know, you will be sleeping on the couch tonight." I slammed the door closed and took a deep breath before turning down the sheets. For some reason, I flashed back to an hour ago when he had been standing less than a foot away from me with clenched fists. I looked at the chair by the window and carefully moved it so that its back was propped up under the knob of the bedroom door. I stared at my handiwork for a moment. Silly, really. Tad wasn't dangerous; he wouldn't hurt me in a million years. But for some reason, I didn't want to move the chair back. Instead, I tucked myself into bed and pulled the blankets over my head.

I actually slept well that night. Not because I was feeling peaceful but because I was so completely emotionally spent. I woke up groggy and slightly on edge, although it took me a few minutes to remember why I was anxious. I looked at the chair propped under the doorknob and was instantly disgusted with myself. I was afraid of Tad? When exactly had that happened?

I looked over at the bed stand and my eyes focused on the *Girlfriend's Guide to Pregnancy*. Somewhere I had read that pregnant women can be excessively emotional during their first trimester. It was kind of like having PMS for three months straight. "Good times for all," I muttered as I swung my legs over the edge of the bed and stretched my arms above my head. Today Tad and I were going to have to have a calm, rational discussion about last night's showdown. The problem was, I was still furious.

I tiptoed across the cold hardwood floor and quietly moved the chair back to the location it had been in the day before. Things were bad enough without Tad accusing me of paranoia. I might be emotionally charged, but what he did would have angered Mother Teresa. But if he apologized I could get past it. We could talk, we could learn from our mistakes and we could move on.

I examined myself in the mirror. I was wearing the Donna Karan pj's Allie had bought me for my birthday last year; not exactly sexy but elegant in a rather understated way. It's important to look good when you're walking into a confrontation. I arranged my hair in a way that was flattering but could still have passed for an I-just-woke-up-with-this-style look. I stuck my finger in the lip balm Caleb had given me and carefully applied it. "I'm ready," I told my reflection. "I'm ready to forgive and move forward."

I walked out to the living room and found Tad thumbing through his date book. The files I had thrown at him had been cleared away. The only evidence of the battle that had been waged was the palpable tension hovering between us. "Hello, Tad." I know it was an overly formal greeting, but it was all I could manage. *As soon as he apologizes, you'll feel better.* I clasped my hands behind my back and waited.

He looked up from his book and nodded curtly. "Don't forget, our appointment at Kaiser Medical Center is at three-twenty today."

Hello? Where the fuck was my apology?

"April? Did you hear me?"

I made a talk-to-the-hand gesture. "I can't talk to you right now." I went into the bathroom and turned on the shower.

That morning Tad and I got ready for work in complete silence. Instead of exchanging words, we engaged in a full-fashion assault. He dressed in a double-breasted suit that he accessorized with a bow tie. It was an outfit I had forbidden him to wear anywhere other than a Tony Bennett concert. In turn, I put on a pair of gray fitted pants and a low-cut dip-dye shirt that he had once said made me look positively edible. Then I sprayed myself with a perfume sample despite his allergy to fragrances.

When I finally moved to leave the house, Tad stopped me. "April, I want you to know that I am happy that you're pregnant."

That was not an apology. It struck me that Tad had never once apologized to me the entire time we had been together. He just tricked me into thinking he had. Like with the ceramic bunny; searching the city for an ugly ceramic-figurine replacement was a lovely gesture, but he had never said, "April, I screwed up and I'm sorry." The revelation just fueled my frustration.

I pulled on my coat and tried to hide my satisfaction as Tad rubbed his eyes and stifled a sneeze. "Nick says we're late on the rent."

Tad sniffed and looked away.

"Why are we late on the rent, Tad?"

"I've been wrapped up with everything that's been happening at the office and a few things fell through the cracks."

"The only cracks our home should be in danger of falling into are the ones that appear along the fault line. Pay the damn rent." I walked out of the house without looking back.

I drove to work. Parking would be marginally affordable since I was scheduled to go home after attending a brief meeting. I stuck a tape in my cassette player and tried to cool off to the sounds of Jewel. I was convinced that all I needed from Tad was an apology. I had listened to Dr. Phil enough times to know that he would suggest that I tell Tad what I required of him so that he could provide it. But did an apology count if you had to ask for it? The answer to that question was a big fat no, and if Dr. Phil was a woman he'd understand that.

I reached into my bag while waiting at a traffic light to see if

I could locate a piece of gum. My hand was stopped by something spongy wrapped in some kind of crinkly packaging. The Twinkie! And I was having such a Twinkie moment. I let my fingers start to close around what I had come to think of as Hostess's version of nirvana when I remembered the baby. I jerked my hand away and put it over my chest. "Be strong," I whispered to myself.

At least the meeting had been called by Blakely, I thought as I pulled into a downtown parking lot. If Liz or Marilyn had been conducting it, the agenda would have included lots of pep talks and lists of unrealistic expectations. Blakely would just give us the information we needed in order to sell her buys, throw out a few token Dawson's phrases like "Be proactive, not reactive," then expect us to leave her office quickly so we could implement her suggestions.

I walked into Dawson's stark conference room a few minutes early. Most everyone was already there. The group consisted of nine managers, one buyer and her assistant, and yet I was still one of only three non-blondes there. Although, by looking at their roots, I could tell God had intended for me to have more company. Even the Latino manager from 537 had bleached her hair. Cherise was sitting to Blakely's right, blissfully ignorant of her impending unemployment. Her jet-black hair hung in delicate braids pulled back from her face. She was wearing bold silver jewelry, a bright red Versus deep V-neck and a pair of black boot-cut pants with a waistband that came just below her protruding belly.

I took the seat farthest from Blakely and pulled out my Day-Timer and pen. I started to make a little preliminary meeting note when I caught the sight of Gigi in the doorway, looking breathless and perfect. She quickly stepped into the room and took a place beside me.

"Gigi, I believe you're supposed to be downstairs setting the floor," Blakely called from her seat, echoing my thoughts to the letter.

"I know this meeting isn't for assistants," Gigi said apologetically. "But I got here at six, so the floor's all set. I just really want to hear about the new product lines."

"And that's why I'm telling the managers about them." Blakely leaned forward, clearly not impressed. The other managers began to exchange meaningful looks and Cherise's expression was heavy with sympathy. Gigi had stepped over the line and she couldn't have done it with a less compassionate buyer.

"I'm sure April will share her notes with you and the rest of the crew," Blakely continued in a tone that could have turned boiling water into ice.

"Oh, I know she will." Gigi beamed, showing no indication that she was the least bit disconcerted. "It's just so totally great hearing about it from someone who's, like, talked to and questioned the vendors. You always make such intelligent buys and I really think it would help if I had the opportunity to ask just a few questions about the FAB so I could presell. You know I'm all about preselling."

Blakely now looked as if she was torn between praising Gigi's dedication and tying her to a railroad track. "The floor's really all set?" she asked warily.

"Totally. And just a half hour ago I got Liz to approve a new contest in which each salesgirl puts together an outfit that totals over seven hundred dollars, and whoever sells their outfit to the most customers by the end of the week wins a one-hundred-dollar gift certificate. The girls are putting together outfits right now. They're, like, totally into it."

Blakely sat back in her chair. "That's the best contest idea I've heard in a long time," she said quietly. Her eyes shifted from Gigi to me and I felt my cheeks heat up.

"Oh, and you should see what Dorita's already come up with," Gigi gushed. "The Vertigo skirt with the Vivienne long sleeve—" Gigi threw up a dramatic hand "—totally hot."

Blakely nodded slowly. "I'm sure it is."

And she was in. Gigi sat by my side through the meeting asking question after question and, wonder of wonders, her questions were actually good. They were the kind of questions I would have thought to ask a few days after the meeting was over. Blakely was so taken with her that she actually made the effort to laugh when Gigi threw out a joke. That was huge since Blakely had a reputation for saving all her insincere laughs for those who were above her on the corporate ladder. And the entire time I sat there quietly holding my stomach and mentally comparing it to Cherise's. I couldn't get myself to pay attention to the meeting at all. The world of prêt-à-porter simply didn't hold the same import as the series of crises that constituted my life.

But my ears did perk up whenever Cherise added something. She was completely in touch with the needs and wants of Sassy's target market. Plus, she was so animated in the way she communicated her suggestions that it was impossible to tune her out. I avoided making eye contact with her. It wasn't my fault that Blakely was evil. *Evil.* The word made me think of my grandmother and everything she had gone through. I shifted uncomfortably in my seat, twisting slightly away from Gigi, who was in the middle of questioning the need to wear boots with boot-cut pants. I had no doubt that if Blakely had lived in Germany during Hitler's reign she would have aligned herself with the Nazis in order to secure her financial success. And this was the woman I aspired to share an office with. What did that say about me?

"So are we all clear on this?" Blakely's voice brought me out of my private deliberations. I took in her dark-gray Vertigo suit showcasing a body that had never been introduced to the pleasures of fatty cuisine. I nodded at her, although I had no idea what I was supposed to be clear on. I would have to get the information from Gigi later.

Upon exiting into the hallway I literally bumped into Allie, who had been hurrying in the direction of the break room. She steadied herself and gave me a quick once-over. "What are you doing here? I thought you had the day off."

"I had to be at a meeting this morning," I said, stepping away from the door and gesturing with my thumb to the managers pouring out of the room I had just vacated. Gigi was still inside asking questions.

Allie groaned empathetically. "I'm working a closing shift today but I got here early for a floor move. Do you want to chill in the break room for a few minutes?"

I glanced at my watch to verify that I still had hours before the prenatal visit. "Yeah, I could use a sparkling water."

"Ugh, you're so good. I'm not sure it's a good idea for me to be seen with someone who makes me look like a gluttonous pig."

I rolled my eyes up toward the ceiling. "This from the woman who isn't big enough to fit into the Gap's smallest size."

"That's not true! I usually fit into their size two."

I groaned and swung my purse at her playfully. Unfortunately I had neglected to close my purse and everything from my wallet to my lipstick went flying. I pressed my hand to my forehead in an act of self-disgust. "Well, this is pretty much in keeping with my week." I knelt down and reached to replace the Twinkie first.

"Hey, don't sweat it. Women in your condition are often a little clumsy," Allie whispered as she got on her knees to help me.

"Ohmygawd, April, is this your stuff? Let me help." I looked up just in time to see Gigi pick up my small bottle of prenatal vitamins.

I froze in my crouching position as I watched Gigi's eyes widen with a new suspicion. From the corner of my eye I could see Allie staring at her own hand, hovering above my purse where she was about to drop my wallet. There was no way she was going to be able to reasonably claim that the pills were hers.

I straightened and flashed Gigi what I hoped was a casual smile. "Can you believe those are cheaper than regular multivitamins? Pretty much contain the same things, too." I quickly took the bottle from her and handed it to Allie who had resumed the act of stuffing my things back into my bag.

"So you get those instead of multis?" Gigi asked. Her voice lacked the note of peppiness that was her trademark.

"Yeah, when they're available."

Allie stood up and handed me my now securely closed purse. "Let's go get that coffee now." She smiled sweetly at Gigi. "Sorry to take her away from you, G, but we were out late last night boozing it up, and if we're going to get through the day we're going to have to get some caffeine in our bloodstreams."

I loved Allie. She was so much faster on her feet than I was. I offered Gigi one last sheepish grin and followed Allie to the break room. "Do you think she bought it?" I whispered after I was sure Gigi was out of earshot.

"Haven't a clue, but we'd better hope so. The only way you can trust that girl with a secret is if she stands to personally gain by keeping it."

"You barely know her," I pointed out. We stepped into a

brightly lit room filled with well-used tables and made a beeline for the vending machines.

"I don't have to know her." Allie smoothed out a dollar bill and tried unsuccessfully to get one of the machines to accept it. "Two of my three buyers are cut from the same cloth. They act like they're your best friend and all the while they're sizing you up, trying to figure out if you're an asset or a threat, and if you're a threat…" Allie shook her head as the machine finally took her money and spit out a bag of Doritos. "All I can say is watch out. She has that whole Nicole Kidman *To Die For* thing going on."

I nodded and extricated a mineral water from the soda machine. "I basically said as much to Tad when he first told me to hire her."

"Tad told you to hire her?" she asked as she selected a table for us by the window with a view of a billboard advertising the lack of virtues of Howard Stern. "Why? Did you show him a photo or something?"

"No, of course not." I rolled my eyes as I struggled to untwist the top of my Calistoga. As angry as I was, I still knew that Tad wasn't the kind of guy who would make eyes at his wife's assistant, particularly if the assistant had the personality of Gigi. "He just thought that if I had ambitious help I could avoid driving myself nuts with work. Apparently there's only room for one dysfunctional lunatic in my marriage."

"Uh-oh." Allie crunched down on a Dorito. "I told you the honeymoon period doesn't last, what's the problem?"

"Just a little argument about money."

"Don't tell me, he wants you to cut back on the shoe shopping."

I squared my shoulders and prepared to unburden myself during a therapeutic bitch session, but something about the expectant look in Allie's eyes stopped me. "Yeah, you know how men can be about shopping," I muttered lamely. "We'll work it out." It wasn't that I didn't think Allie would understand, it was that she might understand too well. Tad was the man I would be spending the rest of my life with. I didn't want her to have a low opinion of him.

I stretched my legs under the table and tapped my nails against my water bottle. "We have our first OB appointment today."

Allie tilted her head questioningly. "I thought you had one appointment already."

"That was just to get my blood work done. We spoke to a nurse who told me to stop drinking alcohol and cut back on the caffeine, but I didn't actually have an exam or see a doctor."

"So this is the one where the guy wearing the plastic gloves feels up your ovaries?"

"I guess. It's not like I've done this before." My anxiety over the upcoming prenatal visit, combined with my lingering anger with Tad, compelled me to pull the Twinkie from my purse. "I want to eat this."

Allie shrugged and started to flip through a *W* magazine that had been left on the table. "So eat it."

"*What to Expect When You're Expecting* says that whenever I bring anything to my mouth I should think about what nutritional value the food will bring to my baby, and if I can't think of anything I should put down the morsel in question."

Allie took the Twinkie from me and read the label. "Ten percent calcium—there's your nutrition." She put it on the table and flipped to another page in the magazine.

"The nurse did say it's important for me to get lots of calcium." I gently rotated the treat around on the table. Suddenly the realization of what I was about to do hit me. "Listen to me. I'm trying to justify eating this lard stick as if the only things at stake are a few pounds! I'm a horrible person, Allie!"

Allie grabbed the Twinkie and held it in front of me. "It's a Twinkie—not a joint, not a vodka tonic—a Twinkie."

"So you think I should eat it?"

"I think you have bigger problems," Allie whispered as she tried to discreetly point to what was behind me. I turned, pretending to straighten the coat draped over my chair. Blakely was sitting four tables behind us sipping a coffee, and Gigi was with her. Their heads were bent together, and while neither of them was looking at us, I got the unsettling feeling that I was being talked about.

I turned back to Allie and mouthed the words *Oh shit*.

I met Tad in the lobby of Kaiser's ob-gyn department. He was busy working away on his laptop and barely acknowledged my presence. Unlike the times he had ignored me in Barcelona, this time I was able to read the blatant hostility in the maneuver. I followed suit and tried to become engrossed in a magazine, which was hard to do since the best reading material available to me was an eight-month-old copy of *Reader's Digest*.

I stared blankly at an article on cutting one's cholesterol. Something about this moment reminded me of my wedding day. Of course on that day Tad had been looking at me with adoration and now he wasn't looking at me at all. But like those moments proceeding the signing of the *ketubah*, I was now acutely aware that my thoughts and emotions were inappropriate considering my current circumstances.

Here I was about to go into my first prenatal visit and instead of fantasizing about nurseries I was stressing out about work. Had Gigi told Blakely about the prenatal vitamins? Maybe she had just been using the time to pry more product information out of her. Even if she hadn't told her, how long could I really expect to hide this?

Suddenly I recalled a fantasy I used to entertain myself with as a teenager. I had used it to pass the time while I sat at home waiting to see if my mother was pulling another all-nighter. In the fantasy I was standing in a large museum after hours. All the visitors had left and on one arm I had my handsome, intellectual-looking husband and in my other arm was a beautiful baby girl that I had named Hanna, after Bobe. In this fantasy I am in my midthirties—even as a teenager I knew I wanted to have kids late. I could see myself holding up my child so she could have a better view of the Degas sculpture that stood in the middle of the room. "This is where I work," I could hear myself whisper to my daughter. "You're going to be surrounded by beauty every day, and when you grow up, Daddy and I will make sure that your dreams come true, too."

I sneaked a peak at Tad who was still busy ignoring me. I tried to change the fantasy to fit my reality. Who's to say that the "me" in my picture couldn't be in her midtwenties. And was there really any reason that the fantasy couldn't take place in Dawson's shoe department instead of some marble-floored museum? There wouldn't be any art by Degas but we could always gaze upon a particularly attractive pair of Stuart Weitzmans.

Nonetheless, the drivel about making dreams come true would have to be nixed. I wouldn't want to lie to my child.

"April Silver…Silverperson? Is that right?"

I could see Tad's mouth twitch. He always found the embarrassment I suffered because of my name to be infinitely amusing. Normally I just responded to his snickers by sticking my tongue out at him, but now I wanted to rip his head off.

We followed a heavyset young woman through a swinging door and I reluctantly stepped on the scale at her instruction.

Tad's brow furrowed when he saw the number. "You've lost weight." He looked at me with concern, and I felt the first twinge of tenderness toward him since the rent fiasco. Of course a twinge wasn't enough to erase an ocean of anger, but it was a start.

"It's not uncommon for women to lose a few pounds during their first trimester, especially if they've been experiencing severe morning sickness. Nothing to worry about."

My morning sickness had been moderate at worst, but neither Tad nor I felt the need to share this. She led us to a little sterile room with a chair, a stool and a patient table. She took my pulse and blood pressure and after assuring me that all my numbers were good gave me a flimsy little paper gown. "I need you to change into this with the ties in front. Dr. Griffin will be with you in a moment."

She beamed at Tad before exiting the room. "It's always so nice to see fathers come to these appointments. So many don't, you know." Tad threw me a triumphant look, but I refused to meet his eyes. I didn't want to be reminded of his attributes.

When the nurse left us alone Tad examined the gown as I made work of my shoes and pants. "You have to tie this in front?" he asked, shaking his head in bewilderment. "Won't that make you uncomfortable?"

"Well, my womb is a lot closer to my stomach than my backbone." I pulled off my top but hesitated before removing my bra and panties.

Tad started to hum the tune of "Sexual Healing."

"Shut up, I'm still pissed at you and you don't get to watch me strip while I'm angry. Turn around."

Tad sighed and did as he was told. "In half a minute a stranger is going to come in here and massage your breasts, but you want your husband to turn around."

"The stranger who will be *checking* my breasts has never lied to me." I grabbed the gown from him as he dangled it over his shoulder and tied the ribbons as tightly as I could, although I was still left perversely exposed.

Tad turned around and was about to reply to my last point when Dr. Griffin walked in. She was a woman who looked to be in her early fifties. She wore her silver hair in a neat bob that she had tucked behind her ears. After introducing herself she flipped open my chart and read through the information. "All your blood tests look good," she said and smiled at me. "Of course, you would have been notified if we found anything unusual. How have you been feeling?"

I looked at Tad and considered telling her that I had recently found myself suppressing murderous impulses. "I've been a little queasy but other than that I'm fine."

"Queasy's good. It's a sign things are going normally." She glanced at Tad and then back to me. "I'm going to do a pelvic exam. Do you feel comfortable with him being here?"

"He'll wait outside," I said quickly. Tad shot me a withering look. I knew he thought my demand stemmed from the same anger that prevented me from getting undressed in front of him, but he was wrong. Even if last night had never happened and instead he had managed to convince me that he was the new Messiah, I still wouldn't have allowed him to watch Dr. Griffin probe me with a set of stainless-steel prongs. I mean, that would be right up there with allowing him to watch my beautician give me an upper-lip wax.

Tad reluctantly agreed to wait in the hallway until that part of the exam was over. Dr. Griffin did her thing and then stepped out long enough to give him a heads-up that he was being allowed reentry.

"Everything seems normal," Dr. Griffin informed us as she checked my breasts for unwanted lumps.

Tad had cast his eyes downward, although I had a feeling the gesture was to prevent my discomfort rather than a response to any personal embarrassment of his own. "I still can't believe I'm going to be a dad," I heard him whisper. I closed my eyes and tried to absorb some of his joyful anticipation. But I couldn't get myself there. What I needed to do was call Bobe and break the news to her. Surely she could raise my enthusiasm. Not so my mother, who had been buying me condoms since I was old enough to menstruate. For Bobe the continuation of the family bloodline was a victory over the genocide that had killed her family. I immediately resolved to call her right after the appointment. I owed this child to Bobe. My doubts about wanting it were not only unnatural, they were selfish.

"Now, let's see if we can get a heartbeat."

My eyes flew open. "You can do that already?" Tad and I asked in unison.

"We should be able to. Looking at your chart, you should be about eight weeks along." She pulled out a flat instrument, attached to a curled-up cord, placed it on my belly and began to slowly move it around. Tad crept closer and I strained my neck to see what was going on. For the first time in almost twenty-four hours our eyes met. He smiled at me with so much love and excitement, for a minute I forgot to be mad and extended my hand to him instead. He instantly grabbed it, moving closer to my side.

It's going to be all right, my little voice told me. How could it not be? Obviously Tad wanted this child enough for both of us. That kind of parental devotion had to be contagious, right?

Together we watched Dr. Griffin move the machine around my belly button. And then something horrible happened—Dr. Griffin frowned.

"What, what is it?" Tad straightened his posture, never letting go of my hand.

Dr. Griffin coughed into her free hand before answering. "I think we should do a quick ultrasound."

The color drained from Tad's face. "Why, what's wrong?"

Dr. Griffin turned to us, her eyes relaying her unease. "I'm not picking up a heartbeat."

FIFTEEN

After that, there was a flurry of activity. I was rushed into a room for an ultrasound, and was poked and prodded with frightening-looking instruments. My doctor examined one murky image after another on a large screen, frowning all the while. Tad never left my side. There must have been a moment or two in which he wasn't holding my hand but those moments were so fleeting that I didn't notice them. I just held on to him and tried to draw comfort from his presence even while the whole world seemed to be crashing around me. Finally we were brought back to the room where all the chaos had started. Now both Tad and I were sitting on the patient table, our feet dangling over the side as we waited for Dr. Griffin to tell us what was going on.

She sat on her metal stool with her hands folded in her lap. It struck me that her pose was a little too practiced, as if she had delivered this kind of news before. "Based on the ultrasound, you have what we call a blighted ovum."

Tad shook his head and stood up. "Tell us in English, please, why couldn't you find a heartbeat?"

Dr. Griffin nodded and took a deep breath. "Something went wrong very early in the development of the pregnancy. Your placenta is developing as it should and the conditions of your body are right for supporting a fetus, but the problem is that the fetus itself doesn't exist. It never developed. That is what a blighted ovum is. You are pregnant but you're not carrying a child."

There was a hissing sound as I sucked air in through my gritted teeth. Surely this was some kind of dream, or some weird sci-fi movie that I had been unknowingly cast in. Things like this didn't happen. At least not to me.

I looked to Tad as if he could somehow make sense of everything. He let go of my hand and used his arm to draw me to him protectively. "I don't understand. Is there any chance that this is a mistake?"

"No, the ultrasound was conclusive." Dr. Griffin crossed her legs and straightened her posture. "It's not all that uncommon." She tilted her head in my direction. "You will most likely experience a natural miscarriage within the next two weeks, but if you like we can schedule a D and C just in case."

"A D and C?" Tad's irritation, brought on by yet another foreign medical term, was evident in his tone.

"Dilation and curettage. A relatively simple procedure in which we remove the placenta and any other tissue that has developed during the pregnancy."

"An abortion?" I whispered. None of this was happening, none of this was real.

"No, there's no fetus to abort," Dr. Griffin explained. "The procedure would just hurry along what your body would most

likely do anyway. There is a three percent chance that there will
be complications, in which case future conception may become
more difficult, but for most women there's about a day's recovery
time and then everything goes back to normal."

I bit my lip and looked away. I still couldn't wrap my mind
around this. I wasn't pregnant. Or I was, but I wasn't with child.
For the last two weeks I had been trying to prepare myself for the
role of mother, when in actuality I should have been preparing
for the role of freak. I put my hand on my stomach and I remembered the moment Allie and I had found out that I was pregnant.
I remembered crying and later praying that it was some kind of
mistake. I put my hand over my mouth and stifled a gag.

Tad tightened his grip around me. "It's up to you, April." His
voice trembled as he said my name.

I shook my head. I couldn't make a decision. I didn't deserve
to make a decision.

Tad raised his hand as if to scratch his cheek, but I had already
seen the tears that he was trying to hide. He turned to Dr. Griffin.
"We need a moment."

She looked at the clock on the wall and made a face. "Why
don't you go home and talk about it. There's no hurry. Call when
you're ready."

"I think we're going to make a decision now but we need a
minute alone beforehand."

She looked at the clock again, but Tad interrupted before she
could voice an objection.

"You just told my wife that the child she had begun to bond
with basically died before it had a chance to live. I'm sure your
other patients will understand if you give us a few minutes to talk
about our options."

Dr. Griffin only hesitated a second before leaving the room to give us space.

"I feel like an idiot," I said to the floor.

Tad stood in front of me and put a hand on either side of my face. "You're not an idiot." He leaned forward and rested his forehead against mine. I could hear the jaggedness of his breathing as he struggled to rein in his emotions. "What do you want to do, April?"

I clutched the table beneath me as if I was in danger of losing my balance. "I don't think I'm strong enough to wait for a miscarriage, Tad."

Tad pulled back and lifted my chin so that I was looking into his eyes once again. "You won't have to go through that. I'll make sure of it."

Tad spent the next forty-five minutes arguing with Dr. Griffin and the receptionists at the front desk. They wanted to schedule the D and C in four days but Tad wanted it done immediately. I sat in a chair in the lobby the whole time, barely speaking. He was so wonderful to look out for me like this. He didn't know that I wasn't worthy of his help.

Tad finally settled on an appointment for the following day. He helped me to my feet and guided me out to the parking lot and to his car. I put my hand on his before he had a chance to pull on the handle of the passenger door. "I have my car here," I reminded him.

"I know—" he carefully removed my hand from his and opened the door "—I'll drive you home. Later I'll take a cab back here and pick up your car."

"You don't need to do that."

"Please, April." His voice cracked. "Let me help you."

I hesitated only a moment before lowering myself into the seat. We didn't say a word on the ride home. At one point the car hit a pothole and I was struck by a wave of morning sickness. I couldn't help but think about what that was supposed to mean and what it didn't mean after all.

When we got home I walked into the middle of the living room and just stood there. Tad came up behind me and removed my coat. "Sit down, April."

I didn't comply. "Do you know what I did when the pregnancy test came back positive?" I asked, staring into our darkened fireplace. "I sat down on Allie's toilet and cried." Now I turned and faced Tad, who was still standing there holding my coat. "I cried my eyes out." I marched past him and grabbed one of the pregnancy books that rested on top of our low bookcase and held it up for Tad's view. "I told Caleb that I bought all these books so that I could do everything right, but that was a lie. The truth was that I thought by reading a whole bunch of 'how to be the perfect pregnant woman' books I would be able to get excited about the whole thing, but it didn't work. All I could think of was how this was going to affect *my* future, *my* career, *my* relationship with you. I never thought about the needs of our baby, and now the baby's gone and I'm relieved. That's how cold I am, Tad...I'm fucking relieved." I collapsed into the cushions of the couch. I wanted to cry but the tears didn't come. The only thing tangible for me was an overpowering feeling of self-loathing.

Tad folded my coat over his arm. "Are you finished?"

"Almost," I said in a barely audible whisper. "You were right about me. I fucked up on the birth control pill. I didn't always remember to take it at the right time and I didn't read the warning label on the minocycline. I'm a screwup, and I am..." I searched for some word that would aptly describe the kind of monster I was, but my vocabulary failed me. "I'm not a good person." I drew my knees up to my chest. "You must hate me."

"I have never loved a woman more in my life." I looked up at him and he crossed the room and slowly lowered himself to my side. "April, you've known you were pregnant for just over two weeks now. It wasn't planned and it was going to make some things difficult. If we had been given time we would have adjusted and we would have loved our kid, but no one in their right mind would question your maternal instincts just because you didn't bond with an embryo." He took both my hands in his and gently caressed them with his thumbs. "I won't lie, I wanted this baby. I wanted to bring a life into this world that was half you and half me."

Once again a tear rolled down his cheek and I freed my right hand in order to wipe it away, but then stopped myself feeling like the gesture would seem false, considering the recent revelations into my character.

Tad sighed and pressed my hand against his face. "It will happen, April. You are going to be a wonderful mom." He looked me in the eye. "When you're ready. Until then you'll just be...wonderful."

I fell into his arms. I loved him so much it literally hurt. "I don't know what I did to deserve you," I murmured as I clung to him.

"We have each other," he said in a voice so low that I wondered if he was talking to me or himself. "That's what's important, everything else will come."

We held each other for what seemed like hours. Finally Tad pulled back from me. He smoothed my hair and then stood up. "I'm going to call a cab so I can go get your car." He cocked his head to the side. "Are you going to be all right? Is there anything I can get you?"

I quickly looked away. There was something I wanted and the pettiness of my desire disturbed me.

"What is it, April?" Tad kneeled down on the couch once again. "Just tell me."

"You promise not to judge?"

"I won't judge. What can I get you?"

"Well, if you have time, I mean you don't have to or anything…"

"Whatever it is I'll do it, but you have to tell me."

I shifted uncomfortably. "If you're sure you don't mind… could you possibly stop by 7-Eleven and pick up a box of Twinkies?"

I did eventually cry. In the middle of the night, snuggled into the crook of Tad's arm while he slept, I let the tears spill. But I wasn't crying over my loss as much as I was crying out of gratitude. How could I ever have been angry at Tad for something as trivial as being late on the rent? Yeah, he had lied to me, but it was so obvious that his faults were nothing compared to his strengths. And now that I was thinking clearly I could see that his arguments made sense. Tad obviously knew me well enough to know that I could be incredibly irresponsible. Perhaps it was predictable that I would mess up on my birth control, in which case it was understandable that he felt he needed to do what was necessary in order to secure a house for us. Really, it was amazing that someone like him would want to be with someone like me. It was like that movie City of Angels with Nicolas Cage and Meg Ryan. Tad was playing Nicolas's role of the angel that fell for the well-intentioned but flawed human. I propped myself up on my elbow and gazed at his sleeping face. He even looked like an angel.

"I'm going to draw you," I whispered. Tad didn't stir. Tad needed less shut eye than anyone I knew, but when he did sleep he was dead to the world. I quietly slipped out of bed and pulled a small sketchbook and pencil out of the night stand. I sat by the window where the streetlamp provided me with just enough light, and began to draw. I was at it for a good hour before I stopped and actually saw what I had created. It was Tad, no doubt about that. But he didn't look nearly as peaceful as he did lying before me, wrapped in our teal sheets. The man on my sketch pad looked anguished, and just a little bit frightening. I glided my hand across the picture before tearing out the page and ripping it up.

First thing the next morning I called Liz. I used the five minutes I was on hold to think up and then discard possible excuses as to why I couldn't come in. Telling her I was sick was useless. I could lose a leg in a car accident and Liz would expect me to put on a tube skirt and hop on in. I could tell her that I had a miscarriage but then she would assume I had been trying to get pregnant and that could only be bad for me. Plus, I didn't want to share what had happened with Liz. Today a doctor would stick some cold instrument inside me and scrape away all remnants of my pregnancy. It wasn't the type of thing that I wanted Liz to cheer me through.

"I'm sorry, she's not answering her page, can I put you through to her voice mail."

"No, no, put me through to Sassy instead."

A few clicks and a lot of elevator music later I was on the line with Gigi. "Hi, April! What's up?"

"Hey, Gigi, I know you're probably wondering why I'm not there since we were going to open together…"

"Oh no, it's only seven and I know you usually get here later. No biggie."

That stopped me for a moment. I never got a lot of enjoyment from my exchanges with Gigi, but that was the first veiled insult that she had ever thrown at me. "I scheduled us to get there at seven-thirty," I said slowly, "but I won't be able to come in today."

"No problem," she said a little too brightly. "I have everything covered. We got the most awesome shipment in today—totally to die for."

"I'm sure." I wasn't even able to fake enthusiasm. It was clear that Gigi wasn't going to ask why I wasn't coming but I felt obligated to give her an excuse anyway, especially since there was a good chance that I wouldn't be there the next day, either. "Gigi, I'm unable to come to work today because…because my father's taken ill."

"Ohmygawd, how awful!" Gigi's voice dripped with false concern. "Is it serious?"

"Um, he needs emergency surgery but I'm sure he'll be okay. I just need to be there for…for support."

"Of course, of course. Is Tad with you?"

"Um, yeah, he's here." I shifted in my seat. For some reason Gigi's use of my husband's name seemed too familiar. But then again what was she supposed to call him? Mr. Showers? "Listen, my dad's in—" my eyes fell to the *San Jose Mercury News* that Tad had left on the table "—the South Bay, so I won't be able to run back and forth to work or anything."

"April, you just take all the time you need. I am totally in control of everything."

I sat up a little straighter. "Excuse me?"

"I said I totally have everything under control," Gigi said

quickly, catching her Freudian slip. "You just take care of your family and I'll take care of the work stuff."

"I'll only be gone for two days." I was not stupid enough to give Gigi a whole week to mess up my career.

"No need to rush. Oh, and don't worry about calling Liz, I'll tell her what's going on. Oh look, there she is! Call you later, 'kay?"

And she was gone. I knew that a career-savvy woman would immediately call back and try to talk to Liz first, but I just didn't have the energy. I had lost my baby and no crisis at Dawson's could compete with that.

I got up and turned the volume of the radio up so I could hear Natalie Imbruglia sing about some man who turned out to be a completely different person than he had presented himself to be. I sat down on the love seat and flipped through the paper while singing the lyrics.

I looked up to see Tad watching me from the doorway of the kitchen. "April, if…if I'm ever like the guy in that song, if I ever change, or stop being the man you fell in love with, you'll tell me, right?"

For a moment I was completely speechless. Tad never questioned himself or invited others to do so. "Of course I will," I said. "Not that it'll ever be necessary."

He stood there silently for a moment. Eventually he nodded toward the wall clock. "We should go soon."

I felt my shoulders tense and I dug my nails into my skirt. "I'm scared."

"You don't have to be scared." He walked over to me and bent down to kiss my hair. "I'll take care of you."

SIXTEEN

It's funny how a person can be hit with what seems to be a series of life-altering events only to find that their life hasn't changed at all. It had been six weeks since I had the D and C and it had been less than three months since I had gotten the positive results on the pregnancy test. After each of those happenings I had thought my life was over, and yet here I was standing in the middle of my sales floor with throbbing feet stuffed into uncomfortable but very cute shoes.

I sighed and looked at my watch: 9:30 p.m. The store was supposed to close at nine but Liz had apparently given the order that we were not to make the closing announcements until we had met last year's figures. We were twenty thousand dollars away from that goal, but it was rumored that two teenagers were milling around the lingerie department, so we had at least a snowball's chance in hell of making it happen. My department hadn't fared much better than the store overall so I had sent the other sales staff home early in order to save on labor. I fluffed an already perfect display and rubbed my eyes with the vain hope that doing so would make it easier to keep them open. Tad had been running me ragged lately, but in a good way. On my nights off, we dined at five-star restaurants, saw the best shows and attended concerts. I honestly had never seen anyone with so much energy. Every night he seemed to knock another hour off the time he needed for sleep.

It was great that Tad was so keen on keeping the romance alive, but every now and again I longed for a night of old movies and pizza. I mean, why did romantic dinners always have to involve duck?

Then again, maybe his attentiveness had less to do with romance and more to do with distraction. We hadn't talked much about the miscarriage since the day of my final procedure. That was more my fault than his. I had told Allie and Caleb about it and then promptly sworn them to secrecy and refused to allow them to comfort or counsel me. My mother and Bobe never even knew I had been pregnant. I still wasn't talking to my mother, but I had passed up lots of opportunities to tell Bobe. I knew that if given the chance these people would have agreed with Tad and told me I was a good person and that my feelings had been natural, but what they didn't understand was that I *wanted* to feel guilty. I couldn't help but think that my remorse was payback for the horrible thoughts I'd had during my pregnancy.

As for Tad's sins regarding the rent, I had dealt with that problem by insisting that going forward he would give me the rent payment to mail off every month. I had expected Tad to argue with me over that but he didn't offer a single protest. I had decided that was a good sign. If he was willing to allow me to be the one to put our housing payments in the mail every month then obviously he wasn't planning any other surprises in that area. So if I didn't die of sleep deprivation everything would be fine.

I took another look at my watch and then glared up at the lights that should have been dimmed a half hour earlier. Remorse aside, I didn't feel that I deserved to be held at Dawson's against my will. Things had been relatively normal here. Gigi was acting like herself, there had been no more slips of the tongue that would have threatened to expose her as a power-hungry bitch. After all, that was Blakely's job. Blakely hadn't talked to me about Cherise or the promotion for a while, which had me a little concerned, but she had also been away on two buying trips in the last three weeks.

I wandered around my empty floor completely aware that there was nothing out of place. When the phone rang, it took everything in me to answer with a standard greeting instead of a curse word.

"April? You sound irritated."

Tad's voice allowed me to bring my guard down. "I'm more than irritated, I'm pissed. They still haven't closed the store or even suggested that the customers bring their purchases to the register."

"What the hell's wrong with them? Do they think their employees don't have lives of their own? Is there someone I can call for you?"

"Great idea—" I pulled out the day's charge slips and started putting them in order "—you can call Liz at home and tell her how ticked you are that your wife is working late hours. I'm sure that will do wonders for my career."

"Maybe I could come over there and sexually harass the customers until they leave."

"Nothing doing—from now on you have to save all of your sexual harassment for me."

"Well, I'm coming down there. You can't work all night, we have nightclubs to hit."

"Nightclubs? Are you serious? We didn't get any sleep last night."

"Yeah, I remember." I could practically hear him grinning.

"Tad, I'm exhausted. All I want to do is go home, watch a *Friends* rerun and hit the sheets."

"Tell you what, we'll pump you full of caffeine, tape *Friends*, and after dancing for a few hours we'll hit the sheets together."

"Okay, let me draw your attention to the big difference in our agendas. Mine actually involves sleep."

"You're too young to be tired. I'm just a few blocks away, I'll meet you by the employee exit."

I started to protest but he had already hung up. I considered calling him back but finally replaced the receiver in its cradle with a resigned sigh.

"Everyone, you may now close your registers." The minute the disembodied voice gave the instructions over the loudspeaker I saw my fellow indentured servants grabbing their blue bags filled with the money from their prematurely closed registers and racing to customer service, where, after a not-so-quick money count, they would be freed. If I got out right now, I might not be the absolute last person in line for a change. The phone rang. I hesitated: *don't answer, don't answer.* It rang again. This is why I'm always late. I have some weird condition that makes it impossible for me to not answer phones. "Dawson's Sassy department, can I help you?"

"Two fucking garter belts."

"Are you serious, Allie? We stayed—" I checked my watch

again "—forty minutes late so they could buy garter belts? Were they really expensive garter belts?"

"Twenty bucks a pop."

"Did you at least make your day?"

"Nope. And since I had to keep my salespeople overtime I probably won't make my selling-cost goal either."

"So basically you're telling me there is no upside."

"Basically I'm telling you I'm ready to go on a killing spree."

"Hey, I have an idea. Why don't you come out with Tad and me and we'll kill people together?"

"Sorry, but I'm dead on my feet, which by the way are about to fall off. I'm just going to go home, get out my laser pen and do some sniper attacks on the neighbors."

Totally unfair. *I* was tired, *my* feet hurt, *I* wanted to do sniper attacks. Why did she get to have all the fun? *Because she's not married to Tad, the master of sweet talk.* "Fine, meet me in front of your department—we'll stand in the customer service line together."

"Gee, with an invitation like that, how can I say no?"

I hung up and looked around. Everyone else on my floor had vacated. I sighed and carried my money bags and receipts up the frozen escalator. Allie was waiting for me at the top looking like she was ready to spit fire. "I hate closing," she hissed as we walked the rest of the way to customer service.

"Sure you won't come out with us?"

Allie shook her head. "Some other time. Hey, I was talking to Jeremiah the other day and he tells me you've been avoiding him."

"I have not. He wants to go to dinner with Tad and me but every time we plan something, Tad's work gets in the way and we have to cancel. One of these days it'll happen."

"Huh…" Allie flipped her hair behind her shoulders. "Tad

never seems to cancel on you when you guys are going out by yourselves. Are you sure he's not putting this whole dinner thing off because he's jealous?"

"Of what?" I asked with a note of amusement. "I mean, my God, Allie, is there a man alive that is less my type than Jeremiah? And I can't imagine that I fit into his little rocker world, either."

Allie shrugged. "Jealousy isn't always based on logic. Anyway, if you do want to hang with him, why don't you come with me to see him and his band practice?"

I felt a stabbing feeling in my stomach. "He asked you to watch him practice? Are you two…moving beyond friendship?"

"Nah, he's not my type, either. I thought he was but now that I've gotten to know him, he's just a little too…"

"Stable?" I asked, thinking of the series of losers Allie had dated over the last few years.

"Funny. No, it's not that. I guess the problem is lack of chemistry, although I'm sure I'll still want to eat him alive next time I see him onstage. But here's the thing, I ran into him at a café near our place and he was with the other band members—"

"I know where this is going."

"Oh my God, April, the second guitarist has serious bedding potential. He's like a cross between Kurt Cobain and Ben Stiller."

"So he's a heroine addict with a knack for physical comedy?"

"Shut up. Anyway, you should come. They'll be practicing at his house at one tomorrow. You have the day off, right?"

I nodded and stepped forward as the line moved. "I don't have anything else planned." I glanced ahead at the cashier sorting through the piles of cash that had been handed to him by the accessories manager. Going over to a guy's house to watch his band practice was so high school, but for reasons that I wasn't willing to examine I found the idea rather thrilling.

Thirty minutes later Tad and I were riding up in the glass elevator at the Saint Francis Hotel. He had vetoed my suggestion that we get our late-night snack at Taco Bell. I allowed Tad to order for us since I couldn't get my eyes to focus long enough to read the menu. The bartender placed a couple of vodka martinis in front of us and Tad raised his glass to make a toast.

"To my wife, the most beautiful woman in this or any other room."

I took a small sip of my drink. "Flattery will get you everywhere."

Tad leaned forward so that his lips were aligned next to my ear. "Does that mean that if I keep this up you'll let me ravish you twice tonight?"

I smiled weakly. The only way he was getting it twice was if he served me a double espresso sweetened with a vial of cocaine. "Jeremiah invited Allie to one of his band's practice sessions. I think I'm going to go, too."

Tad pulled back abruptly. "Why would you want to watch him practice? Wouldn't it be better to wait to see the polished act onstage?"

The edge in Tad's voice surprised me. Maybe Allie was on to something with the jealousy thing. "I think the point is to give Allie the opportunity to pick up," I said. No point in mentioning that Jeremiah was not Allie's intended target.

"Oh…" Tad took a long drink of his beverage. "Can't Allie do better than an out-of-work musician?"

Okay, that had been needlessly harsh. "He's not out of work, he's a personal trainer and, believe it or not, his band is being booked with a certain amount of regularity these days."

Tad grunted and took another drink.

"Tad, why haven't we had dinner with Jeremiah yet?"

"What do you mean why? I've been busy with work and so have you."

"We've made the time to go out together almost every night. But whenever we make plans to hang out with Jeremiah, you have to work late or something."

"You think I've been making up excuses?" Tad snapped.

"Have you?"

Tad swiveled in his seat. "You're accusing me of lying?"

"All I'm doing is asking you a question. Are you avoiding Jeremiah or not?"

"Not."

"Fine, I believe you." We fell silent as the bartender served us the oysters and calamari that Tad had ordered. I didn't really believe him but I was way too tired to fight about it.

I watched him plunge his fork into the calamari and then drench it in a thick red cocktail sauce. "Tad, do you ever get jealous?"

Tad's fork stopped halfway on its journey to his mouth. "Why would I get jealous?"

"No reason. It's just that some people are naturally jealous and others aren't. Where do you fit in?"

"I'm not a jealous person, but if you ever gave me reason to be there'd be trouble."

"I'm not going to give you reason." I gently prodded an oyster with my cocktail fork. "Would you ever give me reason?"

"Don't be ridiculous."

I tentatively placed the oyster on my tongue. "You know, I have never seen you ogle anyone but me."

"You make it sound like that's a bad thing."

"It's not bad but it's certainly not normal. What about movie stars? Like Julia Roberts, what do you think of her?"

Tad shrugged. "She's okay."

"Okay isn't great. What about Nicole Kidman?"

"She's a good-looking woman," he said with little enthusiasm.

"Catherine Zeta-Jones?"

A slow smile crept over Tad's face. "Yeah, she's a…really good actress."

I laughed. "Right, and *Playboy* has got some really good articles." I tapped my fingers to the beat of the big-band music coming from the dance floor. "For me, it's Brad Pitt."

Tad nodded solemnly. "Listen, if you ever have a one-night stand with Brad Pitt I'll understand. No one else, just Brad."

I pressed my hand against my heart. "That is so sweet. And I'll let you mess around with Catherine. We just won't tell Angelina or Michael about it. They're probably not as mature about these things as we are."

Tad laughed and reached out to play with one of my unruly locks. "I'd pick you over Catherine any day of the week." He pulled me forward and pressed his lips against mine before adding, "However, if you ever want to have a threesome—"

I swatted him playfully. "Not gonna happen." My eyes traveled to the dance floor where a woman in her forties with bright red highlights was kicking up her heels with a guy who looked to be barely old enough to qualify for military service. "You know, it's been a while since I've talked to my mother."

"I thought that's what you wanted."

There was something in his tone that made me quickly bring my eyes back to him. "It was. Every week or so she calls my department and my cell and I keep screening the calls and deleting the messages. Eventually I'm going to have to make peace, and since I have Sunday off I was thinking maybe we could use the time to take a drive down to Santa Cruz."

"I don't think it's a good idea."

"Why not?"

"What do you mean why not? She refused to come to our wedding! You don't need to forgive her for that. She doesn't deserve it."

Hello? At what point had Tad adopted this viewpoint? "She and Bobe are the only family I have," I said carefully. "And let's face it, Bobe won't be around forever."

Tad put his glass down on the bar with enough force to cause the alcohol to spill over the sides. "The only family you have? What the hell am I?"

"Wait, that's not what I meant."

"We're husband and wife, April. We're supposed to be there for each other 'til the end. Partners. And now you sit there and you tell me that without your mother and grandmother you would be alone?" Tad slammed the rest of his drink and glared at his empty glass.

"I'm sorry, I didn't mean to upset you."

For a moment Tad looked pacified. He reached over and patted my hand as if to let me know that I was forgiven. Something about the gesture sparked a fire inside me.

I pulled my hand away and sat up a little straighter. "Actually, Tad, I'm not sorry. I didn't do anything wrong."

Tad stared at me with something that looked like shock.

I swallowed. I hadn't challenged Tad on anything since the miscarriage, but I had this gut feeling that I couldn't allow him to make this decision. "I want to see my mother." I enunciated each word carefully, as if our communication problem was due to a language barrier rather than some emotional dynamic. "She and Bobe are my only blood relatives. That's all I said and that's all I meant. I'm sorry if you misinterpreted my remarks, but I really don't think that's my fault."

Tad couldn't have looked more stricken if I had slapped him across the face. He opened and closed his mouth as if he was trying to talk but the words refused to come.

I brought my drink to my lips in order to hide my smile.

"I...I didn't..." Tad stammered. "Maybe my anger was a bit misdirected."

I blinked in surprise. That may very well have been the closest thing to an apology that I had ever heard Tad utter.

"I just don't want to see you get hurt," he continued at a pace that indicated that his words were being carefully selected.

"Why would I get hurt?"

"Because that's all your mother does, she just hurts you over and over."

I winced at the truth of his statement.

"You've been forgiving her all your life." Tad was now speaking with more confidence, which was ironic because his comments were eating away at mine. "You forgave her for not being there for you as a kid. You forgave her for being a bad role model and now you want to forgive her for not coming to our wedding. When does it stop, April?"

I felt my back curve into a hunchbacklike position. "She's my mom," I said feebly.

"Genetically that's true, but when has she ever been a mom in the more real sense?"

I couldn't answer the question. I didn't want to mentally

recount all the times my mother had failed me just so that I might stumble across the one or two memories of times when she hadn't.

"Don't put yourself through it, April." Tad looked directly into my eyes and his expression was filled with so much love that I wanted to just melt into his arms. "You don't need her. You will never have to beg anyone to love and care for you again. You will always have those things in me."

I let my head fall forward onto his shoulder. I did have him, and maybe that really was enough.

SEVENTEEN

Tad was gone by the time I woke up the next morning. I didn't mind; I actually relished having a few moments to myself. I stretched my arms over my head and squinted at the clock: 9:00 a.m. God, I couldn't remember the last time I had been able to sleep in that late. I rolled over onto my stomach and thought about the day ahead. The only thing I had planned was Jeremiah's band practice at one.

I crawled out of bed and threw on a silk Calvin Klein robe that Tad had recently bought me. It was a silly thing to buy a woman who got a thirty-three percent discount at a lingerie department, but the sentiment behind the gesture was nice. I slid my feet into some fuzzy slippers and followed the smell of coffee. Tad had made sure there was enough left in the pot for me to have at least two cups.

The phone rang as I was taking my first sip. I sighed and put my coffee down. Probably Tad; he often called me when I didn't wake in time to say goodbye.

"Hello?"

"Hello, I'm calling for April Silverperson or Tad Showers."

I rolled my eyes, all telemarketers should be sent to some remote island that was equipped with absolutely no long distance phone service. "This is April."

"Ms. Silverperson this is Will, I'm calling from Chase Manhattan Bank in regard to your Visa bill."

"My bill?" I shook my head, trying to clear the cobwebs. I didn't have a card with Chase.

"Yes, ma'am, your payment is now two months late. In order to avoid additional late fees you can make a payment right now over the phone."

"I'm sorry, but there has to be some mistake. I don't have a credit card with you."

"Ma'am, we have records of you opening an account with us five months ago."

"I've never opened up an account with Chase."

"I'm looking at our records here and it looks like everything's in order. We've been sending the bills to P.O. Box 12…"

"That's not my address—I don't even have a P.O. Box. Oh my God, someone's gotten hold of my social security number!" I started pacing the floor.

There was an uncomfortable pause before the man responded. "Our records show that you opened the account last November and added Tad Showers to the account the following month. Is this information inaccurate?"

"Yes, it's inaccurate! How much has it been run up to?"

"The balance is now eleven thousand twenty-three dollars and fifty-one cents."

"Oh my God." My hand flew up to my forehead.

"I'm sorry, ma'am, but could you please hold on a moment?"

"Yes, of course." I tugged at the lapels of my robe. If someone had gotten my social security number, there could be dozens of cards under my name being maxed out all over the country. I had heard stories of things like this happening to people but it never occurred to me that it could happen to me.

"Ma'am, are you still there?"

"Yes, I'm here." I walked out into the living room as if movement could somehow alleviate my anxiety.

"Okay, I'm looking at your list of charges and I'm going to read a few off to you, starting from when the card was first opened."

"All right, I'm listening."

"There was a two-thousand-dollar charge made at the Ritz-Carlton. There was an eight-hundred-dollar charge made to a place called Wedding Limos. There is a six-hundred-dollar charge to Mondavi Vineyards, and three cash-advance checks written to Smith Barney, one for $2,300, another for $4,897 and one for $5,689. The most recent charge was for six hundred dollars to Sibella Brandeis art studio."

I stared up at the painting of me and Bobe.

"Ma'am? Are you there?"

"I think I need to call you back."

"Yeah, okay." The man sounded genuinely sorry for me. He rattled off a number and I used a pen left on the coffee table to scribble it onto the back of a magazine. I might have written a number or two incorrectly; it was hard to see through all the rage.

I promised to call back and then clicked off the phone. Five months. Before we were even married. I had to talk to Tad. Now.

Forty minutes later I was in the elevator that went up to Tad's office space. I had thrown on a pair of jeans and a fitted cotton long-sleeve tee that had been washed and dried a few too many times. My hair was a mess and my makeup nonexistent. For once I really didn't care what I looked like. The elevator made a little *ding* noise to indicate that it had reached the requested floor. I marched out before the doors had a chance to fully open and stormed past the desks of the sales reps, who watched me curiously from their cubicles. I went to the door with Tad's name on it and pounded on it so hard that my fist stung from the impact. But I didn't care. My pain would be insignificant compared to the suffering I was about to inflict.

Tad opened the door. His face was flushed and his jaw jutted forward. But when he saw it was me the anger in his face transformed into confusion and then wariness. "April, is everything all right?"

"No."

Tad glanced nervously at the people sitting at their desks behind me and then quickly ushered me in. He closed the door behind me before using it to lean on as he folded his arms across his chest. He didn't say anything nor did he meet my eyes.

"I got a call from Chase this morning."

"Chase." He drew the word out so that the *s* sounded like the hissing of a snake.

"How could you? How could you forge my name on a credit card? And before we were even married, Tad! My God, did it ever occur to you that you were committing a felony?"

"Keep your Goddamn voice down."

"Excuse me? EXCUSE ME!" I was vaguely aware of being on the verge of hysteria and I didn't care. "You told me that you were putting all the wedding charges on your card and that you were paying it off monthly! But you haven't been paying it at all, and it wasn't even your card! What did you do, go through my mail and forge my name on one of those preapproved deals? Or did you actually go out of your way to get an application? Hmm? Come on, Tad, tell me all the dirty details. How hard was it to rip off your wife?"

"April, this is not the time or the place—"

"Nu-uh, no way. You don't get to control this argument. You charged that painting of me and my grandmother to an illegal account in my name! Oh my God, what kind of person does something like that?"

"I was paying the bills, April." The cool detachment in his voice made me want to walk over and throttle him. "I fell behind this month, that's all. I was going to pay it—"

"You fell behind for two months, but that's not the fucking point! You lied to me, you betrayed me and you fucking stole from me!"

He reached over and grabbed my arm, yanking me forward so that we were only inches apart. "I have been paying the bills. Every cent was going to be paid off."

I looked down to where his hand was cutting off the circulation in my arm. I took a deep breath and met his eyes. "Get your hands off me right now." I heard myself speak the words with a menacing force that was foreign to me. Tad removed his hand.

I stood there for a moment not moving my arm or any other part of my body. Would he dare grab me again? And then I realized…I wanted him to. I wanted an excuse to punch the shit out of him. I took a quick breath in and stepped back. I walked around him and pulled open the bottom drawer of his desk and removed the phone book that he always kept there. I flipped through the Yellow Pages, ignoring Tad's inquisitive stare. Finally

I found what I was looking for and dialed the number on the page and switched on the speakerphone.

"Hi," said the recorded voice on the other end of the line. "You've reached marriage and family therapist Harry Klein. I cannot take your call right now but if you leave your name and number I will get back to you shortly."

"Hello, Mr. Klein, my name is April Silverperson." I glared at Tad, who was beginning to look a little lost. "My husband and I need to make an appointment with you before I kill him." I proceeded to leave my home, work and cell-phone numbers before hanging up.

"I was going to pay it off," Tad whispered, although the statement didn't seem to be directed at me as much as to himself.

I clenched and unclenched my hands in frustration. "It doesn't matter what you—"

"It's Sean and Eric's fault."

"Sean and Eric? What could they possibly have to do with this?"

"They were supposed to approve my business plan. I showed them the plan. It's perfect. They're ruining everything. EVERY-THING!" He raised his fist and plummeted it into the wall, leaving a hole where he had made impact. He pulled his hand back and shook it slightly. I could see drops of blood clinging to his knuckles. My hand flew to my mouth to keep myself from screaming or throwing up.

"I'm going to get them for this. I'm going to make them pay." He turned in my direction, but if he saw me he made no indication of it.

"Sean's fighting to get joint custody of his two-year-old son." With each syllable his tone became more sinister. "I wonder how he would like it if I called his ex-wife and told her about the seventeen-year-old boy he fucked. I bet he'd never be able to get within twenty feet of his son again."

I swallowed and moved carefully toward the door. It was time for me to go. Tad started as if he had suddenly remembered that I was there. I felt his eyes follow me as I walked out of his office and rushed to the elevator.

I didn't go home after that. Instead, I drove to Twin Peaks. I got outside and walked right to the point where the hill makes its dramatic slope downward and looked out at the city spread below me. I needed this, to feel separated from all of it. I needed the perspective.

I had been so angry about the credit card that I hadn't stopped to think about how weird it was. It wasn't a normal kind of betrayal.

I sighed and rubbed my arms to help warm myself. Tad had taken me up here on our fourth date. He had wrapped his arms around me and told me that we were the perfect fit. I had just smiled; I hadn't asked him to explain why he thought so; I understood. Once upon a time I had understood Tad. Now I didn't understand anything.

I pushed aside my hair that the wind was whipping into my face. His reaction to being confronted… My God, what had that been about? For that matter, what had *my* reaction been about? It had been the first time in my life that I had felt completely capable of violence. Never mind the fact that he was a lot bigger and stronger than me. Never mind that I still loved him. None of that had factored into my thinking because I hadn't *been* thinking. I had just been feeling. Feeling the bloodlust.

"Jesus, what if I really am a monster?" I said aloud. I looked around to make sure that none of the tourists had seen me talking to myself, but there weren't any standing close enough to notice, and even if they had, they probably would have just taken a picture. "And here's the schizophrenic woman we saw on the top of Twin Peaks, remember her, Marge?"

I went over to an empty bench and sat with my back against a plaque that sang the praises of a deceased husband and father. I did love Tad. He could be so purely wonderful. Like when I had found out that I was going to miscarry... How would I have gotten through that without him? So how could someone be so incredible one moment and then turn around and forge my name on a credit card the next? And why? I looked up to see a hawk gliding over the mountain, circling some unsuspecting prey. Was there more that I didn't know?

I checked the time on my watch. I was already fifteen minutes late to meet Allie. The guitarist at whose home the band was practicing lived in the Mission District, so even if I left immediately I would be forty minutes late. I bit down on my lip. The last thing I wanted to do was hang out with a rock band. But then again maybe there was another reason I should go.

I got back in the car and drove to the Mission. It took me a little while to locate the address. I parked just a few doors down and took the time to put my Club in place before following the beat of the drums to the correct garage. The garage door was closed but I found a little side door that was unlocked. Judging from the noise level, I knew knocking would be a useless endeavor. I pushed the door open and stepped inside.

At first no one noticed me. Allie's back was to me. She was lying on her side on top of some tattered carpet strips spread across the floor. She had her head propped up with one hand and was fingering the edges of a large red plastic cup with her other. The band was busy jamming away. Jeremiah was on the guitar.

He was the first to see me. He didn't say anything or let on to the others that I was there. He just locked eyes with me and took a step forward. It may have been my imagination but he seemed to have gotten better since the last time I heard him play. A slow smile crept over his rather generous mouth and his eyes slanted dangerously. I watched as his fingers worked the guitar strings as if they had a mind of their own. His body was rocking back and forth and I could tell that he was in a different place. Tad had been in a "different place" when I had seen him last, too, but I actually understood Jeremiah's journey. He could take me along if I just gave in to it. I closed my eyes and let the music enter me. I felt myself sway slightly and my hips began to rock to the bass pounding in the background.

"April!" I snapped my eyes open at the sound of Allie calling my name. Jeremiah let his hands go limp and the music stopped. He grinned at me and for a second I felt as if we had both done something that we should feel ashamed of. But that was ridiculous. He had just played his music, and I had just listened.

Allie got up and draped her arm around my waist before giving me a friendly shake. "Where have you been? I thought you forgot about me."

"No one could forget about you, Allie," I said, struggling to keep my tone light. "I just totally lost track of time. Forgive me?"

"Always." She gestured to the three guys I didn't know, "April, this is Dallas, Gary and Paul. And of course you already know Jeremiah."

We all exchanged quick hellos and small talk. After a few minutes Jeremiah suggested that the group take a half-hour break. Dallas and Gary went inside the house, so it was just Paul, Allie, Jeremiah and me.

I liked Paul. He was funny in a crude kind of way and he was clearly very into Allie. I could tell by the way he smiled at her while fiddling with his guitar pick. "Hey, um, you still want to see those records I was tellin' you about?" he asked. "I even have some old 45s from the seventies. You'll dig 'em." It was clear from the way he angled his body toward Allie that the invitation did not extend to Jeremiah or me.

Allie smiled and looked up at me to see if I was okay with being abandoned.

I nodded and gently shoved her away. "Go, I know you love that kind of stuff." Allie couldn't care less about 45s, but as long as he had a mattress and a naughty attitude she'd be a happy camper.

Jeremiah stuck his thumbs into the empty belt loops of his jeans and transferred his weight back onto his heels. "So you thirsty? Allie's drinking margaritas. I can mix you one if you want."

I started to refuse but then an image of Tad punching a hole in his office wall flashed before my eyes. "Actually, a margarita would be great."

I followed Jeremiah inside. Dallas and Gary had already made themselves a sandwich and were in the living room watching football on a television that was probably a few years older than me.

Jeremiah directed me to the kitchen. He reached into the refrigerator and pulled out a half-full blender of what looked like margarita mix. "You like it strong?"

"What?" I felt my cheeks heat up.

"Do you like your margaritas strong?"

"Oh…yeah…strong is good."

Jeremiah mixed the drink quickly and poured it into a plastic cup identical to the one Allie had been drinking from. He sat down at a small brown kitchen table that someone had probably picked up at a neighborhood garage sale.

I pulled out a chair opposite him and took a long drink.

"You okay?"

I stared at the slushy liquid in my cup. "What's the deal between you and Tad?"

Jeremiah shifted uncomfortably in his chair but remained silent.

"What aren't you telling me, Jeremiah? What part of Tad's past do you think I need to be protected from?"

"I don't think you need to be protected from any of the shit Tad may or may not have pulled in the past." Jeremiah rolled his knuckles along the wood surface of the table. "What's got me worried is the shit he might try to pull now."

I heard a crinkling noise and realized that I was squeezing my cup a little too tightly. I relaxed my grip and pulled on my reserves of courage. "I need you to be a little more specific. Is there a reason you don't like him? Did you have a thing for Jackie?"

"Nah, Jackie and I were buds, but she was a bit much for me. She's a little too emotionally charged."

"Tad says she's a pathological liar."

"Pathological? No, that's overstating it, but she has been known to put a weird spin on the truth. I remember her telling me about this dude she'd been dating—claimed he had smacked her around and she had a bruise on her cheek to prove it. So I went to the guy's house to set him straight. When he came to the door I could see he had been majorly worked over. Jackie'd given him a black eye, busted his lip open and bloodied his fucking nose. Then I find out she threw the first punch. Now, I know that there's no excuse for hitting a woman, but if some chick tried to use my face as a punching bag I'd take the bitch down." He shrugged as if to apologize for any possible offense I might have taken. "So I figured the shit she told me about Tad needed to be taken with a grain of salt."

"All right." I waved my hand in the air impatiently. "I promise I'll take it with a whole liter of salt, just tell me what she said." Jeremiah hesitated again. I leaned forward and grabbed his hand. "Come on, you want to tell me and I think…I think I really need to know."

Jeremiah nodded. His eyes took on that vacant look of someone who was remembering the past. "One of Jackie's problems is that she's a my-way-or-the-highway kind of babe. But what's cool about her is she knows her faults and she owns up to them. What you see is what you get. No manipulation, no guessing games. Tad's the total opposite, or at least he used to be. He comes off as this real laid-back guy who will bend over backward to help his friends. But when you think he's helping you get what you want, what he's really doing is convincing you to *want* what *he* wants. He was just as controlling as Jackie but he hid it a lot better."

The sound of cheering coming from the next room brought Jeremiah back to the present. He got up and pulled a beer out of the refrigerator. "Never understood what the big deal was over football. If you're not going to play the game, then why would you get all excited about watching a whole bunch of grown men roll all over each other?"

"Is that what Jackie told you?" I whispered, ignoring his last comment. "That he was a control freak disguised as a laid-back boyfriend?"

"No, that's just my take on it." Jeremiah used a bottle opener to pop the top off his beer. He sat down again without getting a glass. "Jackie…Jackie told me he was unstable."

I felt my heart skip a beat. "Define unstable."

"See, that's the thing… I can't. Even she couldn't really put her finger on it. She said he'd get seriously wigged out over stupid shit. Like she would ask him if he ever planned to go to Atlanta to see his parents and the guy would just lose it."

I felt my back stiffen, this was sounding too familiar. "Tad's parents are in Georgetown," I said absently.

"Really? Shit, I would have sworn it was Atlanta. Anyway, she thought he was a little whacked, and when they split up he got…weird."

"Weird?" I could barely speak. I could hear Tad making those comments about his partners, and then there was the way he had stared at the wall in Barcelona….

Jeremiah was looking in every direction but mine. "Yeah, but like I said, *Jackie's* weird, so I…"

"Just explain Tad's *weird*."

Jeremiah lifted his beer, and just before drinking he mumbled, "He used to scratch the walls."

EIGHTEEN

The sweet slushy margarita oozed onto my skin as my hand squeezed the life out of my plastic cup.

Jeremiah jumped up and grabbed a few paper towels and tried to catch the spill before it reached the floor. I pushed my chair back without bothering to dry the ends of my sleeves, which were now soaked. "I gotta go."

"April, did something happen?"

"No, no, I was just wondering why you acted so weird around him, that's all."

Jeremiah shrugged.

I had thought I could handle this conversation but he had hit too close to home. I didn't allow myself to think about the scratching and I certainly wasn't ready to hear about it from Jeremiah. Somehow, talking to him about my problems with Tad felt like a betrayal. "Look, I have to find Allie."

"Well…Paul's record collection is in his room and if they haven't come out by now…"

"Got it, could you just tell her that I had to leave?"

I turned to run out, but Jeremiah grabbed my arm. "April, what happened?"

I looked down at his hand, but not with the warning glare I had given Tad. I wanted him to hold on to me. In fact, I realized that I wanted him to hold on to a lot more than my arm, and that was not good. I gently pulled away and Jeremiah didn't resist.

I took a deep breath. "Jeremiah, I'm fine… There's just something I forgot I had to do. I'll see you later, okay?"

"Yeah, all right, if you say so. Look, you call me if you need me, got it?"

"Got it." I walked out to the living room and said my goodbyes to Dallas and Gary. Jeremiah escorted me to the door.

"I'll talk to you soon," he said definitively. He held the door for me and I forced myself to walk—not run—out of it.

When I got to my car I tried to figure out where to go next. Home was out of the question. What if Tad had left work early? How the hell was he going to explain that wall to his partners? I thought about his bizarre comments regarding Sean.

Suddenly I knew who I needed to talk to. I pulled the Club off my steering wheel and headed for Dawson's.

When I got to the cosmetics department Caleb was finishing discussing something with the Clinique counter manager. I pretended to look at the items displayed at an adjacent counter until he eventually noticed me. I mouthed the words *Need to talk*.

He gave me a quick nod of acknowledgment before returning his attention to the manager. A few minutes later he was by my side.

He took a decorative bottle of eau de toilette out of my hand. "Don't try this one, you'll regret if for the rest of the day." He regarded my still-damp wrists and lifted one up to his nose. "This is nice. L'eau de Cuervo, is it?"

"I've had a really bad day," I answered. "Do you have time?"

"For you? Always."

"Yeah, but this isn't exactly a five-minute crisis. I need to unburden on you." I moved my hands over my face and then pulled my skin back in a this-is-me-after-collagen kind of way. "I shouldn't have come—you can't deal with this at work. I can't even deal with this at home."

Caleb furrowed his brow before beckoning to one of the makeup artists behind the Estée Lauder counter. "Denise, spread the word that I'll be in a meeting and am not to be disturbed unless there's an emergency."

"Got it." Denise's brown bob bounced as she vigorously nodded her head.

"I'm talking asteroid-hitting-the-earth kind of emergency, okay?"

Again Denise readily agreed and then scampered off to do Caleb's bidding. He leaned over to me conspiratorially. "It's good to be the king." He then made a sweeping gesture in the direction of his office. "Shall we?"

We walked across the floor and stepped through an unobtrusive-looking door that led to the only Dawson's manager's office (outside of Liz's) that actually looked like an office. Caleb had a real desk, with drawers and everything, and he even had space for two filing cabinets. He gestured for me to sit.

"You're a mess," he noted. "You didn't style your hair, your long-sleeve tee might as well have a sign on it reading Time for Goodwill, and worse yet, you're not wearing any makeup. What happened?"

"Something is wrong with my marriage. And something is very, very wrong with Tad."

Caleb scooted his chair closer to mine. "Tell me."

Where to start? "He scratches the walls."

"Excuse me?"

"When he thinks I'm asleep he takes his nails to the walls and he scratches. It's like a cat sharpening its claws, except cats are more…emotional about it. Tad just sort of—" I searched for the right words "—zones out. He zones out and he scratches."

"Well," said Caleb slowly, "maybe it's just a nervous tic."

"A nervous tic," I repeated. "Right, that could be it."

"Lots of people have them," Caleb said.

"Like that thing Shelley Long did with her face while playing Diane on *Cheers*."

"Exactly."

"Or the way Julia Roberts was always fidgeting with her jewelry in *Pretty Woman*."

"Another perfect example," he agreed.

"Or that thing Jack Nicholson would do with his ax in *The Shining*."

"Oh, come on…" Caleb rolled his eyes. "Unless rivers of blood have been running through your hallway, I think you can rule out the possibility of Tad being possessed."

"He forged my name on a credit card application, had it sent to a P.O. Box, charged it up to eleven thousand some odd dollars and then didn't pay it for two months."

Caleb's eyes looked like they were about to pop out of his head. For a full minute I waited while he struggled to come up with a response.

I buried my face in my hands. How bad was my life that its re-telling left the master of witty repartee speechless?

I felt Caleb's hand on my knee and I looked up at him pleadingly. "How did you find out?" he asked.

I let it all spill—the phone call, the office visit, Tad's weird remarks, Jeremiah's account of Tad and Jackie's dealings with him in the past, everything. I knew that it would skew Caleb's view of Tad forever, but I needed to talk to someone who I knew would never steer me wrong or pull a punch.

Caleb listened intently. A few times during my account his phone rang but he just pressed a button and had the call forwarded to voice mail. It occurred to me that if Caleb would have had the decency to stay in the closet, I would have married him.

By the time I was done, Caleb was staring at the floor. When Caleb avoided eye contact it meant he had a big bomb to drop. Finally he took a deep breath. "April, is there any chance that Tad is doing drugs?"

I froze. Tad on drugs? I reviewed everything that had happened up to that point. The scratching, the erratic behavior and mood swings, the honeymoon, the money issues…drugs would explain all of it. Drug abuse was a serious problem, no question about it, but it also would mean… I felt a small twinge of hope fluttering in my belly; if Tad was using drugs his behavior would make sense! My problems would have a name and a solution!

I stood up, unable to contain my mounting excitement. "You're right, of course, you're right! He's just been hiding it from me, that's all."

Caleb gave me a funny look but I think it was in response to my smile rather than my words. "Have you ever seen him do any?"

"No…well, that's not true—once every blue moon he has a

joint. I've seen him do that." I shook my head. "God, how could I have been so blind?"

"April sweetie, contrary to what those public service ads say, a hash brownie does not a heroine addict make." He swiveled back and forth in his chair. "However, the conduct you've described would be consistent with that of a cokehead. Have you noticed him sniffing a lot?"

I dug my teeth into my lip and tried to conjure up a helpful memory. "Oh!" I snapped my fingers in the air. "Two weeks ago we had dinner at Sean's house—he's one of the partners at SMB. Tad was sniffing the whole time. He blamed it on the cat. God, what an idiot I was to buy that one, huh?"

"Um, is he allergic to cats?"

"Well, he says he is, but addicts lie to cover for their habit. Come on, Caleb, I know you saw that episode of *Oprah*. Maybe…maybe he has been coordinating his drug use with the times he knew he would be in the presence of a cat! That would make sense, right?"

Caleb stared at me like I had begun to grow a second head.

I clapped my hands together impatiently, "Come on, Caleb, I like your explanation—help me make it work!"

He nodded solemnly and tapped his finger against his chin. "Maybe he's not sniffing it. Maybe he's smoking it instead."

"Crack?" I asked doubtfully. Tad wouldn't even touch a scotch that was less than thirty years old, so I had a hard time picturing him forsaking cocaine in order to indulge in a cheaper substitute.

"Who knows, I'm not exactly an expert," Caleb sighed. "Drugs are one of the few vices that I've never really indulged in." He met my eyes. "What are you going to do?"

"Well, that's the great thing about addiction." I put my hands on my hips authoritatively. "There are steps I'm supposed to take. Steps that someone else has already thought up for me. First I confront him. He'll probably respond by getting angry and defensive because that's what addicts do…"

Caleb raised an eyebrow. "*Oprah* again?"

"No, that's from *Dr. Phil.* But who knows, maybe Tad's hit bottom and he'll admit to having a problem immediately. If not, I stage an intervention."

"Now, that's *Oprah*, right?"

"The point is, I can handle this." I leaned down and gave Caleb a tight embrace. "I can handle this, Caleb. It's going to be rough but we'll work it out."

Caleb used the fact that I was precariously balanced to his advantage and pulled me down onto his lap. He wrapped an arm around my waist to help stabilize me. "Hon, you need to think this through a little more. People on drugs can be dangerous and it sounds like Tad is in a real bad place right now."

I flashed back to the moment Tad had grabbed my arm, the fist through the wall, even the argument we had over the rent. I had seen the look in his eyes. He had wanted to hit me. But the important part was that he hadn't. Even while I was threatening to cut off his penis Tad had still managed to control himself. That said something. Tad did pose a threat to me, but not the kind that Caleb was talking about. "Tad wouldn't hurt me," I said with more confidence than I had a right to. "On the other hand, if I don't do something soon my credit might be put on death row."

It was after six by the time I came home. One of the local radio stations was doing a "best of the '80s" feature and "Purple Rain" started blasting through my speakers just as I pulled into the spot in front of our garage. I sat through the whole damn thing, including the two-minute guitar solo. That song did seem to speak to my situation, but I had learned early in life that when on the brink of depression pretty much every sad ballad seemed to be written specifically for me. Plus, I would have been willing to listen to an extended rendition of "Knocking on Heaven's Door" performed by *NSYNC if that's what it took to prolong the inevitable. I nibbled on my nails and looked at the front door.

"On the count of three," I instructed myself. "One, two…" I got out of the car and went inside the house.

The first thing I noted was the sound of Mozart. I hung up my coat and took a moment to see if I could recognize the movement. I wasn't very good at that kind of thing but Tad could name a composer, movement and symphony after hearing three notes. When we were first dating I had asked him what it was about classical music that spoke to him. His answer was that it centered him. I remember being struck by his choice of words; Tad wasn't one of those people who went around trying to find his center. Now I was thrilled to hear the music; maybe it had brought him back from left field.

I found him in the kitchen. He sat at our small wood table with a half-filled glass and a quarter-filled wine bottle. My eyes zeroed in on the red liquid. Maybe the drug was alcohol. It didn't fit as well as cocaine but anything was possible. I tried to envision a future filled with apple cider and near beer.

Tad looked up from his glass and offered me a somewhat apologetic grin. "I know it's in bad taste to drink alone but I'm having a really bad day."

I retrieved a glass for myself and emptied the rest of the bottle into it. "Bad day or bad trip?"

Tad looked genuinely confused. "I don't understand." He was slurring his words. One look at the empty whiskey glass by the sink told me that he had started with something harder than Merlot.

I took a long sip of wine from his glass. Tad would probably feel better about AA if I qualified for the codependents group. I gritted my teeth and forced myself to look at him. "Tad, have you been using drugs?"

Tad wrinkled his forehead. "Wha…?" Then shook his head.

"Don't look at me like I'm crazy. You've been making a good income and yet we can't seem to pay the bills. You basically stole money from me and your moods have been…all over the place." He was no longer looking at me, which made it easier to press on. "Tad, if you have a problem, I'll help you. I won't leave, not as long as you tell me and take steps to effectively deal with it."

He scoffed. "You didn't look like a woman that was ready to stand by her man this morning."

"That was because I was completely pissed off. And I still am, but that doesn't mean I don't love you. Just…let me help, okay? Let's find a way through this."

Tad looked into my eyes and I could see the beginning of tears. "I'm not an addict, April. It's been over four months since I've had any weed and I haven't done anything harder since college… but…April, I haven't been completely honest with you."

I let out a humorless laugh. "I think we've established that."

His mouth began to tremble and he dropped his head into his arms that were now folded onto the table. I felt an aching in my heart and I put a supportive hand on his shoulder. "I…I shouldn't have interrupted," I said. "You can talk to me."

"I shouldn't have lied to you. I shouldn't have sent in that credit card application."

I put down my wineglass and stroked his hair. "Is that an apology?"

Tad pulled himself up a little. "Please, April, if you interrupt me I'll never get through this." He wiped away his tears.

Some of my sympathy fell by the wayside.

"I have these plans for the business. I know where I want to take it. I can see it…in my head." He tapped his forehead. "And once we get there we'll have more money than we'll know what to do with, but you have to spend money to make money and Eric and Sean just don't get that."

"You're losing me. What do your plans for SMB have to do with your acting like a prick?"

"I'm not a prick," he snapped, and I instantly regretted my choice of words. I was going to have to do a better job of balancing my wifely support with my righteous fury.

"Eric and Sean just won't listen—they're ruining everything—and I just feel…anxious. I keep coming up with plans that will make the business better and they thwart me every time. Now I'm at the point that I'm beyond angry. It's like something dangerous inside me is about to be cracked open."

I swallowed and pushed aside images of the Incredible Hulk. "So you ran out of money while trying to advance your business and that's when you opened a credit card under my name—to pay for the things in your personal life." Who would have thought that of all the issues that needed to be addressed, credit fraud would end up being the easier one to deal with?

"I was going to pay it off," he moaned. "I still am… It's just going to take longer than I thought. But I have a large commission check coming in soon that should wipe out everything."

"Why did we have a wedding at the Ritz if the money wasn't

there? I swear, Tad, if you had asked me to hightail it to Vegas to be married by an Elvis impersonator I would have been all over it."

"I didn't want that for us." He pounded his fist for emphasis. "We deserve better, and soon the money thing won't even be an issue. I swear to you, April, we are going to be rolling in it."

"You need help. *We* need help."

Tad nodded. "If you want me to go to counseling with you I will."

"Don't you want to?"

He looked up at me, his eyes bloodshot and pleading. "I want you. I'll do whatever I have to do to keep you with me."

The next morning I had what Caleb would call an emotional hangover, which is five times worse than a hangover induced by alcohol because it takes five times longer to go away. I had resisted the temptation to make Tad sleep on the couch and I even let him hold me through the night, but his hands felt uncomfortable against my skin. I had this sinking feeling that nothing had been resolved. But I wanted to believe differently. As I watched Tad pour coffee into two cheery-looking mugs, I decided that I would have to work on my ability to live in denial.

Judging from Tad's careful movements and whispered words, I assessed that his hangover was of the traditional sort. That wasn't such a bad thing since it provided us with an excuse to keep the talking to a minimum. My mind traveled back to his slurred speech of the night before. It was foolish to rule out the addiction possibility so early on in the game, but it was beginning to seem unlikely. Not that he didn't drink too much at times, but I suspected that the drinking was just a symptom of a much bigger problem. Plus, when I had asked him about drugs he didn't get defensive. Not only was that the MO of most addicts, but it was also Tad's personal M.O. He hadn't even tried to turn the argument around and make everything my fault. And he had been so emotionally raw. I had felt for him, but not enough to really forgive him.

By the time we were standing in the threshold of our front door, I was able to muster up the strength to say something marginally meaningful. "Tad, I need you to tell me if there's anything else."

Tad blanched. He had his briefcase in hand and one arm inside his overcoat. "Anything else?" he repeated.

"I'm going to work really hard on the forgiveness thing but I can't take any more surprises. If there's more that you're hiding from me I need you to tell me now… Otherwise…" I swallowed and looked down at my ring. For the first time I saw it as garish rather than simply extravagant. "If you continue to lie to me and keep secrets, I don't think we're going to make it."

Tad slowly put his other arm in his coat, then after putting down his briefcase he drew me forward, putting his hands on either side of my waist. "There's nothing else. I will never lie to you again, April. I promise."

This was one of those times when it didn't make sense to trust my husband. Even at that moment I knew it…but I really, really didn't want to know it. I pulled back and transferred my keys from hand to hand. "I believe you, Tad." But my inner voice was talking to me now. Screaming, in fact, and the unspoken words reverberated through my head. *You're a fool.*

Work was hell. Allie called down from her department; she was angry at me beyond words. She kept sputtering that by not interrupting her little lovefest in order to tell her I was leaving I had broken the girlfriend's code of etiquette. Maybe she was right, but

I hadn't been in a state of mind that was conducive to hearing her gush about her musician's fine instrument. I apologized and pled a migraine. I simply couldn't tell her the truth over the phone.

Each customer was more annoying than the last, until Gigi showed up and suddenly the customers didn't seem so bad. I watched her ring up a six-hundred-dollar sale for a woman who had sworn thirty minutes earlier that she couldn't afford anything in our department.

I looked at myself in the mirror strategically located by the leather jackets. You had to have a certain look in order to get strangers to pay good money for things they didn't want. Gigi had it and I didn't.

"Shouldn't you be asking the mirror who's the fairest of them all?"

I smiled and turned to see Caleb standing a few paces behind me. He used his thumb and forefinger to check the quality of one of the jackets hanging nearby. "You have time for a cigarette break?"

"We don't smoke."

"Damn, then I guess we'll have to spend the whole time talking."

"Allow me to take you to my parlor." I signaled to Gigi that we were going to my office before leading Caleb back.

Caleb made himself comfortable in Gigi's chair and idly looked through the Sassy on-order book. "So you and Tad talked." The extreme casualness of his tone told me how hard he was working on not pushing me for information.

"We talked."

Caleb looked up from the book expectantly. "Sooo…" he prodded.

"He says he's not doing drugs."

Caleb made a small dismissive gesture. "I assumed he would. What happened when you pressed the issue?"

I looked down at my hands.

"You are kidding." Caleb slammed the on-order book closed. "You asked him if he was on drugs, he said no, and you just said, 'Oh, okay, thanks for clearing that up?' I thought you said you watched *Oprah!*"

"I do! I just…" I rubbed my hands up and down my skirt. "I don't know. You should have seen him, Caleb. I expected him to get angry and defensive but he didn't. He really opened up to me."

"About what? What dark secrets does Taddy boy have?"

"He's having problems at work."

Caleb's body had a small convulsive reaction to my statement. "He's having problems at work? That was the big revelation? That was the excuse he used to justify lying about your rent, forging your name on a credit card and acting like an all-around asshole?"

"He's not always an asshole!" I squared my shoulders and prepared myself for battle. It was bad enough that I had called him a prick. I couldn't allow my friends to compare him to other obscene body parts.

"April, lets get real. If your marriage was even halfway okay you wouldn't have had to qualify that last statement with an *always*."

I started to respond but was cut off by the buzz of my intercom. "April?" Gigi's voice sang. "Line one is for you."

I noticed my hand was shaking when I reached for the receiver. "Hello? I mean, this is April, can I help you?"

"Hello, this is Harry Klein, you left a message at my office yesterday."

"Oh, hi!" I mouthed the word *therapist* to Caleb, who was still looking mystified.

"You said you wanted to make an appointment?"

"Yes, yes, I did." I waited for the long list of questions. He'd probably want to know why I felt we needed marriage counseling, if there were children involved, if I really had homicidal tendencies and stuff like that.

"My first available appointment is 11:00 a.m. two weeks from today. Does that work for you?"

I frantically flipped through the pages of my Day-Timer. What about the questions? "Eleven works. I don't have Tad's schedule in front of me but I'll just tell him he either makes it to the appointment or he makes his own appointment with a divorce attorney."

"Then I should pencil you in for eleven?"

I felt a sinking feeling in my stomach. What kind of therapist didn't laugh at other people's misery? "Go ahead and pencil, we'll be there at eleven sharp."

"Good…" He proceeded to give me directions on how to get to his office while I pretended to listen. As long as I could remember the street number and the Web address for MapQuest I'd be fine.

I hung up the phone and smiled weakly at Caleb. "Well, that's step one…we're going to therapy."

Caleb nodded but seemed unimpressed.

I sighed resignedly. "You're right. My marriage is in trouble. But you've got to understand, when Tad's good he's very, *very* good. When I lost our baby…" My voice trailed off and I looked away.

Caleb rolled his chair closer to mine and he carefully removed a piece of lint that was clinging to my stocking. "I know Tad can be wonderful," he said. "I've seen it. But sometimes…" He hesitated then straightened up. "You know what? I'm being horrible. Marriage counseling is a fabulous idea. So tell me, who's the lucky shrink?"

"Harry Klein, I found him in the phone book."

Now Caleb was on his feet. "The phone book? My God, why don't you just go and get your hair styled at Super Cuts while you're at it."

"Well, forgive me, but I don't travel in the kind of circles in which people go around bragging about their therapist. I had to start somewhere, and the Yellow Pages—"

Caleb held his hand out to stop me. "Fine, just promise me that you won't give up on therapy if this guy turns out to be something less than Freud."

I thought about what I would be left with if therapy didn't work out. I nodded solemnly. "I promise."

NINETEEN

Two weeks later Tad and I sat on the couch in the therapist's office with about two feet of space between us. I had never seen Tad more rigid. His eyes kept darting to the door as if he was toying with the idea of making a run for it.

The man sitting opposite us looked normal enough. His horn-rimmed glasses could have used a little tightening but other than that he was very put together. He was wearing a pair of chinos and a periwinkle-blue button-down shirt, and his salt-and-pepper beard was short and well groomed. He looked like a prototype for liberal Jewish intellectuals everywhere.

"So why don't we start with you two giving me a little history." He looked at Tad and pushed up his glasses. "Shall we start with you? Where did you grow up?"

Tad's eyes widened and for a minute I thought he was going to cry. And then something happened. I could practically see the gears in his head leaping into action. He flashed me a satisfied smile and leaned back into the sofa. "I grew up in a little town called Georgetown. Not the one in D.C.—this Georgetown is in Massachusetts."

"Oh?" Harry raised his eyebrows in curiosity. "I haven't heard of it."

"Not a lot of people have, it has a population under ten thousand. Very rural and woodsy. My dad and I would go camping all the time, sometimes fishing or hunting. My mom would have a homemade apple pie waiting for us when we got home…"

"We got it," I said. "You lived in a Norman Rockwell painting but—"

"April—" Harry looked at me over the rims of his glasses "—Tad clearly wants to share his experiences about his childhood. We need to allow him to do that."

My mouth dropped open. I had just been chastised by our therapist. We had been in his office for all of five minutes and already I was the bad guy. I crossed my arms in front of myself protectively. It wasn't that I didn't want to hear about Tad's childhood. I would love to, especially since the soliloquy he was currently reciting was the only thing he had *ever* shared about his childhood experiences. The racism bit didn't become an issue for Tad until he moved to a town that actually had black people in it, and it was then that he realized that some of the things his parents had taught him were wrong. It must have been painful for him to be forced to choose between his principles and the people who had provided him with such an idyllic childhood, and it wouldn't surprise me if he had issues around it—but that wasn't why we were in therapy. We were there so that we could deal with his issues around credit cards and lease agreements. Surely we could deal with the important things first and save the warm fuzzy stuff for Christmas.

Tad cast me a sympathetic but somewhat patronizing look. "April has a hard time listening to me talk about the joys of my childhood because hers was so difficult. She's had to go through a lot."

"Oh?" Harry looked over at me. "Is that true?"

"No! I mean yes, but that's not my issue. It's true that my mother wasn't the apple-pie type, but—"

"That's an understatement." Tad relaxed farther back into the sofa. "You told me that your mother rarely showed up for dinner." He turned to Harry. "She even refused to come to our wedding. She told April she was protesting it or something. April was devastated. Just a few weeks ago April admitted that she hadn't come to terms with her feelings of abandonment." Tad reached over and gave my hand a squeeze. I wanted to bite his fingers off.

"Is that true?" Harry leaned forward. "Do you feel that you have abandonment issues?"

"I don't know, maybe," I said, not bothering to mask the impatience in my voice.

"Do you feel that it has affected your relationship with Tad?"

"Look, I don't mean to dodge your questions, but I'm not here to talk about abandonment or my problems with my mother."

"But maybe those things are more relevant than you think," Tad said, raising his eyebrows. "I feel like you're always questioning me, both my actions and my intentions. Maybe that's because you expect me to hurt you the way that your mother hurt you, or worse yet, disappear like your father did."

"Oh, for God's sake." I pounded my fist into an adjacent throw pillow, sending up a few thousand particles of dust. "For the last time, I do *not* question everything you do!"

"April, I don't think you're really hearing Tad."

Once again I was rendered slack-jawed. My husband and my therapist were ganging up on me. What kind of dark hell had I stumbled into?

"The key words in Tad's statement were 'I feel,'" Harry continued. "In relationships it's often not always about what we do but how we make our partners feel. Tad feels like you're questioning his every move. Now, how does it make you feel to hear him say that?"

My eyes scanned the room, looking for the hidden camera. This had to be one of those reality show hoaxes. Any moment now an attractive man with a blindingly white smile would jump out and tell me that Tad and my new therapist were really a couple of professional actors hired to make my life a living hell for the amusement of the American people.

But if there was a cap-toothed host hiding in the wings he wasn't making an appearance, and Harry and Tad were waiting for me to respond.

I cleared my throat. "I think..."

Harry put a hand up to stop me. "Not I think," he corrected. "I feel."

I bit back a scream. I gave Harry a level look and then smiled demurely. "My bad." I took a stabilizing breath and turned my body so that I was facing Tad. "Tad, right now I *feel* like telling you to go fuck yourself."

Harry shook his head in disappointment. "I'm afraid that wasn't a very productive statement."

"I'm sorry, perhaps that was a bit narrow." I pushed my purse strap up on my shoulder and stood up. "How's this. I *feel* like telling you both to fuck off. Now, if you'll excuse me, I *feel* like storming out of here."

There was a shocked silence as I left the office. Caleb had been right, I shouldn't have picked a therapist out of the Yellow Pages. I mean, really, what did I know about this guy other than that he had an office that was close to my home? Of course, there was something to be said for that because now even if I didn't catch a bus I would only have to walk for fifteen minutes before arriving at my front door. In fact, a walk was just what the doctor ordered.

I went a block out of my way so that I could walk down Lake Street. Normally I love to dawdle in that neighborhood and I admire the beautiful architecture of the mansions that line the sidewalk, but today I chose the street for its lack of pedestrian traffic. The fewer people around me the better.

I stuffed my hands in my pockets as I marched toward a fog bank that had settled less than a mile ahead of me. How had Tad done it? How had he turned the therapy session around so that it was all about me and my issues rather than his and ours?

Unless the issues really were mine. I slowed my pace. Why had I reacted so violently? Was it because he had hit a nerve when he started talking about my mother? Had I allowed my feelings about her to affect my relationship with Tad? *Did* I question him too much?

I quickened my pace again. Now I was totally confused. I knew that Tad bore a lot of the responsibility for our marital problems, but maybe I needed to own up to my part, as well. Was it possible that I was driving him to do some of the things he was doing? I mean, if a therapist would side with him so quickly then surely some of his points must be valid.

I turned it all over in my mind as I completed my walk. I was somewhat relieved when I got home and found that Tad wasn't there yet. He was probably disappointed in me for walking out on our therapy session. *Good*, my little inner voice said. *Now he'll know what it's like to be let down by someone he loves.*

But maybe I had let him down before this. Maybe—

The phone rang, interrupting my thoughts. I put my hand on my chest in a pathetic attempt to rid it of the anxiety that was restricting my lung capacity. It was probably Tad, and I wasn't ready to talk to him.

"Nobody's home to take your call," Tad's recorded voice said over the answering machine, "but if you leave your name, number and a good time to reach you we promise to get back to you."

The machine beeped and then a male voice spoke. "Yo, April, you there? It's Jeremiah…"

I grabbed the phone with a little too much enthusiasm. "Hello?"

"Hey, you. I haven't heard from you since you ran out of Paul's crib. I just wanted to check and make sure everything was cool."

"Cool? Nothing is cool," I spat out before I was able to censor myself. "I'd say I was having the worst day of my life but there's been so much competition for that title that this day barely even makes it to my top ten."

"Whoa, slow down. What happened?"

"I lost my mind, that's what happened! I am in the middle of a nervous breakdown. Maybe it's my husband that's driven me to this point, but then again it might be my mother. That's how pathetic I've become, I can't even figure out who to use as a scapegoat!"

There was a long silence on the other end of the line. I realized that I was talking to a man who was in no way required to listen to my hysterics. I fell into the chair by the phone. Well, if Allie had been right about Tad being jealous, he certainly didn't have anything to worry about now. As soon as we hung up, Jeremiah would be calling the phone company and requesting to have a caller block put on my number.

"April, do you want me to come over?"

I was so surprised and relieved by his offer that I actually laughed out loud. "I thought I might have scared you away."

"Nah, I don't scare easy. Tell you what, I'm hanging with the guys right now, but we're done rehearsing for the day so I'll ditch them and come over."

"There's no need for you to ditch your friends. I guarantee that they're better company than I am right now."

"Now, why would I want to hang with a bunch of ugly dudes when I could offer a shoulder to a fine woman like yourself?"

"You're not trying to make a pass at a married woman, are you?" *Please God, let the answer be yes.*

"A pass? Nah, just trying to flesh out a fantasy." He laughed, and I could hear the voices of the other band members in the background. "Hey, I got an idea," he continued. "You don't have to go into work this afternoon, right?"

"No, I have the rest of the day off."

"Great, meet me at the Legion of Honor."

I wrinkled my brow. "Why?"

"You got to trust me on this. Just meet me at the front entrance in twenty-five minutes. There are times to question and times to go with the flow. Right now you need to be flowin'."

So it was unanimous. The entire world thought I questioned people too much. Fine, if they wanted me to flow, I'd flow. "I'll be there in twenty-five minutes."

Twenty minutes later I was standing in front of the white pillars that led into the Legion of Honor. It was definitely one of my favorite museums in the city. It had been built to resemble the Parisian eighteenth-century Palais de la Légion d'honneur and held works of art that ranged from ancient to modern. I looked wistfully at the view of the bay. It hadn't been far from here that Tad had proposed.

"There she is."

I turned around to see Jeremiah, Dallas, Gary and Paul walking up to me. Now I was really lost. "You *all* came?"

"Yeah, these guys needed a little culture and I figured you're the chick to give it to them."

"I'm sorry, but what precisely is it that you expect me to give them?"

"Precisely? Well, I would 'precisely' like you to give us a tour of the museum. You know, tell us about the art and the artists… Hell, the building itself looks pretty damn artsy. Is it supposed to look like it's from Ancient Greece or something?"

"Not exactly, it's neoclassical architecture, which basically means that it's the Renaissance era's interpretation of the architectural style of the Ancient Greek and Romans. Neoclassicism was very popular during the reign of Napoleon."

"See, we're already learning shit and we haven't even walked in the door. Aren't we, guys?"

The rest of the band offered their agreement and encouragement.

I shook my head. "I don't know about this."

"So—" Paul stepped up from his place in back "—are you saying that this building is a copy of a copy?"

And that's all it took. I went into a full spiel about neoclassicism and the inspiration for the Legion of Honor, and then I promptly took them into the courtyard and showed them Rodin's *Thinker*. We stepped inside, and to my surprise the guys paid their own way and mine and I continued the tour in the Ancient Art room. I even looked a little like a tour guide since I was the only one in the group not wearing jeans. As we approached each new piece of art I got a little more enthusiastic and the guys turned out to be a great audience. It was obvious that they knew nothing about art, but they knew what they liked and they were clearly caught up in my explanations about the history of the works as well as the tidbits I gave them about the artists themselves. By the time we got to the European paintings of Wateau and Matisse, we had picked up a few stray visitors who wanted to join the party. And by the time we reached the room holding the more modern works, our group had grown from five to eleven.

And I was happy. Really, really happy, like I hadn't been since I had sat in my college art classes learning the information I was now teaching. The earlier events of the day faded into oblivion. Who cared about my unresolved childhood issues? Who cared about my husband's felonious acts? We had the works of Rodin to admire! What more could anyone need?

Eventually I called an end to the tour and the guys and I stepped outside where we were greeted by a rose-tinted sky filled with fluffy pink clouds. I beamed at Jeremiah. "Thank you, thank you for helping me find my sanity."

Jeremiah just looked at me for a moment, then turned to the rest of the group. "You guys go ahead. I'll catch up with you later."

Paul, Dallas and Gary made a few hasty goodbyes and then left Jeremiah and me standing alone in front of the courtyard.

"You took separate cars?" I asked.

"Yeah, for some reason no one ever wants to ride in my Suzuki."

I laughed and pulled my hair away from my face. "I was serious about what I said. You really saved me today."

"Nah." Jeremiah's lips moved into a Mona Lisa-type smile. "You saved yourself. That's the only way to do it, you know."

I couldn't think of a response to that so I smiled stupidly at the ground.

Jeremiah nodded, as if reacting to something that I had not said. "I'll let you have some alone time so you can sort out your thoughts. You call me if you need me, okay?"

"Okay," I whispered.

"Day or night, don't matter what time it is," Jeremiah continued as he walked backward away from me. "Just think of my number as a twenty-four-hour hotline."

"Let me guess," I called after him. "No matter what time I call you'll still be hot."

Jeremiah pointed to me and then his nose to confirm my assessment of the situation. Then he turned around and went off to his car in the parking lot.

As I watched Jeremiah's car drive off into the distance I had a sudden urge to wave him down and ask him to run away with me. The problem was that I wasn't sure what I was attracted to, Jeremiah or just the idea of running away.

My eyes traveled to a clump of bushes about twenty feet from the Legion's entrance. I was all too familiar with what lay behind those bushes and I desperately wanted to avoid it. But as usual, I had to look. I walked over to the area and went down the somewhat concealed curving stone staircase. There it was—San Francisco's Holocaust Memorial.

A pile of colorless stone bodies lay on top of one another. I swallowed and allowed myself to look at the only standing statue with his back to the carnage. He was staring blankly out a barbed-wire fence. The sculptor had not used any color; the engraved quotes about a brighter future were up the stairs and out of sight. This was simply the depiction of despair in its rawest form.

The lights that surrounded the memorial had already been turned on in preparation for nightfall. It gave the whole thing an eerie glow that made the muscles in my neck tense. It was as if the bodies lying before me really had once contained life and the figure standing with his back to them really had forgotten what it was to hope.

How had Bobe survived it? How did you go on after such persecution? I unwillingly imagined what it would have been like. I visualized being forced to stand by while my mother and Bobe were humiliated, tortured and murdered. And Tad, how would I have dealt with the loss of him?

Of course, Tad wasn't Jewish. He might have been able to dissociate himself from me and live a rich life among the other Aryans, but in my heart I knew he wouldn't have. Tad would have done whatever he possibly could to protect me, even if it meant putting himself in mortal danger. The last few months had forced me to appreciate the fact that there were a lot of things about Tad that I didn't know, but I knew *that*, and *that* was the important part.

I looked at the bodies again. I didn't have problems. Hell, compared to the people who'd had to go through this, I was living a utopian existence. He lied to me about a credit card and the amount of our rent, so what? He had been there for me when I miscarried our baby even after I had confessed to the horrible feelings I had been concealing from him. And when my mother refused to come to our wedding, who had been there for me? Tad. There were a lot of women out there who would give their left arm to be with a man like that. A man who wanted to take care of them and hold them close at night. A man who would love them.

And who had been the one to storm out of the therapy session when things got tough? That would be me, the worst wife in the world. My God, a few minutes ago I had actually been tempted to run off with Jeremiah. Was I one of those grass-is-always-greener girls?

I turned around and walked back up the stairs, determined to be satisfied with what I had. I would start by making up with Tad. As for Dawson's, I knew that the last few years of working on the sales floor had drained me of the ability to be an upbeat or even a fully effective manager, but I had an easy out: approach Blakely and push for the promotion she had once dangled in front of me. The buying office would be new enough to keep me as close to satisfied as I needed to be. And last, but certainly not least, I would cross Jeremiah out of my address book. After all, the best way to resist temptation was to avoid it.

I turned around and took one last look at the Legion of Honor. It was also lit up, but unlike the Holocaust Memorial, the museum looked glorious and beckoning. For a brief instant I felt overwhelmed with a sense of longing for what might have been, but then I quickly turned my thoughts to Bobe. She had been through so much and now all she wanted was for me to be happy, and I was needlessly failing her. I had the ingredients for happiness. All I had to do was make something out of them.

When I returned home I was disappointed to see that Tad wasn't there. He had probably gone back to work. Or maybe he just didn't want to face me. Couldn't blame him for that—I didn't want to face me, either.

Finally, at a quarter after twelve, he showed up. I was sprawled out on the sofa when he walked into the living room. We studied each other silently for a minute or so before I finally found the nerve to say something.

"I'm sorry." I was surprised how steady my voice was when I said it. Perhaps all those hours of practicing had been helpful. "I'm sorry I acted like such a bitch."

I stood up and Tad crossed the room to me. He smoothed my hair with his hand. "I was worried about you," he said. "I know how painful it is for you to talk about your mother. You shouldn't have to do that in front of a stranger."

Well, then maybe he shouldn't have brought it up. But I suppressed the urge to say so and continued with my apology. "I shouldn't have stormed out like that. It was childish, to say the least. I know that I make it hard sometimes."

Tad's fingers were now gently caressing my neck. "I don't mind fighting for you occasionally, even if you're the one I'm fighting with. After all—" he swept me off my feet and held me princess style in his arms "—if we don't fight, we can't make up."

"Tad, I'm not finished with my apology," I protested as he carried me to the bedroom.

"Let me make it easy for you. You are now officially forgiven." He laid me down on the bed and pressed his body on top of mine. His lips nibbled at my earlobe. "My God, I love the way you taste."

And I loved being tasted. But I had more to say, and I wasn't going to let him distract me. "Tad, you're not blameless, either. You lied to me and you betrayed me."

He stopped nibbling and rolled over to the side so that he was next to me. "I never betrayed you." There was an icy tone to his voice that caused me to scoot a little farther away from him.

"Forging my name on a credit card and hiding our lease agreement from me was a betrayal, Tad."

He seemed to relax again and lifted my shirt enough so that his fingers could play over the waistline of my shorts. "I would consider those acts more like omissions of the truth. But just because two people pronounce the word *tomato* differently doesn't mean we should call the whole thing off. Besides, I'm never going to keep anything from you again."

I put my hand on top of his to keep him from pulling down my shorts. "I want to believe you. I can't tell you how much I want that."

"It's not hard, April. All you have to do is let go and have some faith in us."

It sounded so simple. Could it be? I studied his face and he looked so sincere and so incredibly trustworthy. "Don't let me down, Tad."

"Never." His hand freed itself from mine and in one smooth movement he removed my shorts.

Cuddled into the crook of Tad's arm, I had to admit to myself that making up had some major advantages over holding a grudge. I toyed with the hairs on his chest and his arm tightened around me. "You know," I said quietly, "that therapy session was beneficial in some ways."

"I'm not sure you can call fifteen minutes of arguing in some guy's office a session."

I cringed with embarrassment. "God, I was so awful."

"No, you—"

"Yes, I was, and I learned from that. I know now that I have some issues of my own that I have to work out."

"Just because you became defensive when asked to talk about your life in front of a stranger…"

"I didn't just become defensive. I paid some poor guy eighty dollars so that I could sit in his office and tell him to go fuck himself. Now, if that isn't evidence of some deep-seated issues, I don't know what is."

"Where are you going with this?" Tad's fingers were beginning to dig into my arm and I winced and pulled away.

"For one thing I'm going to start being happy with my life. I spend more time developing my fantasies about being a curator than I do developing my real career at Dawson's. Well, that stops now."

Tad propped himself up on his elbow and looked at me quizzically. "I know I told you that there were some problems at SMB but they're working themselves out. We're going to be a huge success soon, so if you're still harboring a desire to pursue some kind of art administration job then there's no reason why you shouldn't go back to school and do it. You don't need to work."

I felt my heart do a little flip-flop. Just hearing Tad tell me that my dreams were obtainable made me feel dizzy. I searched his face; he meant what he said. He was willing to support me both financially and emotionally while I went for a Ph.D. For a split second I had a vision of myself back at Berkeley, sitting in the middle of a classroom the size of a small theater, my pen scribbling shorthand with a textbook open to one of Manet's paintings. Then the reality of my situation came crashing around me. I could learn to overlook Tad's faults, but trusting him to support us was a whole different thing. We were over eleven thousand dollars in debt, we had a rent that was just a little less than my current monthly income and there was a big difference between "going to be huge" and actually *being* huge.

I tried to keep the disappointment from showing on my face. I couldn't tell Tad why taking him up on his offer was an impossibility. He would see it as an expression of my lack of faith in his abilities. I would have to find a way of declining while maintaining the delicate reconciliation that we had just established.

You're playing politics, my little voice said, *just like you do at work*. But I buried the thought. I wasn't doing anything that millions of wives hadn't done for centuries before me. I ran my hand across his collarbone in order to give myself an excuse for focusing my gaze on something other than his eyes. "I think it would be better if I worked in the buying office for a while before completely giving up on Dawson's. Who knows? Maybe I'll love it. I'm going to give Blakely another month. If she hasn't handed me the promotion by then, I'll approach her. If Blakely really is going to let Cherise go, I'm going to make sure that I'm the one to take her place."

Tad traced my jawline with his index finger. "Beautiful, ambitious and smart—I knew there was a reason why I married you."

"I'm also going to forgive my mother."

Tad immediately withdrew his finger. "We talked about this."

"What if you were right? What if my issues with my mother are keeping me from being happy in all the other areas of my life?"

"You don't need her, April. You never did."

"You're wrong, but this isn't about needing *her* anyway. It's about needing to be emotionally stable. I think what I need to do is let her back into my life without taking on all her excess baggage."

"Meaning?"

"Meaning that I've got to let her back into my life and at the same time accept that fact that she is deeply flawed and stop taking everything so personally. You were right when you said that my mother's absence at our wedding had nothing to do with me. It really was about her, and I need to accept that and let it go."

He looked less than convinced, so I pulled out the heavy artillery. "Tad, I had to do the same thing in order to work things out with you." He winced and I quickly qualified the statement. "Not that you're deeply flawed, but you did mess up and I had to let go of my anger in order to move forward with you, just like you did for me. Now it's Mom's turn to be forgiven."

Tad eyed me warily. "The two situations are completely different." He slid back down and wrapped a lock of my hair around his finger. "Just think about it for a while before you call her."

"I haven't spoken to her for over four months now. How much longer do you want me to think about it?"

"Give it another month," he said, and let his foot rub up and down my calf. "What difference will four more weeks make? You have other things that you should be focusing on now, like getting your career back on track. Wouldn't it be nice to have all your ducks in a row before tackling the more difficult problems?"

"True," I said reluctantly.

"Between dealing with Blakely and making time for all you need to handle at home…"

"What do I need to handle at home?"

Tad grinned wickedly as he took my hand and pulled it down beneath the sheets.

"Oh, *that*." I giggled. "That *is* a lot to handle…I better get on it right away."

TWENTY

"God, I wish this place served hard liquor."

I looked up and smiled at Allie as she dropped into the seat I had been saving for her at Boudin. Almost a month had passed since that fateful therapy session and I had been working overtime trying to be satisfied with what I had. Apparently I wasn't the only one failing in that area.

I took the chicken Caesar I had purchased for her off the tray and pushed it toward her. "Problem customer?"

She scoffed and violently rammed her fork into a crouton. "I caught two people having sex in one of my dressing rooms."

"Again?" I wrinkled my nose in disgust. "Why do they always pick your department?"

"Who the fuck knows? Maybe they think that any lingerie department that charges twenty dollars for a thong must really be a front for a low-priced brothel." She pressed her fingers into her temples.

I sighed. It really was amazing that I had lasted as long as I had at Dawson's. But things would be better when I got into the buying office. They had to be. "Why do you do it, Allie?" I asked, rotating my plastic spoon in my soup. "You're educated, smart and all that good stuff. Why do you work at that freak show we call Dawson's?"

"Three words—*thirty-three percent discount*. Although after what I put up with today they should be upping mine to forty." She took a long sip of her 7-Up. "Hey, thanks for buying lunch. I know I've been a little removed lately, but I've had a lot on my plate."

She'd been removed? I had barely made time to talk to either her or Caleb since Tad and I reconciled. I had avoided Caleb because he knew too much. He always had questions about Tad, and whenever I told him things were fine he gave me what Allie and I called the "I-don't-think-so-girlfriend" look. I had avoided Allie because I was afraid that if she spent any time with me she would be able to see that under my practiced smile I was really falling apart. But perhaps I'd been so busy avoiding Allie that I hadn't noticed that she was also avoiding me for her own reasons. It's always humbling to know that you're not the center of the universe. "Is everything okay?" I asked before tearing at the edge of my bread bowl.

"Oh, you know, same old same old. My sister just had her fifth anniversary, although judging from the party she threw, you would have thought it was her fiftieth. And you know my family, every time we get together the interrogation begins. 'So, Allie, any new marital prospects? Are you dating anyone?' My brothers' wives are always trying to set me up, and then my bothers find out and go ballistic because in their minds no one is good enough for their little sister. And then there's my mother who wants to make sure that I'm not out there giving away the milk for free. I'm twenty-seven, April. If I hadn't given the milk away by now it would have gone sour."

I laughed politely but I couldn't help feeling envious. Allie had a family full of people who wanted to look out for her. Maybe their tactics needed a little refining but it was still a lot better than not having family support at all—which, I reminded myself, was not my situation. I had Tad and Bobe, plus I had a new pair of CK boots that were almost like family.

Allie sighed, oblivious to my internal monologue. "I really don't see what everybody's so worried about. I'll meet someone, right?"

I lowered my spoon, surprised by the insecurity in Allie's voice. "Of course you'll meet someone. Besides, I thought you were dating that guitarist guy, Paul."

"Yeah, but I can tell that one's not going anywhere. I know my soul mate's out there somewhere. I always wanted to marry before thirty and I can still make that happen."

"Of course you can!" I smiled encouragingly. I had never heard Allie talk about marriage. She had always seemed so content with single life I had just assumed that she was going to be a confirmed bachelorette until she was at least forty. After all, dancing on top of the bars at nightclubs didn't seem like the behavior of a woman who was looking for a husband.

"And look at how it all fell into place for you and Tad," Allie added. "You met, started dating and six months later you were man and wife, so if I use your relationship as an example, then I shouldn't have to worry about finding Mr. Wonderful until I'm twenty-nine and a half."

I looked away. Although things with Tad were better, I wasn't sure anyone should use my relationship as an example. Nonethe-less, the fact that she was envious of me just confirmed my decision to be thankful for everything.

As if on cue Tad rang my cell phone. I held up a finger to indicate to Allie that I would only be a moment and pressed the Talk button. "What's up?"

"We landed another client—a big one, April."

"Tad, that's fantastic!"

"You have no idea. By the fifteenth of next month I'll have made enough money to pay off the credit card with enough left over to buy you a little something special at Tiffany's."

I laughed. "Just pay off the card and I'll be happy."

"This is just the beginning. In another year I should be making well over two hundred thousand a year, and a few years after that, who knows? We could be looking at millions."

I bit gently down on my tongue. Tad was getting ahead of himself again. But still, if he thought he was going to be making two hundred grand then surely he'd be able to pull off a hundred and twenty. That was enough to keep financial issues from causing undue stress on our relationship even if he did charge up the occasional credit card. "I'm thrilled for you, Tad."

"Don't be thrilled for me, be thrilled for us. We're going straight to the top. Sean or Eric won't be getting in my way now. We are going to be rolling in it."

There was something in Tad's attitude that disturbed me but I suppressed my instinct to analyze it. I reminded myself to stop questioning everything and go with the flow. I looked up to see Allie watching me inquisitively.

"Tad, I've got to get going. Maybe we can celebrate tonight?"

"I'm going to be working late tonight, maybe even after

midnight. I have to make sure that this new account is handled perfectly. You understand?"

"Of course," I assured him. "We'll celebrate tomorrow. Oh wait, don't you have that business trip to L.A. tomorrow?"

"No, that's the day after. Tomorrow night's ours."

"Sounds good. I'll call your office when I'm done with work."

"Why don't I call you instead? After six I'm having my incoming calls automatically forwarded to voice mail so I can concentrate."

I gave Allie an apologetic smile. I made a gesture with my hands to imitate Tad's run-on of the mouth. "Fine, you call me. But now I've got to go."

"I understand. I love you, April. I don't think I would have been motivated to do any of this if you weren't a part of my life."

"I'm not sure that's true, but I'm not stupid enough to spend a lot of time convincing you otherwise. I'll talk to you later."

I hung up and returned my phone to my purse.

"What was that all about?" Allie asked before polishing off the last bites of her bread roll.

"Oh, Tad just landed another big client. He seems to think that he's on his way to being the next Bill Gates."

"Men and their egos. If they couldn't brag about their cars, bank accounts, sexual prowess or athletic ability they wouldn't know how to maintain a conversation." She patted the corner of her mouth with her napkin. "Speaking of careers, how're things going with Blakely? Any more word on your imminent promotion?"

"Actually I was planning on going to Blakely's office right after this to make sure that I'm still her favored candidate."

Allie arched an eyebrow. "I didn't know that was in question— Wait, did that little bitch Gigi tell her that you were preg—"

"I have no idea what Gigi told her," I said quickly. "It's just that Blakely hasn't been by the department for a while and I'm beginning to think that something's changed…but maybe not." I shrugged. "Whatever the case may be, the time has come for me to pucker up and get promoted. If I'm going to stay at Dawson's, then I might as well have a higher-paying job."

Allie slid her straw up and down in the lid of her drink. "Just watch out for Gigi. I'm telling you, that one has claws."

"Maybe…it seems like she's been behaving differently around me since she found those vitamins, but then again she's been Miss Congeniality today. She's working the closing shift and she waltzed in two hours early and presented me with a double latte. She even offered to watch the floor so I could enjoy my beverage in peace. As far as I know, nothing's changed at work, so it stands to reason that her attitude is being affected by some outside source."

Allie smiled. "Maybe she got lucky last night. Can you imagine Gigi having sex?" Allie flipped her hair and batted her eyes. "Ohmygawd," she squealed in an exaggerated impersonation of Gigi. "Your penis is, like, so totally big! Oh and FYI, this month's *Details* says that adult circumcisions are all the rage—you should so totally do it."

I willed myself to swallow my Diet Coke before erupting into peels of laughter.

I knocked on Blakely's door tentatively at first and then with some force. Clearly I could no longer assume that I was a shoo-in for the promotion, so if I wanted it I would have to exude a contagious level of confidence.

Blakely opened the door. She shared the office with the junior-wear buyer, but she and her assistant appeared to be out.

Cherise wasn't there either, which meant that Blakely had probably sent her to another store to check up on some poor unsuspecting manager. My timing couldn't have been more perfect.

Blakely raised an eyebrow at me and offered a closed-lip smile that was so devoid of warmth that she might as well have just cut to the chase and given me the finger.

"Shouldn't you be on the sales floor, April?"

I tried not to let her see how much her greeting had cut me. "Gigi's on the floor and I'm at the tail end of my break." That was a lie; my break had ended fifteen minutes ago but what she didn't know wouldn't hurt me. "I was hoping you had a moment."

Blakely nodded curtly and motioned for me to enter. I waited for her to sit in her chair before finding one for myself. I selected Cherise's. After all, I was beginning to suspect that it would be my only chance to sit in it.

Blakely checked her watch and I decided I should get straight to the point just in case she was timing me.

"Blakely, I've come to talk to you about the assistant position."

"Ah, so you heard about Cherise. That was fast."

It took me all of two seconds to gauge her meaning. "You fired her today."

"She should have cleaned out her desk immediately, but she got emotional and ran out. If she doesn't get her things by the end of the day I'll let Housekeeping take care of it."

Was she kidding? Who the hell was this woman, the Bride of Frankenstein? On second thought, she wasn't good enough for Frankenstein; she lacked his humanity. I kept my gaze firmly on Blakely so I wouldn't inadvertently glimpse the family pictures on Cherise's desk. "Well, I'm sorry Cherise didn't work out, but I'm very excited about the opportunity—"

"You're welcome to apply for the position, April, but you should know that I am also considering Nina from 547."

The bleached-blond Latina chick; I should have seen that one coming. But I couldn't give up at this point. If Nina's promotion was a done deal, Blakely would have said so immediately. She never chose to drag things out when the alternative was to stab someone in the heart and be done with it. I took a deep breath. "Nina is a very good manager," I said in my best interview voice. "However, as I'm sure you're aware, my numbers have been consistently better than hers.…"

"Marginally," Blakely said. "And you have location on your side. When you consider that her store is in an area where the majority of the local residents have recently been laid off, her ability to keep up with your successes speaks greatly in her favor."

True. That was the problem with Blakely, she was too reasonable—hateful bigots should always be unreasonable, otherwise they risk screwing up a perfectly good stereotype.

I cleared my throat and started again. "You're right, I do have location on my side and working at the flagship store has given me insights into what Sassy and Dawson's is all about, insights I wouldn't have gotten if I was working at 547."

Blakely studied me carefully. I'm pretty certain that Blakely won all the staring contests in grade school. She crossed her legs carefully so as not to wrinkle her D&G skirt. "I have known that I needed to let Cherise go for some time now, long before I spoke to you about it. I have simply been biding my time until I found a suitable candidate to replace her— No, I take that back." Blakely held an index finger up as if to check herself. "I was looking for someone who was more than suitable. I needed someone exemplary. After watching you for a few months I decided that you were that person. You are a wonderful merchandiser and you have a fantastic eye. Your personal sales are mediocre but that doesn't concern me. I am one of the few people at Dawson's who recognizes that good salesmanship is not a necessity for buying."

I hated it when Blakely made herself seem superior to her peers, and I hated it more when the reasons she gave to support that attitude held up.

"But things have changed," Blakely continued. "Now I think that you may need this promotion more than I need you."

A little spark of anger ignited inside me and I struggled to keep it concealed. "I do want this promotion, Blakely, but if I don't get it I'm happy to continue to hone my skills while managing Sassy."

Blakely shook her head, her eyes never leaving mine. "You won't last much longer on the sales floor. You're slipping, April, and it's only a matter of time before Liz decides to pull the rug out from under you."

"Liz has been very happy with me lately," I snapped.

"She's happy with your department and she's happy with Gigi, but with you?" Blakely raised an eyebrow. "Ever since you got engaged you've been noticeably distracted. I suppose that's normal, but the problem's gotten worse instead of better. Your heart's not in it. I'm not sure it ever really was, but you always managed to hide it well. Now it's obvious, particularly when your enthusiasm is held in comparison to Gigi's."

"So this is about Gigi," I said through gritted teeth. Fucking Napoleonette, someone ought to send the bitch to Corsica.

Blakely gave me another one of her cold smiles. "Gigi is the only reason you've made it this far without being spoken to." She leaned forward. "You know, April, you're not as perceptive as you think you are."

The spark had grown into a full-blown wildfire. "Oh, really?" I asked sweetly. "Well, I know why you fired Cherise."

Now Blakely looked amused. "And why would that be?"

"Because she's black," I shot back, and then gasped, immediately realizing how much that slip of the tongue was going to cost me. I had just completely screwed up any chance I had of being promoted. I briefly entertained the idea of backpedaling but it was hopeless. And if it was hopeless I might as well lay it all out on the table.

I sat up a little straighter and squared my shoulders. "You and I both know it's true, and please don't bother pointing out that Nina and I are minorities, too, because in your mind we're different. Unlike Nina and me, Cherise acts black. She peppers her speech with what I'm sure you consider ghetto slang," I said, moving closer to the edge of my chair. "She has braids, and she's the first one to say something whenever she sees Dawson's security team resorting to racial profiling—which you probably think the company would be grateful for, considering that Dawson's has had to settle out of court over that issue God only knows how many times. But the point is she has a little too much flavor to fit into your lily-white view of the world, so you fired her and now you're trying to replace her with a female version of Colin Powell."

Blakely leaned back in her chair as if considering what I had said. Finally she focused her attention on me again. Nothing in her appearance indicated that I had hit any kind of nerve or even fazed her. "If you're asking if I like Cherise personally, the answer is no."

I hadn't been asking that or anything else but it was nice of her to confirm my assertions. Maybe Cherise and I could get together and file a nice little class action suit.

"However," Blakely continued, "my decision to get rid of her had nothing to do with personal feelings. It's the way the people I work for feel about her that bothered me. An assistant's job is to make her immediate supervisor look good. Cherise can't do that because of the way she is. I suppose you would call that institutionalized racism, but it's much simpler than that. It's just politics."

I felt my heart pick up the pace. I had an inkling that Blakely was on to something and that scared me.

Blakely waved away a small fly with her well-manicured hand. "There's a certain kind of person that the Dawson's powers that be respond to. There's a Dawson's personality-type spectrum. Gigi is on one end—the good end, and Cherise is on the other. In other words, Cherise is not one of us and she never will be."

"And I am?" I asked. For some reason I didn't find the thought comforting.

"You could be. I've seen you fake it before and that's all that's really necessary. Wave an occasional pom-pom at an Appreciation Meeting and tell Liz that the new merchandise is 'to die for' and you're in. It was a learned behavior for me but I've mastered it and, when necessary, I can cheer with the best of them. Every company has its own religion, so to speak. You either convert or you need to move on."

The room went silent. I recognized that Blakely had asked me an unspoken question, but I wasn't sure how to respond. Could I convert? To some degree I already had, but not entirely, and as Blakely pointed out I was quickly losing my ability to fake it. Faking a personality type was a lot harder than faking an orgasm, although in this case the level of enthusiasm expected of me was about the same.

"I meant it when I said you have a good eye, April." Blakely's voice had taken on a coaxing tone that I hadn't heard from her before. "You could be an asset to this office. You just need to put aside whatever has been distracting you and focus your energy on being the kind of person who succeeds here."

I *had* been too wrapped up in the chaos going on in my own life. But that wasn't a good excuse, because Dawson's was supposed to be my life and it wasn't. I wasn't sure I wanted it to be.

"Think about it," Blakely said. "If you can mold yourself to fit the company then I would be thrilled to offer you the job."

"I'll think about it." I rose to my feet and walked out of her office and down to the sales floor.

I stood in the middle of my department and tried to come to grips with what had just happened. Blakely basically told me that she was willing to give me what I wanted. But there was a price to pay, and it was terrifyingly high.

TWENTY-ONE

"Are you kidding?" Allie squealed. "Take it! I would put on a pleated skirt and do backflips in a second if I thought it would get me into the buying office."

She, Caleb and I had gone to our favorite North Beach bar and were currently rehashing the day's events over a round of lemon drops.

Caleb shot Allie a withering look. "You're not April." He rubbed his finger against the sugar that was rimming his glass. "Allie told me earlier that Tad's income has increased. Is that right?"

I nodded. "That's the word on the street."

Caleb watched a young Puerto Rican man in a marginally sheer shirt scoot past our table. "Are you sure that it's enough to cover all of Tad's…expenses?"

Allie gave him a funny look and I kicked him under the table. "This last pay hike has taken care of all that." I still hadn't told Allie about all the financial stuff and I certainly wasn't prepared to get into it now. Besides, things were fine. Tad was still spending money like it grew on trees but apparently his company was a virtual orchard. Each one of his paychecks seemed to be a little bigger than the last and I often witnessed him write the checks to his various credit card companies so we weren't delinquent or anything. We weren't saving a lot but saving seemed to be a concept that was too complicated for most people under the age of thirty-five to grasp. In other words we were normal and that's all I ever asked for.

Caleb raised his glass and saluted the sheer-shirt guy who was now watching him from the bar. "In that case," he said without taking his eyes off his latest object of desire, "why don't you quit Dawson's and go back to school for your Ph.D.?"

Allie looked at Caleb like he was crazy. "But she doesn't want to do that anymore, do you, April?"

I downed my drink quickly and waved the waiter over again. "It's not practical, Caleb," I said after ordering my second drink. "Tad's business is really taking off now and if I truly wanted to be a curator of a major museum I'd have to be open to relocation…"

"You always say that," Caleb said impatiently. "Perhaps you haven't noticed but there are a few museums in San Francisco. There's this little place called the MOMA, and perhaps you've heard of the De Young, and—the Legion of Honor. And those are just the more famous places."

"Yeah, yeah, I get it," I snapped. "What do you suggest I do? Do you think I should abandon a perfectly decent job at a company where I have a promising future in favor of handing over tens of thousands of dollars to some university? Oh, and the fun doesn't stop there…" I shook my head vehemently. "Getting into a Ph.D. program is one thing, staying in it is a whole different ball game. And if I did graduate, then what? I still could end up a docent at some second-rate museum in the boondocks. Thank you but I think I'll stick with the road well traveled."

Allie's eyes widened. "Wait a minute, is that why you gave up on the curator thing? Because you don't believe in yourself?"

The waiter came back with my drink, along with another one for Allie and Caleb. Caleb shook his head. "We only ordered one drink."

"The gentleman at the bar bought you this round," the waiter said as he placed a glass in front of each of us.

We all turned toward the bar and the sheer-shirt guy waved. His eyes locked with Caleb's. A slow smile spread across Caleb's lips. "Allie, you talk some sense into April. I'm going to thank our new friend."

Allie leaned forward as Caleb left our table. "Seriously, April, let's review the situation here. Tad's doing well, right?"

"I guess," I hedged. "I need to figure out exactly how many more dollars a month this new client is going to mean to us."

"But assuming that it's a decent increase, this would be the ideal time for you to go back to school!"

"It's not that simple." I held out my fingers to check off my points of objection. "There are a lot of things you have to do before you get accepted into a Ph.D. program. I'd have to take the GRE, and many programs require you to speak another language...."

"But you speak French, right?"

I held up my cocktail. "Only after three martinis. Otherwise my French is completely incomprehensible."

Allie wrinkled up her nose in wonder and amusement. "Are you serious?"

I finished the remains of my cocktail in one swig. "*Absolument.*"

Allie giggled and slapped her hand on the table. "I love it. Well, would you be comfortable going into an interview drunk?"

"Would you be comfortable leaving a bar sober?"

"Point taken. Oh, I know!" She threw up her hands as if to imply that she had just had a major stroke of genius. "I went out with this marine once—he was Intelligence or something. Anyway, he was here for some summer language program that they had through Berkeley, five days a week, five hours a day of full immersion. If it's good enough for 'the few and the proud' it's got to be good enough for the drunken wannabe bilinguals."

I shook my head and then abruptly stopped when I realized that the objects in the room were beginning to blur together. "I can't do a five-day-a-week program… Besides, even if I did, three months isn't enough…"

"If you can speak when you're drunk then you can speak sober, too—you just need a little confidence and a refresher course. So quit Dawson's, get yourself some weekend volunteer work at the De Young or something and start preparing for graduate school."

"I can't ask Tad to support me," I mumbled. I had drunk those lemon drops way too fast.

"Why not? This is the big benefit of being married. Right now Tad is living his dreams so why shouldn't you get to live yours?"

Good question. I looked over at Caleb, who was now toying with sheer-shirt guy's buttons. I used to really enjoy picking up men. I liked that initial feeling of anticipation and animal attraction. I gave that up for marriage, which was fine, but there was supposed to be a trade-off and maybe this was it. And wasn't it just a month ago that Tad had tentatively suggested that I go back to school?

I felt the flutters of excitement creep inside my stomach. "I'm going to talk to Tad tonight and find out where we are financially."

"And if finances are good?"

"Then you may have to find another person to complain to during Dawson's Appreciation Meetings."

Tad was true to his word and didn't return home until close to 1:00 a.m. He did a little double take when he came in and found me awake and cross-legged on the couch doodling in my sketchbook.

"Why did you wait up?" he asked. I looked up at him in surprise. He sounded inexplicably defensive. Maybe he thought I had waited up so that I could question his latest success, which wasn't far from the truth. I would have to proceed carefully.

I put my paper and pencil down on the coffee table and stood up to give him a hug. "You smell like wine and pesto," I commented as I kissed the corner of his mouth.

"Yeah—" he returned my embrace but with little enthusiasm "—I ordered dinner from Calzones and you know how I can never eat Italian without a glass or two of Chianti."

I pulled back a little. "They delivered a bottle of Chianti?" I asked. "Can they do that?"

"I went down the block and got a bottle at the liquor store." He pushed me away. "What the hell is this, the Spanish Inquisition?"

"No, I was just wondering." I wasn't going to get in an argument over this. "Tad, I am just so excited about this new deal you landed."

That seemed to soften him up. "This is just the beginning, too. I'm going to make a fortune, April." He smiled and pulled his tie off, then wrapped it around his hand only to quickly unwrap it again. "Our future is going to be filled with all the things we ever wanted—new cars, boats, expensive jewelry for my beautiful wife." He put a hand on the outside of my arms and gave me a gentle shake, no longer able to contain his mounting enthusiasm. "I'm telling you, in a few years the sky will be the limit, so start making your wish list now."

This was my moment of opportunity. "I wish that I could go back to school."

Tad's grip loosened as he stared at me in surprise.

"I know what I said last month," I said quickly, "and I know it's a long shot. Berkeley has a good Ph.D. program but they require that candidates be fluent in one of the romance languages, which I'm not. They're offering a language course this summer, and if I just found a weekend sales job somewhere, or something that allowed me to start my shift late in the day, then I could take it." I stopped long enough to catch my breath and continued, "Of course, even if I got my Ph.D. I might never land a curator job in the Bay Area. But I want you to know I wouldn't take a job in which we would have to relocate. Your business is here and that comes first—"

"Do it."

I blinked. "I'm sorry, did you say—"

"Quit your job at Dawson's and go back to school. You can make it happen, April. You're the smartest, most talented woman I've ever met in my life and we don't need the money from Dawson's anymore." Now he was grinning like the Cheshire cat. He walked over to the fireplace and then back to me. "Everything's going to be great. Better than great. All those people who've tried to hold us back, or didn't believe in us…we're going to show them, April. We're going to be on top and nothing can stop us."

That sounded suspiciously like the line the villains in the Batman movies always used, but I pushed aside the thought and focused on the issue at hand. "This is a really big decision, Tad. If I tell Liz I'm quitting, then that's it. I might be able to get rehired as a salesperson but it will be years before they let me manage again."

"April, listen to me!" He grabbed me by the shoulders. "You don't need to work there anymore!"

"Well, I wouldn't quit until I found a part-time job. I should be bringing in some kind of income just in case…"

I saw a dangerous cloud cross over Tad's face and I immediately amended my half-spoken sentence. "Just in case I got bored. I've been working since I was fifteen—longer if you count babysitting—and I wouldn't feel right if I wasn't making something."

The cloud dissipated and he laughed gently. "Far be it from me to stand between you and your need for financial independence. Hey, I have an idea. My admin, Cathy, is going to China next week to adopt a little girl. She's been looking for someone to share her job responsibilities so that she can leave early two or three days a week. Why don't you take the job?"

"You want me to work for you?" I asked doubtfully.

"It wouldn't be more than fifteen hours a week," he pointed out. "It's a fairly basic job, not exactly stimulating, but you'll be paid over twenty an hour and you'll have weekends off. That beats any retail-sales job you could line up."

Weekends off! My God, those had to be the most exciting words any man had ever said to me. But I had to think about this clearly. "There's one possible problem." I put my hand on his chest and pushed away from him so I was in a better position to meet his eyes. "If I took that job there's a very good chance that I would end up sleeping with the boss."

Tad flashed me a wolfish grin. "I would hope so."

"How would Eric and Sean feel about me working for you?"

"Eric's wife comes in every month to help us with filing and other stuff, so that won't be a problem." He placed a lock of hair behind my ear. "Tomorrow I'll tell them that in a few weeks you'll be coming in to assist. Cathy will be thrilled. Just remember that, for you, work is a choice, not a necessity. This last deal that I cut guarantees we'll be making upward of one hundred and eighty thousand this year."

I gasped. "Seriously?"

Tad nodded vigorously and gave me a loud kiss on the forehead. "Just wait, it will end up being more then ten times that, I promise. I'm telling you, I'm on top of my game."

I felt a little faint. Was I really doing this? Could I chuck everything I had worked for at Dawson's in order to chase the impossible dream just because Tad said we could afford it? What if he was wrong? What if we didn't make anywhere near that much? Of course he had used the word *guarantee*. He wouldn't have said that if he didn't mean it, right? I needed to stay calm; I had to make sure that Tad understood what he was agreeing to. "Tad, this is going to require a lot of sacrifices on both our parts. I'm going to have even less free time than I do now, and even if you're making a lot of money we're going to have to budget more. We should be cutting down on the expensive nights out, and—"

Tad's lips had moved to my mouth. He kissed me and then gently bit my lower lip. "You worry too much. We'll do whatever we need to in order to make this happen. Everything will be great." He worked his way to my shoulder. "You know, I was disappointed that I didn't have time to celebrate with you earlier," he murmured between kisses. "Maybe I can make it up to you now?"

He had already made it up to me one hundred and eighty

thousand times. I lifted my hands and let them run through his hair. Maybe we could have it all. Tad's business was obviously living up to its full potential, and if I could pursue a career as a curator... "Everything could be perfect," I whispered aloud.

Tad straightened up and gazed into my eyes. "April, it already is."

The next morning I went into work with a letter of resignation in my hand. Tad had been too amped to sleep so he had typed it up for me at three in the morning. He spent the rest of the night writing up new business objectives for SMB and waxing his car. When I woke up at six and found him sorting through old paint samples to help him determine what new color we should paint the bookshelves (that didn't need painting) I began to worry. But his restlessness was understandable. He was on the road to major success. I tried to imagine what it would be like to be a member of the Silicon Valley Multimillionaire Club. I had a hard time mentally casting myself in the role of socialite, but Tad helped fill out the fantasy: exotic vacations, beautiful houses furnished by Crate and Barrel and Pottery Barn (I'm aware that there are more prestigious brands but neither Tad nor I is familiar with them), a pool in the backyard and a fountain in the front. It would be the perfect palace for Cinderella and her prince to take up residence. Of course, these were still fantasies, but five to ten years down the road it could be our reality.

That morning while setting the floor, Dorita talked incessantly about all the details of her upcoming ten-day trip back to her boyfriend's hometown in Argentina. She was so excited about the adventure she didn't notice that my hands were shaking so much I could barely tie a scarf around a mannequin's neck. What I was about to do was so impulsive. I didn't really do impulsive—that was Tad's area. Of course, I did rush into marriage after only three plus months of dating, but once again the credit for that one really belonged to Tad.

Maybe I did need to slow down and think about this. I waited until the store opened before calling Caleb in Cosmetics.

"Well?" he asked as soon as he determined it was me. "Will we be needing reservations at the Bubble Lounge in the near future?"

"It seems I have access to a part-time office job and Tad says the money's there." I kept my voice hushed in case Dawson's version of the Secret Service had the register area bugged.

"Tad says the money's there," Caleb repeated slowly. I knew what he was thinking.

"You think I should wait?" I asked reluctantly. "Maybe I'll just see what the next paycheck looks like."

"No, do it now," Caleb said with new definitiveness. "I know you. Given forty-eight hours you'll have come up with forty-eight reasons why you shouldn't pursue your dreams. Go to Liz's office today and call it quits."

"And if the money isn't as good as Tad thinks it is?" I didn't want to go down that road, but this decision required some thought.

"You'll still be able to afford graduate school. You'll just have to start shopping at Payless."

"Bite your tongue!"

"Yeah, yeah, tell it to the starving children in Africa. Besides, if they're good enough for Star Jones they're good enough for you. Talk to Liz."

I felt my heart pound against my chest just at thinking about the conversation. "If this doesn't work, can I blame you?"

"Absolutely. I'll even blow up a picture of myself so you can use it for dart practice. Now, go get yourself unemployed."

I smiled and clutched the phone cord in my sweaty hand. "I really am doing this, aren't I?"

"At this very moment you're really *not* doing it, which is why I'm hanging up the phone. Call me when it's over."

I continued to keep the receiver pressed to my ear long after I heard the click. Putting it down meant that I had to move to the next step in my game plan.

"Are you all right?" I turned to see Dorita's doleful brown eyes looking up into mine with concern. "You look like you just survived a major earthquake."

I shook my head. "No, but I think I'm about to cause one."

I told Blakely first. The buyers she shared her office with were in, so she came down to my office in the interest of privacy. She stood next to my desk, her arms crossed confidently in front of her. "So I take it you've made your decision."

I cleared my throat and met her gaze. "Blakely, I want to thank you for being so honest with me. I know it was a risk. But you really opened my eyes to what it takes to make it in this company and helped me determine what my future is with Dawson's."

Blakely smiled. "So tell me about this Dawson's future of yours."

"I don't have one."

Blakely's smile froze in place.

"I can't be who they want me to be and so I've decided that it's time to move on." I had to struggle not to swoon as I said the words. "I'm turning in my two-week notice today. I wanted you to be the first to know."

Blakely's smile had now turned into a thin straight line. I

waited for her to throw out fifty reasons why what I was doing was idiotic.

She uncrossed her arms and smoothed the crinkles out of her blazer. "You're wasting my time."

And with that she strode out the door. I stood alone in my office, unsure of how I felt about that little exchange. Obviously I wasn't an employee worth fighting for. I ran my hand over the customer holds that Blakely had been so emotional about several months back. I had been single then, or at least unmarried. So much had changed in such a short time.

Gigi burst through the door, abruptly putting an end to my stroll down memory lane.

"Hi, April, what's up?"

"Hmm?" "What's up" isn't really an invitation to drop a major bomb.

"You okay? You seem, like…I don't know…nervous." Gigi removed her jacket and carefully hung it on a spare hanger.

"Well, I came to a major realization." I lifted my chin up and offered her a quivering smile. "Actually, it concerns you."

Gigi dropped the hanger. She looked down at her coat that was now splayed across her feet as if she was unsure of where it came from. "Um, like, what did you realize about me that would make you upset?"

I let out a shaky laugh. "No, that's not what I meant. The only realization I've come to about you is that you're a better manager than I am, which is one of the reasons I met with Blakely earlier."

Gigi exhaled audibly and quickly retrieved her jacket. "Okay, sorry…I just thought I had done something wrong by mistake. You know I try to give one-hundred-and-ten percent and all but even I have my 'oops' moments and… Wait, you decided I was a better manager so you went to see Blakely? I don't get it." She wrinkled her perfect brow and perched herself on top of her desk.

"Gigi, when you found those prenatal vitamins, what did you conclude?"

Gigi looked understandably thrown by the change in topic. "What did I…um—"

"What did you think, about why I had them?" I clarified.

"I know what *conclude* means." Gigi's eyes narrowed. "I *concluded* that you were preggers."

I looked down at the floor, unable to meet her eyes. "You know…I'm not. Not anymore."

Gigi crossed and uncrossed her legs at the ankles. "Yeah, I kind of figured that out. I am, like, so totally sorry about that. I mean, it is just so totally unfair…"

"Did you tell Blakely?"

Gigi's eyes widened in surprise. "No!"

"No what? No you didn't tell her I was pregnant, or no you didn't tell her I miscarried."

"None of it. Like, Blakely is the last person I'd tell!" Gigi tossed her hair behind her shoulders. "You know, people always assume that I can't keep a secret just because I'm, like, so totally chatty, but it's completely untrue. If a secret's important enough I'll totally take it to the grave."

"I saw you talking to Blakely right after you found the vitamins."

"Is that what you thought we were talking about? You so should have asked me! I just figured that with you being preggers I needed to work extra hard to get you into the assistant-buying chair before you started to, like, you know, show." She whispered the word *show* as if she was articulating the name of a particularly loathsome venereal disease.

I didn't say anything. My eyes traveled to her desk. She had decorated the bulletin board in front of it with pictures of her and her friends, along with pictures from various magazine layouts, and a few ticket stubs from a Christina Aguilera concert. A small mirror was propped up next to a pink unicorn Beanie Baby whose legs were sprawled out in a manner that suggested he had just been dropped from a ten-story building. There was nothing personal on my desk. I had never bothered to make it my own.

"I'm going to recommend to Liz that you be my replacement. You'll make a great Sassy manager."

Gigi jumped to her feet and pulled me to mine. "Ohmygawd, ohmygawd, ohmygawd! You got promoted! I knew it! I heard a rumor that Blakely had let Cherise go, and really, who could blame her, and then I just knew you would end up with her job. Ohmygawd, this is, like, so totally awesome! Can we tell yet? Or is it a secret because as you know, I can totally keep—"

"I'm quitting."

Gigi dropped my hands. "You're…"

"Quitting." I sank back down into my chair. "I'm just not cut out for this. I need a fresh start somewhere else, where I have a better understanding of the corporate religion."

"Corporate religion…" Gigi's voice trailed off. She was clearly not as interested in understanding my obscure reference as she was in trying to grasp the overall implication of my announcement. "Are they forcing you out?"

I shook my head. "No, in fact, if I had told Blakely what she wanted to hear I might have been able to convince her to give me Cherise's job."

"What did she want to hear?"

"That I would be less like myself and more like you."

The corners of Gigi's mouth twitched, but she refrained from breaking into a full grin. "Are you sure about this? I mean, are you going to tell Liz today?"

I nodded. "Right after we're through, I'll give her two weeks' notice."

"They might want you to leave right away," Gigi said more to herself than to me.

"Under different circumstances maybe, but with Dorita's vacation coming up I'm sure they'll want me to see the two weeks through."

Gigi smiled absently. "Nice of you to offer to recommend me."

But we both knew that my recommendation was an unnecessary formality. The job was hers and she probably wouldn't have to work it a year before she was promoted again. Gigi didn't have to convert to Dawson's religion. She was already practically a priestess.

Gigi lifted her mirror and checked her lipstick. "I'm going back to the floor. I won't tell the girls anything until you chat with Liz. It's totally cool with me if you want to be the one to break the news."

I blinked. How could Gigi switch so easily from treating me like a boss to treating me like an employee? "I'll tell them," I said quietly.

Gigi shrugged indifferently. "Wish you had given me a heads-up sooner." She put the mirror back down on her desk. "I would've bought balloons."

The rest of the day was like a dream. Liz asked me a few times if I was sure this is what I wanted to do, but I could tell that she wasn't too broken up. We agreed that I would stay two weeks and then my career at Dawson's would be over. I looked over my shoulder as I exited her office and caught her reaching for the phone. I knew she was calling Gigi. It hurt a little to think that I could be so easily replaced, but this had been my decision. My heart began to pick up speed. This was so out of character for me. It was…well, it was the kind of thing my mother would have done, and that thought in and of itself was enough to make me want to run into Liz's office and beg her for my job back.

And that's when it hit me. Pure unadulterated elation. No more pom-poms for me! Liz, Blakely, Marilyn, Gigi, all of Dawson's was behind me now, and in front of me was everything I ever wanted. I had been wrong about my need to settle. I might just be able to have the career of my dreams, too, and thanks to Tad there was no real risk. Caleb was right, even if we fell a little short of the hundred-and-eighty-grand figure it would still be fine. Like we couldn't get by on a hundred and fifty?

I went to Lingerie first and found Allie neatening stacks of bras and panties. She looked up as I approached. "You did it, didn't you?"

I nodded and bit down on my lip. "It's over."

Allie's mouth formed into an awed smile. "Holy shit."

"You're telling me!"

"You know I want all the details." She put down the panties that she had been holding. "Did Blakely burst into a blaze of flames or did she turn into an ice princess? Did Liz take it like an adult or did she make you sing some kind of special Dawson's resignation song? Did Gigi merely jump up and down and break into cartwheels?"

"Why don't I tell you everything tonight at the Bubble Lounge."

"You got it. Are you going to call Caleb or shall I?"

"I'm headed down to see him now." I did a few jumps of my own, and Allie laughed.

"You know, if you had shown that kind of enthusiasm at the Appreciation Meetings, Liz would never have let you go."

I giggled and went to the escalator where it took all my willpower to keep myself from pushing past the throngs of shoppers in order to take the moving steps two at a time down to Cosmetics.

Unfortunately, I was paged before I got to the first floor. I reluctantly made a pit stop at Sassy and dialed the operator from the phone at the register.

"April Silverperson here, you paged me?"

"I have a Tad Showers on the line for you, shall I put him through?"

"Oh, yes!" I said with enough zeal in my voice to cause Dorita, who was across the floor, to look over at me curiously.

"April?" Tad's voice floated through the receiver.

"Tad," I said in an eager whisper. "I did it! Can you believe it? I did it!"

Tad let out a gleeful laugh. "I'm so proud of you. Everything's going our way."

"It is, isn't it?" I shook my head, still having a hard time wrapping my mind around the idea.

"We have to celebrate tonight," he said.

"Oh, you're not working late?" My mind went to the invitation I had just extended to Allie.

"Not tonight. Tonight's about us."

"Well, I was going to go to the Bubble Lounge with Allie and Caleb, do you want to make it a foursome?"

"Can you tell them that you're going to have to reschedule? I have a surprise for you and I want to be the only one there when I present it."

"Why's that?" I asked suspiciously.

"Because when you see what it is you're going to want to thank me properly."

"Properly, huh? Does properly involve a conspicuous absence of clothing?"

"Just meet me at home after work and we'll see where it leads."

I hesitated, but only for a moment. Tad had been swamped at work lately and I knew that his taking this time to be with me meant that he was making some sacrifices. "I'll meet you at home then," I agreed. I hung up the phone and tried to take a deep breath. I didn't want to tell the staff just yet, which meant that I was going to have to keep it together a little better in order to avoid questions. But they knew something big was up. How else could they explain my new smile that simply wouldn't go away?

TWENTY-TWO

When I got home Tad's car was blocking our one-car garage, violating our rule that whoever got home first parked in the garage so that the other person could have the spot behind it. But Wednesday evenings in Laurel Heights weren't the worst in terms of parking and I found a spot less than half a block away. It didn't matter. Nothing mattered except that I was on my way to making my dreams come true. I bounced in the door and smiled when I heard Everclear's "I Will Buy You a New Life" coming out of our speakers.

Tad was waiting in the living room with a chilled bottle of champagne. I caught a whiff of something scrumptious coming out of the kitchen. He instantly pulled me in for a kiss. It was long and eager and full of promise.

When he finally let me go I smoothed out my shirt and walked around him, examining his efforts. "A home-cooked meal, champagne." I clucked my tongue appreciatively. "I guess this makes up for making me park on the street."

"I think you'll forgive me." Tad snatched the champagne out of its decorative ice bucket. "I have a little congratulations present for you."

I held up a protesting hand. "Now let's not get ahead of ourselves. I haven't even been accepted into a program yet." But I couldn't stop smiling. It did feel as if a token gift was appropriate, if only to commemorate my moment of courage.

Tad shook his head. "You're always so cautious." There was a gleam in his eye that spoke of his mounting excitement. I was touched that Tad would be this happy for me. I had never believed he understood how I felt about all the things I had given up in the name of practicality, but watching his movements as he popped the cork and poured the champagne it was clear that he was having to work extra hard to keep himself from breaking into a jig. He seemed even more hyped than when he had announced his own accomplishments.

He handed me a glass and grabbed my free hand, nearly crushing it in his current state of exhilaration. "We need to toast."

I lifted my glass. "To fresh starts."

Tad shook his head. "To mind-boggling success. To showing all the assholes who held us back what we're really made of."

I didn't like that toast. But I didn't want to break the mood, so I managed an appeasing smile and drank.

I then promptly spilled half my drink down my shirt as Tad yanked me through the kitchen. "Are you ready for your surprise?"

I didn't answer. If I had been ready, my silk Theory top wouldn't be saturated in Dom Perignon.

He stopped in front of the door to the garage, his face alight with…with what? A little chill traveled up my arms. This wasn't just excitement. This had an edge to it.

"My surprise is in the garage?" I asked carefully.

Tad nodded with the vigor of a little child. He grabbed the doorknob and threw the door open.

I gasped. Parked in my spot was a BMW Z3. The chill was gone, now I just felt ice cold.

"You…you bought that?" I whispered. He couldn't have. Surely it was a rental, a loaner; there was some reasonable explanation.

"Yep! I saw a woman driving one today and I knew I had to get one for you. So what do you think?" He ran down the three steps that took him to the car. He whirled around and made a little "ta-da" gesture. "Is this great or what? We are now a two-BMW family!"

"B-but," I stammered, still glued to my spot in the doorway, "I don't need a car."

"April, this isn't about needing, this is about wanting! Don't you get it? We can get the things we want now! Our days of penny-pinching are over!"

"Penny-pinching?" I heard my voice rise an octave. "Three days ago we had a two-hundred-and-fifty-dollar dinner at Maas!"

"And now we can do that every weekend!" Tad exclaimed. "And next time you can give this baby to the valet! And they'll know! They'll know what kind of people we are!"

"You mean crazy? Or were you aiming for bankrupt?"

Tad stepped back as if I had just dealt him a physical blow. "What are you talking about?"

"I just quit my job!" I screamed. "We should be saving! You said you would support me if I went back to school!"

"And I will!" he shot back. "What the fuck is your problem? I bought this for you!"

"But I don't want it! Take it back! Take it back! Take it back!"

The words kept tumbling out, each syllable hitting a new note of hysteria. He couldn't return it, not a car. I turned and ran back into the kitchen, slamming the door behind me. I gripped the back of a kitchen chair and tried to calm myself. Okay, we couldn't return the car, but we could sell it. This was fixable.

I heard the door slam against the wall as Tad shoved it back open. He grabbed my arm and whirled me around. His other hand went to my opposite arm and he pulled me to him, almost lifting me off the floor with the force of the movement. "You bitch," he seethed. "You still don't believe in me. You've never believed in me…."

The shock of his violent behavior had an odd steadying effect on me. "This isn't about my believing in you, Tad." My voice sounded cool and detached. "Now, let go of my arms."

He pushed me backward, releasing me as he did. I fell, knocking over the chair as I hit the floor. Tad flinched but he didn't offer his hand in assistance. Instead, he turned on his heel and stalked toward the front door.

"What are you doing?" I asked, pulling myself to my feet and following him despite the sharp pain in my ankle. My heart stopped as I watched him retrieve an old baseball bat from the hall closet. "Tad…"

He didn't respond, just opened the front door and disappeared outside. *Let him go.* But I couldn't stop myself from following him. There was something very strange going on and I knew it wasn't over.

When I stepped outside I could see Tad on the sidewalk looking this way and that. "Tad!" I called after him.

He didn't turn. He was staring at something that I couldn't see. Then he turned to the right and ran down the street. "Tad!" I screamed again. I hobbled after him and then stopped in horror as I saw the baseball bat make impact with the windshield of my car.

No. I mouthed the word but no actual sound came out. I stood paralyzed as he smashed every single one of my windows. Then he turned around and walked back in my direction.

Run, my little voice said. *Get out of here now!* But where should I go? Into the house? To the home of a neighbor I didn't know? Tad was getting close. I started to back up, wincing as I inadvertently put weight on my injured ankle. Tad stopped when he was only a few feet in front of me. I looked him in the eye, expecting to see rage. But all I saw was pain.

He dropped the bat and I stood speechless as his face twitched with the effort to hold back his mounting tears. Then he walked past me, stepped into his car and drove away.

Less than a half hour later the police came to my door. They claimed to have gotten a call about a possibly violent domestic disturbance, and seeing that the vandalized car down the street was registered to me they thought I might know something about it. I leaned against the door frame in order to hide the fact that I was favoring one leg and shook my head. I told them that I had seen my car, but only after the fact, and had written it off as the work of some drunken teenagers.

The police officers seemed satisfied with my account. They babbled something about how I was welcome to report the vandalism at the station and then wished me a pleasant evening.

As if that was possible.

That night I packed and unpacked my bags five times. At ten I was standing in my bedroom looking over an empty suitcase. What should I do? Leave? I could stay with Caleb or Allie but then I'd have to admit to them what had happened. If they knew...

I shook my head. I couldn't share any of this until I was sure of what I was going to do. I looked down at my ankle. The sharp pain had mellowed to a persistent ache. I wriggled my toes. It was twisted but not broken or sprained.

I looked around the room. Everything was neat and in order. Everything except my life. "Think, think, think," I muttered to myself. If I could just find a way to put what had taken place into logical terms, I could figure out how to deal with it.

But you can't make the illogical logical. As usual my little voice was right. Nothing that had happened had made sense…unless Caleb had been right, and Tad was on drugs.

I immediately turned to the dresser that contained Tad's clothing and started opening all the drawers. I pulled all the clothes out of each one, unfolding the socks while looking for a little plastic bag containing a white powder, a syringe, papers to roll joints—anything. My breathing quickened as I tossed the searched items on the floor and reached for the next. There had to be some evidence of a reasonable explanation. I couldn't accept anything else. I wouldn't.

The phone rang and I straightened up, clutching a pair of Tad's jeans in my hand. "Tad," I whispered. What felt like a wave of ice water rolled from my chest to the pit of my stomach. I walked to the phone, counting the steps as I moved, nine, ten, eleven… "Hello," I said quietly into the receiver.

"I'm glad to hear that you're not dead."

I squeezed my eyes shut. "Not now, Mother. I can't do this with you now."

"Have you gotten my messages? Do you understand how—"

"I understand that I can't talk to you now."

"April…"

"Not now!" I screamed so loud that my throat hurt from the effort. I slammed the phone down and then quickly took it back off the hook. I sat down on the chair by the phone and a single tear trickled down my cheek. I quickly wiped it away and blinked back the tears that threatened to follow. I needed to go over the facts. Tad had bought a car… How much did it cost? He had to have gotten a loan. But were we even eligible for a loan, considering the recent delinquent credit card payments?

I retrieved my purse from the coatrack by the door, pulled the navy checkbook out of my wallet and examined the balance. Five thousand four hundred and nineteen dollars were in it last I checked, and we had another nine hundred in a savings account that was exclusively in my name. I went back to the phone and put the receiver in its cradle long enough to get a dial tone again. Then I dialed the number at the bottom of my check.

"Hello, you've reached Bank of America's automated account services," said the recorded voice. I pressed the necessary numbers until I got to the part that recited our balance. "You have an available balance of fifty dollars and three cents in your checking account…"

My stomach did a flip-flop. I checked the savings account. "You have a balance of zero dollars…"

I hung up the phone. Okay, okay, I could deal with this. I would have to hold off on getting my car fixed but I could still sell the Z3. It might take a few days but that was okay. I had two weeks left at Dawson's, so I could focus all my energy on selling, and collect as much commission as possible.

The phone rang again. I pressed my fingers into the bridge of my nose. Of all the nights for my mother to try to reach me she had to pick tonight. I picked up the receiver. "Listen," I started.

"April."

I stopped at the sound of Tad's voice. I racked my brain for an appropriate thing to say. "Where are you?"

"I just needed to drive around. April, did I hurt you? God, if I hurt you—" His voice broke and I could make out his muffled sobs.

"I twisted my ankle, but other than that I'm okay," I said, unsure if it was my duty to reassure him. "Tad, I don't understand what's going on."

"I never wanted to hurt you." His voice was weak and shaky. "Please, tell me how I can make things right. Please…"

"I need you to help me make sense of this. Can you do that, Tad?"

I could hear him begin to cry again and I struggled to keep my own throat from constricting. I didn't want revenge. I just wanted all of this to go away. But since there was no magic genie around to grant me impossible wishes, I would settle for understanding.

"I promise we'll talk," he said. "But not tonight, okay, April? Please, we can't talk tonight."

I hesitated. The suggestion that we put this off seemed like a colossal joke. Tomorrow he would be going on a two-day business trip, and in the meantime every window in my car was broken and my bank account was practically empty. What was I supposed to do, plant my ass on some broken glass and pay for my gas with chocolate gelt? On the other hand it seemed like a very unwise idea to push Tad tonight. Better to allow him some time to calm down and then strategically approach the problem.

"We'll talk about it when you get back from L.A.," I agreed. I took a deep breath before I asked the next question. "Are you coming home tonight?"

"Would it be all right if I stayed at a motel—just for tonight?"

"Yes!" I cried, and then instantly regretted my unbridled enthusiasm. "I mean, sure, if you think the alone time will help you."

"Yeah, I think it will."

There was a long pause on the line. Finally, I spoke up. "So we'll talk in two days."

"Yes, I promise. I love you, April."

I was silent.

"April?"

"I'll see you in two days." I hung up the phone.

I walked back to the bedroom and surveyed the disaster that I had created there. I didn't need my little voice to tell me that the dynamics in my relationship with Tad had drastically and permanently changed.

THE
UNRAVELING

TWENTY-THREE

I stumbled into Dawson's the next day in a daze. I was working a midshift but the luxury of coming in late in the morning was wasted on me since I hadn't slept at all the night before. I hadn't even tried. Instead, I cleaned the house, and when the smell of Pine-Sol failed to make me feel better I turned on the television and watched infomercials. From this I learned that the right exercise program could change your life. I subsequently did three hundred sit-ups and six sets of push-ups.

But my life didn't change. And now I had to deal with the hellish new reality that I was drowning in. I stepped into the elevator and pressed the button for my floor. I was supposed to meet Allie and Caleb tomorrow night, which was also when Tad was coming home. I needed to cancel but I was sure that the minute they heard my voice they would know something was wrong. Plus I'd already canceled on them to spend my "celebration" night with Tad—how could I explain to them what I didn't understand?

I walked out of the elevator and observed my department. It was already busy. Good, I could distract myself and make some much-needed money at the same time. I stepped onto my floor and immediately made eye contact with Gigi, who was finishing up with a customer at the register. For a split second I thought I saw a flash of hostility in her expression, but it disappeared so quickly that it could have easily been an illusion. She smiled sweetly at the customer and handed her two garment bags full of merchandise before trotting over to me. "I am *sooo* glad you're here. I have, like, the best news!" she said as she dragged me toward the back room.

"Great," I said softly as the door to the office closed behind us. "I'm due for something good about now."

"Then be prepared to totally love me because I'm about to make your day!"

I raised my eyebrows as a way of prompting her to continue.

She flipped her hair behind her shoulders and smiled. "Dorita's boyfriend has pneumonia!"

I looked at her blankly, then looked around to confirm that I had indeed fallen into the twilight zone. Gigi now seemed to be waiting for me to respond. I cleared my throat. "Okay, sooo… how is this a good thing?"

"Hello! Don't you get it?" Gigi cocked her head to the side. "Now she can't go to Argentina! You don't have to finish out your last two weeks!"

My stomach did a nauseating flip-flop. "I really don't mind staying.…"

"Don't be ridiculous. You've worked so hard for so long, it's time for some serious 'you' time. You can spend your days getting pedicures and facials." Her grin turned into what looked suspiciously like a sneer. "You could even spend time with your husband."

Oh God, anything but that. "I would prefer to stay." I looked up at Gigi. Her almond-shaped eyes seemed to be narrower than usual. A cruel smile formed on her lips and I took a step aside. *Oh God,* I thought. *This is the part where she sheds her human form and eats me!*

Instead, she just leaned back against her desk and crossed her arms over her chest. "I've already talked to Liz about it. She thinks it would be less confusing for the staff if you left right away."

"Hello? What is so confusing about me handing in my two weeks' notice and then actually staying for those two weeks?"

"Your presence on my floor undermines my authority."

So the claws were now in view. I felt my hands clench into fists. "*Undermines* and *authority*, those are pretty big words, Gigi. Do you know what they mean?"

Gigi laughed. "Yeah, they mean you're out of here." She turned around and walked out, allowing the door to swing back and forth behind her.

She couldn't fire me. I was her manager until my two weeks were up and no way was I going to allow her to treat me like this. I stormed up to Liz's office and found her at her desk poring over a stack of printouts with lists of figures and statistics. She greeted me with a serene smile. "Hello, April. Did Gigi tell you I wanted to see you?"

I sat down opposite her. "Gigi and I had a discussion of sorts, but no, she didn't mention that you wanted to see me."

"Ah…" Liz folded up the printouts. "Well, I hope by 'discussion' you don't mean argument. Managing is a lot like parenting. It's important to always show a united front."

As far as I knew, the closest thing Liz had ever had to a child was a pet Chinese fighting fish that she forgot to feed. "Liz, as you know, I plan to stay and work for my remaining two weeks—"

Liz held up her hand to stop me. "That is just so sweet of you to offer, but Gigi's informed me that Dorita will not be going on vacation after all, so the department is very well staffed. Why don't you take a few extra days to yourself."

"You don't understand, Liz, I *want* to be here."

Liz put her hand on her heart. "Wow! I'm so impressed by your work ethic, but here at Dawson's we've found that once someone quits it's better that they leave sooner rather than later. It's so hard to give a hundred-and-ten percent when you're counting off the days 'til your next venture."

"Liz…"

"I've arranged to have your final paycheck prepared. It's waiting for you in HR."

My jaw dropped. I was being fired. I quit yesterday and yet somehow I was being fired today. I swallowed and rose to my feet.

Liz followed suit and extended her hand. "It's been so great working with you. I do hope you'll keep in touch. And remember, just because you're not an employee doesn't mean you shouldn't feel free to shop here anytime you like. We still consider you part of the Dawson's family."

In less than a half hour's time I was standing outside of Dawson's with a shopping bag filled with various personal belongings and a final paycheck for seven hundred dollars. I looked down the street as if expecting to see some sign telling me which way I should go or what I should do. I walked out into the hordes of tourists and followed their migration to Powell Street, where they rushed to get in line for the cable cars. There was a man on the corner holding a large wooden cross over his head screaming that the end of the world was near. Maybe he was right. I looked around at all the people milling about. They didn't seem to be taking him seriously, but just because the general public thought that everything was fine didn't mean it was true. It didn't mean that everything they had worked for and depended on wouldn't fall apart in the blink of an eye.

My heart started pounding against my chest. I looked back at the man with the wild eyes and wooden cross and suddenly I knew I had to get as far away from him as possible. I turned and rushed into the Gap store behind me. I stood ten feet away from the escalator and watched as frenzied women destroyed the perfect fold of dozens of scoop neck tees.

My heart was beating even faster now. I didn't have a job, my husband was spending all the money we had left on fois gras and BMWs, and I had no idea what my next move should be. My breaths started coming out in short little gasps. If I had just been sensible enough to tell Blakely what she had wanted to hear I could have been an assistant buyer. What had I been thinking? I grabbed on to a fixture as I fought off a dizzy spell. What was happening? Why was everything spinning?

"Excuse me."

I turned around to see a headset-wearing Gap employee. "Are you all right?" she asked.

I used the back of my hand to wipe away the beads of sweat that were dampening my forehead. "I'm just a little dizzy," I said weakly.

"I think you should sit down." She led me through the crowd of shoppers to a simple metal bench. "Can I get you anything?" she asked.

"Can you get me anything?" I repeated. For some reason I was having a hard time making sense of her words. I squeezed my hands together, which were shaking uncontrollably.

The woman's eyes widened with concern. "Would you like a glass of water?"

Water? How the hell was water going to help me? My heart was still picking up speed; I was going to have a heart attack right there in the Gap. The woman was still standing next to me. She had to help me. I grabbed her arm and yanked her closer to me. "An application. Please! I need an application for employment!"

Now the Gap employee looked really freaked. "Um, I'll be right back with that." She quickly removed her arm from my grip and in her rush to get away almost knocked over a middle-aged woman wearing an "I Heart SF" sweatshirt.

I squeezed my eyes shut and tried again to steady my breathing. Even in the middle of a panic attack I knew that I had better get out of there quickly before the poor salesgirl I had accosted had a chance to point me out to security. I managed to stand up and stagger out the door.

The man with the cross was still there, so I immediately averted my eyes and started speed walking up Powell. I hurried past Union Square and past where all the major stores were located. The upward slope of the street turned into a dramatically steep hill and I felt the strain in my calf muscles as I sped to the top. The physical effort that I expended helped clear my head and the sharp pangs of anxiety dulled to a manageable ache. At the hill's crest I reached the Fairmont Hotel and I allowed myself to slow my pace. I wasn't aware that I was heading anywhere in particular until I went another few blocks and noticed that I was on a street that led to Allie's apartment building. She was at work, but Jeremiah might be home and it hit me that he was the one person I could talk to. He didn't have an existing relationship with Tad and it was doubtful if the three of us would ever manage to sit down for that once talked-of dinner. I could tell him what was going on and it would never come back to bite me.

I hesitated in front of the building. Which apartment was it again? His name wasn't next to any of the numbers, but that didn't mean anything since he had four roommates. Was it number four? My finger was hovering over the doorbell when the door to the main entrance flung open.

Jeremiah lifted his eyebrows in surprise and then broke into a large grin. "Hey, I was just thinkin' of you. You here to see Allie?"

"Um, yeah," I lied, "but she's not home and I was wondering if you'd like to get a cup of coffee."

Jeremiah studied me. His smile disappeared. "Something's off. What's up? Is it—"

"Tad?" I finished for him. "You were going to ask me if there was something up with Tad because you know there is." I sucked in a deep breath and willed myself to lock the tears inside.

Jeremiah sighed and looked down at a large backpack that he was holding in one hand. I hadn't even noticed it until then, which said something about my state of mind, considering it was the size of Arkansas. "Are you going camping or something?" I asked. Had I really thought that he would just be sitting around waiting for me to unburden my problems on him? He had a life, and he didn't need to put it on hold for me.

"Cat-sitting."

"Cat-sitting," I repeated. I eyed the backpack again. "Is the cat…in there?"

Jeremiah laughed. "Yeah, he was bugging me so I just stuffed him in here and decided to take him for a walk."

I smiled for the first time in what felt like days. "Bad puns aside, I think the time has come for you to let the cat out of the bag."

Jeremiah laughed again. "You can still make jokes—that's a good sign." He pulled the backpack up and supported it with both arms. "My friend took off for a month-long trip to Europe and he's got a cat. So I'm going to crash at his place while he's gone. I was just loading up the car. You wanna come check out the place?"

"Yes!" I said a little too quickly. But Jeremiah didn't seem to notice. He simply ushered me in the direction of his Suzuki, which turned out to be three city blocks away. We walked in silence, but it was a comfortable one. I felt myself begin to relax. A light breeze had picked up and it had a calming effect. When we reached the car Jeremiah threw his bag in the backseat before helping me into mine. It occurred to me that going to Jeremiah's friend's place alone might not be the wisest of moves, not because I didn't trust him but because I didn't trust myself. But I could no longer stand the idea of being alone right now.

We didn't talk a lot during the drive, either. It seemed that although Jeremiah's car was a piece of junk his stereo was fairly decent. He popped the Black Crowes into the CD player and I listened to Chris Robinson croon about a junkie who spoke to angels.

That's when I broke the silence. "So do you think Tad's on drugs?"

Jeremiah's eyes didn't leave the road as he shook his head. "I seriously doubt it. He's not the type."

He pulled the Suzuki into a parking spot adjacent to a man sitting in front of a shopping cart full of clothes. Jeremiah got out first and I opened my door carefully.

"Hey, Elijah," he called to the man who was now busily chewing on his knuckles. "How's it hanging?"

"The Lord knows, Jeremiah," he said inexplicably. "The Lord knows all."

"Yeah? Does the Lord know if my car's gonna be safe here tonight?"

"The Lord knows."

"Right, tell you what, I'll come down with a sandwich for you in an hour or so and in the meantime try not to do anything to mess with it, okay? No more eating in it, and though it looks like shit it's not a toilet, got it?"

"The Lord knows it's not a toilet. I follow the Lord."

That was apparently good enough for Jeremiah. He took his backpack in one arm and gently took my arm with his free hand and led me across the street.

"Your friend lives here?"

"Yeah, he lives on his own, but the trade-off is a neighborhood that's a bit dicey."

"It's the Tenderloin," I pointed out. The Tenderloin was one of the poorer areas of the city and usually had the most crime.

"Yeah, but it's the outskirts of the Tenderloin. I like to call it Tenderloin Heights."

I laughed despite myself and followed him up a very narrow and somewhat precarious-looking outside staircase that led to a small apartment with bars on the window. Jeremiah pulled some keys out of his pocket and opened the creaky door. Inside, a Siamese cat was curled on top of a Victorian-style cushioned chair. He lifted his head as we walked in, and then after gracing us with a disinterested stare, settled himself back to sleep.

Jeremiah dropped the bag by the small television and went to the kitchen. "You like cognac? Dave's always got a supply of cognac around."

"Your friend drinks cognac?" I asked doubtfully as I surveyed the worn state of his furniture.

"It wasn't always like this for him," Jeremiah called from the kitchen. "He was doing okay when he was married, but when he got divorced, things got messy and he lost pretty much everything with the exception of these very fine snifters." Jeremiah walked out of the kitchen and handed me an elegant glass filled a quarter of the way up. "Here, you look like you need this."

"He had the money to go to Europe," I said, taking the drink from him.

"Yeah, he's doin' the Eurorail and pensions deal. He just needed to take some time to find himself again." Jeremiah sat next to me and looked into my eyes. "How 'bout you? Are you lost?"

I bit my lip. "I…I don't think Tad is okay."

Jeremiah's gaze remained steady. "Neither do I."

I turned my head away and closed my eyes. "Jeremiah, what have I got myself into?"

"Hey…" His voice was soft and he draped his arm over my trembling shoulders. "It's okay. Whatever it is, you'll find a way to get through it."

"What makes you so sure?"

"I know a survivor when I see one."

A survivor. My grandmother, she was a survivor, but me? I shook my head. "I don't know…I might not be as strong as you think I am."

"Or you might be a lot stronger." I felt his hand tighten around my shoulder. "Lay it on me. What exactly went down?"

I took a deep breath and told him everything, save the

physical push Tad gave me in the kitchen. That was the one thing I couldn't admit to anyone, not even Jeremiah. It was too pathetic-battered-wifeish. But the credit cards, the car, the rent, his unreasonable outbursts coupled with his intervals of hyper-activity—that all came spilling out. Jeremiah listened without interrupting or asking questions, and as I spoke I began to relax into him more and more. He felt so secure and comforting, which was odd because this was completely contrary to the image he projected. Tad was supposed to be the provider, the safe choice, and yet right now it felt like, of the two, the bad-boy title went to my husband.

When I was done, Jeremiah let out a heavy sigh and leaned his head back onto the back of the couch. "April, are you familiar with the word *bipolar?*"

Without disturbing the position of Jeremiah's arm I twisted so that I was angled toward him. "Bipolar? I think…I've heard the term before, but I don't know a lot about it. Is it like schizophrenia?"

"Nah, not that bad. The worse cases can get close, though. The brother of one of the other trainers at work is bipolar. I've met him a couple of times. He's this bigger-than-life dude and smart as hell, but then he makes all these crazy decisions…like he got a hair up his ass and went out and bought a fifty-thousand-dollar horse. He didn't even have a place to keep her. Then when things get bad he goes into these really dark depressions."

"How dark?"

"He downed a bottle of sleeping pills with a cup of straight-up vodka."

"Oh my God." My eyes widened. "Wait…you're not saying…" I stood up. "Tad's not actually insane. I mean, he might be on drugs and he has issues, but there's nothing wrong with his brain."

"Maybe not, but the shit you're describing isn't normal, April. You know that. That's why you're so freaked."

"I'm freaked because…" I scrambled to come up with a logical reason that didn't allow for the possibility of mental illness. But there wasn't one, not unless I stuck to the secret-drug-addiction idea, and I had found no evidence of that, despite the deep cleaning I had given the house the night before. I shook my head and turned away from Jeremiah. "He can't be insane," I whispered to the bare wall in front of me. "My husband can't be insane."

"Hey, you can't think of it like that. He's sick. Lots of people get sick, April. Then they take their meds and get better."

"Medication." I said the word slowly as if to test the feel of it on my tongue. "What kind of medication do they prescribe for this?"

"Well, they used to prescribe lithium."

"Oh, God," I gasped and tried to stave off another panic attack.

"But they got other stuff now, better stuff. Look, I may be completely off on this, but I think you should check it out. At least get him to a shrink.…"

"We already went to a marriage counselor. It didn't go so well."

"Not a therapist, April, a psychiatrist."

"Oh, God."

"Hey, going to one doesn't make you crazy. It can just be a place to make sure that you're not. And if there is something off in his head then maybe he can find a way to deal with it."

"How 'bout me?" I asked, my voice so faint that I could barely make out my own words. "How will I deal with it?"

Jeremiah walked up behind me and put his hands on my shoulders. He positioned his head so that his mouth was just inches from my ear. "You believe in yourself, April. That's how you deal with it. You get through this by knowing that you can."

* * *

The morning after my second sleepless night I went to Golden Gate Park and found a seat in Shakespeare's Garden. There, I spent two hours writing and rewriting what I was going to say to Tad when he got home. His plane came in at five-fifteen, which meant I had plenty of time to practice. Basically I had to find a way of suggesting that he see a psychiatrist without setting him off. But how does a person tell her husband that she would like him to get evaluated by a mental-health professional in order to verify his sanity? Hell, that would set *me* off.

I finally settled on a two-page script. I would say that I suspected that the pressure of his work was getting to him and that maybe he should see a psychiatrist so that he could get a prescription for Valium or some such thing to calm him down on the nights that he's feeling particularly amped. I wouldn't even mention the word *bipolar*. If he was bipolar let him hear it from the psychiatrist.

Of course, I still didn't believe that was the case. There had been so many special moments that Tad and I had shared. There had been times when he had been there for me in a way that no one else ever had. Like when I had lost our baby. Surely someone who had a severe mental disorder couldn't have functioned so well in a time of crisis.

I shook my head. There had to be another explanation. The psychiatrist was just a precaution. I shoved my notebook into a large tote bag that I had lugged with me and walked to the hated Z3. I didn't yet have the money to have the windows fixed in my car. That seven hundred dollars didn't even amount to half our rent and God only knew what Tad was going to do with his paycheck. I wanted to have some time alone in the house before he got home. I still hadn't called Caleb or Allie to cancel our plans for the evening, although I knew I should. I needed to spend some time with Tad so that I could work out what was going on, but the truth was, I wanted the excuse to leave the house. I wanted to be able to confront Tad and then make a quick run for it. That didn't make me the bravest little toaster around, but it did speak to the survival instincts that Jeremiah had credited me with.

I drove home and pulled the car into my miniature driveway. That was when I first noticed the woman who was sitting on my doorstep. She was wearing almost all black and was hunched over so that she was hugging her knees. I stepped out of the car but kept the door open with the keys in the ignition just in case she was hiding a sawed-off shotgun under her leather jacket. "Can I help you?" I asked.

The woman stood up. At full height she was probably an inch taller than me. And she was wearing a black twinset and a knee-length, A-line floral skirt. Her hair was thick, brown and wavy and fell just below her shoulders. Her eyes were a piercing shade of green. Kind of like Tad's.

"Are you April Showers?" she asked. Her voice was kind, but also a little nervous.

"Yes, I mean no, my last name is Silverperson."

"But you're married to Tad Showers?"

"Yesss…who are you?"

The woman stepped forward, extending her hand as she did. "I'm Maddy Showers, Tad's sister."

TWENTY-FOUR

I stood motionless, staring at the woman's hand. "Tad doesn't have a sister.

"Ah, he didn't tell you about me." It was more of a statement than a question. She dropped her hand and rubbed it against her skirt. "I hadn't really suspected that he would, but I hoped… Oh, well. I suppose I can't fully blame him."

"Tad would have told me…" My voice trailed off. Did I know that for sure? For that matter, was there anything about Tad that I knew for sure?

The woman nodded and started rummaging through her large purse. "I wouldn't believe me either if I were you. Here." She pulled out her wallet and a miniature photo album. "Here's my license, and you can see my name really is Madeline Showers. I'm sure you'll agree that Showers isn't a very common name."

I stared at the license.

"And here's a picture of us as kids. That's me, Tad, our mom and the little one on her lap is our half brother, Otis."

My eyes darted back and forth between the four figures in the photograph. It was one of those quasi-professional photos you bought at Sears. The backdrop was made to look like the North Pole depicted in children's Christmas stories, and the eldest child was a boy of about fifteen. His hair was cut in a militaristic fashion, his mouth was set in a straight line and his arm was flung protectively around the shoulders of a girl who looked to be four or five years younger. I studied the cut of his jaw, the way his ears stuck out just a little too much, making his hairstyle less than flattering. He was wearing a sweater that brought out his eyes. There was no way that the boy in the picture was anyone other than Tad, and the girl was a perfect miniature of the woman before me. I swallowed and looked around me. I *was* in a soap opera.

My eyes went back to the picture. The older woman…the one Maddy had said was her mother, was attractive, most likely in her midthirties at the time the picture was taken. She was laughing in the photo. Her long mane of chestnut hair was tossed behind her and she was looking up at the camera with the kind of joie de vivre one would expect from a woman who had just won the lottery. Her high spirits were in sharp contrast to the apparent mood of everyone else in the photo. While Tad looked somber and determined, Maddy just looked frightened. She was leaning into Tad as if silently pleading to be safeguarded against some unknown force. And the little boy couldn't have been more than six. He had jet-black curly hair and his skin was the color of milk chocolate.

"The little boy…" I began.

"I know, he doesn't look much like us. His father's Haitian."

"Your mother had a child with a black man?"

Maddy nodded, clearly finding my surprise puzzling. "I'm sorry, but you're biracial, too, aren't you?"

"Isn't your mother racist?" I asked, ignoring her question.

"Mom?" Maddy laughed. "She had a lot of faults but racism wasn't one of them. I think the father Tad and I share was the only white man she ever got involved with."

"But there aren't a lot of minorities in Georgetown, Massachusetts, are there?"

"Georgetown? Tad and I are from Reno."

My fingers tightened around the edges of the photograph so that my fingertips turned a shade of white. "I need to sit down," I whispered.

Maddy rubbed her hands against her skirt again. "Perhaps you'll allow me to come in? I promise I won't stay long."

I nodded numbly and led her into the house, only taking my eyes off the photo long enough to unlock the front door. We walked into the living room and I stood by the fireplace as I contemplated the somewhat grotesque smile on Tad's mother's face. I had seen that smile before…on Tad's lips.

"May I sit down?"

I looked up, inexplicably surprised to see that Maddy was still there. I motioned toward the couch and Maddy sat down without letting her back touch the pillows. "I know this must be weird…"

"I believe that's what one would call an understatement."

Maddy rung her hands and looked down at the carpet. "I'm so sorry about this. I had hoped that Tad would be the first to arrive. He should be the one to explain things to you. But I didn't know a good time to reach him, and it seemed better to show up at his home instead of his work…perhaps that was a mistake."

"He didn't know you were coming?"

Maddy let out a bitter laugh. "If he had known he probably would have moved out of the city just to avoid speaking to me."

"You two had a falling-out? Is that why he kept you a secret?" But even as I asked, I knew that a falling-out didn't even begin to explain the photo that I was still holding.

Maddy was now scrunching the fabric of her skirt into her fist. "Not a falling-out, not with me anyway. Tad… He left the family. He got his GED at sixteen and then he just disappeared."

"What do you mean, he disappeared?"

"He ran away, he and his eighteen-year-old girlfriend at the time."

I felt the spark of indignation on Tad's behalf. "Didn't you and your parents look for him?"

Maddy shrugged. "My father had been out of the picture for a very long time by then, and my mom wasn't in any shape to go searching for Tad. We knew he'd be okay. Tad's always been resourceful and he's incredibly smart…." Maddy's face took on a faraway expression and I could tell that she was reliving something…something traumatic.

I looked at the painting above the fireplace. If I had run away as a teenager Bobe would have been out personally turning over every rock, pebble and leaf trying to locate me, but would my mother have expended that kind of effort? My mind traveled back to the one and only play I had ever performed in. I had been a freshman in high school and I had landed the part of Ursula in my school's production of *Much Ado About Nothing*. I had only tried out so that I had an excuse to be near the boy who was playing Don Pedro, and when it came time to actually perform in front of other people I had nearly panicked. Three hours before opening night I had confessed my fears to my mother. I knew she wasn't coming since she had a date with our building's new super, but I needed to talk to someone and she was there. She had listened and nodded and told me all the standard stuff about picturing the audience in their underwear and so forth, and I remember thinking that was a pretty paltry defense against a roomful of critical strangers, but I had pretended to be comforted. That night I stepped onto the stage ready to make a complete fool of myself. I looked out at the audience and there she was…my mother, smack-dab in the middle of the front row, no date in sight. At that moment I knew I had what it took to get through my scene. She ended up coming to every performance, and every time it was my turn to bow she screamed and cheered like I had just won an Oscar. Would my mother have come looking for me if I had gone missing? The answer was an unequivocal yes.

I sat down on the opposite side of the couch from Maddy and handed the picture back to her. "There has to be more to this story," I said. "What do you mean when you said your mother wasn't in any shape to look for him? Was she ill?"

Maddy took the picture and examined it as if seeing it for the first time. "Ill…yes, in a way. Our mother was bipolar."

I sucked in a sharp breath. There was that word again. That horrible, terrifying word. I bit down on my lip so hard I almost cried out in pain.

"Tad doesn't know that," Maddy continued. "She wasn't diagnosed correctly until shortly after he left…after she…tried to hurt herself again. She had been called a whole bunch of other things of course…irresponsible, flighty, eccentric, an alcoholic. Those were labels we all became familiar with during our early-childhood years. But bipolar…that was a new one."

"But she got help, they fixed her, right?" I scooted closer to Maddy. I needed to know that this thing was curable, that it didn't have to destroy my life.

Maddy flashed me a sarcastic smile. "'Fixed her'? It's not as if she was a car with electrical problems." She must have seen the fear in my eyes because she immediately looked apologetic. "I just mean that you can't exactly *fix* a psychiatric condition. You can treat it and make it manageable, but you can't make it disappear."

"And did she? Make it manageable?"

Maddy's head bent forward so her hair hid her face. "They tried...they put her on lithium, and then later Depekote. Horrible drugs, both of them. My mother went from being this larger-than-life beautiful woman to being fat and lethargic. She couldn't even stay awake during dinner. I remember trying to talk to her...tell her about my day, but she just couldn't follow a conversation anymore. I didn't blame her when she stopped taking the pills. Why trade one hell for another?"

"But there has to be a solution." My throat began to constrict and I had to struggle to get the words out. "You said that the illness could be managed!"

Maddy gave me a funny look. "It can be managed. But it's not easy. For one thing, every person responds differently to the various meds. Secondly, the doctors rarely prescribe the medications with the least amount of side effects first." She shook her head in frustration. "The better meds are always newer and the doctors are often afraid of them. Patients really need an advocate in their corner, someone to do the research for them and motivate them to keep trying new meds when the first ones don't work for them."

"But if they had someone to do that, can they get it under control and live a happy, normal life?"

Maddy offered the first genuine smile I had seen since she arrived. "It's definitely possible. After all, it worked for me."

"For you? You're—"

"Bipolar," she finished for me. "I was diagnosed about eight years ago. But thanks to Lamictal and a lot of therapy, I'm doing okay. Better than okay, really. I'll be starting law school at NYU in the fall."

I took a moment to study Maddy. She seemed a bit uncomfortable, which was understandable, but other than that she seemed very even-keeled. "Did you get help as soon as you got diagnosed?"

"Hardly. Mostly I didn't want to take the medications. Plus, I kind of liked my manic episodes. I felt like I was on top of the world, and in some ways I was. I didn't have the desire to sleep, so I was able to accomplish twice as much as everyone else...I was totally self-confident—to a fault really, but I didn't know that. All I knew was that I was on top of my game."

I swallowed hard. Tad had used that term before. All of a sudden all the nights that he had forgone sleep in favor of work and entrepreneurial activities took on a whole new meaning. A cold chill crept up my arms and I rubbed them in order to warm myself.

"But I had Otis to think of...he depended on me, and one day I took him on one of my whirlwind shopping sprees and he grabbed my arm and said, 'Maddy, you're acting exactly like Mom.' He looked so scared. It was enough to get me to make another doctor's appointment. Unfortunately it wasn't enough to get me to *keep* the appointment. It took Otis refusing to talk to me, coupled with those horrible, horrible depressions..." A dark cloud passed over her face. "The depressions were unbearable. I totally understand why my mom tried to kill herself so many times."

I blanched. "How many times did she try?"

Maddy closed her eyes as if to block out the image. "The first time that I know of was when I was four and Tad was eight. She swallowed a whole bottle of pills and had to have her stomach pumped. I don't remember much of that. My dad was still around at the time. But he left a few years later. He said he just couldn't deal with her. Of course, he could have had the decency to deal with his kids, but that's just the kind of person he was." Maddy spit out the last words with such venom that I instinctively inched farther away from her.

"Our mom and dad used to think they were kindred spirits... both of them fun and spontaneous. Unfortunately for him spontaneous translated to irresponsibility, and for her it was another word for insanity." Maddy put her fingers on her temples as if attempting to massage away a memory. "I'll never forget the day he left...but I'm getting off topic. Her second suicide attempt was right before Tad ran away. He walked in on her while she was in the middle of slipping a noose over her head."

"Oh my God."

"Yeah, I understood his need to leave, but I resented him for it for a long time. It was really just jealousy on my part. I had spent my life watching Tad deal with the worst of our mom, due to the fact that he was the oldest. With him gone that burden fell on me and I didn't want it. Not at all."

"I can't imagine you did." I studied the pattern on the rug. "So was that it? She tried to kill herself two times?"

Maddy flinched. "Actually, that's..."

We heard the front door open and close. "April? April, are you home?" Tad stepped into the living room and instantly his eyes fell on Maddy.

There are no words to adequately describe the expression on

Tad's face. Anger, despair, terror, those terms don't even come close to doing it justice. Maddy rose from the couch and took a step forward and Tad simultaneously took a step back.

"You can't be here." His words came out mechanically, like a robot programmed to warn a thief that the car they are about to steal has an alarm. "You're not allowed here."

I cringed and looked to Maddy, but all I saw on her face was sympathy and understanding. "I know what you said on the phone. I came anyway."

"You have to go away."

Now I was just plain scared. Who was this man who spoke like a five-year-old child? Surely he couldn't be my husband.

Maddy sighed and took another careful step forward. "Listen, I need to talk to you about Mother."

Tad shook his head vehemently. "She's not my problem anymore. I don't have to deal with her anymore."

"None of us do, Tad. She committed suicide last week."

A strangled cry pushed its way out of Tad's mouth. He backed up farther so that he was nearly out of the room. "No. No, no, no, no, no, no!"

With three large steps Maddy crossed to him. I watched as he crumpled against her and sobbed as she stroked his back and whispered words that I couldn't hear.

Maddy was at the house for over an hour. I used the time to go for a run. I ran around my block a total of thirty-nine times. Each time I completed the circle I picked up the pace a little more until the only thing I could concentrate on was the strain of my breathing. I ran until I was too physically drained to feel anything intangible like the pain of betrayal.

When I finally went back into the house Tad was sitting on the sofa with his head in his hands. Maddy had her purse pulled over her shoulder and her eyeliner was badly smudged. She motioned for me to walk her out.

I stood on the doorstep with her and prayed that all she wanted to say to me was goodbye. I couldn't bear any more revelations. Even soap opera characters had their limits.

She looked up at the gathering clouds in the sky and for a moment I thought she wasn't going to speak at all. But eventually she cleared her throat and began. "April, I don't think Tad is okay."

I wiped away the sweat that was beginning to trickle into my eyes.

"He needs help. Professional help. But…I'm not sure he's going to be willing to get it." She finally turned her gaze to me. "Try to convince him otherwise, but please remember, there's only so much any one of us should be willing to sacrifice. He needs someone to tell him that if he doesn't get help he will lose everything that's important to him. But April—" she leaned forward and her voice lowered with a new level of gravity "—he does not need a martyr."

I stared at her, unsure of what to say. Apparently she hadn't expected a response because she simply nodded and then walked past me to her rental car, which was parked across the street. I watched as she got in, pulled out of her spot and then disappeared around the corner.

I looked back at my front door. "Go on, April," I whispered to myself. "Go conquer your demons."

I walked in and there he was, my demon, sitting in the middle of the couch looking absolutely devastated. His head was still in his hands and I could make out the sound of quiet sobs, the kind of sobs that leaked out after you no longer have the strength to wail.

I was a sweaty mess. I could practically feel the blackheads and pimples forming under my skin. It would be so easy to excuse myself to take a shower, thus putting off the inevitable confrontation for a few more minutes. But looking at Tad I knew he needed me now.

My eyes traveled to the phone. I should call Allie and Caleb and tell them that I wouldn't be making it for drinks later on, but I knew that was one call that would be left unmade. I couldn't be here all night, no matter how much Tad needed me. My sanity depended on it.

Tad looked up as if noticing me for the first time. "My mother's dead."

I pulled on the edges of my T-shirt. "Yes, I know…I was here when your sister told you."

Tad met my eyes and I could see fresh tears threatening to break through. "I should have told you."

"Yes, you should have." I had yet to go to him, and the ten feet that separated us felt like a mile.

"I just wanted to leave that part of my life in the past. What happened back then has nothing to do with who I am now."

It was such a ridiculous statement that I actually laughed. "Do you really expect me to believe that you're the first man in the history of the world who was in no way affected by his upbringing? Please. In one way or another our past shapes all of us, whether we like it or not."

"Not me." His voice had taken on a hard edge and I bit my lip and waited for the fireworks. But they didn't come. Instead, Tad just slumped over once again. "I wish Maddy hadn't told me. I thought that when I left I wouldn't have to deal with this again. Goddamn her, why did she have to come?"

I bit down on my lip. Wasn't he getting upset over the wrong thing? I suppose we all deal with grief in different ways. A good wife would put her arm around her husband's shoulders about now, but something stopped me. What other secrets were there? How much of the story did I know? But I couldn't ask these questions, not in the wake of his mother's death. So I swallowed them and tried to focus on the issues that I knew couldn't wait. "Tad," I said carefully, "Maddy told me that your mother was bipolar."

"Yeah, she told me that, too. I knew there was something wrong, but I just thought…" Tad ran his hand through his hair. "I don't know what I thought."

"Maddy's bipolar, too."

Tad didn't say anything.

"It seems to be a hereditary illness, Tad, and I think… maybe…"

"You think I'm crazy," he said.

I felt all the muscles in my body tighten. His lack of defensiveness felt like an admission.

"Sometimes I feel it," he said quietly. "It's like there's something inside me, something dark that's struggling to break out and take over."

He had said something to that effect to me before but I hadn't understood what he meant. It had always been there; I just hadn't seen it.

"I can't explain it well," he continued. "It's just that at times I feel like…like…" Unable to find the words to demonstrate his emotions, he raised his left hand and curled it into the formation of a claw and simulated the act of scratching the walls.

It took all my restraint to keep myself from running out the door. Who was this person I'd married? I looked away in an attempt to hide the fear that I knew must have been written all over my face. "First thing tomorrow I'm going to make an appointment with a psychiatrist—not a therapist, a psychiatrist. I'm going to get you help."

Tad nodded but didn't say anything.

"So you'll go to the appointment and if the doctor diagnoses you as bipolar then we'll get you some medication and you'll get better." I knew I was oversimplifying things, but I was pretty sure that both Tad and I needed a few deceivingly easy answers right about then.

Tad nodded again. "I'm so sorry about the other night… when you fell."

You mean when you pushed me, but I didn't say the words. Instead, I just tried to reap some satisfaction from the fact that Tad had learned how to say the word *sorry*.

"I'm so tired, April, I don't think I can talk about this anymore tonight."

"That's fine," I said a little too quickly. "I'm going to take a shower and then I'll go out so you can have some space."

"Where will you go?"

"I'm going to meet Caleb and Allie. I still have to tell them the gruesome truth about my Dawson's exit."

"Liz had no right to push you out."

I wrinkled my brow. "I didn't tell you that Liz pushed me out. That happened when you were on your business trip."

Tad straightened up and his eyes darted from one end of the room to the other before he settled on looking at his wedding ring. "I called your work. I got Gigi on the phone and she filled me in."

"Gigi? That little bitch is the reason I was pushed out in the first place. Liz rushed my exit to appease her. Did she tell you that?"

"No," Tad said, the misery in his voice palpable. "She didn't tell me that. She must have felt threatened by you or something."

"I don't have any idea why she would have. Anyone can see that she's the new darling of Dawson's. I'm just the evil step-mother who was standing in her way." I could have gone on with my rant, but one look at Tad's face held me back. No matter what lies he had told me, the fact was he had just lost his mother—it was no doubt devastating. Even an estranged mother had a special place in her children's hearts. I should know.

I walked to him and squeezed his shoulder, feeling like I owed him some kind of demonstration of affection. He seemed to be grateful for it but made no indication that he required more from me, so I got up, took a shower and got out of the house as quickly as I could.

TWENTY-FIVE

Caleb and Allie were already at Bubbles when I got there, and had somehow managed to snag a table. A bottle of champagne was chilling in front of them.

Caleb waved me over. "We were beginning to wonder if we were going to have to start the party without you," Allie chided as she tried to make eye contact with a harried-looking cocktail waitress.

"I'm five minutes late," I snapped and sat in the chair they had saved for me.

Allie and Caleb exchanged quick looks. "Hard day?" Caleb asked.

I shook my head. "Of course not, I'm free from Dawson's. I never have to deal with Gigi, Blakely, Liz or any of the others again. How could I have anything but great days?"

Allie shrugged. "I don't know, but I get the feeling that we need to get this champagne uncorked pronto." She finally succeeded in getting the attention of the waitress, who quickly came over and popped open our bottle before pouring it into the waiting flutes.

I tried to take a deep, cleansing breath. I needed to get myself together, otherwise Caleb and Allie were bound to start asking questions that I wasn't ready to answer. I took a sip of champagne, resisting the urge to down it in one gulp, and forced myself to smile. "Sorry, I'm just working off a little road rage—some idiot nearly killed me on the way over," I lied.

Allie leaned back and draped her arm over the top of her chair. "You know, I might go get myself a degree, too. Any excuse that gets me away from Liz is a good one. She fully laid into me today. Apparently my department isn't doing enough to turn the returns into exchanges. Half the merchandise that I'm forced to take back are stolen goods. What should I do? Invite the person to steal something else?"

I managed a polite laugh. I wanted to tell her that Liz was an evil bitch who deserved a horrific fate, like being forced to wear comedogenic drugstore-bought cosmetics. But I knew that in the eyes of Caleb and Allie that kind of sentence would be the equivalent of cutting off someone's hand for stealing, and my extremism would only invite the inquisition I sought to avoid.

Caleb leaned forward. "Enough of the Dawson's talk. I have some important news to tell you guys. Actually I'm *making* some important news." He paused dramatically before continuing. "A whole bunch of people are going to Sacramento to protest the state's refusal to recognize gay marriage, and guess who's helping to spread the word amongst the ever-important San Francisco gay community?"

Allie clapped a hand in front of her heart. "You're helping to organize a protest? Why, Caleb, that's so Susan Sarandon of you!"

"Let me get this straight," I said slowly. "You are going to fight for the right to marry?"

My tone alerted both Allie and Caleb that I had a problem with this. "Yesss," Caleb said. "You don't have a problem with gay marriage, do you?"

"No, except...well, gays fighting for the right to marry is kind of like women fighting for the right to be drafted. Why would you give up a perfectly good excuse to avoid that kind of hell?"

Allie and Caleb exchanged more looks but I ignored them.

"I mean, maybe you think that marriage will solve all your problems." My voice was getting higher pitched but I had lost my ability to control it. "Maybe you think that if you get a seemingly nice, normal guy to put a ring on your finger you'll gain some normalcy in your own life. But—" I leaned forward and waved a finger at Caleb "—how do you know that Mr. Normal really *is* normal? Because he told you he was? Because he's romantic and has a good job? Do you think that means something? Well, let me tell you something, it doesn't mean shit. Everyone thought Jeffrey Dahmer was normal until he started eating people. So I ask you, how the hell is a person supposed to know that their Mr. Normal isn't a cannibal?" I fell back into my chair and downed the rest of my champagne while Caleb and Allie gawked at me.

Allie shifted uncomfortably in her seat and Caleb crossed his arms over his chest before speaking up. "April," he said, "is Tad...eating people?"

I squeezed my eyes shut. I was going to have to give up on the idea of keeping Tad's behavior a secret. "No," I said, "but I kind of wish he was, then I would have a great reason to get divorced. No one would be able to accuse me of walking out on my husband without good cause if he was chopping up the neighbors and marinating them." I opened my eyes. "It would be such an easy decision."

"Wow," Allie said quietly. "I don't know what to react to first—the fact that you're talking about divorce, or how incredibly frightening that statement was."

Caleb held up his glass and swirled the liquid around gently. "I don't know everything that's going on with you two but—" he locked eyes with me "—there are plenty of valid reasons to divorce a man…even a man who isn't a murderous psychotic."

"He has a sister," I said as I poured myself some more champagne. "The bastard I'm married to has a sister."

Allie shook her head so that her red hair fell flirtatiously over one eye. "Sorry, that's not a good enough reason."

"He told me he was an only child, and then today I come home and, surprise, surprise, there she is on my doorstep. It turns out there's a brother, too, and a messed-up mother and a dad who abandoned all of them when they were little. Everything Tad ever told me about his childhood was a total lie."

"Are you kidding me?" Allie's eyes widened in horror. "Who does that?"

"Wait a minute." Caleb absently tapped his finger against his glass. "Why does this sound familiar to me?"

I sighed. "You're thinking of last season's story line on *One Life to Live*. Sam had led everyone to believe he was an only child from this upper-crust, pedigree family when he was really the son of some mafia guy. He had a brother, a sister—you name it, he had it."

Caleb snapped his fingers in recognition. "That's it! Wait, Tad isn't mafia, is he? Because that would be good grounds for divorce, too."

"No, he's not mafia. He's just crazy."

Allie smiled. "Aren't we all?"

"Well, if I wasn't before I'm definitely getting there now," I retorted. "But this is different. He says he feels like there's a dark force inside him that's struggling to get out. He's going to see a psychiatrist and hopefully the shrink will be able to tell us something, but I'll bet the family gene pool he's bipolar."

Both Allie and Caleb were frozen in place, clutching their drinks as they struggled to come up with a response.

Their silence forced me to contemplate what I had just said. "Oh, God," I whispered. "Oh, God, how am I going to handle this?" I folded my arms onto the table and let my head fall on top of them. Obviously, crying into my champagne was not the way to go.

I felt Caleb's hand pet my hair. "Okay, why don't you start from the tippy-top."

"Yeah," Allie added, "because I am completely lost."

I told them everything. Except of course for the scene in the kitchen in which he grabbed me and I "fell" to the ground.

"What do I do?" I asked when I had finished my account. "What's the right thing to do?"

Caleb and Allie both quickly looked away. They didn't have any answers. The things I was describing happened to guests on *The Ricki Lake Show* all the time but they didn't happened to people like us. We were too normal. Or at least I used to think we were.

Caleb pulled himself together first. "You're doing the right thing," he said with an assurance that I knew he didn't feel. "You're going to call a psychiatrist tomorrow and you're going to be supportive of him." He paused as if to weigh his own words. "And then…then you're going to apply to that summer language program at Cal."

"Are you crazy?" I let out a humorless laugh. "I can't go to Cal now. I can't afford it."

Caleb held my gaze for a full thirty seconds before saying, "My treat."

I gasped, then looked at Allie to see if she had heard what I had. She straightened up in her chair and quickly finished off her glass of Cristal. "I'll chip in, too."

Caleb held up his hand in protest. "No, no, this one's on me," he said. "No offense, ladies, but I make a lot more than both of you and I have a lot more saved."

"Caleb, that's so sweet," I said, fresh tears springing to my eyes. "But you know I can't accept. It's too much."

"You have a birthday coming up, right? Consider it an early birthday gift."

"Um, the tuition for that summer session is three thousand dollars."

"Okay, so consider it an early Hanukkah gift. What would that come out to…three hundred and seventy-five dollars for each of the eight nights."

Allie shook her head in disbelief. "That beats the hell out of chocolate gelt."

I smiled dismissively and split the rest of the champagne between our glasses. "I really appreciate the offer, Caleb, but it really doesn't make sense for me to enroll right now. I don't know what's going on with my finances or my marriage—any aspect of my life. So for me to invest a lot of your money into a language program on the off chance that I'm going to be able to pursue a doctorate any time within the next decade is just irresponsible and stupid."

Caleb rolled his eyes. "Oh, God forbid we do anything that

could be perceived as irresponsible or stupid. We should always take the safe route, right, April?" He leaned over the table so that it was difficult for me to avoid his eyes. "We should always take the road more traveled. Isn't that right? We should marry the nice guy with a good income, take the job that offers us a steady income, even though we hate it, and we should always give up our dreams for the sake of practicality. After all, that is the philosophy that got you where you are today, right?"

My face heated up and I tightened my grip around my glass stem. "I don't want to throw your money away," I whispered.

"And I don't want you to throw your life away. When I get home I'm going online to get you an application. You're going to Berkeley this summer and that's final."

When I got home that night I felt an odd sense of relief. Caleb had given one aspect of my life some unexpected clarity—attaining a Ph.D. I would still have to find a part-time job, but that was doable. I'd need to learn French…but of all the things I had on my plate that one seemed the easiest to accomplish.

The rest of my life was another story. The next morning after Tad went to work I called Kaiser Medical Center and asked to be connected to the psychiatric department. The earliest appointment I was able to schedule was three weeks away. And those three weeks turned into some of the most difficult of my life. I didn't know what to say to Tad so I avoided saying anything at all. Every morning when he woke up to go to work I pretended to be sleeping late. Then I would spend my days filling out job applications and contacting temp agencies. Then I would pray that Tad would work into the evening hours, which he almost always did. When we did speak it was strained. I would ask him

how his day went. It was always fine. He never gave me any
details, and I was too afraid to ask for any. Tad was falling asleep
in front of the television with increasing frequency and when
that happened he almost never made it to the bed, which was a
major relief. Why would I want to share my bed with a stranger?

My mother called a few times. She never caught me at home
and I never listened to her messages. I knew I needed to talk to
her, but I couldn't deal with her drama just then. I could barely
deal with my own.

The day I drove Tad to his appointment was beyond awful.
I sat behind the wheel of the Z3 that I had yet to sell despite
the ad I placed in the paper. Tad sat beside me staring glumly
into space.

I glanced over at him. He looked so forlorn. So totally de-
spondent. I reached out and gave his knee an awkward pat.
"Are you okay?"

"Yeah."

"You know, this is the first step to making everything better."

Tad didn't say anything. I pressed my lips together and turned
on the radio.

We drove in silence as Beck explained to the world that he
was a loser who needed to be killed. The song faded out as we
approached Kaiser.

It seemed that the psychiatric department was located in the
most remote corner of the building, which would have worked
in favor of those patients who wished to be discreet, provided
they knew where they were going. Tad and I were not so well-
informed. Instead, we were forced to expose the reason for our
visit to a handful of strangers as we repeatedly asked directions.

Finally, we found the right lobby and I announced our presence one more time to the receptionist.

The woman behind the desk smiled warmly at me. "Has he been here before?"

I glanced nervously at Tad. He was standing right next to me. "No, um, this is our first time."

"How about other Kaiser departments? Has he been to this facility before for any reason?"

Tad was glaring at her now but the woman didn't seem to notice. I shifted my weight from foot to foot and tried to wait for Tad to answer the question for himself, but the pause went on for too long and I couldn't stop myself from answering. "No, he's never—" I stopped myself remembering all the things that I had not known until recently. I looked up at him questioningly. "Have you been here before?"

"No."

The woman seemed not to hear him and was still watching me with an expectant smile while she waited for me to repeat his answer.

God, this was uncomfortable.

She gave me the forms, I handed them to him, he filled them out. She asked me for his card, he gave it to me, I gave it to her and so on. It was absolutely horrible. He was a psychiatric patient, not a child. I would complain. Or at least I'd add it to my three-page list of customer-complaint letters that I planned to write sometime in the next few years.

Eventually, we sat down in the sparsely populated institutional-looking waiting room. I took note of the other individuals in the room. There was a woman in the far corner who was about a hundred-plus pounds overweight. She had a magazine in her hand, but it kept falling into what might be considered her lap as she sporadically dozed off. Across from us was a middle-aged man with thinning hair who was biting his fingernails and looking around the room anxiously.

"I don't belong here," I heard Tad whisper. I didn't answer for fear I might be forced to agree with him. But if he didn't belong here where *did* he belong? Where did the people that were marginally crazy get help? Were there support groups for that?

I sighed and studied the gray carpeting under my feet. This had to be the right place. I had spent a good fifteen minutes on the phone with the psychiatrist who would be seeing him. It took some doing to arrange that phone conversation, but I thought that it was important the man who would be analyzing Tad talk to me first, particularly since Tad had told me that he didn't want me in the room during the appointment. If the psychiatrist just talked to Tad and Tad didn't feel like telling the whole truth, where would that leave us? The doctor would believe him (everyone believed Tad when they first met him) and we would be back to square one. I couldn't go back to square one. At least this way the psychiatrist would be able to ask him about specific events and that would make evasion difficult. Of course, Tad could choose to out and out lie, in which case we were screwed.

"Tad Showers?" A man called his name from the doorway. Tad stood up and the man made eye contact with him and nodded in greeting. He looked friendly and kind. That was good; the receptionist hadn't been representative of the rest of the staff. Tad looked so scared. I smiled at him for the first time in ages. I didn't want him to be scared. I just wanted us both to be okay.

He gave me a curt nod and then disappeared through a swinging door.

TWENTY-SIX

The car ride home from the appointment was excruciating. I wanted to ask so many questions, but it felt wrong to immediately begin an interrogation. For some bizarre reason I had assumed that Tad would volunteer some information on his own. But that was a stupid assumption. If nothing else, the experiences of the last few months should have taught me that Tad didn't volunteer unpleasant information.

I sighed as I put the stick in Neutral at a red light. I eyed Tad without turning my head in his direction. He was staring fixedly at the road in front of us. I had to ask. "Tad, what did the doctor say?"

"He thinks I'm bipolar."

My heart sunk. It shouldn't have—we had predicted the diagnosis—but to hear that a licensed professional of the medical community agreed with our diagnosis scared the shit out of me. *If you're scared, think of how Tad must be feeling right now.* It was probably the most empathetic comment my little voice had ever made. The light changed and I pushed the car into gear. "So now what?" My voice was barely above a whisper.

Tad shook his head. "He wants to put me on medication."

I glanced at him before quickly returning my eyes to the road. By his tone one would have thought the doctor had recommended he take a daily swim in a pool full of leeches. "Um, isn't that a good thing? I mean, if you can fix it with a pill…"

"I don't want to take pills. I don't need to be drugged up, and I'll be damned if I'm going to take lithium."

My eyes widened. "Did he say you needed to be on lithium? Did you ask about Lamictal?"

"He said he wanted to try Depekote first."

"Oh…" I slowed to allow a car to change lanes in front of me. "Do you have anything against Depekote?"

From the corner of my eye I could see the tightening of his jaw. "I don't need meds."

That was it. With a jerk of the wheel I made a frighteningly sharp turn onto a side street and screeched to a stop in front of a fire hydrant. I took off my seat belt so that I could better angle my body in his direction. "Listen, I know you're sick. You have a chemical imbalance that affects your behavior. I can accept that. I can even forgive you for all the shit that you've pulled up to this point, but only if you're willing to try to get better. So here's your last chance. Come clean with me about all the lies that you've told me and follow your doctor's orders, or get out of my life."

"Don't talk to me like that!"

I wanted to smack him, but then I saw his eyes moistening. I turned away and stared out the window as the cars rushed by us. What was wrong with me? Had I really thought that yelling at a man who had just been diagnosed with a mental illness was going to be helpful? My mind went back to my miscarriage. Tad had been there for me when I needed him and I wanted to be there for him now. But he had to meet me halfway.

"I'm…sorry," I said. "I don't mean to be bitchy. But I need you to understand that I'm at the end of my rope." I turned back to him and tried to gauge the effect my words were having on him. "Try the medication. If it's awful, we'll try something else. Promise you'll at least try it."

Tad nodded. "I'll try it."

"One more thing…" My voice wavered, my next request could result in confessions that I didn't really want to hear. "I meant it when I said you needed to come clean. Are there more secrets?"

Tad shook his head but did not meet my eyes.

"Are you sure? Right now I'm offering you a 'get out of jail free' card. Tell me what you've kept from me, lied about or whatever, and I will forgive you. We'll work through it. But, Tad, if I find out later on my own, things will get ugly."

He turned toward me and his eyes met mine. "No more secrets. I'm not going to do anything that could cost me you."

I felt my shoulders relax. I hadn't even realized that I had been holding them in an elevated position. I refastened my seat belt and pulled back onto the street. I could breathe now. Tad loved me; he was going to get help for his illness. Everything was going to be okay.

But that horrible little voice inside of me had a different take on the situation. *All Tad did was tell you what you wanted to hear.*

I tried to cuddle up with Tad and watch *The Wedding Singer*, which was playing on Comedy Central. It felt like a normal-couple kind of thing to do, but I hated it. Not the movie, but the feeling of being close to Tad. He was busy laughing along with Adam and Drew and he threw me an occasional loving look. But there was something forced about his laugh, and something desperate about his looks of love. Nothing was right, which was why I got panicky when he changed position and started sucking on my neck.

I felt his teeth gently graze my ear as his hands began to explore the rest of me. I knew all his moves and had given most of them Olympic 6.0 scores or at the very least 5.6's. But that night the only desire he was drawing out of me was the desire to flee to my room and barricade the door…again.

Tad's hand moved under my shirt and over my bra. I sucked in a sharp breath. Okay, I could do this. He was my husband, I was his wife, we were supposed to want each other. I could do this.

I closed my eyes and tried to enjoy the sensation as he gently pinched my nipple.

The image of Jeremiah popped into my head. He was onstage, sweaty, sexy, but there was no audience…only me. It was his hands I felt against my breast, it was his mouth on my neck, his erection pressing against my upper thigh….

"I can't do this." I pushed Tad away and jumped off the couch.

The shock on Tad's face looked almost comical. Almost.

"I…I don't understand," he stammered.

"Today was just…draining. Would it be okay if we just held each other tonight?"

"But…" Tad was sitting up now. I noticed that the bulge in his pants had deflated. "You were enjoying yourself, I could tell."

What was I supposed to say? *Sorry, hon, but the only way I can deal with your touching me is if I pretend I'm with your old workout buddy, Jeremiah.* I swallowed hard. "It's not that I wasn't enjoying myself, I'm just so tired and—"

The doorbell rang and I nearly fell to my knees and thanked the Lord for the last-minute reprieve.

Tad glanced at the wall clock before getting up and straightening his shirt. "Nine o'clock, kind of late for Jehovah's Witnesses, isn't it?"

I smiled and shrugged. Maybe it was a band of robbers and they were going to take everything, including the bed *and* the couch! Then I wouldn't have to have sex with my husband for weeks!

I waited in the living room as Tad went to see who the late-night caller was.

"Sean," I heard him say, "I thought you were in San Diego."

"I just got back tonight. What's this shit I hear about there not being enough money to pay the partners this month?"

A chill crept up my spine. I had spoken to Sean on several occasions but I had never heard him use this tone before, and I had a horrible feeling that his words were indicative of another Tad-made disaster.

"Well, as I explained to Eric, the funds are a little tight this month with—"

"Last month we were rolling in it and this month things are so tight that I don't get to bring home a paycheck? What happened to the money, Tad?"

"It's not my fault that you spent half the company's expense fund on wining and dining the guys at UMW," Tad snarled. "They're not even a big account and you spent—"

"This isn't about UMW, and you know it. This is about the mismanagement of funds, Tad."

"I don't know what the fuck you're talking about, unless you've been using company funds to woo some of the young boys at the YMCA. Tell me, Sean, did your ex-wife ever find out about that little incident in college? Does your pious Catholic family know that you're a faggot?"

I gasped. Tad couldn't have said those things. He wasn't capable of it. Yet it had been his voice, and the silence that followed his statement told me that I had not misheard.

"That was one incident in college. I was nineteen. One incident, Tad. One incident I told you about in confidence. I wouldn't have told you at all if we hadn't been drinking."

"If you want me to keep your dirty little secrets then I suggest you refrain from banging on my door in the middle of the night accusing me of mismanagement of company funds. Now get the fuck off my doorstep." I heard the door slam and Tad stormed back into the living room and sat in front of the television. I had forgotten that it was on. I looked over at Adam Sandler, who was berating some woman for wearing a Van Halen T-shirt. I looked at Tad. He wasn't laughing. His face was twisted into a menacing grimace.

"Tad?" I whispered.

"Can you believe that asshole? If he thinks he can fuck with me he has another think coming."

I took a step back, almost tripping over the coffee table. "I'm um…" What? What was I? Horrified? Frightened? Enraged? I looked at Tad's hands. They were now curled into tight fists. "I'm going to bed," I finished. I turned around and went into my room. And for the second time in our marriage I locked the door.

I couldn't sleep that night so I did push-ups instead. And when my arms could no longer support me I started work on my abs. I found my Walkman tucked into the corner of my closet and chose to listen to Offspring while I worked my muscles to the point of exhaustion. I welcomed the emotional release that exercise offered me and I liked the idea of being strong, the idea that one day I might be able to kick Tad's ass.

I finally went to bed at 5:00 a.m., and at 7:00 a.m. I was awakened by the smell of pancakes. For a few sleepy moments I imagined I was still dreaming. I hadn't had pancakes since I was pregnant.

I pushed myself out of bed and put on a robe and slippers. Tad had a lot of problems but his pancakes were always perfect.

That thought gave me the courage to open the door and tiptoe into the kitchen. Tad stood in front of the stove dribbling batter onto a sizzling skillet. He looked up at me and his lips formed a rather strained smile. "Good morning, birthday girl."

Birthday girl? I checked the wall calendar. Well, what do you know, it *was* my birthday!

Tad furrowed his brow. "Did you forget? That's unlike you."

"I've been distracted." I sat down at the kitchen table and watched as he flipped a pancake over.

"I was thinking that to celebrate, we'd—"

"What's going on at SMB?"

Tad was silent. He carefully transferred a short stack over onto a clean plate and put it in front of me, along with a small creamer full of maple syrup and a big slab of butter.

I spread the butter on with a circular motion. "Tad, did you hear my question?"

"You know, I woke up early this morning to cook a special breakfast for you and you don't even have the courtesy—"

"No." I put my butter knife down. "You don't get to turn this around or avoid the question. What's going on at SMB?"

Tad frowned and walked back to the stove to prepare some breakfast for himself. "Sean's an asshole. He doesn't understand business."

"He said the funds were being mishandled."

"That's bullshit. There were a few extra expenses last month, that's all. It happens when companies expand."

"And then you called him a faggot."

Tad's back was to me so I couldn't see his expression, but I could see his shoulders tense up. "You know I'm not homophobic…I was just very, very angry."

It wasn't Tad's homophobia or lack thereof that concerned me, it was the violence of his reaction. "You know what I want for my birthday?"

"What?" Tad's voice no longer sounded friendly.

"I want you to call the psychiatrist and get a prescription for the medication he recommended."

Tad put a few pancakes on his plate and took a seat beside me. "He gave me the prescription yesterday. I just have to get it filled."

I picked up my fork and stabbed my meal. "Then why didn't you fill it while we were at Kaiser yesterday?"

"I wanted to talk to you about it first."

Bullshit. I squeezed my eyes closed and silently counted to ten. "I'll fill the prescription for you this afternoon."

"You don't need to do that. Today's your birthday."

"I want to do it. Where's the prescription?"

"Jesus Christ, April, I'm trying to have a nice breakfast with you."

Did he think that was possible? Was he under the misguided impression that my increasing age would trigger some short-term memory loss? "Where's the prescription?" I repeated.

Tad looked as if he wanted to tear my head off. Instead, he pulled his wallet out of his pocket and handed me a folded-up piece of paper, which I stuck in the pocket of my robe. "I'll fill it today."

"Fine," Tad said sulkily. "Can we eat now?"

I took another bite. The pancakes were great but for some reason I no longer had an appetite. I just wanted Tad to go to work so I could have some space to breathe. So when Tad kissed me before leaving and asked how I wanted to celebrate my birthday that night I told him that I had made plans with Allie. "Girls' night out." Tad knew it was a lie and I could see the hurt in his eyes. I felt horrible, but I couldn't celebrate with him. I could barely stand to be in the same room with him.

About an hour after he left, Bobe called. "Happy birthday, *mummala*. So how does it feel to be such an old lady?"

"Tiring," I answered. Bobe laughed. She thought I was joking. Over the last few months I had managed to keep my conversations with Bobe brief and infrequent. If she knew about everything that I was going through she'd be devastated, but lying to her was beyond awful.

"So what plans do you have for the day? Perhaps Tad is taking you out for a proper meal for a change?"

"For a change?" I plopped myself on the chair by the phone. The one thing I had been able to consistently count on Tad for was a good meal.

"Last time I saw you, you were too skinny. You need to eat more."

I looked down at my ever-thinning figure. The last time Bobe had seen me I was getting married, at which time I was probably seven to ten pounds heavier than I was now. How had that happened? "I'll have a large meal tonight," I said.

"Good. Tad will be wanting children soon and it's not good to become pregnant when you are malnourished. Very bad for the baby."

My neck muscles tensed. Bobe had no idea that I had already

lost one child. She didn't know how understanding and caring Tad had been, and she didn't know how much I wanted out of my marriage.

I put my hand over my heart and stifled a gasp. *I wanted out of my marriage.* When I had thrown the word *divorce* around at the Bubble Lounge I had told myself that I was joking…just being dramatic in the face of controversy. But I had meant it. I had sworn that I would stand by him in sickness and in health, and now he was sick and I wanted out. I hated myself.

"*Mummala? Mummala,* are you still there?"

"Yes, Bobe, I'm still here but I have to get going. Tad took the day off work for my birthday and I'm supposed to meet him at our favorite breakfast spot." It was frightening how the lies rolled off my tongue.

"Oh good, you go and eat," she said. Then more tentatively, "When will I see you again, *mummala?* It's been so long."

It had been quite a while. A lifetime. "I'll come down next weekend. Tad won't be able to come due to a new business deal he's putting together, but I will." I looked up at the painting Tad had purchased with my credit card. "I actually have a gift for you."

"It's your birthday and you're giving me gifts?"

"I bought it awhile ago, and have been meaning to give it to you."

"Nothing too extravagant. Don't waste your money on me."

"Don't worry, it's just something to hang on your wall. Look, Bobe, I really have to go. I'll call you in a few days?"

"Of course, *mummala.* You go meet that husband of yours. Such a handsome man and a real mensche, too."

I winced and muttered a last goodbye before hanging up. A real mensche. A real sick mensche married to a real selfish bitch.

The phone rang again. It was unlike Bobe to call back… "Hello?"

"April, it's Mom."

I bit my lip. I had been waiting for things to settle down before trying to reconcile with her, but I now realized that by the time that happened we'd both be dead. "Mom," I said in my best professional voice, "I've been meaning to call you."

There was a long pause before she spoke again. "You're not going to hang up on me?"

"No, I'm not."

"Really." Another silence. "I wasn't expecting that."

"I'm sorry, did I throw you off? If it would help I could hang up on you now."

I heard my mother sigh into the receiver. "I called to wish you a happy birthday."

"Thank you."

"I got you something. I had my astrologer do your chart."

"Of course you did." The words slipped out before I was able to check them. I really didn't want to be sarcastic. I cleared my throat and decided to throw her a bone. "What did my chart say this year?"

"It says that this will be a year of self-discovery and…well, it just says lots of stuff."

Now, *this* was different. Usually she couldn't wait to give me the details of my horoscope. "What did my chart say, Mom?" I asked again, this time with genuine interest.

"It said that the year would be filled with self-discovery and that a relationship will end while others will become stronger. And in September, Saturn will be entering your seventh house and, well, that's bound to stir up lots of trouble."

I slumped back in my chair. "That's just fucking great."

"These things aren't always right, you know."

My eyes flew open. My mother had broken up with men based on their sign and now she was telling me that "these things aren't always right"? Was she saying that to spare my feelings? That would be a first. "Is everything okay, Mom?"

"I want you to have a nice birthday. We used to have so much fun on your birthdays when you were little. Do you remember how we tried to make a vegan ice-cream cake for your ninth birthday? We even tried to make the ice cream ourselves."

"But the cake never rose and the ice cream never hardened so we made giant milk shakes and ate the cake with a spoon."

My mother laughed. "I never could bake anything."

"You did okay with the hash brownies."

There was another long pause and again I regretted my words.

"I want you to have a nice birthday. I know I owe you that."

I furrowed my brow. She was acting as if she had a lot more control over my day than she really did. "Okay," I said carefully. "I'll have a nice birthday."

"Good. Look, I need…or… Can we talk tomorrow?"

"Sure." I could tell that there was something going on, but it was also obvious to me that neither of us wanted to get into it right now.

"I'll call you tomorrow then. Happy birthday, April."

"Thanks." I put the receiver into its cradle. That had been weird. Granted, I hadn't spoken to her for over four months now, but there was more to it than that.

I shook my head. I had other things to deal with. I pulled out Tad's prescription and looked at the chicken scrawl that was written across the white paper. This was the answer to my problems. Tad would take his medicine and everything would be back to normal.

It had been normal once. Hadn't it?

TWENTY-SEVEN

My mother did call the next day but only to set up a face-to-face meeting, but she had just started a job with some medical marijuana advocacy group and her work schedule wouldn't allow her to get into the city until the end of the week. So now, five days later, I sat at a little two-person table at Herbivores and waited for her to arrive. She hadn't wanted to meet at my place, which had been fine with me. Even though Tad wasn't home very often I still didn't feel comfortable being there. Caleb and Allie had ended up taking me to a movie on the evening of my birthday and afterward Caleb had handed me the enrollment papers for Berkeley's summer language program. The forms had a box to check if you needed housing. I had been *soooo* tempted. How sad was it that living in a dorm at the age of twenty-seven seemed preferable to living in a house with my husband?

When I saw my mother's figure appear in the front entrance, I took a moment to study her before waving her over. She was wearing a long A-line tie-dyed skirt and an orange tank top with an open oversize denim shirt hanging over it. Her burgundy highlights had gone red but it looked as if she hadn't touched them up for a while. She was tugging at the end of her shirt and looking around as if she expected to see a gunman pop out from under a table and take her hostage. I had seen her behave like this before and I knew what it meant; she was in trouble. Shit. Shit, shit, shit, shit. I did not need this. She had probably gotten involved with another idiot who didn't take kindly to being dumped, or maybe she had been busted for possession and had skipped bail. Whatever it was, I didn't want to deal with it, and I resented the hell out of her for having the nerve to drop it in my lap after she had skipped my wedding. I considered ducking under the table but it was too late. Her eyes caught mine and she managed a shaky smile. She crossed over to me and I stood up to give her the hug I knew she expected.

"April, you're so thin!"

I pulled back. My mother never noticed my weight. I smoothed my shirt and realized that my rib cage did seem a little more pronounced.

I motioned for her to take a seat and pushed a menu in her direction. "The vegan dishes are marked with a star, so you don't need to quiz the waiter about the ingredient list."

My mother didn't even look at the choices printed in front of her. "Does Tad know you're meeting me?"

Deep in the recesses of my mind a little warning bell went off. "No, I didn't get around to mentioning it to him." I had barely gotten around to speaking to Tad.

My mother nodded and finally looked at the menu. "I'll have mixed green salad," she announced.

Now I knew something was wrong. The mixed green salad was the most conventional thing on the menu. It didn't even have tofu in it.

The waiter came over to our table and I ordered, despite my complete lack of appetite. The minute he left, my mother leaned forward and took my hand. "April, I know you're angry with me and maybe you have a right to be—"

"Maybe? Are you kidding?"

She shook her head and continued as if she hadn't heard me. "I just need you to know that I really liked Tad. I wouldn't ever say anything bad about him if it wasn't…if it wasn't true."

The warning bell had turned into a siren.

"Mom, what do you know about Tad?"

She looked like she was going to cry. "The whole calendar and bumper-sticker thing…it's just a mess, April. He promised he would give everyone a refund for the calendars or at least redo them, and the bumper stickers, well, those still haven't arrived, and now the other congregants think that Tad and I conspired to take their money or something. I mean, the Children of the Earth are the most forgiving and patient people in the world but everyone has their limits and now I'm afraid…"

"Whoa, whoa, whoa." I held up my free hand to stop her. "What are you talking about? What calendars? What bumper stickers?"

"The ones that he was supposed to make for the Temple of the Earth Goddess. You knew he was going to make them."

"No, he promised me that he wouldn't."

My mother's eyes narrowed. "Then it's you? Are you the reason that he didn't fix the calendars?"

"There weren't supposed to be any calendars to fix." My voice went up a few decibels. "He was never supposed to start the project. He promised me before we were even married."

"Oh…" My mother looked puzzled. "But he did do some work on them since then. I got the first shipment a month after you got back from Spain. April, they're horrible. He got all the holidays wrong, and some of the pictures show these horrid man-made structures…"

"Tad sent you the calendars a month after our honeymoon?"

"Yes. I suppose everyone could have lived with the pictures, but the holidays…instead of putting the Day of the Bear on May fourth like it's supposed to be, he put it in December. December! Bears hibernate in December! And he completely forgot about the Day of the Amphibian, and that's one of the biggest holidays of the year!"

Was this seriously happening? I withdrew my hand from hers and nibbled on what was left of my fingernails. I had bitten them to the quick weeks ago. "So you're saying that Tad made these calendars for you and then when they weren't up to snuff he refused to fix them?"

"No…not refused exactly. He said he'd fix them. He just didn't. Oh, and the order was short by twelve calendars, and the bumper stickers never came in at all. We paid him up-front for all of it, April. He said that it was necessary to cover his production costs. Now whenever I try to call him his secretary puts me through to his voice mail and he never returns my calls.…"

"You could have called me!" My voice carried through the restaurant and a few heads turned in our direction.

"Sweetie, I did call you but you never returned my calls. I left you lots of messages explaining everything. Didn't you listen to any of them?"

She had left several messages on my cell and I had listened long enough to determine that it was her before pressing the delete button. "You could have tried my home," I mumbled, knowing damn well that I wouldn't have listened to those messages, either.

"What are you talking about? I left at least ten messages on your answering machine last month and at least that many the month before."

"No you didn't or I would have gotten them...."

I felt a stabbing sensation in my chest. Tad always checked the messages from his work. And if he was checking the messages he could have been deleting them, too.

One by one, more of the puzzle pieces were fitting together. Tad had good reason to encourage the recent estrangement between my mother and me. He hadn't wanted me to find out that he had conned her and her friends. Once again he had been trying to conceal the true nature of his character.

"How much money have people shelled out for this little business venture?" My voice was icy. I was beyond angry. I was beyond any emotion that I had ever experienced.

"A little over three thousand."

"For calendars and bumper stickers?"

"Well, there were about a hundred and thirty or so orders for calendars and almost two hundred orders for bumper stickers..."

"I'll talk to Tad."

My mother shifted uncomfortably in her chair. "April, I'm picking up some very bad vibes. Have there been other problems between you and Tad? You just don't seem as...as shocked as I suspected."

"You were trying to shock me?" I let out a humorless laugh.

"You should have shown up with a French manicure and an Ann Taylor suit."

"There have been problems, haven't there? The few times I talked to Tad on the phone, he had a lot of negative energy."

I met her eyes and considered my options. Telling the truth about Tad's illness might buy him some time with the jilted Earth Children. That would be a good thing, especially since California was a community-property state, which meant his debt was my debt. "Tad's been going through a hard time," I said slowly. "He was recently diagnosed as being bipolar."

My mother gasped. "Bipolar? Who diagnosed him with that? A western medical doctor, I bet."

"Well, it wasn't his acupuncturist."

"They're always trying to diagnose people with things these days. I bet they put him on medication, too. That's why he's acting this way." My mother shook her head in dismay. "Listen, April, Tad's just a free spirit. I'm sure he's simply having a hard time harnessing all his creative energy while working in that corporate job of his."

"SMB isn't a corporation, it's a private partnership."

"Private partnership, corporation—" she waved her hand in the air dismissively "—it all falls under the same evil capitalist umbrella. He needs to find a career more suited to his enlightened mentality. It's the medication, I'm sure that's why he hasn't been able to fill the product order. When you were a little girl I hooked up with this guy named Jordy. His doctor told him he was bipolar, too, but he didn't buy it. He never took a pill and he was just fine."

"Jordy…I think I remember him. He was the one who was arrested for writing bad checks, right?"

My mother tapped the table thoughtfully. "I forgot about that."

I threw some money down on the table and got up. "Mom, I've got to go. I'll call you as soon as I talk to Tad, okay?"

She flashed me a relieved smile. "Thank you, April. I knew I could count on you."

It took me exactly sixteen minutes to get home. The first thing I noticed was Tad's car. He was home early. Good. That saved me another unpleasant trip to SMB. I stormed inside and found him sitting in the living room listening to Mozart while staring into a glass of what looked like whiskey or bourbon. He didn't even bother to look up as I entered. So it was Barcelona all over again. Wonderful. But this time his behavior didn't scare me as much as it just pissed me off.

"Tad?" I spoke his name at a volume that would suggest that we were separated by a football field rather than a coffee table.

His eyes rolled up in my direction but he didn't say anything.

"Why are you home?" I asked, although I wasn't at all sure if I cared.

"I decided to call it an early day." His voice sounded hollow. "It was just a bad day, that's all."

"You had a bad day? What a coincidence, I had a bad day, too. I bet if we compared notes we might even find out that we both have the same problem."

"What would that be?" Tad asked.

"You."

He straightened up. Now I got a real good look at him. His face was flushed and his eyes were glazed over and red. No doubt he had been drinking for a while now.

"What are you talking about?" With an unsteady hand he lifted his glass and slammed the rest of his cocktail.

"I just had lunch with my mother."

Silence.

"You son of a bitch," I hissed. "All this time you were telling me that I needed to cut my mother out of my life because it was the best thing for me but it wasn't about me at all, was it? It was all about you, as always."

Tad shook his head and clumsily pulled himself to his feet. "No, I didn't want you to talk to your mom 'cause she's bad for you."

I took a step back in disbelief. I wasn't sure if I had ever seen Tad this hammered before.

"She's bad for you, April," he continued. "You don't need her."

"Oh, really? So I should just disappear from her life the way you disappeared from your mother's life?"

"Yes!" Tad nodded enthusiastically.

"Because that worked so well for you. I mean, look at you. You're just the poster boy for mental health, right?"

Tad didn't answer, just gazed at his empty glass.

"And your advice didn't have anything to do with the fact that you ripped off my mother's Earth Goddess cult to the tune of three thousand dollars?"

Again, no answer.

"You are amazing." I crossed my arms over my chest and looked up at the ceiling. "The bipolar piece is just the tip of the iceberg isn't it, Tad? I mean, your problems go way beyond that. You're a full-blown sociopath."

"I'm not a sociopath," Tad growled.

"Really?" I raised an eyebrow. "Let's see what Webster's dictionary has to say about that." I marched over to the bookcase, pulled out the dictionary and flipped to the correct page. "'Sociopathic—characterized by asocial or antisocial behavior or exhibiting antisocial personality disorder.' So let's think about that. Do you think you were being very social when you were staring at the wall of our hotel room in Barcelona? Do you have a healthy social relationship with your sister or brother? Oh, that's right, you're an only child."

Tad snatched the dictionary out of my hand and threw it to the ground. "Listen, I didn't—"

"No," I said, cutting him off. "I don't want to listen. You'll just lie to me. You know I could have forgiven the unfilled bumpersticker order, but for you to try to convince me to disown my mother just to protect yourself…that you could erase her messages…" I shook my head and fought back the tears of hurt and anger. "I'm leaving you, Tad. I'm going to pack my things right now and I am leaving you."

Tad's eyes widened. He looked shocked. Shocked! Had he actually thought that I was going to just stand by while he hurt my family and lied about it?

"April." He grabbed both of my arms, but the gesture was one of desperation rather than violence. "April, you can't leave me. I love you."

"Maybe you should have thought about that before." I pulled away and went to the hall closet where we stored the suitcases.

"April, wait, it's the bipolar disorder. It makes me do crazy things. Just give me a few more weeks on the medication and everything will go back to the way it was."

"How was it, exactly?" I pulled out the largest bag and lugged it into the bedroom. "As far as I can tell, everything about our lives together has been one cleverly orchestrated lie."

"That's not true." Tad stumbled after me and I turned to see him wobbling in the doorway. "I've always loved you and I always will."

I glared at him and started to remove my clothes from my dresser.

He grabbed my hand. "No, you have to know it hasn't all been a lie. You remember when we lost our baby, right?"

I swallowed and looked away. I didn't want to remember that.

"I stood by you, April, you know I did. Now all I'm asking is that you stand by me."

I yanked my hand away. "I've been standing by you. I stood by you when I found out that you lied to me about the rent. I stood by you when I found out about the credit card. I stood by you when I found out that you had been lying about your family. I was there for you when you had to face your own mental illness. I even stuck it out after you trashed my car and threw me on the kitchen floor. But now you've hurt my family. And I can't stand by you while you do that."

"So I'll stop!" Tad screamed. I shook my head and continued packing.

"I'll stop, April, I will. I didn't mean to hurt your family. I'm just sick, but I'll get better. You have to give me some time to get better."

I ignored him and continued packing. I couldn't let him weaken my resolve.

"April, I can't live without you. You're my life. You're everything to me."

I bit my lip and kept packing.

I didn't look at him but I could hear him sobbing. I wanted to go to him, but I knew that if I did I would have to stay, and I couldn't do that. I couldn't survive it.

I listened to his heavy footsteps as he left the room and traveled to the kitchen. Was I being unfair? Should I give him another month or two on the medication? I looked around the room. *You need to get out,* my little voice screamed. But didn't my little voice remember all the times Tad and I had laughed together? And where had my little voice been during our love-making sessions? Probably shocked into silence. I glanced at the door. I would talk to him.

I put down the clothes in my hand and went to the kitchen. I was still leaving but I would try to do it on a better note. Tad was standing over the sink with his back to me. He was shaking and I could still hear his little sobs. I stepped forward quietly. "Tad," I said gently.

He turned and that's when I saw the blood coming out of his wrist. His eyes were wild with fear and pain.

"Oh my God." They were the only words I could think to say.

"April, help me. Please help me."

I rushed to his side and noted that only one wrist was cut and that the slash was horizontal not vertical. He wouldn't die. But still, there was a lot of blood. "Sit down," I ordered and ran to the bathroom and yanked open the drawer where we kept the first-aid supplies, and then ran back to the kitchen with a long strip of gauze that I wrapped around his wrist. He was crying too hard for me to understand him, but every few sentences or so I caught "can't live without you," and "want to die."

I knelt in front of him. "Tad, listen to me. We have to get you to the hospital."

"I want to die," he cried.

"No, you don't. You know you don't. We're going to the emergency room now, okay?"

He didn't answer, so I gently took his elbow and guided him into a standing position. I led him to the Z3 parked in front of the house. I opened the passenger-side door and he obediently got in. I went around to my side and stuck my key into the ignition. Before I pushed the gearshift into Reverse, I took a second to look at him and for a sudden and brief moment I had my first full-fledged out-of-body experience. But unlike the out-of-body experiences that you hear about on Lifetime, there was nothing wonderful or enlightening about this. I didn't feel like a free spirit or an angel. Oddly enough I felt more like a Holly-wood *producer*, studying a film that I needed to edit. I could see Tad and I could see April and I could see the chaos and the pain that those characters were both in but I was watching the scene with an impassive and detached eye. It was the visual details that had my attention…like all the blood, Tad's blood. It was still coming, soaking the bandaging. If the blood leaked onto the interior of the car it would be a lot more difficult to sell. April would be stuck with it. She would have to learn to live with it and accept it even though the audience would know that she wanted to be free of that car so badly she could taste it.

And the audience would shake their heads and give each other knowing glances because that was life. Sometimes you get stuck with the things you don't want.

TWENTY-EIGHT

The emergency-room doctors fixed up Tad, interviewed him, interviewed me and then sent us home. In their professional opinion Tad was suffering from severe depression and needed therapy. Thank God we had medical insurance, because if I had to pay for that advice I would have been seriously ticked. On the flip side I was freaked out enough that I was able to score myself a prescription for Paxil.

I love Paxil. It had been seven weeks since Tad cut his wrist, nothing had improved but thanks to my miracle drug I wasn't perpetually on the verge of a major anxiety attack.

I flipped through some merchandise at Macy's that I couldn't afford. I was waiting for Allie, who was taking me to dinner at the Cheesecake Factory.

I had told both her and Caleb about Tad's little accident several weeks ago. They had both been appropriately appalled and offered to help me move. But I had postponed my marital separation. I desperately wanted to leave him but I didn't want him to commit suicide on account of something I did. Somehow I had to find a way to make it work, or at least give it a last try.

He was taking his medication now. I knew because I counted his pills every morning after he left for work. He had gained some weight and was somewhat lethargic, but other than that I didn't see a big difference in him. He was still depressed to the point of being borderline suicidal, although he hadn't had a manic episode for a while. After all, that would require exuberance and joy and Tad didn't have a lot of that these days.

I held up a sheer DKNY shirt. It was a beautiful dip-dye, totally my style. I checked the price tag. Totally out of the question. I reached for my cell as I heard the musical notes come out of my purse. "Hello?"

"I'm at the elevator, where are you?" Allie asked.

I looked at the shirt in my hand. "One floor up from you, torturing myself."

"I thought the reason you left Dawson's was because you didn't like torture."

I giggled. "Be there in thirty seconds." I clicked off the phone and took the escalator down to where she was. When she saw me, her eyes ran over my figure. "Shit, you're skinnier then I am."

"I haven't had much of an appetite lately," I said as we joined the crowd piling into the elevators. "But I have been taking care of myself in other ways."

"Such as?"

"I've been working out a lot. I may be unemployed, on the verge of bankruptcy and married to a masochistic nutcase, but I do have defined abs and that's got to count for something."

Allie laughed as our fellow elevator passengers struggled to put more distance between themselves and us.

At the restaurant Allie gave our name to the hostess who escorted us to our table. She sighed and looked down at the square from the wall of glass adjacent to our seats. "I love this place—the view totally rocks."

"Mmm, of course, the way my life has been going there'll probably be an earthquake momentarily and we'll plunge to our deaths amongst shards of glass."

Allie shook her head in sympathy. "So I guess things are not well on the home front."

"Things on the home front are never well. They're always sick and twisted. Tad's business is having problems and his partners think he's embezzled some money or something. He's a mess over the whole thing and he's scared to death I'm going to leave him."

"Are you?"

I diverted my eyes and shrugged indecisively. "I have no immediate plans to do so. Before I came out tonight we got into it. He said he was so afraid of losing me he wasn't sure if he could take it. He even threatened suicide again."

Allie shook her head in bewilderment. "What do you say to something like that?"

"Well, I'm on Paxil, so I told him that if he must do it he should at least have the courtesy to do it in the kitchen where it'll be easy to clean up."

Allie smiled and looked up at the ceiling. "I don't know how you do it, April. If I were you I'd be losing it about now, and here you are cracking jokes."

I shrugged again. Tad had been threatening suicide about once a week since our little hospital visit. At first the threats had scared me to death, but after a while the novelty wore off and I had sort of become reconciled to the idea that on any given day I might walk in to find my husband dead on the floor. I wasn't happy about it, but in order to survive you have to take the horrors of life in stride. Just ask my grandmother.

"So how about you?" Allie pushed. "You say you've been working out…have you been doing anything else for yourself?"

"Well, I've been making one hell of a lot of bumper stickers."

"I still can't believe you did that."

"That makes two of us. But it ended up being cheaper than giving everyone a refund, and since they all agreed to take the same sticker…"

"Bugs are people, too?"

"Bugs have rights, too," I corrected. "Anyway, it's done. And they agreed to accept the calendars as Tad made them, man-made structures and all."

Allie narrowed her eyes. "And what has Tad done?"

I smiled. I appreciated that Allie was bitter on my behalf. After all, the stuff with the Temple of the Earth Goddess was not my mess to clean up. But it was clear to me that the other problems Tad was dealing with took priority over my mother's grievances. Embezzlement—that could actually go hand in hand with jail time. I could end up being married to a convict. Wow, life just got better and better. The waitress came by and took our orders before I had a chance to answer Allie's somewhat rhetorical question. I waited to see if she was going to push the issue more, but instead she casually unfolded her napkin into her nap and ran her fingers through her hair.

"So any luck on the job hunt?"

I shook my head. The job hunt had been dismal. All the jobs

I was qualified for that paid a halfway decent wage required that I work during the morning hours when I was to be in the language program, and although I often considered giving up on the whole French thing, I couldn't quite get myself to do it. Caleb was paying for my summer classes, but whether or not I did well in them was entirely up to me. I liked the idea that in at least one aspect of my life I was in control of my own success or failure.

"So you haven't found anything at all?" Allie pressed.

"Nope, I'm just a big loser."

Allie grinned from ear to ear. "Good."

"Good?" I sat back in my chair. "Why? Does my sad excuse for a life make you feel better about your own, or is there another reason that you are reveling in my misery?"

Allie rolled her eyes. "And they say *Caleb's* a drama queen. I'm glad you're unemployed because I've found you the perfect job."

I lifted a bottle of olive oil off the table and held it threateningly. "If you even start to suggest that I return to Dawson's this oil goes right onto that BCBG shirt of yours."

Allie reached forward and guided my hand and the olive oil back to the table. "I wasn't going to say the *D* word. I was out on a date last night and I ran into Artsy. You remember him, right?"

I nodded enthusiastically. Artsy was the brother of one of Allie's ex-boyfriends. His name was Arnold but Allie and I called him Artsy because he had a gallery in New Mexico.

"Well, he's back in town and guess what? He's opened a gallery here and according to him he's been raking in the dough. He's looking for a part-time salesperson, preferably an attractive woman who has some training in art history."

I practically jumped out of my seat. "Are you kidding! Why

didn't you call and tell me immediately? He could have already given the job to someone else!"

Allie put up a hand to stop me. "Chill, I already told him you were looking and he said he would love to meet with you. He has an opening on Friday at one if you have time. Of course, you might have to miss your soap opera."

"Ha. Ha. Oh my God, Allie, do you really think he'll hire me? What should I wear? I was thinking of getting my hair cut short. Should I do that before or after the interview?"

"You must have a few decent outfits that you haven't sold to Crossroads yet."

"A few," I said. I had taken to selling my things to consignment stores in order to pay the bills.

"And my hair?"

Allie toyed with her own hair as she considered mine. "You don't want to risk a bad cut before the interview, so I'd hold off." She smiled and leaned forward. "April, you're a shoo-in."

I clapped my hands together and laughed. I hadn't been this excited about something since…well, for a very long time. Maybe I could manage to have a little happiness in my life after all.

That Friday I waited for Tad to go to work and then spent the entire morning preparing for the interview. I had settled on a William B button-down with three-quarter-length sleeves and a teal Theory skirt. I finished the outfit with a Hermès scarf that Caleb had gotten me for my birthday last year.

I hadn't told Tad about any of it. I was too excited about the opportunity, and I was afraid that if I told him he'd just look at me as if I was reciting the grocery list and then turn back to whatever was playing on the Discovery Channel. Or worse, he would ask me if my getting a new job was the first step toward leaving him.

I shook my head and checked my reflection one more time. I refused to think about any of that now. I had an interview at an art gallery and I wasn't going to screw up my eyeliner by crying.

THE
TURNING POINT

TWENTY-NINE

I walked into the gallery office in my William B blouse and Hermès scarf and forty-five minutes of small talk later I was hired. *I got the job!* He hadn't even bothered to check my references. It seemed that of all his brother's love interests Allie had been his favorite, and so as far as he was concerned, Allie's recommendation was golden.

I had sat across from him in his small but fashionably appointed office and smiled and nodded and tried my damnedest not to jump out of my seat and kiss him. Not just because he was giving me the opportunity of a lifetime, but because he was kind of cute.

He had salt-and-pepper hair, and broad shoulders. His skin was kind of blotchy and he was about twenty pounds overweight. Okay, maybe he wasn't cute. But lately I had found myself attracted to every man who wasn't my husband. I had even started flirting with the pimple-faced kid who sold me Slurpees at the 7-Eleven—he was kind of scrawny but he had a certain nonsuicidal quality that I found very sexy.

After the interview I skipped to my car. I was dying to tell someone about my good fortune. Allie had gone to San Louis Obispo for her cousin's wedding and I knew Caleb was in meetings all day. I plugged Bobe's number into my cell, but she didn't pick up. Okay, who was left…? Tad. I obviously needed to tell my husband about my new job.

The thought of talking to Tad immediately took the wind out of my sails. How had Tad become the person that I most sought to avoid? I closed my eyes and tried to conjure up images from our wedding. There had been a man standing under the chuppah. He had been strong, although his strength hadn't been enough to keep the tears of joy from moistening his eyes. I had loved him and I know he loved me. Could that possibly have been the same man I was married to now?

I opened my eyes again. Enough with the morbidity. I had just landed a job in an art gallery and that was something that needed celebrating. I pushed the car into gear. I knew where I was going and I knew I shouldn't go there. But I didn't care.

I was able to park right outside the Tenderloin apartment. I would just walk up to his door and knock. If God didn't want me to see him he wouldn't be home.

I carefully climbed the stairs. It was silly of me to feel guilty; I mean, it wasn't like I was going to make out with him or anything. I just wanted to tell him about my new job, that's all. I knocked three times.

Jeremiah answered the door wearing jeans and a black shirt that he was still in the middle of buttoning. My eyes immediately went to the hairs that were splattered over his very defined pecs. I flushed and forced myself to look at his face.

He was grinning from ear to ear. "Hey, April, what's up?" He ushered me into the apartment as if my presence there was the most natural thing in the world.

"Hey, I was just in the neighborhood and I thought I'd stop by."

"Glad you did." He threw the newspapers that were covering the couch onto the floor and made a gesture indicating that I should make myself comfortable. "Can I get you anything?" he asked.

"No, I'm good." I carefully treaded over the newspapers and sat in the center of the sofa. "I got a job."

"Oh, yeah?" He sat down next to me and I felt this wave of desire wash over me. *Be good, April,* warned my little voice. That voice was such a killjoy.

"What's the gig?" Jeremiah asked. His tone was casual but I knew he was feeling something, too. Something in his eyes told me so.

"I got a sales job at an art gallery."

"No shit." He pulled me into an enthusiastic embrace. "April, this is fucking huge!"

I laughed nervously. "Yeah, I'm pretty happy about it. I mean, the pay is purely commission, but when I'm excited about a product I can usually sell it."

Jeremiah pulled back enough so that he could look me in the eye. Oh, if only he would button his shirt! "You're gonna rock. I was there at the Legion of Honor, remember? You got this way of making other people appreciate paintings even when they don't know shit about art. Besides, look at you. What guy is gonna say no to you?"

I reluctantly disentangled myself. "Yeah, well, the only thing I'm selling is art."

"Don't matter." Jeremiah's eyes didn't leave mine. "Guys are simple. When a beautiful woman tries to sell us something we buy. And when that woman also happens to be smart, funny and—"

"You know, I should get going." I stood up abruptly. "Tad will be home soon and I want to tell him about the job." I had been there for approximately half a minute but if I listened to Jeremiah sweet talk me for another thirty seconds I might conveniently forget that adultery is wrong.

"Yeah, okay." Jeremiah got to his feet. "How're things going with you two?"

I looked away. "Fine, I guess. Where's the cat?"

Jeremiah was quiet for a moment. I knew he wanted to ask more questions about Tad, but he didn't. "The cat's in the bedroom. Hey, before you go I got something for you."

"You did?" I tried not to look as shocked as I was. Jeremiah should not be buying me presents. And I should not be so thrilled that he had.

"Yeah, hold up for a sec." He disappeared into the bedroom and came out with a box the size of an encyclopedia wrapped in the comics section of the newspaper.

I giggled and took it from him. "Nice wrapping paper."

"I'm not a ribbons-and-bows kind of guy."

I hesitated for a mere second before sitting back down and ripping into the paper. I lifted the lid of the box and stared at its contents.

"They're catalogs and applications," he stated needlessly, "to all the universities with the best Ph.D. programs in the country. At least the best in art history. I did some research on the Internet."

"I can't believe you did this."

He shrugged sheepishly. "Hey, it's not like it cost me anything."

"It's the nicest thing that anyone's ever given me." My mind went to the painting Tad had commissioned for me—the one I had paid for and recently given to Bobe. "The nicest thing," I said again.

"Yeah, well, you still gotta fill 'em out and everything, but I figured I'd make it easy for you."

I looked up at him and there it was. That tingling feeling that went right from my heart down to my nether regions. Clutching my applications, I got up again. "I'm going now."

Jeremiah nodded but he didn't immediately move to get out of my way.

I took a deep breath, scooted around him and ran out the door.

When I got home Tad wasn't there. I sighed in relief and put my applications on the bed. I walked over to the answering machine to check the messages. Eight. Usually we were lucky to get three messages in an afternoon. I pressed the play button.

"April? April, it's Mom. Where are you? Damn it, why didn't I bring your cell number with me? You need to get down to Monterey. Bobe's had a stroke."

In a ten-second span of time my entire life had been re-prioritized. When I left Jeremiah's everything had seemed so complicated. Now it was very, very simple. Bobe was in the emergency room struggling to stay alive and that was the only thing that mattered.

For once I was glad to have the Z3. That and a lead foot got me to Monterey in two hours. Since Carmel was too small a town for its own hospital I knew without asking that Bobe would be taken to the nearby community hospital of Monterey Peninsula. Now as I stood at her bedside it was all I could do not to collapse onto the floor sobbing. She was asleep. Maybe that was better since my mother said that she couldn't speak. Nor did she have the use of her left side. Seeing her lying there wearing the standard-issue hospital gown, I couldn't help thinking that she looked unnaturally small. I reached forward and gently touched her hair. It was the only part of her body that looked as if it wouldn't break the minute my fingers made contact. How could this frail thing be my bobe? She had survived the Nazis, traveled halfway around the world by herself, moved to a new country, raised a child, survived the death of a husband, cared for a grand-child and now she couldn't even hold a pencil? That wasn't the way it was supposed to be. I walked in a daze out into the lobby connected to the emergency room. My mother sat slumped in a chair. Her hair hid her rosy-tipped nose and bloodshot eyes. I sat next to her without speaking and stared into space.

"They say we might not know for a few days," I heard her mutter.

I didn't respond. There was nothing to say.

We sat in silence for a few more minutes. I was aware of my mother straightening her posture next to me. I still did not turn my head.

"As a child," she said, "I never felt like I was able to breathe."

I felt myself stiffen. Although my mother had never said the words before, I knew what was coming and I wasn't sure I wanted to hear it.

"She had me sleeping in the same bed as Dad and her until I was five. Then I remember…I remember being in kindergarten and asking to have my own room. She didn't want to give in but Dad made her. I was so excited."

"Mom…"

"But then sometimes I would wake up in the night and she would be sitting at my bedside, like she was standing guard or something."

I finally looked at my mother. She didn't look like herself. She lacked her standard air of vivacious rebellion.

"She wouldn't let me go to friends' houses unless she was a close friend of the parents, which was rare since she was so reclusive. She didn't let me date, she didn't let me drive. I…I think I hated her."

"Shut up."

My mother winced but she shook her head obstinately. "Please, let me share this. I know how you feel about me. I know you hate me, too."

"I don't hate you." It was all I could give her right then. This was Bobe's moment. I needed to focus on her, not my mother. Why did my mother try to make every crisis about her?

"Well, maybe you don't, but you're angry, and I don't blame you. I was…I was a terrible mother."

Now she had my attention. I shifted uncomfortably in my seat but I didn't interrupt.

"I was so anxious to break all the rules that had been placed on me during childhood. I just wanted to live. Really, really live. And when I found out I was pregnant it just seemed so perfect. I was a single woman who was carrying a love child. I wanted to give you all the freedom that I'd missed as a girl. But you didn't want freedom. Instead, you wanted to take my freedom away."

I snapped my head in her direction. "Are you fucking kidding me? I was a child, Mother. Children need supervision. I'm sorry if that cramped your style, and I'm sorry if you felt suffocated as a kid, but in case you've forgotten, Bobe's a Holocaust survivor. If she has issues she has a pretty damn good excuse, and yet she worked through a lot of them. You, on the other hand, were just a little overprotected as a kid, and yet you don't seem to have been able to work through any of your issues."

My mother blinked her eyes rapidly and then quickly looked

away. I wanted to feel sorry for her but I was just so drained. I closed my eyes and pressed the base of my palms into my forehead. "What is it you want from me, Mom?"

"I want your forgiveness. I messed up, April. I really messed up with both you and Mom and now I may not have a chance to fix things with her. And I want to."

I put my hand on her knee. "Okay, I got it." My mother leaned over and put her head on my shoulder and we fell silent again. I watched the tired and frantic people come in and out of the glass door that led to the parking lot.

"Look at these people," I whispered. "Everyone here is facing something that they don't want to face." I shook my head in amazement. "I bet every single one of them is at a turning point, and for some of them the whole outcome of their lives could depend on what happens in the next few hours."

My mother sat up and looked around the room before turning to me. "*We're* at a turning point. What's going to happen to us?"

I thought about it for a moment. What choices would I make? It would be so easy to hold on to my resentments against my mother, but in the end where would it leave me?

"I don't know if I can forgive you," I said slowly. "I can't just pretend that our history is different than what it is, but I think I can let go and move forward."

"What does that mean?"

Good question. I thought about it a little more. "If we can't have a normal mother-and-daughter relationship maybe we could kind of pave our own way. You know, we could be like friends who are related to each other."

"Like sisters?"

"Sort of…but different. I don't know, we'll have to figure it out as we go along." I paused as we both thought about that. "It won't be normal," I added, "but I'm beginning to think that normal isn't all it's cracked up to be."

My mother smiled. "I've been telling you that for years."

"This isn't a really good time for the 'I told you so' speech."

"You're right." She took my hand and we looked at each other. And for the first time I saw her. She wasn't the mother that I had always been embarrassed about, the woman who I blamed for all my problems. She was a woman who was a little lost and confused but who, deep down, had a very good heart. And she loved her daughter even if she didn't always know how to show it.

She took a deep breath. "I think I'm going to like being your friend."

I had been in Monterey for two days before the doctors announced that Bobe seemed to be out of the woods. My mother and I were so excited we rushed to the gift store and bought the biggest teddy bear we could find. It had a Band-aid above its left eye and was holding a big red heart with the words "We Love You" embroidered across it. We had been staying in Bobe's apartment together. The first night I slept on what must be the world's most uncomfortable couch, while my mother took the bed. But on the second night my mother pointed out that there was room in the bed for two. It was weird sharing a bed with my mother but it was also kind of fun. Bobe had a television in her room and we stayed up late with a bowl of popcorn between us watching old *WKRP* reruns on TNT. We almost turned it off at 1:00 a.m. but then the Thanksgiving episode came on and neither of us was willing to miss seeing Les Nessman report that Mr. Carlson was dropping live turkeys from the sky. We laughed so hard that we scared Bobe's cat and he refused to come anywhere near us for the rest of the weekend.

Not all of our interactions went that smoothly. After spending twenty-seven years driving one another crazy, we weren't able to suddenly turn around and become best friends, but we were trying, and that was more than we had ever done in the past.

I had called Tad to tell him where I was. He had been sympathetic until I gently refused his offer to come down and meet me. Then he'd accused me of not wanting anything to do with him, which was true, but I had additional reasons for not wanting him there. It had become clear to me that the weekend was going to be about my mother, Bobe and me. There was no room for him.

I sat by Bobe's bedside while she tried to talk to me, but it was hard to understand her. However, she still had full use of her right side and so she wrote notes to both me and my mother. She noticed the change between my mother and me and I could tell by the faint sparkle in her eyes that it pleased her. When she fell asleep, Mom and I went to lunch in the cafeteria.

"Look—" my mother pointed to the refrigerated beverages "—they have beer."

"I think we've earned one of those," I said. "In fact, we should probably have a bunch. If we suffer from alcohol poisoning they won't even have to call an ambulance."

Mom giggled. "I think we should stick to one. I've been kicked out of a lot of bars in my life but I'm not sure I want to be kicked out of a hospital cafeteria."

"That would be a new low," I conceded, and put one Budweiser on each of our trays.

We found a seat and munched on our respective salads. Mom took a sip of her beer and then pushed it aside so that there were fewer items between us. "April, what's going on between you and Tad?"

"Nothing good," I said in between bites.

"Is it fixable?"

I put my fork down and let my finger trace the rim of my beer. "I don't know. I thought that if he just took his medication, things would get better, but I think that his problems go a lot deeper than being bipolar. He has some issues that he is either unable or unwilling to deal with." I lifted my beer to my lips before continuing. "He had told me that he had a falling-out with his parents after he reached adulthood but that his childhood itself had been idyllic."

"It wasn't?"

"No, that was a total lie. I know this doesn't seem possible, but I seem to have married a man whose family is even more dysfunctional than ours."

My mother laughed. "Amazing."

I stabbed a crouton. "I think I was willing to stick it out because I had my own issues that I was avoiding."

"You know, your chart said this is a year of self-discovery and change."

"Yeah, you told me. No offense, Mom, but I'm not going to make my life decisions based on what my horoscope says."

"All right, what do you want this year to be about?"

I thought about it, then laughed. "Self-discovery and change?"

"Aha! The stars never lie."

"Yeah, well, anyway…I'm going to have a long heart-to-heart with Tad when I get home."

"And if the talk doesn't go the way you want it to?"

I shook my head. "I don't know, but I think I will when the time is right. I guess we'll just have to wait and see."

THIRTY

The wind whipped through my hair as my car raced down 280. It was Tuesday night and I was finally going home. I had to admit, Bobe couldn't have picked a better time to have a stroke. I was going to start classes next week and start my new job a week after that, so the only thing I had missed by spending five days in Monterey was time with my husband, and I was okay with that.

Bobe was recovering surprisingly well considering her age. With some effort she could manage intelligible speech, and though she was presently in a wheelchair the doctors predicted that with the help of a walker she would be back on her feet by the end of the month. There had been the question of how she was going to manage once she left the hospital, but my mother had settled that issue by offering to move in with her. Apparently her job with the medical marijuana people didn't work out so she was free to relocate. I had serious doubts about how well that arrangement was going to work, but my mother's horoscope had reported that she was supposed to reach out to others, so I figured Bobe had at least until next month's reading before she would have to find a new roomie.

I hadn't called Tad to tell him I was on my way back. I wanted to wait to talk to him in person, although I hadn't even decided what I was going to say. Maybe it was okay to call it quits. What was my obligation at this stage? It was so difficult to identify the right thing to do.

When I pulled in front of my house I saw that the lights were on. I got out of the car but I didn't immediately go to the door. I was a little scared. Tad was so unpredictable it was impossible to surmise what I might be walking into. I took a deep breath. Whatever it was I could handle it. I was strong.

I opened the door and walked into the living room, expecting to find him prostate on the couch, watching some documentary on the Discovery Channel.

What I did not expect was to find him on the couch underneath a half-naked Gigi. I stood in the living room for a full minute too shocked to speak. Finally Gigi looked up and saw me. She gasped, scrambled off my husband and wrapped her arms around her bare breasts.

Tad looked horrified. He jumped to his feet and looked from me to Gigi and then back at me. His face was flushed and his eyes had a kind of wild look to them that I hadn't seen for a while.

I closed my mouth and met his gaze. "That," I said, "is not Catherine Zeta-Jones."

He cleared his throat uncomfortably. "This isn't what it looks like."

I laughed. I couldn't help it. "Well, Tad, it looks like you were about to fuck my former assistant. Is that an incorrect assertion?"

Again his eyes darted between the two of us. "Yes," he said with a shaky voice, "that's incorrect."

"Okay, so maybe you could explain to me why Gigi's here with her top off."

Tad flushed. I could tell that he didn't have an answer and I was kind of disappointed by that. I really wanted to hear what possible excuse he could have come up with.

"It's your fault, April," Gigi spat. She was now trying to get her bra on without further exposing herself. "You've been, like, totally awful to him. Awful!"

I raised an eyebrow but my eyes stayed locked on Tad.

"He told me all about how you ignore him all the time. You are, like, the worst wife ever! You lay all this stuff on him, you even told him that he was antisocial!"

"No, I called you a sociopath," I said, directing my words at Tad. "That's an entirely different thing—antisocial people almost never screw their wives' assistants."

"Um, hello! You can't just pretend that I'm not here!"

I gave her a withering look. "I am aware that you're here, Gigi, you're just not important enough for me to acknowledge."

Gigi looked as if she was about to combust. That wouldn't do at all. I did not want to have bits of Gigi all over my living room.

"I am, too, important!" she screeched. "You may not like it but Tad and I are in love, we have been for months...."

"Gigi!" Tad snapped. His eyes bored into her as if he expected the animosity in his glare to shut her up. He obviously didn't know her very well.

"I'm sorry, Tad, but, like, we have got to get this out in the open." She turned to me again. "Tad and I started talking for the first time when he was coming in on your days off to leave you gifts. I mean, he is, like, the nicest husband in the whole world and you totally don't even appreciate him. Tad and I—"

"Gigi, shut the fuck up," Tad shouted.

Gigi's eyes nearly popped out of her head. "Tad, how could you—"

"Gigi, you need to go now," I said calmly. "I know you think that we have a triangle going on here, but the fact is that if you were to list Tad and my marital problems in order of severity, this little affair wouldn't even make it to the top ten."

"I am important!" She actually stamped her foot like a five-year-old. Tad looked as if he wanted to sink into the floor.

"I'm sorry, Gigi," he said with a bravado that I was pretty sure he wasn't feeling, "but I don't love you. I have always loved April. You really should leave now."

"What!"

I sighed and shook my head. "I understand how that could have been confusing for you considering he was speaking in Standard American English, so allow me to translate his statement into your language." I flipped my hair the way I had seen her do a million times before. "Your boyfriend is, like, totally not into you. So you need to get out of my house before I, like, totally kick your ass."

Gigi advanced on me and I was really beginning to think that I was going to get to hit her. But then she stopped. Tad had stepped up to my side and his posture was defensive.

Gigi swallowed. She straightened her shirt and grabbed her purse, which was on the floor by the fireplace. She looked at us one last time and then turned on her heel and ran out of the room.

We listened to the front door slam and I prayed that there weren't any more broken car windows in my future. Tad tried to put his hand on my arm. I didn't jerk away. I just stepped out of reach.

"April, I know this is bad but…I was really upset. I thought you were going to leave me and then when I came home and saw those applications…some of them were for schools that are across the country, April! I just got upset, and the side effects of the medication…"

"You're not going to tell me that sleeping with Gigi is a side effect of the medication."

"Actually, I stopped taking the medication a little over a week ago. It just didn't seem to be helping and—"

I held up my hand. "Tad, it doesn't matter."

"Of course it matters! I know how you must be feeling right now."

"That's just it. You don't know how I feel. If I was really upset by what I saw we'd have a place to work from, but when I saw you with Gigi… I didn't care."

Tad stared at me.

"No," I continued, "it was worse than that. I was relieved."

"You don't mean that."

"Yeah, I do. I felt that I owed it to you to stay. I didn't want you to commit suicide or hurt yourself, and I do take my marriage vows seriously, but you have broken every single one of yours. You have officially released me from my contract, and I'm out of here."

"No, no, April, you have to give us another chance. I'll do anything. I'll take my medication. I'll never spend another cent. I'll—"

"You're not getting this. I don't want to work it out. I just want out, period. I have a change of clothes in the car, so I'll get the rest of my stuff later. I'll make an appointment to file for divorce tomorrow."

Tad shook his head so hard that his features became a temporary blur. "You can't just turn around and walk out!"

I thought about that for a second. "You're right." I walked into the bedroom and did a quick survey of the room. There by the window was my box of college catalogs and applications. I picked them up reverently. "I might need these. At least I hope I will."

"April."

"Okay, now I'm ready to turn around and walk out." I started toward the front door.

"No!" He grabbed my arm and whirled me around. "You can't give up on us. You have to remember the good times, the times I was there for you. Like when you miscarried."

I shook my head. "Tad, I am really grateful for the times you were there for me but it doesn't balance out anymore." I gently peeled his fingers off my arm. "I still don't think you're a bad person, but you really are a mess. Not only are you a liar and an adulterer, you're also totally self-destructive, and self-destructive people always end up destroying the people closest to them." I stepped backward, putting more space between us. "I can't let you destroy me, Tad."

"I won't! I would never hurt you, April!"

I bit my lip. I felt sorry for him. But I didn't love him anymore and now I knew it. I had stopped loving him a while ago. "Goodbye, Tad."

I turned back toward the door. My hand was on the doorknob when I heard him call out my name once more. I hesitated a moment and then, against my better judgment I turned around. He was standing behind me and he was holding a gun.

My lungs jumped into my throat and my heart stopped beating.

This must be fear. But even my little voice wasn't sure. The emotion I was experiencing was so much more extreme than anything I had ever previously felt that I didn't recognize it.

The gun wasn't pointed at me. It was pointed at the floor. But he was holding it and his finger was on the trigger. Where had he been keeping it? I noted that the drawer in the console we kept in the hall was open. I had always dismissed that drawer as being to small to keep anything of significance in but Tad had proved me wrong. I forced myself to look him in the eyes. "Are you threatening to kill me?"

"What?" Tad's eyes widened as if he was shocked by the question. "No! I would never hurt you. I love you. I don't want to live without you."

"So you're threatening to kill yourself."

"I don't want to live without you," Tad said again. "And I don't... I don't want to go to jail."

"Jail," I repeated.

"I think Sean and Eric have gone to the police. I think they've searched the office. I can't get through this without you, April. I don't want to live without you."

The full reality of my situation came home to me. "You're holding me hostage."

"No! No, I just... I don't..."

"Yes, you are. You're saying that if I leave someone's going to get shot."

"Me! Not you! Not anybody else! Just me!"

"Oh, and suddenly you don't count?" My voice was rising. My anger was eclipsing my fear and I wasn't sure if that was a good thing, but I couldn't control it. "So you did embezzle that money."

Tad shook his head, but it wasn't in protest as much as it was in confusion. "I messed up. I can get through it, though, if you stand by me. I can find a way out. I don't want to go to jail."

"And I'm going to be dragged through this, too, right? I mean, the police are going to be questioning me, as well?"

"I don't know. Probably."

"Well then, you are going to have to get yourself a criminal defense attorney and get something written up that says that I knew nothing about any of it and never saw a cent of the money. And then you are going to have it signed and notarized or whatever else you have to do to make sure it will stand up in court, and you are going to do all of that before you kill yourself."

"I have to see a lawyer before I commit suicide?"

"Yes!" I slammed my fist against the wall. "You have been screwing me over from the moment you put the engagement ring on my finger! Now the least you can do is put your suicide off for one week so I don't get saddled with more of your shit!"

"I…I don't want to live without you."

"So don't! I can't save you, Tad. I tried and I failed. So now I'm going to save myself. If you want to shoot yourself in the head that's your choice, but you're going to have to wait until you've seen a lawyer and signed some papers. Trust me, hell will wait."

Tad started crying. Then wailing. If Edvard Munch's *The Scream* could actually make a sound it would be the sound that Tad was making right then. He fell to his knees and started rocking back and forth. The gun fell to his side and I knew I should grab it, but it was too close to his hand and I couldn't be his hostage any longer. I took a steadying breath, turned around and walked out the door.

About a half hour had passed and I was in my car watching the police take Tad away. I had called and told them Tad was bipolar and threatening suicide. He would be taken to a psychiatric ward now and I would be filing for divorce. Maybe doing so while he was in the hospital wasn't the proper thing. But I had had my fill of proper things. I had taken the safe job, married Mr. Perfect and look where it had gotten me. A psychotic husband who was screwing the bitch who got me fired. From now on I was taking the road less traveled. Obviously it was a safer way to go.

I looked at my hands, which were clutching the wheel of the Z3 despite the fact that the engine was off. It wasn't really over. There would be a divorce and it would probably get ugly. There would most likely be more threats of suicide. And then of course there was the mountain of debt, probably more than I knew about. I would have to call one of those debt-consolidation places or declare bankruptcy. Either action would make getting a loan for a Ph.D. program close to impossible. I looked at the box of applications resting on the passenger seat. Somehow I would make it work, and this time I wasn't trying to convince myself of it, I just knew it.

But what about Tad? I wanted him to be okay. Maybe now that he had hit rock bottom he would find the motivation to get his act together and seek help. Maybe he would end up like his sister rather than his mother. But whatever direction he ended up going in he was going to have to go without me.

I sighed, reached into my purse and called Allie.

"Yello," she chirped.

"Allie, it's me."

"Hey, April, what's up? I haven't been able to reach you since I got back from my trip."

"I've been busy. Tonight, for instance, I left Tad."

There was a moment of silence before Allie spoke up again.

"What can I do? Do you want to come over? You can stay here for as long as you want."

I smiled and rested my head against the leather seat. "Thank, you Allie, you're awesome. But I can't come over tonight."

"Why not?"

Good question. I didn't know how to explain that what I was feeling was way too intense to allow me to sit still in Allie's living room while we quietly talked it out. I needed a physical release, something that would help me let go of the horrible image of Tad falling apart. In a flash I knew exactly what I needed to do.

"Allie, I'll explain it all tomorrow, but tonight there's just one more thing I have to take care of."

"All right, if you're sure. Come over tomorrow. Caleb and I both have the day off. If you give me an approximate time, I'll ask him to come over, too."

"I'll be there by twelve-thirty at the latest."

"Okay..." She paused. "April, are you sure you're all right? If you want me to meet you somewhere I can."

"No, I'll be fine. Oh, and Allie?"

"Yeah?"

"Thank you for being such a wonderful friend. I don't know what I'd do without you."

"Probably drink less. I'll see you tomorrow."

THIRTY-ONE

I made one quick stop at the drugstore before I went over there. I knew he'd be home. Don't ask me how I knew, I just did. I parked the car and took the creaky steps two at a time. Jeremiah answered on the third knock. His shirt was buttoned this time, but he still looked incredible. His dark hair hung loosely around his face and the beginning of a stubble clung to his chin and upper lip.

"April."

I nodded and walked past him into the apartment. Mick Jagger was singing "Beast of Burden" on the stereo.

I heard the door shut behind me and I turned in time to see him checking the clock. It was almost midnight. "Did I wake you?"

"No, I was just sitting up reading." He looked at me and he must have seen something in my face. "What happened?"

"I've had a really bad night. No, scratch that. I've had a really bad six months."

"Tad." He stepped closer to me but didn't make any move to touch me. "What did he do? Did he hurt you?"

I shook my head. "It's over, Jeremiah. It's all over."

"You left him?"

I nodded.

"And you're okay?"

"I'm getting there."

Yeah, well, you're strong."

"Yes, I am."

We stood in silence. The music changed. Now it was the Black Crowes singing "Seeing Things." I don't think Jeremiah moved but suddenly he seemed to be closer. I took a deep, cleansing breath. "I need to be on my own for a while, I need to…to make this a year of self-discovery." I smiled to myself. My mother would be so proud. "But tonight I need something…"

"What?" And now he did step closer. He was so close that there was barely an inch of space between us, but he still wasn't touching me. "What is it that you need, April?"

"You," I whispered. "Tonight I need you."

Jeremiah smiled. His left hand slipped around my waist and his right hand grabbed mine. "Let's dance."

We moved slowly to the music. We were face-to-face and I could smell the scent of something vaguely minty on his breath. His hand left mine and he gently ran his fingers along my collarbone, then up my neck until they reached my face. He tilted my chin upward and he gazed into my eyes. "You are the sexiest woman I have ever seen."

He leaned in and his lips touched mine, so very gently at first, and then he parted my lips with his tongue. He started slow and then the urgency increased. I felt his arm tighten around me and

I was crushed against him. There wasn't one part of my body that didn't feel the impact of that kiss.

He plunged his fingers into my hair and then gently pulled my head back and attacked my neck. He started by kissing that hollow spot at the base. Was it possible to have an orgasm while necking? My fingernails dug into his back. I was probably scratching him. Oh well, he'd have to deal because I was totally out of control by that point.

He let go of my hair and then his fingers went to the buttons of my blouse. He leaned in so that his lips were next to my ear. "I've always wondered what you would feel like."

I remained silent since I had lost the ability to speak. His left hand was still firmly on my back, holding me in place, guiding me as he moved me to the beat. He easily undid each of my buttons until my shirt hung open revealing my Victoria's Secret push-up bra. His fingers gently grazed the top of my breasts and then worked inside the left cup. I felt my nipple harden as he lazily toyed with it. His other hand was now moving up my back, and with one easy move he had unclasped the bra. In a matter of seconds both the bra and shirt were on the floor. He stepped back and looked at me as his breath caught. "Jesus, you are incredible."

I didn't have Jeremiah's patience, I wanted him now. I tore at his shirt and greedily ran my hands over his pecs and his perfect six-pack abs. Oh yeah, I could see why people would pay this man money in order to learn his fitness secrets.

He grabbed me and pulled me in for another kiss, this time pushing me against the wall as he did. He parted my legs with his and pressed against me. A gasp escaped my lips as he pulled my arms above my head and then let his hands slide from my hands to my wrists to my forearms, all the while his mouth was also working its way down over my neck, my shoulder…my breasts. I cried out as he tortured my nipples with his tongue.

He released my arms and moved to a crouch so that we were nose to waist. He undid the button and zipper on my pants then slowly guided them off my hips until they were piled around my ankles. I stepped out of them and kicked them aside along with my shoes.

Jeremiah rose to his full height. I had always thought that he was only a few inches taller than me. But now with my heels off and him so very close he seemed to tower over me. Then again maybe it wasn't his height. Maybe it was his sheer presence.

He kissed me again and I felt his fingers slide inside my panties. A shudder went up my spine. "Oh, Jeremiah."

He brought me to the brink and then pulled back.

"What! What are you doing? Come back here now!"

"Ah, ah, ah. If you want this to be a one-night deal then we're gonna have to drag this out."

"Oh, really?" I stepped forward and undid his pants and worked them down to the floor. I got to my knees and kissed him along the waistband. I took my time about it.

"You're killing me," Jeremiah moaned.

"Don't dish it out unless you can take it," I teased. I pulled his boxer shorts down and then let my hand run over his erection. I reached over to my purse with my other hand and pulled out the condoms that I had just purchased and carefully put one on him. But to his ultimate frustration I stopped there. I worked my way up his stomach and chest until I was standing upright in front of him.

"So how's this? Am I dragging this out enough?"

"That's it. You're going to get it."

"That's what I'm counting on."

He whipped me around and pushed me against the wall again. In seconds my panties were gone. His mouth was on mine and the kiss was becoming more and more demanding. "Now," I heard him growl. And then I was off the ground and my legs were wrapped around his waist as he plunged inside of me. I cried out and I think he did, too, but I was too caught up in what Jeremiah was making me feel to notice much of anything else. My back banged against the wall again and again, causing the pictures hanging around us to shake. Then he lifted me away from the wall and, without ever breaking our connection, brought me to the bed. We fell on top of the comforter and he dived inside me with more and more force. Somewhere along the line I rolled on top of him and then him on me again. If this was what it was like to give in to temptation, why did anyone ever resist?

Finally, after what seemed like blissful hours of pleasure, I could feel that I was close to what was clearly going to be the most intense orgasm of my life. I grabbed on to the headboard and Jeremiah drove inside me again. I heard myself scream his name and he answered with a guttural moan. And then my world exploded into a series of fantastic fireworks. I arched my back and felt him shudder against me a second after I had met my full climax. I had never climaxed at the same time as a partner before. And now it had happened with Mr. Wrong, who as it turns out, was a lot better than Mr. Right.

Jeremiah and I made love no less than five times that night. The second time was more gentle and caring, and after the third time I let him take a nap. I lay awake and listened to his steady breathing. This was exactly what I needed. I almost regretted that it had to be temporary. Almost. As much as I cared about

Jeremiah, I was looking forward to being on my own for a while. Still, it would be nice if there was something from our night together that I could take with me. "My sketchbook," I whispered aloud. I crept out of bed and pulled it out of my overnight bag. I sat in the doorway that separated the bedroom from the living room and started drawing. But after a few seconds I realized I wasn't drawing Jeremiah, I was drawing a woman. She was beautiful and strong, a little scared perhaps, but she knew how to take care of herself. I smiled at my self-portrait. I really was going to be okay.

The next morning Jeremiah and I took separate cars to Mama's on Washington Square. I would be leaving when breakfast was over. We laughed over omelets and ate each other's hash browns and toast. We didn't talk about Tad. We just enjoyed the morning.

After the check was paid he walked me to my car. I stood in front of the door and he took both of my hands in his and let his thumb caress the insides of my palms. "There's something I didn't tell you."

"Let me guess…there's a wife and kid hidden away in Utah?"

"No wife and kids. A record contract."

"No way!" Instinctively I threw my arms around his neck. "Jeremiah, that's wonderful!"

He returned my embrace. "Yeah, I'm pretty psyched. Here's the thing, I gotta move to L.A."

"Oh." I pulled back. "Well, I guess that makes sense."

"Yeah, you know…the industry's there." He looked down at his shoes. "I hear UCLA has a great Ph.D. program…."

"I can't do that, Jeremiah."

"Right, right, you need some time on your own. I got that." He looked up at me and then pulled me forward. His lips found mine and I melted against him.

Reluctantly, he released me. "You better get going before our one night turns into a twenty-four-hour thing."

I nodded silently and pulled the keys out of my purse. Jeremiah watched as I positioned myself behind the wheel of the car.

"April?"

I looked up as I pulled the seat belt across my shoulder. "Yeah?"

"If you ever get tired of being alone you look me up, okay?"

I smiled. "You can count on it."

I drove to Allie's and was greeted by both her and Caleb. Caleb took my overnight bag and put it on the couch while Allie led me to the dining-room table where they had placed an unopened bottle of wine along with three empty bowls with spoons.

"We're having break-up food for lunch," Allie informed me. "Wine and Ben & Jerry's."

I laughed and sat at the table. Caleb sat opposite me and Allie prepared to uncork the wine.

"Okay," said Caleb, "tell us exactly what happened."

"Well, after my interview I found out that my grandmother had had a stroke so I drove down to Monterey. She's going to make it but her speech is slurred and she doesn't have full use of her left side. So then I came back home and walked in on Tad and Gigi getting it on."

"Gigi?!" Allie and Caleb cried in unison.

"Gigi, sans top and everything. When she took off, Tad and I had it out. It turns out he's been embezzling money from his company. Oh, and then when I tried to leave he pulled a gun on me."

Allie gasped, and Caleb clapped a hand over his heart.

"Well, not on me so much as on himself," I amended. "He said if I left he'd shoot himself. Anyway, he ended up just completely melting down. I walked out, called the police, and the last I heard they were taking him to a psychiatric ward. That's pretty much the whole story."

There was a long silence. Then Allie wordlessly took the wine and the bowls away and returned from the kitchen with a bottle of Absolut Citron and two more cartons of Ben & Jerry's. She placed one pint in front of each of us and held up the vodka.

"We need shot glasses," Caleb said.

"I'm on it." Allie did another quick trip to the kitchen and returned with the glasses, which she immediately began to fill.

"So now what?" Caleb asked.

I opened up my carton of Everything But the Kitchen Sink ice cream and dug my spoon in. "Well, thanks to you I'm going to learn French this summer, and thanks to Allie, I'll also be starting that gallery job next week."

"You got it!" Allie slammed her hand against the table in triumph.

"Yep. So at least I'm employed. Of course, I'm also broke."

"That's temporary," Allie said.

"And I'm homeless."

"No, never homeless." Caleb waved his finger at me. "Allie and I have been talking it over and we've decided that you are going to be living with me."

Allie shrugged. "I lost the coin toss."

"We'll convert my living room into a bedroom."

"You don't have to do that...."

"Ah, ah, ah, not another word. I have always wanted a woman to play Grace to my Will so now the part is yours. And I know that this whole divorce thing is going to mess with your credit, and mine's perfect, so if you need me to cosign on a student loan just say the word."

"I can't ask you to do that, Caleb. You're already paying for the French lessons."

"I didn't say I would pay your loan for you, I just said I would secure it."

"Yeah, he knows you're good for it," Allie said. "And if you try to stiff him, he knows where you live."

I laughed. "Well, we'll see what happens. In the meantime I think a toast is in order."

Caleb and Allie lifted their glasses. "What shall we drink to?" Allie asked.

"To vodka and ice cream?" I suggested.

"No," said Caleb. "To new beginnings and for having the courage to be true to ourselves."

And that was a toast that we were all willing to drink to. Tad and I were never going to have the happy ending that I had originally anticipated. He wasn't my Prince Charming and my marriage had fallen short of being a fairy tale. But fairy tales are so predictable and mundane. Life is much more exciting.